DANCE OF DESTINY

The pulsing music of carnival filled the hot tropic night as young Lily Ledoux was swept up in the crowd of masked revelers.

Then, suddenly, it was as if she were alone, facing one other human being.

A man. Tall and powerful in stature. Incredibly sensual in movement. His face masked but his eyes gazing almost hypnotically into hers as he drew her with him into the now orgiastic rhythm of the pounding music's beat.

Lily knew that this night she would discover all she most wanted. All she most feared. All that her life had been leading up to until now—and all that her life would seek from this moment on.

The path of love that would lead this incredibly beautiful woman so far and through so much was opening up before her—and there was no turning back. . . .

Rapture's Mistress

Big Bestsellers from SIGNET

- [ ] **SONG OF SOLOMON** by Toni Morrison.
  (#E8340—$2.50)*

- [ ] **GIFTS OF LOVE** by Charlotte Vale Allen.
  (#J8388—$1.95)*

- [ ] **BELLADONNA** by Erica Lindley.
  (#J8387—$1.95)*

- [ ] **THE BRACKENROYD INHERITANCE** by Erica Lindley. (#W6795—$1.50)

- [ ] **THE DEVIL IN CRYSTAL** by Erica Lindley.
  (#E7643—$1.75)

- [ ] **PRESIDENTIAL EMERGENCY** by Walter Stovall.
  (#E8371—$2.25)*

- [ ] **THE GODFATHER** by Mario Puzo.
  (#E8508—$2.50)*

- [ ] **KRAMER VERSUS KRAMER** by Avery Corman.
  (#E8282—$2.50)

- [ ] **VISION OF THE EAGLE** by Kay McDonald.
  (#J8284—$1.95)*

- [ ] **CRESSIDA** by Clare Darcy.   (#E8287—$1.75)*

- [ ] **DANIEL MARTIN** by John Fowles.
  (#E8249—$2.95)

- [ ] **THE EBONY TOWER** by John Fowles.
  (#E8254—$2.50)

- [ ] **THE FRENCH LIEUTENANT'S WOMAN** by John Fowles. (#E8535—$2.50)

- [ ] **RIDE THE BLUE RIBAND** by Rosalind Laker.
  (#J8252—$1.95)*

- [ ] **THE SILVER FALCON** by Evelyn Anthony.
  (#E8211—$2.25)

*Price slightly higher in Canada

If you wish to order these titles, please see the coupon in the back of this book.

Rapture's Mistress

by

Gimone Hall

A SIGNET BOOK
NEW AMERICAN LIBRARY
TIMES MIRROR

NAL BOOKS ARE ALSO AVAILABLE AT DISCOUNTS IN BULK QUANTITY FOR INDUSTRIAL OR SALES-PROMOTIONAL USE. FOR DETAILS, WRITE TO PREMIUM MARKETING DIVISION, NEW AMERICAN LIBRARY, INC., 1301 AVENUE OF THE AMERICAS, NEW YORK, NEW YORK 10019.

COPYRIGHT © 1978 BY GIMONE HALL

All rights reserved

SIGNET TRADEMARK REG. U.S. PAT. OFF. AND FOREIGN COUNTRIES
REGISTERED TRADEMARK—MARCA REGISTRADA
HECHO EN CHICAGO, U.S.A.

SIGNET, SIGNET CLASSICS, MENTOR, PLUME AND MERIDIAN BOOKS are published by The New American Library, Inc., 1301 Avenue of the Americas, New York, New York 10019

FIRST SIGNET PRINTING, NOVEMBER, 1978

1 2 3 4 5 6 7 8 9

PRINTED IN THE UNITED STATES OF AMERICA

Part I

Picnic on a Volcano
(1889)

1

"Will I see him again tonight? I mustn't! I daren't! Will he come again looking for me? How can I live, not even knowing if he came?" Lily had been tormented all day, ever since dawn, when she had slipped into her father's plantation house, Acelie, and removed the mask that had protected her through the long night of dancing.

If only she could have seen his face! If only she could have shown him hers! But without the mask it could never have happened at all.

"Oh, there is a devil in me. A *diablesse!*" She trembled and put on a lamp against the growing darkness of her bedroom. She was French, a Ledoux, but she had lived all her eighteen years on the island of Martinique, and she had not missed acquiring something of the natives' fear. She knew as well as they that two fireflies in the night might be the eyes of the deadly fer-de-lance. To her, as to a *fille de couleur*, a tree was not just a tree, but a being, its leaves whispering in the wind, "I am here. I am me." Even in the daylight, in the awesome luminosity of tropical sun, there was something that spoke of apparitions, as indeed the apparition of the man had haunted her through the brilliant noon and on into the sunset.

From her pier glass, brown eyes that had gleamed with amusement for so many suitors now leaped with coppery fervor. The little mouth so given to laughter was pursed with worry, and the cheeks which she had too often allowed to pinken in the sun bore a flush of a different sort. Only the dark hair was the same, except that at this time of day it should not have been flowing loose about her shoulders like soft wings to bear her spirit to disaster.

Oh, it had seemed a harmless prank to sneak away to Carnival disguised in a beautifully calendered turban, her slender body supple as a servant girl's beneath the trailing skirts of a silk *douilette*, the white skin of her throat concealed by a shoulder scarf, the *foulard*. There had even

3

been gloves to cover her long, delicate fingers, gloves that concealed not only their pale color but also their softness, which proved she had never wielded a knife in a canefield or suffered the scratches of the tough leaves in binding.

She was not the first girl on the island to conceive such an escapade. From the time she had been old enough to understand, she had been hearing the stories, sifting like devilish little breezes past the stern figures of the nuns at her elite school. Third and fourth hand she had heard how someone's cousin or someone's sister's friend had stolen away to unimaginable adventure, to dance the forbidden *bouèné* in the narrow, cobbled streets of Martinique's capital, St. Pierre. And sometimes she had known who these daring older girls were; and when she passed one of them, she had looked with curiosity, hoping to discover their secrets in their faces.

She had never said to herself, "I will do that, too, when my turn comes." But on the other hand, she had not said, either, "No, I would never do that." There had been a force working in her, growing with her, a force she was aware existed, yet dared not recognize, a force at odds with everything warm and familiar. It was a thing that delighted her and frightened her, and she had denied it by ignoring it. Now she knew she must learn to ignore it again. She was engaged to be married. The brief sun of girlhood was nearly over.

Already she could see her future in every detail. And why not? How many generations had lived the same life before her, sliding from the splendid morning of youth into the tropical stillness of womanhood? Of course, there had been exceptions.

Josephine had gone from Martinique to triumph over the heart of Napoleon. Her statue in the *savane* of Fort de France was one of Lily's favorite spots. As a child it had seemed to Lily that the statue in Empire robes was her friend, that it sighed with the palms in the evening wind as it listened to her whispered dreams. Dreams Lily was too old for now. Shadowed desires she must forget. But she knew she could never forget her night at Carnival!

Tonight was the last night. "If I go tonight, will this fever burn itself out?" she wondered. "What if it doesn't?" It was a question for which there was no answer except the lifetime of modesty and respectability to which her aristocratic French Creole heritage destined her.

"Oh, what is wrong with me? Shall I go to find a witch who can exorcise this malefice?" She paced the balata-wood floor of her room, the airy folds of her butterfly-imprinted *chinoise* sailing behind her. A knock came on the door, and, preoccupied, she carelessly called out permission to enter.

"I am going now, missy," said the reveler who appeared. "I thought you would like to see my costume."

"Cyrillia, you look marvelous!" Lily cried, glad of the distraction. It was, if anything, an understatement. The girl had a rare red color of skin and blue-black hair that fell in untamed abandon. Her tint marked her as a *capresse*, but her features were fine, the cheekbones betraying French ancestry. She was the daughter of Yzore, who had been the closest thing to a mother Lily had known and who had rocked them in a double cradle after Lily's mother had died of childbirth fever. They were like sisters—almost. Cyrillia did not have to hide *her* love of Carnival! Twirling for Lily in her embroidered chemise decorated with bright ribbons, she knew Lily's secret without being told. She knew what Lily had done, understood her dilemma.

"Shall I be danced with, missy?" said Cyrillia with an insolent grin, and raised her arms languidly behind her head so that her young breasts lifted. Her skin flashed and glowed like bonfire embers, and her dark eyes teased and mocked her own words. She was a sight no man would be able to resist, and well she knew it! She would be more than danced with. There would be other things—things she had communicated only vaguely to Lily, for they were improper for a French girl to know.

"Oh, Rilla, it's perfect!" cried Lily, clapping her hands. "You go *en bébé* tonight!" She felt, as she often did with Cyrillia, a rush of something like envy. The lace-edged pantalets, the child's cap perched on the *capresse*'s hair, the tinted stockings displayed on smooth legs beneath the short chemise, suggested nothing of the babyhood the costume portrayed. Instead, the outfit emphasized how far its wearer had come from infancy.

"I myself would look silly in it," Lily admitted with a sigh. "I have not the flair."

And if I were caught . . .

The words hung unspoken between them. "Oh, missy, I cannot bear to think of you all alone on the last night of Carnival!" said Cyrillia.

Lily was all too aware that Cyrillia's sudden look of mournfulness was really a sly smile. "Next year it will all be different," she answered. That, too, bore a double meaning.

Next year Papa would be well again. The smallpox epidemic, *la vérette,* brought on a steamer from Colón, would have passed, along with the accompanying typhoid that had felled her father. The cold, stone-bedded Roxelane, polluted now with the refuse of death and dying, would run pure again; and there would be parties at Acelie. Then, too, she would be married, and if her demon still lived, she could not indulge it, even though it might sicken her like her own special plague.

Tonight is your last chance for all your life!

How alike the two girls were—Lily had risked disgrace to dance; Cyrillia had risked death, for *la vérette* affected only natives. It had a liking for *capresses,* as though it sought special beauty to kiss with its hideous mark.

"Well, I have brought you a gift to comfort you," said Cyrillia. "It's for your jupe dress." She opened a palm and Lily gasped in delight at the great gold-beaded necklace that glowed on the saffron blanket of the girl's hand.

"Rilla! You cannot! It's your *collier-choux*! It's valuable, and it was your grandmother's!"

Cyrillia grinned. "It's no matter. I have a prettier one now. It has four strands instead of three."

Lily gazed at her in disbelief. "You have no money, Rilla!"

Cyrillia laughed, her full lips parting like a hibiscus blossom opening. "I got it the way any woman gets something that is pretty. I pleased a man."

"Rilla!" Lily had heard of such things, and as the shock passed, it occurred to her that her friend was being practical. They were grown now and their lives were separating. Marriage among her kind was rare, and if a newspaper listed one legitimate birth on any day, it would list two dozen *naturels.*

As usual, Cyrillia read Lily's thoughts. "It is no different for you, missy!" she said with a prideful toss of her head.

"For me! But I am to marry Edmond Beau Clair!"

"And he will buy you Acelie and keep it from being auctioned away. When the vows have been read, you will pay in all the ways he demands, because he will have a much stronger hold on you than does a man who merely buys a girl a necklace."

"But I love Edmond!" Lily protested. She should be angry, but something in Cyrillia's manner made her feel only confused.

The *capresse*'s eyes went blank as she fastened the beads

around Lily's neck. "This shall remind you how lucky you are!"

Lily studied her reflection in the mirror. She knew that the magnificent beads were intended for her to wear this very night. She imagined how they would shine on the prohibited jupe costume that no one but Cyrillia knew she owned. "Your grandmother sold herself for these," she said, feeling the necklace like the heavy hand of the past on her bosom.

Was it true that the slavery of women to men could not be denied? Was she selling herself to Edmond because he would buy Acelie as part of the marriage agreement? It was difficult to think of gentle Edmond as a master. Would that be different, somehow, after their marriage?

"My grandmother was the pet of Monsieur Bon, and she used the only thing she had, herself, to make him set her free. Yzore says that if the big wind had not come and blown him away because he was so evil, Grandmother would have made him change his will, too. And we should have been rich as well as free."

Lily was familiar with the gist of this story. She knew that Cyrillia considered herself better than others like her because her family had been free before abolition, because the blood of the fabled Monsieur Bon ran in her veins. But tonight Lily realized that Cyrillia was planning to finish what her grandmother had started. She intended to find a colonial to make her rich, not rich with the passing affluence of a mistress, but with the wealth of a wife, for generations.

"The man who gave you the necklace—is he the one?" Lily did not have to wonder if her friend would understand the question.

"Oh, no!" Cyrillia shook her head gaily. "He is only for fun. I must get more pretty things before that, and this one is married. In the meantime, I must dance, mustn't I? I shall think of you tonight when I am dancing." Her eyes flashed wickedly with knowledge, and she slipped from the room.

Lily trembled. Outside the window the sun was setting beyond the blunt ridge of the mornes. She heard laughter down in the gardens of yams and couscous where the workers lived in their *ajoupas* built of trunks of arborescent fern and canestraw thatch. Her carved wardrobe loomed in the duskiness. Inside, beneath her traveling cloak, lay the violet jupe costume. She remembered how she had known she must have it as soon as she had seen it in the secondhand shop in St. Pierre.

She had said to the clerk, "For my *bonne*, my servant, for her birthday," but even as she was taking money from her purse, she had known that yellow was a *capresse*'s color. Cyrillia could never wear that wonderful violet.

As if in a trance, she was moving toward the wardrobe. She could almost see the sway of his body in the glow of the old-fashioned oil lamps, the way his gaze had attached to her from behind his mask, willing her with his eyes to follow him, to be consumed in the dance.

A commotion in the courtyard below broke the spell, brought her running to the window. Before the doorway, beneath the ancestral ceiba trees, a bay horse was stirring up clouds of dust as its rider shouted a command to halt.

Edmond! She had not expected him. She put her hands to her cheeks, spun on her heels, her world spinning with her. The suitor was at the door, and here she was in her *chinoise*! Everything she did now was pure instinct. The door of her wardrobe crashed back. The dressing garment fell to the floor, and instead of the exotic jupe costume, out came a blouse bodice, a skirt of printed delaine with its straw bustle stitched inside. She pulled a bell cord, forgetful that Cyrillia had gone and that Yzore sat at Papa's bedside.

Nobody came. She struggled with the fastenings herself, plaiting her hair into a low, looped braid and tying on a grosgrain bow. Then quickly she ran down the stairs. Had anyone even opened the door for him? She stood on tiptoe on the staircase and peered over, straining to see into the sitting room. He had let himself in. His tall form was so familiar, so suddenly comforting, that she was filled with gratitude.

Dear Edmond! He had come when she needed him! It was as though his love for her had told him, she thought with the mystical romanticism of young girls. It was as if in his male supremeness he had known she needed his protection tonight. She was bathed in relief, the question of the Carnival dance having been wrested so simply from her incompetent woman's hands. She had been saved from all manner of danger into which she might have foolishly cast herself. She drank up the sense of well-being he gave her, the warmth she felt at the sight of his tall, straight back, the wavy chestnut hair above the collar of his twill jacket.

He turned and saw her. She read in his eyes how pretty she was, standing there, poised, on the stairs. She came toward him, both hands outstretched, her every movement unconsciously skilled.

"Lily!"

She heard rapture in his voice, but there was something in his tone that frightened her. Then his hands were in hers and she sought reassurance in their strength. They were rougher than the hands of other young gentlemen, and it was one of the things she liked about him. His strong hands had spoken for him in his wooing of her, telling her how dedicated he was to the land, how he worked his cacao himself, never content to trust his destiny to underlings. Each time his hands had touched hers, she had felt he was right for Acelie. She could trust him with her heritage, and so, with herself.

"Edmond, there is no one about! You must go! This is not at all proper!" This from the girl who only a dawn ago had danced the *bouèné* with a complete stranger. The words fell effortlessly from her lips; the horror she felt was genuine. She had an unrecognized talent for changing worlds. She did not yet realize that inside her were many Lilys, many spheres she would have to explore before finding to which she really belonged.

Something of Edmond's agitation communicated itself to Lily in a sort of excitement. She had never been entirely alone with him, and she wondered what she might expect, especially since they were engaged. He looked past her, up the stairs. "Lily, I have come to see your father."

"Oh." She was crestfallen. "A matter of business, then."

"It is more than a matter of business!"

"Papa is too ill, Edmond. You will have to tell *me*." At once she wondered where these words had come from. It should not have been in the scenario for her to suggest he discuss such things with her. It had been, she supposed, the great urgency in his voice, this new appetite she had for venturing beyond the perimeters of her small world. Edmond was looking at her oddly, and she flushed beneath his gaze.

"Tell *you*, Lily! Well, I suppose I must, then. It is something that concerns you—us."

"Do you mean our marriage, Edmond?" Her face was turned up toward his. She fancied he shuddered, as though his spirit tried to surge from his body and clasp her.

"Yes, dearest." The muscles of his lean face were taut with strain. She was certain now that he was holding himself in check, and sure, too, that it was not only because they were alone together. Still holding her hands, he pushed her gently down in a velvet armchair and sat across from her. Lily became thoroughly alarmed. She pressed his fingers, unable to guess this new peril.

"Lily, Joe has come home!"

"Your brother!" She hardly noticed that he had dropped her hands and sat miserably back from her. Through the shock waves she did not grasp the symbolism of that movement. How long had it been since Joe Beau Clair had left Martinique? Ten years? She scarcely remembered him, a reckless young man in control of all the Beau Clair fortune and destined to come to no good end.

In those days Beau Clair and Acelie had been two of the strongest estates on the island in the aftermath of abolition. Beau Clair had been strong because of its vastness; Acelie, because of the loyalty of its *affranchies,* who had stayed on, accepting its welfare as their own. She remembered the fine estates divided and auctioned, the rich red acajou-wood furniture traveling with the Louis XIV down to steamers bound for Mother France. She remembered the tears shed indiscriminately by those of all colors.

Lily's father had planted bananas and had been laughed at for his descent to native crops. And Joe Beau Clair had stuck to sugar and cacao and women, had professed himself bored with it all, and as times had grown worse, he had disappeared, leaving Beau Clair to the younger, but willing Edmond.

These things Lily had heard about Joe Beau Clair, though she had been too young to really understand. And after he had gone, everyone had begun to say that he was dead. He had had too much passion for danger to remain alive, and each year had reinforced the idea. Now this ghost had come home.

"Lily, I am penniless! I release you from your promise to be my wife."

She stared at his agonized face, remembering sharply Cyrillia's insulting view of her engagement, and suddenly through the tumult of emotion, anger took hold. She would prove beyond doubt that she was made of better stuff. She would prove it to Cyrillia, to Edmond—to herself.

"Do you think my love grows and diminishes with your pocketbook?" she cried furiously. "Is your brother to come courting now? And am I expected to marry him? Am I to be sold to the highest bidder? I will stay with you, Edmond, no matter what!"

She had the joy of seeing hope reborn in his eyes. "Are

you certain, Lily? Joe does not want to buy Acelie; he says it is a bad investment, and he's right, of course. I have pleaded our cause to him already, and I must speak to your father. He may not want this marriage now."

"I want it, Edmond. More than ever."

He was overcome, then, by their aloneness and crushed her to him, kissing her fiercely on the lips. She felt him quaver, and she trembled, too, in a kind of surprise. It was true that she wanted to marry him more than before. The return of Joe Beau Clair had given challenge to her life, a flux, an unknown quality. Far inside her she felt a heaviness slide away from her existence. Then Edmond was gone, and she was left there in the sitting room, aquiver with excitement, filled with an enormous energy.

At last she rose and went up to her father's room, where the setting sun filtering through closed shutters made a red halo around the turbaned head of Yzore, who sat beside the sick man. Lily crept to her father's bedside, looked down into his white face.

"Why is he so still, Yzore?" she whispered, feeling a chill.

"He is the same, missy. He is only sleeping."

"I will sit with him, then. It is the last night of Carnival, and you should go. They are all leaving now."

"I do not want to dance, missy."

Yzore's words filled her with a strange sense of release. She tiptoed to the door; then her feet flew as she ran to her own room. Eagerly she pulled the violet jupe costume from its hiding place, hugged its silken folds against her.

She smiled to think that once she had wondered what she would do with this primitive slave garment with which some wealthy plantation owner had once adorned his favorite property. And even as she had slowly made her other purchases, she had not known. She had bought the scarlet foulard to wear about her shoulders, the brilliant madras turban and trembling pins of gold to fasten it, and, most daring of all, a chemise with half sleeves and five rows of lace. She had not known—it had been as if the *diablesse* inhabited the dress itself.

How willing she was for it to lead her now as she donned her treasures one by one over her bare skin, according to native custom. She hesitated a moment, then fastened the great *collier-choux* around her neck, catching her breath at the sight of its gleaming gold against the violet silk. Over all she fastened the traveling cloak, tying its hood carefully to conceal the yellow turban.

Outside she heard singing. The creaking of wooden wheels, the joking cries to stragglers, were all for her. She hurried out into the sweet fresh air of the new night. In the stable she flung off the cloak and hid it under a pile of straw. When she stepped out again, the white wire mask was over her face, and the violet and red of her costume blazed like the sunset itself just fading over the wind-torn banana trees, the hedges of rose d'Inde.

Now she was a different person, for whom all the rules were different. She ran into the road and swung herself onto a high-wheeled cane cart loaded with revelers.

"Forgive me, Papa," she whispered. She knew he could never understand, should he learn of her adventure, but she could not help it that she was young and the call of life was too strong for her.

And then with tropical abruptness the sun slipped below the green, vine-tangled hills. In the moment just before, the glare faded and the light was pure. It was the only time of the day when things could be seen for their true color. Lily looked back at Acelie, at its walls of washed yellow stone, its irregular roofline broken with small unglazed dormer windows, its piazza trimmed in purple bougainvillea.

For that terrible instant, Lily saw Acelie as it was, a hulk of somnolent, aging grandeur. She saw herself as she was, and two great waves of feeling met and crashed within her—one chill and fearful, the other hot with excitement.

And she saw Edmond. He, even more than her father, would never understand.

2

The glow of tallow-colored moonflowers spun a trail beside the road in the soft night. And then St. Pierre, the gayest of West Indian cities, with its theaters, its cafés, its Lycée, and its shops that rivaled those of Paris. Lily jumped from the cart at its gates and wandered the narrow cobbled streets among the three-story, gabled houses.

Great caldrons of tar burned on the main street, Rue Victor Hugo, each one tended by an Indian laborer, to purify the air of the dreaded smallpox. Lily shuddered as a procession went past which was not the sort she had come to see—a coffin balanced on the heads of black men. She heard moans, sobs, snatches of laughter, Carnival song. The *dégringolade* would begin soon, she thought, but she could not bear the wait and started to head for the *savane*, where dancing might already have started. Then she heard the drums.

With a gasp of anticipation she turned her eyes up the street and saw the maskers gathering, a storm of blue, rose, and yellow clothing poised above the town. It would be the same now at the top of every street that led up to the mountains. She heard drums in the north answer drums from the south. The complaints of the dying seemed to cease. French gentlemen who had been drinking at a sidewalk café put aside their rum punches with smiles. Lily had not looked for her partner among them. He would not be there.

She could not imagine him sitting indolent. He would come as though he had been borne on the drumbeat, yet he would not sweep down with the hordes of maskers. She did not know where he would come from or when. It was almost as though he were a vision that came to her in the delirium of music.

Suddenly the street swarmed. The racketing clash of two great bands buffeted the balconied buildings. The peaked caps of the dancing societies, the Intrépides and Sans-souci, tossed like golden candle flares against the dark. The crowd swayed, fluttered, and preened itself like a flock of wave-borne seabirds. Then a smoothing, an emergence of order, the procession forming, dancers skating backward before the musicians. Lily let herself be hurled into the crystallizing line.

Vampire-bat headdresses leaped among mock-religious costumes, and tin cans clattered from the black robes of *diablesses*, portrayed by the tallest women. Their black masks were an eerie contrast to the ghostly white ones. Loinclothed men, representing the original African ancestors, gleamed with their smearings of soot and molasses, and there were women in Congo costume, old-time plantation garb—gray calico shirt and coarse skirt of percaline, a handkerchief worn beneath an enormous hat.

But some needed no costume. The pox had made their faces unrecognizable. As the procession wound through Rue Peysettes, Tut de Petit Versailles, sick people staggered from the doorways to join the dancing. Lily tried to look away from these grotesques, but there were too many of them. They were somehow compelling, these revelers with the mark of death upon them. Near her a girl in crimson spun silently to the cobblestones like a withered flower. For a moment the sound of wails was louder than the blowing horns, the drums, the clapping hands. There was an outcry to send for a priest.

Lily lifted her eyes to the starry sky, determined not to spoil this night with thoughts of death. "It will not help her if I look at her, if I am sad," she thought. "It is all I have, this one night, to feel this way and dance the *bouèné*."

It was all she had, too. The similarity struck at her, and involuntarily she looked down into the ruined face, feeling a kinship, as though her own life would end in a way with this night. Then the procession drew her on, and she felt a touch on her arm.

She whirled to see him smiling at her beneath his black eye mask. Never had she been so glad to see him, and she was almost overwhelmed by a need to rush into his arms. She could not, of course, not a *fille de couleur* with a French gentleman in the middle of the street. But then he lifted a hip toward her, the expression of his mouth knowing. She answered with a swish of her limbs beneath the violet skirts, and she was telling him things she did not even know she said—that this dance with him had become as life itself to her, that it had become everything essential in her being.

The procession went on. She was aware of nothing but him. The beat of the drums was as unnoticed but as vital as the throbbing of her pulse. She had forgotten that the night must end; she did not wonder what thoughts were in his mind. She accepted unquestioningly the language of his amazingly supple body. How was it that he danced as he did, he whose expertise should by rights be confined to the waltz?

He belonged here no more than she, though his sex made *his* transgression a mild one. It spoke of impatience with pretense, and though she did not realize it, a certain similar quality in herself was what caused her to dance as well as he. Both of them had unleashed something within them which never should have been allowed its freedom.

The air grew brisker, and she saw that they were passing the *savane*, moving across the new bridge over the Roxelane to the old quarter of the Fort. Then the drums stopped. Her soul screamed with frustration. She felt that her very breath had been snatched away. The crowd scattered. Demons and goblins ran into houses, up alleys.

"It is the Good God who comes!" someone cried, and a priest walked by followed by an acolyte ringing a bell. She understood then why the drums had stopped, why the revelers had run. One could not appear masked, as a goblin or devil, before the priest. She shuddered and thought of the girl in the crimson gown who had fallen dead on the cobbles. Was it to her that the priest went? If not to her, then to someone like her, surely.

The drums began again, and she lost herself in the music. She did not know how much later she felt him tug at her hand, lead her out of the dance. "No, don't stop," she said simply, and tugged back.

He laughed. "Come, there are better places for a wanton like you on Carnival night."

She followed, excited, her heart reeling. "Where are we going, monsieur?"

"Where you shall dance so that your soul will shake itself from you in shame, little one," he said. She knew what he meant and went cold with fear. She had heard of the ballroom, with its unspeakable forces of evil.

"Monsieur, I cannot go to the ballroom!"

But her words were lost in a blare of horns. What would he have thought if he had heard? He might have guessed that she was an impostor. And then what? She intuited that he would have a terrible temper. Or he might have laughed at her and packed her off home. She did not have time to think which would have been worse. He was leading her into a long room hung with lanterns and paper streamers.

She had a moment to take in the forbidden scene as he paused to pay at the door. A few French Creoles and their mistresses sat in a gallery above the dance floor, and she was relieved that she was not the only one of French blood in the room. Then, just as he led her out to dance, the music changed. The gallery emptied at once, and Lily knew that she was in the depth of hell.

None of those sisters and cousins of friends who had run away to Carnival had ever participated in the *danse du pays*, and not even the debauched French gentlemen intended to watch. She thought of fleeing, but the crush was thick. She thought of Acelie and Edmond and wondered how she would face them after this.

She did not doubt what was going to happen. A strange certainty was growing over her, and at the same time, she did begin to feel that her soul was leaving her. Her body had become a thing in itself; she knew she had become incapable of directing it. It had an essence of its own, and it seemed to flow joyfully away from her like wine poured from a bottle.

It was not that the music grew louder or faster. It became only franker, more savage. The lightness, the teasing of the *bouèné* disappeared, replaced by an insistent fierceness. Suggestiveness gave way to explicitness. And as she had known it would, her body followed the music. She felt her mouth grow moist and her lips fall open. She gazed into her partner's face and saw the violet flash of her dress mirrored in his ravenous eyes. She saw the extent of his appetite for her, saw the power of his lust as she had never seen lust on a man's face before. The fear she had felt when she had begun to dance was replaced by a wave of triumph. She laughed aloud, pleased with herself, with him, with the barbaric music.

Then, hardly knowing how it had happened, she found herself outside again, his arm familiarly about her. Even Edmond had never embraced her so, with a hand cupped beneath the swell of her breast.

She felt his touch as if in a dream. She was so intoxicated with the music that it did not seem at all untoward.

"How you danced, my sweet!" he cried. "I have never danced with anyone like you! I do not even know your name!"

She would have liked to leave it that way, but instead she floundered briefly and then said, "My name is Mimi. I am a coaling girl."

She could not have said why she took this additional

plunge into untruth. Perhaps out in the street the sense of her old self had begun to creep over her, and she had wanted to wrap herself more tightly in her Carnival identity, to protect herself against the passing of the hours.

"A coaling girl! And you load for the steamers of the Compagnie Generale Transatlantique, of course! Well, we shall probably see each other again, then. My ship lies anchored in the roadstead."

"You are her captain, monsieur?" She knew he could be no ordinary seaman.

"Her owner, Mimi."

"I am not surprised, monsieur. Will you be long in Martinique?" She wondered why it mattered. She would not see him again after tonight, though if she had really been a coaling girl she would have studied every face on the landing to see if she could discover the one that had been behind the mask. She knew she was not supposed to ask where he was taking her. A bargain had been struck, though she did not understand the exact nature of it. Had it something to do with the way her body had tingled as they were dancing, with the unusual stirrings she felt from the light pressure of his fingers through the silk of her bodice? The touch made her skin flame; she let him command her steps as though she had been bound to him with shackles.

"I will not be in St. Pierre long, Mimi. I have come for a wedding. We will make the most of our time, eh?"

"Not *your* wedding!" The words were out before she thought.

"Mine!" He gave a shout of laughter that echoed from the rubblework houses. "You are afraid that I shall be playing the ardent bridegroom, and you shall be cheated of your due! Oh, little Mimi, I could never treat you so badly. No, I shall not be the bridegroom. I shall never be caught by any demure little thing in a crinolette. They do not interest me with their pretty manners. It is women like you who have the only claim to me!"

"I am glad, monsieur," she said, so solemnly that he laughed again. She would have liked it so much better had he said "you" instead of "women like you." "Will you tell me your name, monsieur? I have told you mine."

"What! And have you search me out nine months hence to beg money for your child?"

"But I have no child," she said innocently.

He lifted his eyes to the sky, and this time his shoulders

shook with silent merriment beneath the cashmere of his coat. Lily was bewildered, not at all sure she was happy to be the source of so much amusement to him. In the evil miasma of the ballroom she had had ideas, wicked ideas that might have included embraces behind the great concealing trunk of a silkwood tree or kisses on the twinkling phosphorescence of a beach. He was hatless, and his soft hair was the color of cinnamon sticks in the market. A thrill shot through her as she wondered how it would be to touch it.

"Perhaps your Good God will give you a child soon, Mimi. Indeed, if you dance as you did tonight often, he will not be able to help it."

She did not understand what dancing had to do with it, but she knew there was much of which she was ignorant. She was hungry and thirsty and thought of asking him to buy her a mango or a little pot of cocoa water. But she would have to remove her mask to eat or drink, so she walked along beside him, waiting to see what would happen.

He turned in suddenly at a ramshackle tin-roofed building and led her through an empty lobby, up a flight of stairs. The hallway was musty after the fresh night air, and Lily drew closer to him, suddenly ill-at-ease. He took a long iron key from his pocket and opened a door. "Here, Mimi. I shall put on a light in only a moment." The soft glow of a kerosene lamp illuminated a shell-carved chest of drawers, a floor covered in rush mats, a simple but substantial-looking bed, the washstand with a *dobanne*—the heavy, thick-lipped red water jar—and his shaving mug. The breeze through the open slats of the long Demerara windows was as fresh as outside and tasted of salt.

"This is private, Mimi," he said. "No one will complain, and in the morning there will be a fine view of the ocean and a servant to bring good coffee and plenty of hot water to wash."

"It's a nice room, monsieur." It was unlike any room she had ever seen, but it was not that the furnishings were very different so much as that it had a delicious secretness in the lamplight, a quality much like the man himself. She knew all at once that what she had wished to happen beneath the silkwood or on the beach sand would occur here instead. It would be more than she had imagined, and better. She felt it in the atmosphere, and she began to pulse with disquiet.

He bent and blew out the light, as though he had put it on only to show her the room. Moonlight sifted through the window slats, alternating with shadow like icing and chocolate cake. She saw him coming toward her through the light and the dark, tried to read the expression in his eyes as the moonglow warmed his face.

Then he was beside her, his arm clasping her waist impatiently. She knew that what was to happen was forbidden, even more forbidden than the *danse du pays*. She knew that after it she would never be the same, and inside her a small voice told her it was dangerous, for she must live her life as if tonight had not happened. Tonight she was living a lie, and hereafter she would lie by pretending to be her old self. Somehow Lily knew that that masquerade would be far more difficult than the one she played in the jupe gown.

And yet Lily was not afraid. To her own surprise she seemed to have become Mimi. Her life at Acelie, her engagement to Edmond, had grown so distant she did not connect them to herself at all. Lily was someone a friend, like Cyrillia, had only told her about, someone they had laughed and wondered about as they walked barefoot in the line of *charbonnières*, balancing the baskets of coal easily on their heads.

His breath blew warm as a trade wind about her neck; she felt his lips at her throat and with a strangled cry turned to give herself to him as Mimi would have. He was pressing her to him. She felt her breasts flatten against the hardness of his chest; her thighs were locked against his. Had he not been holding her, she might have swooned away from the delight of it. His fingers reached behind her and unfastened the golden necklace Cyrillia had given her. The great *collier-choux* came away, and they surged even closer. She had not realized that the beads had been wedged between them, boring into both of them, blocking the embrace from completeness.

Now she felt him working among the trembling pins of her turban. It was not the first time he had ever undone a madras, for he moved quickly, expertly. Nonetheless she raised her arms to help him and felt a rush of pleasure as the weight of her hair tumbled into his hands. He kissed its coils with a sigh, and laid them against his cheek.

"Ah, Mimi," he muttered, "you are a beautiful octoroon or a *sang mêlée* to have such hair. Come, let us see what other marvels you are hiding."

One hand was on the brooch that held her scarlet shoulder scarf. The other reached for her mask to lift it away. If he succeeded, she would be Mimi no longer! With a shriek she pushed his hand away from the brooch, wrestled him lose from her mask. His astonishment was such that he hardly resisted.

Her heart thundered. She hadn't realized that undressing would be part of this thing. She should have known at least about the mask! She had never thought when she had imagined the kissing—she had only wanted it so! Perhaps she had hoped for embraces stolen in utter darkness; yet the moon had been shining every night of Carnival. What a fool she had been!

Before she could make some plan, his hands were on her again, this time incredibly on the buttons of the silken jupe gown. A current of air ran against her hot skin, and she gasped as she felt his hand caress the small of her back beneath her clothing. It was a singular sensation—rough and demanding, at the same time soothing, so that all her caution almost dropped away. Writhing against desire, she twisted around and seized his wrist. It was almost more than she could manage not to push him to some deeper intimacy. He withdrew and she sensed the rising of the temper she had guessed that he had. Behind his mask his eyes were furious.

"What is it, Mimi? Do you want money first? Is that all you think of me—that I will not give you any? I thought we understood each other better than that. I intend to make you many pretty presents, Mimi, and, do you know, I believe that if you have a child, you may come to me, and I will make it presents, too. Mind you, I must be sure it is yours and not a borrowed child. The time of its birth must be right. There! What have you done to me, Mimi? I have never told a woman that before."

Still she hesitated, keeping a terrible grip on his wrist, clenching her teeth in an effort not to be overcome by this incomprehensible urgency she felt. His other hand still caressed her. How very large and important it seemed, pressing the nipples that had become taut and obvious under her corsetless garments. She could not move his hand; indeed, she dared not move at all for fear she might detonate responses in herself that would carry her over the precipice.

He, mistaking her reason, went on, "Let me see. What can I give you to show you my intention?" His hand left her bodice, making her quake with a mixture of relief and deprivation. He reached into his vest pocket and brought out an engraved pocket watch on an Albert chain. Opening the cloth purse that hung from her waist, he placed the watch inside. Then, with a sigh of satisfaction, he lifted her off her feet, strode across the room with her, and dropped her into the center of the bed.

"There, Mimi," he cried happily. "Now you will keep the promises you have made me!"

"I made you no promises, monsieur!"

"You did, Mimi! With your body. It is a sin not to keep promises."

She gave up, clinging only to the white wire mask as he slid his hands under her gown, across her quivering stomach. "Come," he cried, "I cannot make love to a woman whose face I cannot see! I cannot love a woman without kisses!" He reached again for her mask, and she fought him off, weeping.

"*Atô bô!*" he whispered. "Kiss me now!"

Everything was lost! He was stronger than she!

Then his hands were gone. She thought at first he must have discovered her, but the mask was still in place. She raised herself weakly on her elbows and saw him hunched on his knees, looking at her. His trousers were gone, and so was his mask. She saw that his eyes were a shocking blue. There was humor in them, a mixture of anger and concern and, above all, a quickness.

"Mimi, you have had the pox," he said with decision. "It can be nothing else. Let me see you! Only be glad that *la vérette* did not kill you! I will understand. I have seen so much beautiful about you already, and these scars often fade. You will see, Mimi, in a year or so."

Lily wept wordlessly and held tightly to her mask. There was something about his face—she felt he had always been part of her life. It was as though he had materialized from her thoughts, her daydreams, from all that was most hidden within her. He was so perfect, so familiar, so distant. She would never be able to touch him, she knew; and she wept harder, wishing she had not seen him at all.

He put his hand on her hair again, thinking he understood.

She longed to throw herself into his arms and confess the greatness of her lie, to tell him of the misery she was destined to carry all her life, a burden worse, she thought, than smallpox scars. Would his voice be so gentle then? Would he gather her to him and do at least this once whatever he had been about to do?

More likely he would cry out that she was making him game for a duel and would deliver her like a chattel to her father's house. Why should he take chances with her when there were so many Mimis?

Without warning, even to herself, she leaped from the bed and ran for the door. Disadvantaged in his underclothes, he gave a shout, grabbed for her. She felt a piece of her trailing skirt come away in his hand. Then she was in the dim hall, stumbling down the steps, her dark hair streaming.

She did not pause when she reached the street, but ran on hellbound in the darkness. She turned a corner, and a hideous figure jumped at her, clad all in red, with a blood-colored mask and a white horsehair wig. His headdress, topped by a red lantern, made him seem to leap in fires of damnation. It was the Carnival devil making his rounds. He gave a cackling laugh at Lily's fright, rapped out something she knew must be obscene, and cavorted away, followed by a crowd of boys.

"Bimbolo! Zimbolo! Et zimbolo! Et bolo-polo!

She stood trembling while the chant grew farther away. It did not seem to be coincidence to her that she had met the devil, and the sensible part of her nature began to reemerge. She must save herself! She must get home to Acelie. She walked until she came to a landmark, a park with a luxury of ravenalas, rubber trees, and palms, and went toward Rue Bouille. There, thankfully, she found what she was looking for, a horse from Acelie. The worker who had been allowed to ride it would have to walk home in the morning and would blame the "theft" on various ones among his peers, but Lily minded none of that.

She drew close to the horse, spoke to it, unhitched it from the iron ring of its post. Then, swinging quickly astride, she rode away through the narrow streets, away from the balconied rooms where soft lamps still shone, away from the smoking tar pots, from Carnival and from Mimi, away from the passion of her life.

3

She galloped away from St. Pierre along the beach; the sea breeze, pungent with salt and the aroma of cod *akras* drifting from some campfire, whipped in her hair. Now and then the shadow of a crab skittered across the sand or moonlight flashed on the red and yellow bands of a perroquet fish, washed up dead by the tide. She rode as though the devil chased her, and indeed she believed he did. "Only let me get home to Acelie, and I will transgress no more!" she prayed.

By the time she turned away toward the mornes, the moon had set. Now the only light came from the shrines along the way, and as she reached one niche lamp she looked ahead, focusing her mind on the glow from the next Virgin or white Christ. And each time she was safely at her new destination, she whispered her vow once more.

The night was full of voices. Tree frogs chanted, wood crickets racketed, birds piped among the broad-leafed balisiers and the Indian reed. At last came the shelter of Acelie's avenue of cacao trees. They reached for her like a mother's arms as she slipped from the horse and led it into the stable. She found her cloak where she had left it, and tying it about her once more, she went quietly into the house through the kitchen entrance, where, if anyone saw her, she might still be taken for a returning reveler.

In her room she tossed her purse on the dresser and shed the torn jupe costume. Then in her virginal white cotton nightdress she knelt beside her great boat-shaped *bateau* bed and thanked God.

But even in her own bed the gentleman from Carnival pursued her. And all her prayers had not subdued him. In her uneasy dreams she felt his hand caress the contours of her body, making her aware of herself in fascinating new ways. In her dreams she did not push his hand away, and there was no mask to hinder kisses. Strange emotions grew in her, spreading along her spine until she was tense from head to toe. She tossed in her bed, thrusting the covers away from her, believing them to be her clothing. She knew vaguely that she was reaching for something beyond; she knew he was leading her. She moaned, struggling to find the thing he seemed to tell her was so desirable. His hand was on her shoulder, shaking her.

"Please, no," she murmured, just as she had when he had tried to pull her away from the street dancing. This rough motion, so unlike the smooth caresses, was distracting her from her quest.

The shaking did not stop. She tried to roll away. "Missy! Wake up!" Lily opened her eyes and saw Yzore gazing down at her speculatively. The eyes of Yzore had always been worse than the priest's confessional when you had sinned, and instinctively Lily knew she had sinned, even here in her bed where she had slept each night from childhood.

But Yzore was not looking at her accusingly tonight. There was something else—pity? And it was not yet time to rise, for outside the wood crickets still sang.

"Missy, your father is dying!"

She leaped from the bed, the dream falling away where she was grateful it could never be retrieved. "But he was all right—"

Yzore shook her great turbaned head sorrowfully. "I do not understand it, missy."

"I must go to him, Yzore!"

The *bonne* put out a hand and stopped her. Yzore's eyes told her that much would be required of her, and even in her confusion and grief she wondered what it would be. "I have sent for the priest," Yzore said.

Lily shuddered. "For the last rites," she whispered.

Yzore shook her head. "For more than that. He is to fulfill your father's last wish. He wants to see you married to Edmond."

Lily drew in her breath. "Married! Tonight!"

Yzore sighed, and there was a hugeness of meaning to it, like the soughing of the sea wind. She put her hand gently on Lily's shoulder. "Ah, missy, there were things I was to tell you, and now there is not time. There is no time to spare at all. You must ride for Edmond yourself. Everyone is still at Carnival."

"I, Yzore! Ride to Beau Clair!"

"There is nothing else to do. I have laid out your riding habit."

Picnic on a Volcano 25

Lily let Yzore fit her into her stays and fasten her into the gabardine jacket and skirt. "I must see Papa, Yzore!"

Yzore hesitated, then nodded. "Do not stay long. Remember, it is his last wish, and he will be gone before dawn."

She knelt at her father's bedside, buried her head against the covers to stifle the sound of her weeping. She had been everything to him all her life. And she had had no mother or sister or brother—only him. He had made a companion of her, overruling Yzore to teach her to swim with him in iridescent green lagoons and to talk to her about things he would have with his sons. She had learned from him the business of cane and cacao, and she had helped him survive these difficult times.

She felt her father's hand in her hair, where last she had felt the lustful fingers of the man from Carnival. She remembered how he had stroked her tresses and thought her a beautiful octoroon. Those moments had happened in another life, and this, too, was a nightmare from which she must awaken.

"Papa, don't leave me alone!" she cried.

"You will not be alone, Lily. You will be with Edmond. You will be at Acelie, as you have always been."

"Yes, Papa." The rasping voice made her suddenly ashamed of her outburst. She rose steadily to her feet. He had made her stronger than most women, but she had never had the chance to test herself. "I will go for Edmond, Papa." She was rewarded by a sigh, and only when she was once more on the dark road did she remember Joe Beau Clair.

The house lifted whitely from the night, lightless, but imposing, an enormous ghost trimmed in pommiers roses. It had not the friendliness of Acelie; it was less to Lily's liking with its marble pillars and great ballrooms. Always in coming here she had felt intimidated. Her footsteps echoed on the stones of the portico. She lifted the brass knocker and let it fall, hearing it sound against the heavy balata-wood door. No servant came to let her in. Like Acelie's, they were all at Carnival.

"Edmond!" she shouted wildly. What if he were not here? What if he had gone to watch the Carnival dancing? What if she were to meet Joe, who was master now? She thought of Joe Beau Clair as matching the house—arrogant, powerful, self-serving. He was a person, she thought, who could take what he liked and destroy what he didn't. She knew that someday she would have to meet and deal with Joe Beau

Clair. She had already recognized that Edmond was too in awe of his brother to be effective in his own behalf. She would have to do it herself—somehow—but not tonight, please.

"Edmond!" she shouted. The door burst open, and he was there, his necktie still unfastened. How thankful she was that he had been home abed instead of reveling as she had been!

"Oh, Edmond! Papa is dying!"

"Dearest!" He reached for her, pulled her into his arms. "Whatever can I do?"

"You must marry me, Edmond!"

"Of course. I am pledged to."

"It must be done tonight. It is Papa's last wish."

He gazed at her, and to her horror, she saw doubt come into his eyes. "We must tell him about Joe, Lily."

"We cannot!"

"Are you afraid he would forbid us, then? I cannot promise to keep Acelie for you."

She drew herself up, shook back her uncoiffed hair. "You must promise not to tell, Edmond. I demand it of you. It is the price of having me."

She saw the way he looked at her. The desire she saw in his eyes was not unlike that she had seen in the eyes of her dancing partner.

"You ask this against my honor, Lily?" he said.

"I ask you to let my father die at peace, Edmond." She knew she had won; he could not help himself against her. What power she had over him, greater than that of honor between men!

"Oh, Lily," he murmured, "we shall save Acelie, somehow, you and I."

"Yes, Edmond," she complied, and she waited while he brought his bay horse.

The priest was waiting for them in her father's bedroom. She knelt with Edmond, thinking how odd it was to be married in a riding habit. She had known, without being told, that she did not have time to change into the trained white satin gown that had taken so many careful fittings.

She marked the time exactly when they were pronounced husband and wife. It was four-thirty, the precise moment at which the wood crickets always ceased to sing. In the silence she looked triumphantly to the bed for approval of a thing well done.

Papa was gone. Before she fainted she had just time to notice the smile he had left behind.

Above her Lily saw the blades of a ceiling fan waver in the pale light of dawn. The fan should not be turning, she thought. It was so very cold. Then her vision cleared, and she saw that the fan was still. Someone was bending over her. Edmond. How could it be that he was in her bedroom? She felt the unaccustomed touch of silk against her breasts, and glancing down, saw that she was wearing, instead of a muslin nightdress, the low-necked gown with Honitron lace and yellow ribbons that had been intended for her wedding night.

Everything came back to her then. "Come and lie here beside me, Edmond," she said.

"I shall wait, Lily," he said. "You are not well."

But she knew that he should. Otherwise Yzore would not have dressed her in this gown. "I wish it, dearest," she said. "Come, I am your wife."

A little smile played at his mouth at the sound of the words on her lips. He adored her. He was the happy bridegroom despite the circumstances, despite the fact that within the hour the wedding night would be day. "I shall lie beside you, then, and make you warm. You are shivering, Lily."

She watched as he shed his clothing to his undergarments, only half aware that she was comparing the sight to her view of her Carnival partner without his trousers. Then Edmond opened the covers and pulled her to him. She felt the great tremor that ran through him as she pressed against him. His heat comforted her more than she had expected, and in release she began to sob out her grief. He held her gently, as he had promised, forbidding himself to explore the new wonders that were his to own.

Before long she began to feel that it was not enough. Unbidden memories returned. She thought of the way she had felt when she had been pinned on the bed in St. Pierre. She remembered the dream she had had only hours ago in this very bed, the reaching toward some paradise. Surely if she could reach it, her grief would be washed over, swept away. And now that she was married, she intuited that this ecstasy might not be forbidden to her. Edmond, dear Edmond, would take her to that heaven, and her two worlds would merge. Her *diablesse* would be stilled.

She raised herself on an elbow, bent over him, kissed him boldly on the mouth, while her clouds of dark hair stormed against his face. With a groan he let his hands begin to move—over her breasts, her back, her hips. She moaned after him, a tight sensation of well-being starting to grow in the depths of her. Then suddenly she was tossed onto her back. She felt him spread her legs, and his weight on top of her took away her breath. She did not resist, although it was somehow not what she had expected.

There were probings—hot, urgent, demanding. She struggled instinctively, tried to push him away, embarrassment superseded by awful panic. She looked to his face for reassurance, but it did not seem the same now. The familiarity had vanished.

And then, pain. She felt betrayed. She had never expected Edmond to cause her pain, he who had always taken care to bring her a footstool or find her a spot out of the sun. She cried out, little guessing that the sound was as basic to life as the cry of a newly born baby, not knowing that Yzore listened for it in a room close by, just as she had kept vigil through the illnesses of childhood.

Astonishingly, the searing, commanding thing which must be part of her husband gained entry to her body, seeking and ransacking secret regions of which she had had no inkling. She felt her body disunite, wrenched apart as mountains by a great rush of the sea.

And then he was done. She wondered what had happened to the sensation of promise she had felt at the beginning. It had been a lie, that paradise she had sought.

Or had it? While Edmond slept, her thoughts turned again to the man for whom she had danced so shamelessly. It had, after all, been he, not Edmond, who had seemed to make her the promise. A peculiar certainty grew in her that with him she would have found it.

At last, in the growing day, she crept from bed, opened the purse she had carried at the waist of the jupe costume. He had given her a watch. It was all she had of him now, just as he had only the gold *collier-choux* that she had abandoned in her haste.

The watch lay cool and heavy in her hand. She studied its every engraving minutely, knowing she would always be searching.

Without expectation she flipped open the back. And read the name inscribed there. JOE BEAU CLAIR.

4

Shutters snapped at Yzore's brisk touch. Beyond the red-tiled roofs of the plantation buildings an enormous rainbow shimmered from horizon to horizon over the green hills. Beneath, everything seemed small, lost in the wide grandeur of its colors.

Lily moaned and pulled herself onto her elbows. Her head swam as the sweet warmth of the day breeze swirled around her, and her senses reeled at the sun's blue blaze against her eyes.

"I am not well, Yzore," she muttered, dropping again into a crumpled heap amid the bedclothes. She had cried herself to sleep, and she ached with the exhaustion of spent emotion. "Why didn't you tell me, Yzore?" Her words were heavy, her accusation drugged with despair.

"Tell you what, missy? About men?" Yzore's calico skirts rustled efficiently, but secret compassion glimmered from her eyes. "It is better that you not know, a proper Creole girl like you. Come, I have your bath ready. You will feel better then."

Lily sat up, thrust a toe into the steaming tub Yzore had placed beside the carved bed. The water was a balm, and trancelike she stripped away her stained gown and lowered her bruised limbs into its heat. Her head cleared and the details of her deflowering rushed over her. She flushed as she thought of the brazen kisses she had bestowed on Edmond, of her invitation to the inconceivable indignities he had dealt her. *He thought I wanted . . . He didn't know that I had no idea. Yzore should have told me; yes, I know she should have!*

"Why, Yzore? Why is it different for me?"

"Because it would happen anyway. It is better not to know, like a sea snail when it comes into the net. It is better, missy."

"And it will happen again, Yzore? It is what marriage is all about?"

"Yes, missy. And you must allow it. That is the duty of a wife."

Lily shivered, though the water was still warm. "And it isn't the same for a girl of color?"

"She doesn't marry in church with a priest. She loves when she likes, and who she likes. And when she doesn't like, she shows him a sharp cane knife."

"But isn't that wrong, even for her?"

"She buys flowers for her Virgin, and the Virgin understands her prayers. The Virgin is a woman, too, missy."

"Yzore . . ."

"Yes, missy?"

Lily reached for a towel and stood up, water streaming over her firm breasts and her finely molded stomach and thighs. Again the breeze touched her, cooling this time, after the steamy bath, and she was reminded of another such breeze, rushing against her skin when it had been fiery from the touch of a man—a man not only not her husband, but the brother of her husband, the man with whom she would have to deal to keep her beloved Acelie.

She had wanted to tell Yzore, to go to her as she might have her dead mother, but she realized it was impossible. Yzore was like a mother, but not a mother. There would always be that gulf between them—the distance of culture and position that no amount of affection could quite bridge.

If *she* prayed to the Virgin, would the Virgin understand? And what of the longing that rose within her at the thought of the hands of Joe Beau Clair, at the memory of those bice-blue eyes that seared into her, unclothing her very soul? How should she hide from that gaze when next they met?

She had not known the ways a woman could feel; and when she had learned, it had been too late. *If I had known . . .*

But as soon as the thought formed, she knew that Yzore was right. It would not have made any difference. Joe Beau Clair would not have married her. He would not have pledged to save Acelie. He was a man who loved, freely and boldly, women who did not hold back, those who gave themselves without scruple in the ghostly tropic moonlight, as though the sun would never shine again to illumine their deeds.

Why should a man like Joe Beau Clair, an adventurer, a wanderer, tie himself to a woman any more than to a plantation like Acelie? One alliance would be as unprofitable as the other. But Edmond had, without hesitation, tied himself to both.

She thought with a little thrill of the moment there on the steps of Beau Clair when he had agreed to compromise his honor by marrying her without telling her father of the disaster of Joe's return. "It is the price of marrying me," she had told him. She had not been quite aware then that she, too, was paying a price.

Papa had died thinking that she and Acelie were safe. Edmond had kept his bargain, and she would keep hers, too. Edmond had dedicated himself to her, and it was Edmond to whom she owed her love. It did not occur to Lily that an obligation of love could not be discharged as easily as a debt for a monkey orange or breadfruit from the tray of a *porteuse*, an island carrier girl.

She turned for Yzore to lace her into her crinolette, and drawing in her breath to make her tiny waist smaller yet, thought with determination: "It cannot be that I care for Edmond's rogue of a brother! Edmond is well worth a dozen of him. I despise a man like Joe Beau Clair, a rootless vagabond who consumes women as carelessly as he downs his white rum. Last night he wanted Mimi. With morning he has forgotten his appetite. When the wood crickets sing again, some other shall satisfy him. He will have forgotten Mimi, and I will have forgotten her, too!"

She looked with distaste at the dress of black shot silk that Yzore had brought out. How different from the violet jupe gown she had worn such a short time before! But she was no longer the same person who had slipped away to Carnival. That person had been a mere girl, drunk with the excitement of discovery. Today she was a woman; she felt the reality of womanhood before her. The time of frivolity had slipped from her, spinning as it went like a pretty pebble swept to sea, its pinks and lavenders shining as the tide sucked it down where it might never glisten again.

The dress suited her mood of purpose. She let Yzore drop it over her head like the robe of a penitent, and gazing out the window, thought she matched two butterflies with black velvety wings that fluttered over the red foliage of the rose d'Inde, silhouettes against the yellow light. Death's butterflies, the natives called them. Yzore, seeing them there, did not think it coincidence. She leaned over the sill and flapped an apron vigorously.

"It is because we must bury your papa today, missy. They are the little spirits of death."

"Perhaps they have come to carry his soul away," said Lily, falling easily into the native manner of thinking. "Do you think they mind, Yzore, that they aren't bright like the others? I should, if I were a butterfly."

"I do not like them, missy. Hurry, now. Monsieur is waiting for you. It was he who said you must be allowed to sleep so late."

Lily watched in the mirror as Yzore braided her hair and secured the plait in tight loops at the nape of her neck. Then she bit her lips to bring color into them and rubbed at her pale cheeks to make them rosy.

"Yzore, does it happen every night?"

"Perhaps, if a man is young and in love."

Then tonight he would do those things again, she thought with certainty. And even as she promised herself it would be better, she felt a current of dread steal over her. She gave her skirts a shake and went down to greet her husband.

He sat waiting for her at the dining table. When he saw her, he leaped to his feet, seized her hands in his, and kissed her cool cheek. In his eyes were triumph, ardor, concern.

"Dearest!" The single word on his lips conveyed the thousands he could not find to say. He pulled out a chair for her, rang a little silver bell to summon Cyrillia.

"Croissants, Rilla, and rum punch for madame."

"Oh, no, Edmond, I cannot drink rum punch so early!" She could not meet the gaze of her friend, though she could feel Cyrillia's knowing eyes upon her.

"It's not early, Lily. And we will have a hard day. Rilla, be sure to use plenty of sugar syrup. Madame will need the energy."

Lily looked out the window and saw the wagon waiting with the coffin, which must have been made only this morning, and she did not protest further about the rum punch.

"We must go at once, Lily," he said gently. "It's a long way, and we mustn't be on the road after dark. We can't risk the snakes."

"I know, Edmond." She drank the punch gratefully and fetched her domed parasol. The great palms rustled and soughed as she took her place beside Edmond on the wagon. The scent of freshly sawed lumber drifted to her nostrils, and she shuddered, thinking of the body covered in quicklime lying beneath the new-smelling ceiba wood. She did not need to be told that the burial must be at once, any more than she had needed to be reminded of the menace of the fer-de-lance on the road after dark. In ordinary times there would have been a funeral, a procession winding its way to the cathedral at St. Pierre. But with every family touched by the pestilence, Edmond and Lily would be the only mourners. The workers gathered silently on the drive to watch them go, and in their faces she read tribute to a Frenchman who had always treated them fairly.

"We will not need to worry about our workers, Edmond," she said. "They will stay with us, if the pox doesn't take them." Her eyes swept over the brown canefields and the rows of banana trees, her mind filled with the need of work to be done.

"There will be trouble about the banana crop if the quarantine is not lifted. It will not keep like the sugar," he replied thoughtfully.

"But we will need the bananas to have any hope of saving Acelie. It is a long time off, Edmond. Surely you don't think—"

"When you pray for your father's soul today at the cathedral, Lily, pray that the ships will sail again as well."

It would have startled Edmond to think that he loved Lily for more than her beauty, that he had chosen her as much because he had always been able to talk to her of the things that interested him most—of cane and coconut groves and things ripening under the dazzling sun, of the feeling he had of belonging to the land that his forefathers had claimed from the tangled slopes of Pelee.

He had a sense of destiny on Martinique, and only a cruel fate had sent him to his beloved island as a second son. He had thought to have Beau Clair; he was still staggering beneath the blow of his brother's return. But when he had pledged to Lily, "We shall save Acelie, you and I," the two great passions of his life had joined into one.

The graceful Acelie, its plumed cane swaying, its palm crowns lifted toward the purple mornes, would be the foundation of his life. And Lily, no less beautiful, would be as much at the center of his existence, for it was she who would mother the next generation, sealing the plantation solidly to his line. He was content, even on his grim errand. He had a dream, a challenge, a woman who moved him more than the brilliant landscapes. Joe had made his task more difficult, but he intended to make good his promise to Lily. He would keep Acelie or he would die trying. He would never reconsider; he would never throw up his hands in despair. It was his nature.

No more suitable successor could have been found for the man whose coffin jounced over the limestone road on its way to its grave.

It was a good road, broad and well-graded, with embankments carpeted in moss and vines. Where it ran along precipices, shadows beyond its stone walls rippled the mountains with violet and indigo, and paler heights reached into the tender frosted pinks of clouds. There, far off, grew the virgin forests, those that had not already been destroyed in the making of charcoal. Nearer were slopes of young bamboo, furry and green, and stands of baby ferns like flocks of emerald-feathered birds in the grass.

"Drink enough to last you, Lily," her husband advised as they stopped by a fountain piped through bamboo from a spring. "This water is pure. We can't be sure when we reach St. Pierre."

She shuddered and took such a deep draft of the water that she felt dizzy from its coldness. One wrong sip in St. Pierre and she might be dead of typhoid like her father, but it was not that of which Lily thought. It was the mention of St. Pierre itself that unnerved her.

Could she see those streets where she had danced without betraying herself? It had been another lifetime, when she had been Mimi, who teased and loved where she pleased. She was not Mimi now; it was finished and done with, and yet . . .

As they came down the crescent hills into the narrow streets of red-roofed houses, Lily felt the stirrings of a wild excitement inside her, where some part of her could not be so easily told that Carnival was over, that all was ended. She gasped as they turned into Rue Victor Hugo, horrified to know that her devil still dwelt within her as she had feared.

But how different the city looked today! The clear light was stained with the smudgings of the tar pots, and there were no drums to blot away the sound of the death agonies. The water supply, which ran gurgling through open stone gutters, dropped in dirty little waterfalls down the steep streets, and even the silk-cotton and mango trees seemed limp with grief.

"Are you all right, Lily? It's not a sight you should see." Edmond's arm moved about her solicitously.

What else would he think would make her so pale? He could not know that she had seen it all before. He could not guess that even now she saw, in her mind's eye, death cheated by life in this same street. She saw the dying rising to dance; she saw herself turn to the man for whom she had been waiting all evening—no, since some eternity before her birth.

The cathedral loomed before her. The great statue of the Virgin looked down upon her, and she made confused obeisance in her heart. "Oh, Mary, mother of Jesus, help me!" she cried.

Edmond was going in to look for a priest. "Father Jacques," she told him, "the one who married us. I want no other."

"I will fetch him, Lily."

She watched as he disappeared through the middle one of three arched doorways. As she sat waiting, a sense of quiet began to come over her, as if her prayers had been answered. "He is not here now," she thought. "I am safe as long as he is not here." A small bird flew from an ancient tamarind tree in the little park nearby and diverted her attention from the new mounds in the churchyard, where even now several crews of gravediggers were working.

She had come here so many times, all of them happy, and the place itself began to exert its influence. It would be good to see Father Jacques, who had not only married her but also presided at her first Communion. "I will go in now and light a candle," she thought, longing for the cavernous gloom she had always liked. She gathered her skirts and jumped down from the wagon in time to see Edmond coming toward her. Beside him was a priest, but it was not Father Jacques.

"Lily, Father Jacques is dead."

"Dead? But only last night—"

"Only last night, after he married us, he was at the lazaretto administering the last sacrament. It must be that he wasn't vaccinated, because this morning he was seized by what they call the *vérette pouf*. It's a form of the disease that strangles its victims in a few hours. One of those graves they are digging out there is his."

She dissolved in tears then, sinking against Edmond's arm as the coffin was unloaded and carried away. It sat inelegantly on the ground as the native diggers carved a spot beside Lily's mother in the gray volcanic earth. The proper prayers were said, the grave filled, and still she sobbed fervently, crying for all that was lost to her—her father, her innocence—and for Acelie, which without a miracle would be lost soon. And then a shadow fell across the bench where she sat half shaded by a pair of pineapple palms.

"Edmond, what are you doing out at this time of day? It's uncivilized in this heat. Is this your lady?"

She turned her tearstained face up involuntarily at the sound of a voice all too compelling, too familiar, and looked at the author of a large part of her grief—Joe Beau Clair, who would take from her her birthright, Acelie, and who without even having claimed her body had ruined her for other men. It was incredible to think that he did not even know her.

5

"My wife, Joe. Lily, this is my brother."

"Your wife! But I expected to stand with you at your wedding!"

"It was sudden. Lily's father, whom we have just buried, wished to see his daughter wed before he died."

Joe's eyes swept over her like the sapphire ocean beyond the beaches. She felt herself lifted on the crest of his gaze. And yet he was not looking at her in anything like the way he had the night before. He was cool, appraising, as though she were a pumpkin for sale in the market.

"She is lovely, Edmond," he said at last. "I can't say I blame you, even though your prize comes attached to a bankrupt plantation. Lily, I am pleased to know you. We shall be good friends, you and I."

"I think not, sir," she said softly.

He gave a whoop of laughter. Ordinarily it would have seemed irreverent at a gravesite, but with so much dying everywhere, it hardly seemed to matter. "So you hate me already, Lily! Come, it's only business. I can't invest in every plantation with a pretty mistress!"

"You could help your brother, sir!"

"Oh, do cease to call me sir! I can't abide it. And as for my brother, he has chosen his path. The thing is his to do. If he wins, I shall be the first to cheer, but we cannot celebrate a wedding with a funeral! I must toast the bride at a wedding supper. It shall be my treat." He put out a hand and took Lily's, pulling her to her feet. Her skin tingled at his touch, and she drew her hand quickly back. He looked at her quizzically, as though he had noticed something, too.

He led them to a plush restaurant with velvet chairs and white linen tablecloths behind its yellow-tinted, awninged front; and he ordered them all *cocoyages* to drink, made with gin, coconut milk, egg, nutmeg, and sugar. The Demerara windows had been drawn shut and locked, and music blotted out any unpleasant sound that might drift through from outside. Here Creoles could still forget the plague beyond the doors, forget as they dined that they might return home to find a favorite *bonne* dying or their crops untended by stricken field hands. Someone was playing a guitarlike banjo and singing a French song much in vogue.

> Little feathered lovers cooing,
> Children of the radiant air
> Sweet your speech, the speech of wooing,
> You have not a grief to bear.

She had heard it at Carnival the night before, and she watched with satisfaction as a secretive smile stole across Joe's features. He was thinking of Mimi now, of the pleasures he had but tasted. "Ah, if I were to tell him!" And unknown to herself, she smiled a mysterious little smile of her own, which both men found delightful.

The meal Joe ordered set before them abounded in lobsters, rosy little West Indian crabs, yams, fried plantains, and tropical cherries. Lily had not eaten since morning, and suddenly was ravenous in a most unseemly way. The *cocoyage*, which she had sipped too quickly while awaiting the food, had made her giddy. Otherwise the reckless solution to her problems might not have occurred to her as she studied Joe from beneath lowered lashes.

There he sat—so relaxed and self-confident, that devil of a man with the soft, rich hair she had wanted so to touch, with the lively impatient eyes that seemed always ready to fly like two bright birds from beneath the shelter of his brows.

Her smile grew as she assessed the lean limbs flung so easily out from the ornate chair. Oh, he had not been so calm and self-possessed without his trousers in the moonlit room last night! She had had him in her thrall as Mimi. He had been so beside himself he had given her his watch, payment far too great, she guessed, for one romp with a coaling girl.

What Lily could do as Mimi, she could do as Lily. Oh, not that she would take him to her bed, of course. She was a married woman! But she would have him in her power again, and when she did, he would pay and pay for his cavalier evenings with Mimi! She would have of him far more than a fine watch—she would have the price of Acelie.

She did not quite know how she would accomplish her goal, but she felt a new sense of purpose, a beginning of hope. And she felt a growing sense of excitement as she consumed her food with appetite. She was forever setting prices when it came to men—for Edmond the price of marriage had been a compromise of honor; from Joe, she would exact a bank draft for the mortgage of Acelie. But Lily did not reflect that the practice might prove dangerous. She did not, in fact, think about it at all.

She turned her attention to the conversation of the two brothers. Joe was holding forth on his journeys around Cape Horn to San Francisco. Edmond listened, interested but detached.

"The winds in the Strait of Magellan blew us onto Tierra del Fuego, and I lost two men overboard reefing the mizzens. Another was saved only because he fell into the belly of a sail. We were marooned for a week at Port Tamar for repairs."

"What is it like, Joe, Tierra del Fuego? I have heard it spoken of with fear, and I know it means 'land of fire.' Is it a volcano like our Pelee, and is it forever erupting and spewing flame and rock on any ship that ventures too close?" Lily's voice was breathless. He had caught her imagination at once, as she pictured him clinging to the helm of a ship half-submerged in great green waves, hellbound for a mountain of flame, murderous winds straining the sails with fire-whipped breath.

He laughed, pleased at having stirred her fancy. "It's not like that at all, Lily. It was the many bonfires of the Indians that gave the island its name."

"Indians!" she exclaimed.

"They are a treacherous lot, it's true. But when we are at anchor we spread carpet tacks on the decks. It proves effective when they come creeping barefoot in the dark, ready to split our skulls. There are magnificent mountains, higher than Pelee, and passages so splendid and terrible that many a sailor believes he has met God."

"Oh, I should like to see it!" she cried enthusiastically.

"Perhaps you shall travel someday, you and Edmond. You shall have free passage on any ship of mine. But by that time you may not need to go such a route. There will be Panama—"

"Ah! Panama! I shouldn't care for that," Edmond put in, draining his glass. "There have been tales enough of the railroads across the isthmus! They are forever breaking down, and the jungles are rife with yellow fever."

"I don't mean the railroad, Edmond. I am speaking of the canal, of the syndicate headed by the great Ferdinand de Lesseps. Think of the glory for France if he should manage to divide the continents! It will make fortunes for those who invest in it."

"Have you invested in it, Joe?" Lily asked.

He leaned back and thrust his thumbs into the armholes of his double-breasted brocade vest. "I am not one to miss out, Lily," he replied with satisfaction.

She sighed, thinking of how she had wanted him to invest in Acelie. She intuited that he had refused, not because of the large element of risk, which might even have appealed to him, but because of the lack of other elements—those of adventure, of grandeur. "I think I would like dessert now," she said. "Do you think I might have some of those dear little coconut cakes?"

"A fine idea. I had forgotten them while I was away. I was fond of them as a boy." The success of the dinner had put Joe in a pleased mood. He was somewhat intrigued with his new sister-in-law, and rather glad that she had softened a little toward him. But he did not doubt that she had married Edmond only to save her family's hold on Acelie—as if generations long dead and those undreamed of could matter so much.

He did not quite blame her; she was only a woman, and he himself had been subjected to such arguments from his family before he had taken flight from a society in which he had felt too firmly rooted. He had felt imprisoned here, one spring's leaves caught on a tree of antiquity. What an ache he had felt, tasting the wind on his face! And with a mighty flutter he had swept free on the ocean current. He did not expect her to have the same alternatives as he, of course; but she represented a society and a set of values he abhorred. He did not intend to make life easy for her.

She bit greedily into the cake, her mind turning, forming plans she did not know how she would implement. *It is not exciting enough for him to risk his money in Acelie,* she thought. *I will change all that someday. I will see to it that he finds his adventure.*

All too soon Edmond was hurrying her again, telling her they had already stayed too long. "I didn't notice the lateness with the shutters closed."

Joe dug into his watch pocket. "And I should have kept

track for you," he said ruefully, "but I have misplaced my watch."

So did he remind her again of what had passed between them as they went out into the glow of afternoon sun.

"Perhaps a hotel, Lily?" Edmond suggested.

"There are rooms where I am staying, Edmond, though it might not be fine enough for your bride."

She thought with a sudden start about the coming of night. She had forgotten, as she listened to Joe's tales, as she plotted her happy revenge, that soon she would be subject once more to the dark marriage ritual. A wife must allow it, Yzore had said. But not in St. Pierre! Not in Joe's hotel, knowing he lay only rooms away, his view to the sea the same as hers. She wanted only to be away from the city with its strange, overwhelming mixture of plague and passion. Away from here she could put aside the memories of Carnival, and set herself to learning to love her husband in the demanding way that marriage required.

"Edmond, I want to go home!"

"But I think Joe is right, Lily. We could never reach Acelie by dark."

"They are fast horses, Edmond. You don't know how fast, and no weight is in the wagon to hold them back." She tugged at his arm, and he surrendered, throwing a grin back at Joe as he handed her aboard.

She looked back once as they drove away and saw Joe still standing there, watching them speculatively. Then, with a lift of his shoulders he sauntered away, bound, Lily reckoned, for the kind of evening in which she could never again play a part.

Shadows were long as they left St. Pierre; the sea and sky melded into lavender oneness, and the ocean's sound became louder and more important as it hissed over the black-sand beach. Masts of ships and supple royal palms swayed against the great orange sunset, and bright birds shot now and then from the tall crowns of trees, like embers from the dying sun.

On the high road she clung to the wagon seat as Edmond urged the horses to a gallop, and the darkening mornes led her to a full realization of what she had done. Faster they raced while the night came sliding down, so quiet and beautiful. It was the time of day that Lily had always loved best, and even now she was half-mesmerized as the mountains facing the light began to glow a fiery phosphorescent green, and distant peaks glowed iridescent violet through a vapor of gold.

Then suddenly the island seemed to sigh like a body relinquishing its soul, and a velvety murk rose from the valleys to join the dark of the hills. Now only the highest peaks glowed crimson, like the wicks of just-extinguished candles.

Edmond muttered beneath his breath, words she knew a lady must not hear. She felt his tension, felt anger rise in him with the growing night.

"I'm sorry, Edmond," she hazarded.

"You should be! You have risked the lives of two very good horses to the snakes! Do you imagine we can afford to lose horses in our financial condition?"

She was silent. It was strange to hear him speak of "our financial condition." Only yesterday it had been her father's plantation, and she its pampered only daughter. Now, oddly enough, the plantation was hers and she was Edmond's. The only thing that had not changed was the absence of money.

"There is so much to get used to," she said. "I only wanted to go home, and I gave in to the whim. I will be more careful in the future."

She heard him sigh. "Never mind, Lily. It was I who gave in to your whim. I was being the bridegroom, pleasing you when I must have known the horses could never make it so quickly. It is I who mustn't give in to your whims again."

"We are better than halfway," she replied. "Let the horses have their heads. They will know better than you if there is a snake."

"I have done that, Lily! Don't advise me!"

She did not understand what she had done wrong. "Why shouldn't I advise you?" she asked meekly. "I know Acelie's horses."

"Acelie is my responsibility now," he said, turning toward her, and even in the darkness she could sense the set of his jaw, the fire of resolution in his eyes. "If you know what is to be done, it's only chance. It's I who must make the decisions!"

"And I, Edmond? You said I should help. You said we would save Acelie together."

His gaze softened. "You shall help indeed! You shall bear Acelie's sons and be the inspiration for all that I do."

She did not have time to wonder exactly what was involved in being an inspiration. At that moment the horses whinnied and reared. She caught at the wagon bed as she was thrown backward, and she felt her skirts rip against the wheel as they plunged from the road down the embankment across a grove of coconut trees. She did not scream; she did not have breath for it. She thought with certainty that the wagon would be smashed. The sky rushed near; she saw a firefly's flash of light that to her was the lantern of a mountain specter. She heard a sound that might only have been the call of a bird, but to her was the laugh of a malefice.

Tomorrow she, too, would be in the churchyard, where she could never again be tempted by Joe Beau Clair. And then everything was still. She heard the drowsy ocean and the night voices of numberless little beings.

"Lily! Are you hurt!"

She lay shaking, too weak to answer. He clambered down beside her and laid his hand against her breast to feel the terrible beating of her heart.

"It's all right, Lily. The horses have taken us to the beach. We'll be safe from snakes here. The fer-de-lance doesn't care for the open sand."

Suddenly she was grateful to have him there; she felt protected by him as even her father had never protected her. "What will we do now, Edmond?" she asked.

"We'll stay here until daylight. Are you cold? Come close to me."

She let him gather her in his arms, welcoming the pillow of his shoulder. She did not dream what feelings such proximity might arouse in her husband, here in this rough wagon that had carried her father to his resting place. Still clothed in shards of innocence, she thought this part of marriage would always be contained in the bedroom as decently as such things could be.

But then his hand moved differently against her bosom, and her heart pounded for other reasons. He parted the fastenings of her bodice and laid his palm over her soft nipple. His kisses tasted different in the open air, as though the tumultuous ride had lent them a certain spice. Her thighs offered no resistance as he pushed them hungrily apart, and she felt the urgency of her own mysterious quest. But Edmond did not seem to notice her searching. Her movements against him were like those of a trapped butterfly, and out of nowhere came the terrible fear, immobilizing her beneath him. And still Edmond continued to worship her with his desire. He had not expected response. He had expected only that she should satisfy him and that he should be eternally grateful. And when he was done, he kissed her lips gently to show her, and pulled her clothing over her as one might cover a child from the cold.

The moon rose as he slept with an arm heavily across her, as if to punctuate the fact that she was his forever. A violet came into the sky and then a rose hue, almost like the heralding of a northern dawn. The huge tropic moon made Lily uneasy. Always she had slept behind closed shutters to avoid its brilliance, but last night this same moon had peeked in on the scene between her and Joe; and now it seemed to mock her with the knowledge, as she lay beside the man who had possessed her. The sound of night creatures had grown muted, too, as if they were affected by the moonlight, and by contrast the sound of the ocean seemed louder, more enticing, as if the sea were making her an offer of company and friendship.

At last she lifted Edmond's arm from her and jumped silently down from the wagon. Walking across the beach, she stood for a moment looking at the sparkling water. All her life she had loved to swim, and with a sigh of surrender she plucked off her shoes and stockings to dig her feet into the warm sand. Then she stripped altogether, lifting her bare white body to the creamy moonglow as the dark mourning clothes dropped from her. With a tingle of delight she padded onto a crescent of tawny wet sand and splashed into the emerald water. The sea rocked her, giving her surcease, and she turned on her back and looked up at the familiar Southern Cross in the sky. Somewhere across these waters were winds that could blow a ship stern-over-bow, and shores ablaze with the fires of savages. And suddenly she realized that the difference between the brothers was not so much that one was principled, the other a rascal; or that one was steady, the other irresponsible. The real difference was that one had a single dream; the other, many.

6

She was proud of the way Edmond took charge of Acelie. Each night she suffered his desires, but each morning when she looked from the windows at the endless rows of green shoots growing in the sun and heard the songs of the workers, the terrors of the dark seemed inconsequential dreams. No, he could not have done those things, not this man who sat over his black coffee and delicate fruit of *corossol* in such an ordinary way.

"It is going well, Edmond," she would say happily, and they would stand together, hand in hand, looking out on his one dream, which he was making come true for her.

But underneath their happiness there was still trouble. Their cheerfulness over the plantation was a masquerade they played for each other. The bananas were ripening, and still no ships sailed from St. Pierre. In the city the death rate had reached six hundred a month; whole streets had been depopulated. If the ships did not sail, they would lose Acelie. They would need the bananas to meet the payments due. But Edmond and Lily did not speak of it. Every few days Edmond rode to St. Pierre. She would look at him inquiringly on his return, not really needing to hear him say, "It is just the same, maybe worse."

She would ring the bell for Cyrillia and order rum punch for the master, and then she would sit on the arm of his chair, and brushing his hair from his forehead, she would whisper that it could not last and that the ships would sail in time.

"We must only have faith, Edmond," she would say, but she would think then of Joe, who could so easily save them. And every afternoon when she spent an hour praying for the souls of the dying before the little olive-oil lamp of her Virgin's ivory *chapelle,* angry thoughts of Joe would intervene.

They were almost isolated on the plantation now. The theaters and restaurants of St. Pierre were closed, and everyone was too beset by problems to give entertainments. Edmond had ordered that none of Acelie's workers be allowed to go to the city.

Now and then Joe came and stayed to dinner. When this happened Lily would wear a dinner dress with a bit of lace about its low, square neck, and a little pair of jet mourning earrings would flash against her cheeks. She did her best to please him, though she knew he thought she had married Edmond expecting to have the Beau Clair fortune. But even had that been true, it had not been a one-sided bargain. As Cyrillia had predicted, she had paid and paid.

She wished he had seen how willingly she had married Edmond when he had become penniless. She wished he understood her determined loyalty to her husband, this virtue she clung to in the face of passion far beyond the bounds of her schoolgirl comprehension. She smiled and blushed for him, bent on making him like her—for Edmond's sake, she told herself. But she hung helplessly on every word of his stories; and as he told of his scrapes with Moorish pirates or of dodging coral reefs in the South Seas, she was far more in his power than he in hers.

He did not trust her. He did not trust women of her kind. Hadn't he told her that night in St. Pierre he did not care for demure Creoles with their pretty manners? But she could not act like Mimi *now*! She must think of something. . . .

She would see that the table was set with the best Vincennes china, which had come long ago from France, and candles would shine in the bronze-stemmed *verrines*. Having pestered her brother-in-law to learn his favorite dishes, she would send a worker up the mountain to gather palm hearts for a salad. Afterward would come a *blaffe* made of fish served with pimiento, lemon, and spices; or a chicken-and-rice mixture called *poule-epi-diri*, which Joe said he had often eaten in New Orleans, where a similar concoction was known as *jambalaya*.

He was usually berthed in New Orleans, he told them. It was very French, and the narrow streets of the Old Quarter reminded him of St. Pierre.

"So! You do get homesick, Joe," Edmond would say triumphantly.

"No. It is precisely because I have New Orleans that I don't. It is familiar."

"But after all, you are here," Lily persisted. "Why have

you returned to Beau Clair now, if you don't love it? You know they call this island Le Pay des Revenants."

"The land of comers-back. That silly idea that Martinique enchants!" Joe frowned. "It was only a matter of poor timing. I was nearby at Grenada, and I heard that Edmond was to be married. I had a sudden curiosity, and then there was the quarantine."

"That is our hope, Lily," Edmond would say when Joe had gone. "My brother cannot stay put. Even now, he's restless. When the quarantine is lifted, he will go, and not only will we load our bananas, but we will be in charge of Beau Clair again. If only the quarantine is lifted in time!"

The quarantine would be lifted, and he would go! Perhaps she would never see him again. Or if she did, it would be in ten years, and she would be different, worn to resignation with the passing of thousands of nights.

Yet if the quarantine were not lifted soon, Acelie would be lost. She scarcely knew what to hope.

But Cyrillia did not agree with Edmond about his brother, and one day as they worked together steaming one of Lily's dresses, she told Lily why.

"Monsieur Joe, he's caught in a trap just like a little jungle possum. He sticks his head up to look around at Martinique, and what happens but a pretty coaling girl snatches his heart."

"Oh! I can't believe that, Rilla! Monsieur Joe can have any woman he fancies. He wouldn't let himself be snared by one. Why do you say these things?"

Cyrillia laughed. "Because I hear what you do not. I know he looks for one he cannot find. She is smart, that one, who hides from his kisses. She will get her pretties!"

"Rilla! How you talk! How do you know he looks for her?"

"I heard it among the coaling girls when I last was allowed to go to St. Pierre. He will give twenty francs to anyone who finds her. Everyone is out of work with the quarantine, and the money would be a fortune. But she is nowhere to be found. They say she is the ghost woman."

"The one who lures men to follow her and leads them over cliffs in the night?"

"Yes, missy. She has put a spell on him, and he can never leave Martinique until he finds her."

Lily smiled, thinking how annoyed Joe had been when she

had suggested to him that he was enchanted by the island. "Did she have a name, this woman?"

"She told him her name was Mimi."

Lily was in ecstasy to know she had had such an effect on him. She slipped into her bedroom, and locking the door behind her, she took the beautiful jupe dress and held it against her, twirling in little dance steps before the mirror. It would not be as striking now, if she were to wear it, since she no longer had the gold necklace that had set it off so well. She wondered what he had done with the jewelry. Did he keep it close to him, perhaps in a box in his bureau? She wished she knew.

She went about singing:

> Little feathered lovers cooing,
> Children of the radiant air . . .

She could not help herself. Each morning was incredibly perfect with its cool, light air. Beyond the blossoming granadilla the mountains rose like thin blue smoke, almost transparent against the sky, and a halo of gold hung over the ripening cane. Then she would force her gaze to the banana trees, where the elliptical red blooms had given way to curving clusters of green. And she knew the time was coming . . .

She was alone in the house when the men from the bank arrived, two of them in a shining brougham, wearing top hats and tight-legged trousers and coats of fine diagonal. She saw them look about at Acelie's antiquated yellow walls, and at the broken red tiles on its roofline. She saw one lift a walking stick at the burdened banana trees and shake his head at the other.

There could be no doubt as to who they were.

She had sent Cyrillia to the stream with laundry, and Yzore was visiting among the workers' cottages. She had to open the door herself. "Gentlemen, my husband is not home."

They looked at her in embarrassment and said they would come back later. She knew what would happen if they did. Edmond was a simple man with no ability to dissemble. "Lily, he would say, "we have failed to meet the payment. We have lost Acelie, and that is all there is to it." Edmond was never devious.

"Oh, but do come in!" she said. "We have so little

company in these terrible times. And you cannot return without refreshment. It's a dusty journey."

They sat uncomfortably as she poured the best brandy, and she realized with irritation that she would have to broach the subject herself.

"Come, gentlemen, tell me your business," she said at last. "Acelie is *my* inheritance."

"It is a matter of delicacy, Madame Beau Clair. The payment is due."

She let her mouth fall open in a pretty little gasp of astonishment, and she laid a hand against her heart. "Oh, dear me! I have not heard anything about it. My husband didn't tell me."

"No doubt he didn't wish to worry you so soon after your father's death. We should not have spoken of it." They rose to go.

She stopped them with a touch at the arm of each. "But my husband has no money," she said disarmingly. "The bananas . . . You must give us a week at least."

They shook their heads like doctors pronouncing a sentence of death. "The quarantine will not be lifted in a week, Madame Beau Clair. And in longer than a week it will no longer matter about the bananas."

"But there is something besides the bananas," she said, thinking fast, letting her voice grow conspiratorial. They heard the change and they became very interested, interested in something they intuited was more exciting than Acelie's doomed bananas.

"I have jewelry. I will pawn it. You must give me time."

They sighed together. "Forgive us, Madame Beau Clair. You are not to be blamed for trying to save your plantation, but we know you have no jewelry. Your mother's diamonds and even her coral have long since been sold. Your father had no more such valuables to offer."

"My father didn't know of these. And my husband must not either. I must tell him I sold silverware I found in the attic, something that had been lost and forgotten." Lily blushed. She was not used to such lying, but her flush fit the situation perfectly.

The gentlemen from the bank cleared their throats and looked at each other. "Oh, do hurry and go now!" she cried with sudden urgency. Her gaze spun toward the window. "I am afraid he is coming! He mustn't find you here—he mustn't find out . . ." She pushed them along to the door.

"Oh, it is so kind of you! I will never forget it. You must come again and have tea with me when this is all only a memory."

This last she uttered with a hint of promise, and she was rewarded to see a certain licentiousness come into their expressions as they hurried down the steps to their carriage. She tried not to imagine the things they must be saying about Lily Beau Clair as they drove away. What had happened was sure to have a certain effect on her reputation, and later she might have to deal with the bankers in a different way.

But later was later. Lily gave a whoop of triumph and threw herself down against a tufted sofa. Then quickly the savoring of the moment passed. She had no jewelry. And certainly there was no silverware in the attic. She ran upstairs and changed into the trained skirt and trousers of her riding habit. Out in the stable she found a native boy and had him saddle her favorite dappled mare.

She remembered as she approached the white columns of Beau Clair that she had come here another time not so long ago, her horse steaming, her request urgent. But that time she had faced only Edmond; that time she had had something to barter—herself! Today she had nothing. She knew of no reason why her brother-in-law should help her. She was spared having to knock, having to wait to be shown into his presence. Joe was watching her from the palm-and-ceiba-shaded porch as she flung down from the saddle.

She wasted no time on pleasantries. "You must help me, Joe. They have come from the bank."

"I have made it plain I wouldn't."

"But you must! I've told them I had jewelry given me by a man. I have wrecked my reputation for the chance to save Acelie."

"You did *that*, little sister?" He looked at her with renewed interest. "You are resourceful; I give you credit. You are a minx, Lily. I didn't know."

She felt tears sting her eyes. "Oh, you are heartless! I hate you, Joe Beau Clair! Edmond has worked hard. He doesn't deserve to fail!"

"You hate me, Lily? When you have gone to such trouble to make yourself beautiful for me when I come to Acelie? And the table is laden like a feast day? I should have know, Lily," he mocked, "you have done these things because I have money."

Her anger welled over. It was true in part, of course. But

he did not guess how difficult it had been to hold herself back, and how delightful to her these ploys had been. But the ploys had failed. He felt no more tender toward her than on that first day they had met over her father's grave.

"Do you rate yourself so poorly, sir?" she cried, letting her rage burst forth. "I quite agree with your judgment! Surely no respectable woman would find you attractive. They may lift the quarantine too late for the bananas, but we shall be rid of you then at least! I don't know which I will be gladder to see the last of—*la vérette* or you!"

He laughed, throwing back his head with its wonderful cinnamon-colored hair. "Oh, Lily, I swear I am tempted to help you when you are so honest and angry! You are a hundred times more appealing with your eyes blazing than smiling sweetly over a candleflame. Tell me, has Edmond seen you this way? I am sorry you squandered your reputation with the bankers. And squandered it for nothing. Acelie is doomed. It has lived past its time, the time of slavery; and if I were to save it this time, it would only need saving again and again. It's a shame your father didn't foresee the smallpox when he planted bananas. It's a judgment—Frenchmen were not meant to grow bananas."

"But I will ask you only once, Joe. If you arrange the payment, I will find your Mimi. But it will cost you more than twenty francs."

She saw the effect the name had on him. She saw color drain from his face as his lips formed a circle of astonishment. She felt herself going pale as well.

What I can do as Mimi, I can do as Lily. The thought came back to her as she ran for the mare, and throwing herself gracelessly onto its back, galloped away, aghast at what she had done.

7

"We will start picking today, Lily." Edmond spoke quietly, as if it were of no importance.

"That is good," she answered, sipping her tea at the breakfast table. She had not needed to be told. Long before the sun had begun its daily assault on the bananas, she had heard the sound of the plantation drum, the *ka*. Later the drum would beat to a song. She would hear it all through the working hours as the golden fruit was cut down by the men and carried away on great flat trays on the heads of women.

She watched from her window as Edmond directed the labor, inspecting the bunches as they were brought to be stored. And then she closed the shutters, and wishing she could blot away the sound as well as the sight of the harvest, she rocked herself in a dark balata-wood rocker.

Where would they go, those bananas? Would they be dumped into the sea to rot? At last she could stand the inactivity no longer, and going to the kitchen, she sent Yzore and Cyrillia to the fields and cooked supper herself, a simple meal of codfish stewed with potatoes and pudding of manioc flour, molasses, and milk.

Edmond was furious. "What is this, Lily?"

"It is not much, but I cooked it myself," she replied uneasily.

"What! A wife of mine—cook! We aren't bankrupt yet, Lily!"

"But . . . I would like to be useful."

He calmed and touched her cheek. "Lily, dearest, you are not supposed to be useful."

"I am supposed to be your inspiration?"

He smiled, glad to feel she understood. "Yes, my beautiful inspiration. That is, in its own way, useful."

"Oh, but I am bored with being an inspiration!" she burst out petulantly. "And you shall eat what I have cooked or go hungry!" She flounced away up the stairs and lay, wakeful, wondering at all she did not know about being a wife. Her father had always allowed her to spend time in the kitchen with Yzore. She had not been able to help learning. . . . In the morning the dishes of cold congealed food told her what choice he had made.

She did not cook again. Edmond had troubles enough without her adding more, and it seemed she could help him most by doing least. No labor could have been harder. Each evening he came into the house long after she had eaten, and she would pretend to sleep as she watched him undress, shedding his stained clothing for a cool linen nightshirt. He would lean across and kiss her gently, stroke her loose, dark hair. He was too exhausted to do more these nights. And somehow she was more touched by these devotions than she had been by anything else in their marriage.

In the morning she dreaded the coming of light, knowing that not only had no miracle occurred to save the crop, but that the week she had bought so dearly had one less day to run. If only she had work to keep her busy! If only she could be as cool and single-minded as Edmond! In the afternoon she would pluck purple bougainvillea blossoms and bring them carefully to her Virgin's altar without smelling them— to smell them was to rob the Virgin, Yzore had always taught her. She would pray, but without the candor of a native girl. She hid the truth from the Virgin just as she hid it from herself, and perhaps because of that, she sensed no answer to her prayers.

She would lie on her bed in her chinoise and try to nap while the sound of the drum throbbed on and on. Finally she would go to the window to watch the *ka* player, as he sat astride his instrument, beating it with the fingertips of both hands. Beside him a boy with a stick kept striking the uncovered end of the drum in a clattering accompaniment while the drummer pressed his naked heel against the drum head to change the tone of the music.

In other days this same drummer had won many a match with his performance. And he had played each Sunday while the workers had danced the old African caleinda. If Lily had not been so infected with the spirit of that dancing, if she had not watched so closely and imitated the dancers behind the door of her room, then perhaps she would not have acquitted herself so well as Mimi.

Did Joe want Mimi enough to pay Lily's price? And what, dear heaven, would she do if he did? One moment she laughed to think that she might use one incarnation of herself to help the other; the next, she went damp with fear. Suppose she did not produce Mimi? She did not doubt that Joe's anger would be colder than any she had ever witnessed. She did not doubt that he would punish her soundly. And yet how could she give him Mimi?

He had said she was resourceful; he had said she was a minx. She had never thought of herself in such terms, and already it seemed unbelievable to her that she had confronted the bankers and that she had dared this awful bargain with Joe. But since it had been Joe who had applied these descriptions, she gave them some credence. Perhaps she would find a way, after all, when the time came. *If* it came—for it seemed more and more likely that it wouldn't.

He had not been so enraptured of Mimi as the coaling girls had thought. Mimi had not the hold of the ghost woman upon him. She was worth twenty francs, no more. She bothered him because he had not satisfied himself with her. She was like a rum punch left undrunk; he had a thirst he would soon slake elsewhere.

Lily would never have admitted it, even to the Virgin, but such thoughts upset her more than thoughts of the doomed banana crop or the payment due the bank. The *ka* beat on. She marveled that they kept picking, knowing as well as Edmond that there would be no money for wages. But they seemed to believe he had some talisman that would save him. The force of his steadfastness overwhelmed them, and they called friendly greetings to him as he rode about the plantation on his bay horse.

She was unprepared for the moment that the drum stopped. In the silence there was a strange emptiness. She stood rigid, feeling that the earth had stopped moving. The bananas were picked; now there was nothing. What could the future hold for them? What comfort could she offer Edmond, when she herself had suffered a defeat even greater than his?

"Lily!"

It was a voice not full of despair, but of jubilation. She whirled to have her husband close her in his arms. "Lily, there is a boat! It will come to Grande Anse for the bananas!"

She thought of that village of roaring winds and thunderclap seas that lay on the far side of the island, and she looked with fear at Edmond. She had heard of the delusions that came to Creoles who exerted themselves too long in the sun.

"Edmond, ships do not come to Grande Anse," she said gently. "Only the small boats, the pirogues, that carry the rum that the surf swimmers bring them in barrels."

"You are right, Lily," he exulted, "but this time will be different. There is no quarantine in Grande Anse, and you have reckoned without my brother, Joe!"

The meaning of it swept over her; joy and fear surged. She felt the world begin to move again, spinning faster and faster, and before she fainted she saw that the sun around which it traced its course would always be Joe Beau Clair.

He had sent the message by a native boy from Beau Clair. The ship, which he had ordered up from nearby St. Lucia, would stand that very afternoon to await the loading of the bananas. He had also arranged for the line of *porteuses* who filed barefoot and graceful into Acelie's drive. When Lily had recovered from her swoon, she wasted no more time on feminine weakness. She put on a simple shift of Cyrillia's and went out to help with the loading of the trays.

The carrier girls were the main means of transport between Grande Anse and the other side of the island. Once oxcarts had been tried, but the tortuous roads had exhausted the animals. Now, what oxen could not do, the *porteuses* did swiftly and well. They were selected for their speed and endurance, and most could walk fifty miles in a day. Lily worked steadily hour after hour, stacking incredible weights atop the trays on their turbaned heads. Time after time she was overcome with worry at the great burdens, and would pause to ask, "Is it too heavy? Shall I make it lighter?"

And just as often, she would hear a soft laugh. "No, missy. I will tell you when to stop." And when Lily could not imagine adding another stalk, the girl would move away beneath her tray, her hands clasped gracefully behind her head, her fruit-tinted arms lifted, her fine breasts thrust forward as she joined the column of walkers. At the other end of her journey, someone would have to unload her, for a *porteuse* could never unload herself without rupturing a blood vessel or breaking her neck.

Before noon the job was done. Edmond led a disheveled Lily into the house and kissed her grimy face. "Oh, Edmond, not now," she cried. "I look a fright!"

"I *must* kiss you, Lily! We have done it!"

"You aren't angry, Edmond?"

"Angry?"

"I've been helping, not just in the kitchen, but in the field."

"I'm not angry, isn't that odd? Though when I first saw you I thought you were one of the girls in that dress. Come, we must get it off you."

He led her upstairs and ripped it away. "This is not worth saving!" he said as he pushed her backward onto the bed. There was in this lovemaking a hint of something that had not been before, an acknowledging of her in a new way. For a glorious moment she let herself be swept along. Then, as if he were shocked at himself, he drew back and put her in her place again, using her as he always had.

"You won't go to the fields ever again, Lily?" he said. "I will forgive you this time."

"Yes, Edmond." She sighed.

"Come, dress yourself in something suitable. I will have the horses hitched."

"Are we going somewhere?" Her delight at the idea banished the disappointment of the bed. They had not been away from Acelie for many weeks.

"We will go to Grand Anse and watch them load."

"To Grand Anse!"

"Yes. Where else is there, with this wretched smallpox? We are in need of a change of scene at least."

She searched through her wardrobe and chose a gown of apricot-and-white-striped India cloth, with kilted skirts and a small bustle. She added dainty shoes of black patent and white buckskin, and brushing the dust from her hair, she plaited it into a shining coil about her head. Finally she selected her best parasol edged in lace, with a handle of painted china.

Edmond stopped in amazement as he returned to find her preening before the mirror. "You are not in mourning clothes!"

"Oh, just for this one day!" she cried. "It is a celebration, and at Grande Anse no one will know the difference." She posed for him prettily. "You don't take me for a native girl now, Edmond!" she declared.

He drank in the sight of her, and she knew she had won.

Seated beside him in the carriage, Lily was happy as only a girl who looks her best can be. She had never been to Grande Anse; few Creole girls had, and the prospect of the unknown excited her.

For a while the road went steadily up, until they reached the top of an enormous ridge that divided the east side of the island from the west. Here they paused to climb a little hill with a stone cross, where for the first time in her life Lily saw the sea on both coasts. From there the road plunged down frighteningly between mornes wooded in arborescent ferns and grasses. It bridged torrents, skirted gorges from which great virgin forests loomed through streamings of lianas. Once they passed a barefoot native postman carrying his bundle at the end of a stick.

The palms grew taller as they descended, and with the descent Lily began to worry again. Joe had not paid the bank note as she had intended, but he had certainly helped her. Would he attempt to hold her to her bargain? Would she have to face him at Grande Anse? She supposed the fear of that was, as much as any, the reason she had discarded her mourning. The pretty clothes would make her more confident, not that she might expect her looks to have any effect on Joe.

She supposed she should not be surprised that his help had come as it had. There had been nothing to interest Joe enough to pay the note, not even finding Mimi. But the ship—that had appealed to him, never mind that it might founder at the edge of the terrible surf. It must not founder! She read the same thought in the tenseness of Edmond's hands on the reins.

They had left the woods now, but the road continued to twist and drop among low hills of cacao and cane. They passed the deep, rocky channel of the Riviere Falaise, and then at last the sea appeared, and a warm trade wind nudged their faces. The wind grew stronger, and as the road gave one last drop that sent the horses sliding, they drove into the town of Grande Anse.

All the buildings were gray, as if they had been exposed to coal smoke, and the pebbled streets were a dark ash color from the volcanic soil. Lily wondered if her bright clothes would soon take that hue if she remained in the beating wind. But in a moment she had forgotten the thatched-roof cottages of the town as she caught sight of a speck against the turquoise sea.

"There! The ship! It has really come!"

Edmond hurried the horses down to the black-sand beach. She saw the great green leap of the waves, and over the sea wind came the deep, mellow sound of the spiraled lambi shell being blown to call the swimmers. She saw that the bananas were being lashed to rafts and covered with tarpaulins as quickly as the carrier girls were unloaded. And then across the midnight sand galloped Joe Beau Clair, silhouetted darkly against the sea. His hair flung out like a battle standard; his magnificent body seemed as one with his great muscled stallion, as they shot over the beach. She could not take her eyes from him as he rode straight to the carriage. The brilliant blue eyes were more alive than she had ever imagined eyes could be; she felt herself whirled to their hurricane depths as though the violent sea winds were only zephyrs of his passage.

His horse pranced in front of her, and the eyes teased her triumphantly. *See, I have done my part. Now you must do yours.* She shuddered, almost believing he had spoken the words aloud. But no, he was talking to Edmond about the chance of the venture's succeeding.

"It is only an experiment, of course. It has never been done, and we could lose everything to the sharks and the flying fish. But if we succeed, many planters will want to ship from Grande Anse. It will make me a fine bit of money, brother."

"It will be enough for me that the crop is sold," Edmond replied.

"It's true we each have a lot at stake. You, your plantation; I, the ship. I was compelled to buy it to bring it here. Do take your wife away. I cannot give the order to begin until she is gone."

Lily gave a cry of indignation. "Go! But I came to watch!

"The professional swimmers do not wear any clothing, Lily." Joe laughed.

"Oh!" She flushed deeply, as Edmond turned the horses, driving her away from the beach while Joe Beau Clair grinned insolently after her.

Edmond left her at a large wooden house with a wide, low veranda, where he had arranged to take rooms; and he went back to the beach. Behind the house the long sloping yard was bounded by a bamboo fence and a hedge bright with pink and white butterfly blossoms of *loseille-bois* begonias. On the grass were drying nets and fish traps made of tough liana stalks.

In her room she poured water from the full *dobanne* and for the second time that day washed her face free of grime. Then she rested her head against a soft pillow stuffed with sugarcane plumes and stared across the room at an ancient

Picnic on a Volcano

print of Lamartine's *Laurence with Fawn,* which had been well-nibbled by paper-destroying insects. Cries came to her ears, shouted instructions and advice, calls of encouragement and dismay. She discovered a fine view of the not-too-distant beach, and pulling her chair close, sat riveted for hours as the small banana-colored men pushed the rafts toward the waiting ship.

Sometimes the rafts seemed suspended above the great sapphire crests. Sometimes they seemed to shatter into the fans of crystal spray. She would see them plunge down into a trough, as if to be dashed to the center of the earth. Some were lost. But more were reaching the ship. Each was a victory for Acelie, for her and Edmond and Joe. The sun yellowed, richer and more golden as evening approached. The light became lemon, and then orange, and the sea turned its dusky lavender. Edmond returned and kissed her wearily. "It has gone well," he said.

They dined on lobster-sized crayfish trapped by lantern light and little pancakes made of sweetened palm cabbage. Darkness fell, and the clock of the church tower burst into a moonlike glow above the ash-colored houses. They lighted the candle, but the sea breeze from the broad, sashless windows extinguished it at once.

"Shall I close the shutters?" Edmond asked.

"No. I like the feel of the wind." She watched as he matter-of-factly shed his trousers and crawled into bed.

"Edmond, where is Joe? He didn't come to eat with us."

The plume stuffing rustled as Edmond turned onto his back, arms behind his head. "Joe was still at the beach when I left, and probably had not thought of eating. You might have liked to thank him if he had joined us."

"That would have been . . . pleasant." She felt a pang of fear. Was there something in her husband's tone? She had never thought of Edmond as an especially observant person. But where his wife was concerned? When she had seen Joe racing so masterfully at the edge of the bursting surf, she had lost control of her feelings for the first time since her marriage. Did Edmond suspect?

"My brother has helped me, but in such a way that I saved my pride. I should like you to show appreciation, because he and I must pretend it is only business."

"Are you so sure it is not?"

He gave a low laugh. "Do I detect a bit of sarcasm, Lily?

I'm not surprised. I should like you and Joe to be good friends, but it's true he hasn't the proper regard for women. I have seen you try to please him for my sake."

She flushed and turned her face to the night glow of the window. "Are you implying, sir, that I am upset with a man because he has not responded to my charms?"

"Why not? What has a woman but her beauty and charm?"

"Her virtue, I should hope!"

He gave a whoop of laughter. "Lily, you have hit on it! Virtue is exactly what a woman must *not* have if she is to please Joe. Where women are concerned, he has only low appetites, which he does not bother to control. All the same, I would like you to thank him for today. We shall have enough money to meet the bank payment because of him."

"He said Acelie would need saving many times," she said uncertainly.

"He told you that? It must be because he cannot understand, as you and I, why anyone would work so hard for a bit of ground, even one as beautiful as Acelie."

She trembled, though the breeze was warm. "You don't see any problem with the cane, Edmond?"

"None at all. Come to bed. It has been a hard day, and tomorrow we will have the long ride home."

"I will come in a minute. I want to sit here for a while. It's an enchanting place."

He did not answer, and in a moment she heard the sound of the slow, steady breathing of sleep.

Nothing seemed as far from Lily as slumber. The soft night, filled with the susurrant ocean and the chorusing of tree frogs, awoke in her a furtive excitement. Opening the wide door, she slipped out into the yard, drifting past the forms of trees and bougainvillea bushes to the gate of the bamboo fence. Beyond lay the beach, its sable sand matching the sky. Above the growling water she glimpsed the Southern Cross as a gray veil of clouds fell across the stars and moon, shimmering like an unearthly spider web. She pulled off her shoes and stockings before walking onto the sand; and then, not far away, came the low sound of a man's idle song, sung in a vibrant voice she recognized.

> Little feathered lovers cooing,
> Children of the radiant air . . .

Picnic on a Volcano

She knew she should turn back at once. Instead she backed quickly against the curved trunk of a royal palm. She could not resist the temptation to spy on him, to try to see his face as he murmured the song that had such memories for them both.

He saw her almost at once. He came toward her, hands thrust into his pockets. His white linen shirt was unbuttoned halfway, so she could see the forest of nut-brown hair that lay against his chest. His trousers were the blue pantaloons of a plantation worker, turned up over his fine, strong calves, and his lean feet were bare, like hers.

She was glad that in the night he could not see the emotion his appearance aroused in her.

"Good evening, Lily." The words were matter-of-fact. There was nothing of the mocking tone he had used when he had called her a minx, nothing of demand to recall the promise she had made. Nevertheless her heart begin to beat furiously for more reasons than one.

"Is the ship all loaded?" she asked, knowing already that it was.

"Yes. It will sail at dawn."

"It was kind of you, Joe. We are grateful."

He laughed shortly. "You exacted a high price from me, Lily. I salute you. I have never before been outdealt by a woman."

She remained silent, feeling that her voice had fled. She would have liked to follow it, wherever it had gone, but her knees had become too weak to bear her away.

"You would not go back on your word?" he said. "You have made me a promise."

You have made me a promise. He had accused her with those words once before. And only by the thinnest margin had she prevented his collecting. Joe Beau Clair was not a man to be easily cheated. Could she be so lucky a second time?

"What is she to you, Joe, this coaling girl named Mimi?"

"Oh, Lily, you could never understand, a girl like you! You do know how to find her? I shall find a way to punish you if you were bluffing."

"Does it astound you that I know my way about the island better than you? That I can ferret out a coaling girl where you cannot? I can find Mimi. But whether you can bed her will be up to you. I cannot help you there."

He gazed at her agape. He was forever being surprised by

this starched, corseted young sister-in-law. From the very first time he had seen her tearstained face over her father's grave, he had thought her too beautiful to be the wife of a man like Edmond. Imagining her white body beneath his brother's, he counted it a shame that it could not be put to better use. But she was the sort of woman she was, and such ideas would have horrified her. He had had to force himself to remain cool toward her when her interest in his conversation had seemed so intense. Had he had less strength of will, she would have him paying Acelie's debts just as she wanted. She was a witch, this Lily! She was different from others of her kind. There was something about her he did not fathom.

And now she was taunting him with her knowledge of his need for the native girl. He felt a sudden urge to lash back at her and hurt her.

"I shall bed her, Lily. You can be sure. She has about her a beauty as natural and profound as that of the sea. She is as free and unhampered as the wind and gives herself to her passions. When she dances, a man comes to think she is love personified. She is a thousand times the woman you can ever be!"

Strangely, she was not crushed by his words. "Ah, Joe, you admitted one time that *I* was beautiful!"

"You are beautiful like a vase on a shelf, to be dusted each week and passed from generation to generation." Suddenly he had had enough of her. He stripped away his shirt and tossed it onto the sand. He grinned at her sharp intake of breath. "Don't worry, little sister. I am only going for a swim. You may keep the shirt to remember me by."

"Remember you?"

"I am going with my ship. I am bored with Martinique, and it is my only chance. There is no quarantine here at Grand Anse, and even though I've been in St. Pierre, I can't spread the disease. I've been vaccinated. I will be back. And then you can keep your bargain."

Even as relief filled her at her reprieve, she was gripped by a new fear. "Joe, the waves are very high. Even the professional swimmers don't swim at night."

He regarded her as he stepped into the warm surf. She did look lovely, even in that ridiculous bustled dress. Before today he had not seen her in colored clothing, and he almost wished for daylight so that he could see once more the way the apricot tones of her gown brought out the delicate rose tints of her cheeks. Like a finely painted vase—that was what he had thought then. It was the basis of the comparison he had used to insult her.

"Don't be concerned for me, Lily," he said. "Certainly it would be easier for you if I drowned and Beau Clair were Edmond's again."

"Can't you give me a signal when you reach the ship?"

"A signal? Very well, if you wish, I will light a flare."

"I would like that."

"You said once that you should be as glad to see the last of me as of *la vérette*. Don't worry. I shall be harder to lose than the plague, I promise." And he swam away into the night.

She paced the sand nervously. "A vase on a shelf indeed!" she thought. "I will show him! I cannot let him escape so easily. I will bring him low some way!"

With Mimi? The idea sprang unbidden. Lightning flashed, warning of a storm, and then a spot of flame on the dark horizon told her he was safe. He was safe, not she. He would be more difficult to lose than the plague, just as he had said. He would return and demand his coaling girl to bed. She smiled for a moment at the memory of his description of Mimi—of herself. As the first big raindrops splashed down, she trembled, not knowing what she could do.

8

It was quiet at Acelie now. The bank was temporarily subdued, and the growing cane gleamed and sighed in the sun. It was difficult for Lily to believe that the pink clouds that drifted over the fields at dusk heralded the last of the plantation's troubles. Like a native, she felt a prescience—a zombi or a malefice, Cyrillia would have said. With the weather sense of a sailor, she intuited a gale. She did not know from what direction it would come nor how to set her sail to avoid it.

Edmond had begun to use her again nightly. And each evening as she sat sleepily on the veranda, she would begin to think of the one weary chore that lay between her and slumber. She would play her banjo and sing softly to postpone the moment as long as possible. The very spot that in girlhood had been her sanctuary had become a usurer's purse into which she paid and paid. She thought ruefully of the expression "as safe as in one's own bed." Surely that saying had been invented by a man! Whatever price she eventually paid to Joe for his saving Acelie could not be higher than the one she paid to Edmond. She saw her life stretching out before her, and a discontent grew. She must have something more, she decided, and she began to think of something that would make her happier.

She was supposed to be an inspiration and the mother of the next generation. A mother . . .

"Edmond," she said one night when he had finished with her, "do you think we shall have a child soon? I should like that very much."

He lay away from her, sunk heavily in his lethargy of satisfaction. "When the time comes, we shall have many children, Lily."

"When will it be time?" she persisted. "We have been married for months. I should have thought by now . . . Do you think there is something wrong with me?"

"This is not a fit matter for us to discuss," he warned. "When you find yourself with child, then you will know it is time."

"But why not now? I so want a little baby to love. I am a woman and meant for children."

He sat up and looked at her, and his voice snapped with anger. "Would you want a baby now, with the typhoid and the smallpox? We would be burying it in the churchyard in St. Pierre."

"Oh!" she gasped in horror. "You are right, Edmond! I didn't think of that. After the smallpox, then? Shall I look forward to that?"

"It shall be time when we have paid every sou of our debt," he said, his face hard with determination.

"That might be years!" she cried, filled with dismay.

"Yes. But you are young and have many good years for children. We shall give our children their heritage, Lily. I shall not risk having to ask charity of my brother for my son."

Hysterically she rose onto her knees, her hair wild where his fingers had tangled it in his passion, the breasts he had so recently fondled spilling voluptuously into the cradle of her low-necked bodice. "That is unreasonable! I do not care for your pride! I shall not wait so long as that!"

"You will wait," he said. "I am your husband. You have no choice."

Tears of outrage choked her throat. Babies came from God, and God had control, not husbands. But Edmond was so certain that she knew there was something she did not understand. She could not find words to demand an explanation, and then, without her asking, he told her.

"There are ways, Lily, if a man cares for a woman but doesn't want to get her with child."

She fell down against the pillows, weeping. When he removed himself from the bed and slept on the sofa that was used only for naps, she was not sorry, and shifted her body, glad to have her bed her own again. And she enjoyed that luxury with the luxury of her tears.

In the morning she was wan, walking about the gardens with Cyrillia, watering the lobelia and hibiscus from a great tin watering can. She was dressed again in her mourning black. It didn't matter. She felt like wearing it.

"Missy is not happy." Cyrillia, in a dress of indigo cotton and a new madras painted a sulfur color between its crimson checkered bands, looked at her mistress from beneath lowered lashes. "I should be happy if I had all you have!"

"You do not know what I have, Cyrillia." Lily sighed.

"You have a fine husband and a beautiful home."

Lily brushed back a strand of hair that had fallen from her chignon and looked at the girl. Cyrillia was as bright and uncluttered as the morning, she thought in a moment of envy. Even her red *capresse*'s skin glowed as though fired from the sun. Lily had no mother or sister, and she was deeply in need of someone to talk to. "Rilla, we are still friends, aren't we? As we were before I married?"

"Yes, missy, of course."

"Then we can talk of things that concern women, just as we talked of dolls when we were children."

The girl hesitated. "It isn't done, missy. We are still friends, but it isn't the same as when we were children. You are the mistress, and I am the servant."

"It is not a role you care for, Rilla."

The girl's dark eyes flashed. "No."

"Well, then, come. Let's be two equals this morning. Your grandmother, who freed herself from Monsieur Bon, would be proud of you."

Lily saw the mention of the admired grandmother take its effect, and removing a pair of shears from her pocket, said quickly, "Come, we'll cut a bouquet of roses, and no one will ever guess we are not talking flowers." They bent over the pink and yellow blossoms, Lily choosing a bud, holding it away from the others for Cyrillia to snip.

"Rilla, you have been with men—in their beds?"

"Yes, missy, I have."

"Is it only for the pretties that you do it? Only for the money and presents? Do all women hate it as much as I?"

Cyrillia's laughter tinkled as she cut a pair of yellow buds together on the same stalk. "So that is it. That is what makes missy unhappy. But all women do *not* hate it. Women are different, just like these pretty flowers are the same, but different colors, like you and I. There is a simple solution to your problem."

"What?" Lily's heart lifted. Cyrillia had always had more knowledge of this sort than she.

"I should not mind the bed of Monsieur Beau Clair. I shall take care of his wants, and he shall cease to bother you."

Lily pricked her finger on a thorn in shock. "Rilla!"

The girl's eyes went misty, clouding Lily's vision into her

thoughts. "Why not? I fancy him. And it would not be the first time anyone had such an arrangement."

"Should Edmond have nothing to say about it?" Lily, still agape, was amused. Cyrillia was being as peremptory with Edmond as he had been the night before with her.

"No. He should never know we had agreed. He would find himself desiring only me, and he would never know how it had happened."

"As simple as that!" Lily, her face flushed, gathered the blossoms, ready to hurry away to the house. "I shall make no such bargain, Rilla! It would be a sin to plan that a man commit adultery."

"Ah! Missy would have to confess to the priest!" Cyrillia mocked softly after her. "Or perhaps missy does not hate it as much as she says. But if missy doesn't agree, and it happens anyway, *then* her conscience will be clear."

Lily went into the gloom of the house, and her fingers shook as she arranged the flowers in a bowl. Outside, she heard Cyrillia's laughing song pierce the air. It had been a mistake, after all, to cross the natural barrier that lay between them. What would come of this peculiar conversation?

She knew with sudden fervor that she was not ready to give up on the bedroom. Other women knew pleasure there. It was, as she had suspected, not impossible. She thought again of her wedding night, when Joe Beau Clair had so aroused her, and she had tried to finish the journey with Edmond. It had not been all bad in the beginning, not even with Edmond.

He apologized to her that night as he stepped out of his clothing. "Lily, dear, you know it is that I want what is best for both of us. The debt will be paid sooner than you imagine. And you shall have so many babies the house will be bursting. Only be patient and trust me, dearest."

And then she felt his heaviness on her. The repugnance of his entry was less than usual. He was in a gentle mood this night.

"That is pleasant, Edmond," she whispered.

He looked surprised. She had never spoken to him during lovemaking, and the words seemed to set him aflame. Quickly she was left behind, her enjoyment drowned in the wake of his passion. He rolled away from her, leaving her dazed and miserable.

Always before at this moment she had comforted herself with the idea of a child. Now there was nothing—only an emptiness that her best efforts had not filled. She knew she could not live this way, with no one to love. When he slept, she put on her chinoise, and before the olive-oil glow of her Virgin's shrine, she prayed for a baby.

All these nights—for nothing! As she prayed, a course of action occurred to her. She could go to Yzore. She would have nothing to fear from the old woman who had raised her, dressed her for her wedding night, and protected her from knowing before it was necessary. Because she had had the thought while kneeling before the *chapelle*, she was certain it was the right thing to do, and in the morning as soon as Edmond had left the house, she went to the kitchen, where Yzore was peeling breadfruit to cook into a mush.

The native woman nodded at the breadfruit pods she had put into sugar to candy. "Those shall be for you, missy, if you tell no one."

Lily brightened. Yzore had kept pods for her from childhood. It was one thing at least that had not changed with her marriage. "I have a problem," she confessed, seating herself on a wooden stool as she always had as a girl.

Yzore said nothing of their roles as mistress and servant. She would never be able to think of Lily as anyone but the child in her charge. "Tell Yzore," she said, and the dark hands kept moving, cutting the breadfruit.

Lily took a deep breath and said swiftly, "Oh, Yzore, I am longing for a baby and Edmond doesn't wish me to have one."

Yzore's face showed surprise beneath her turban, and she paused in her work. "This is not possible, missy. All men wish their brides to have babies. The French gentlemen especially cannot be easy until they have a son."

"It's different with Edmond. He says there are ways to prevent it."

Yzore snorted. "I have heard of none. He is not telling you the truth."

Lily was aghast. Edmond not tell her the truth! "Oh, no, Yzore!"

Yzore nodded, and now that she had figured it out, the pale breadfruit began to fly into the pot. "Something is wrong that he cannot get you a child. He is afraid you will think him not a man, so he tells you this. I will fix it, missy. I will make you a charm to hang above the bed."

"And then I will get with child?"

"It will be exactly what the witch doctor himself would give you."

Lily shivered as she thought of the strange sorcerer in his hut beneath the calabash trees halfway up the mountains, the man to whom the natives went with their ills, and whom they dared not anger. "You are sure it will be all right, Yzore?"

"Haven't I told you?" The old woman was becoming impatient. "I will make it of palm leaves and dried flowers from the Corpus Christi procession. They are blessed and will keep the zombies away."

"Yzore, I am afraid the smallpox will kill the baby—"

"Hush. The smallpox is in St. Pierre. It has not come to Acelie."

"Yes, I suppose you are right. And anyway, it would be a long while before it was born. . . ."

She put out the lamp that night before Edmond had even come into the room. She was hoping that he would undress in the dark and would not notice. But he turned up the wick with a grunt of irritation, and immediately his eyes locked onto the amulet attached to the wall behind the carved bedstead.

"Lily, what in heaven's name is that doing there?"

She cowered in the covers. "It is a charm to keep away zombies. Yzore put it there."

"I know what it is for. I am not ignorant of native ways." He reached over her head and tore the fronds and flowers down. Bits of papery debris fell into her hair, onto the coverlet.

"Edmond, stop! Those are blessed flowers!"

He did not stop. "Lily, I have told you I will make the decisions at Acelie! Now you are even trying to thwart me with foolish native superstitions!"

Suddenly she was not cowering anymore. She sat up in bed and lashed out at him. "I think you are not a man and cannot get me a child!" She stripped away her gown and offered him her ripe, naked beauty.

He was laughing. He could not remain angry in sight of those inviting breasts, quivering and taut with trepidation. He ran a hand across her stomach and below, and a sob tore from her throat as she felt his hands on her thighs. "Please give me a baby," she begged as she let her body open to him.

"Dear, innocent little Lily! You cannot command it, though you are so desirable. A man has only to turn aside in time, before his seed is spent. I shall make you a mama a dozen times when I am ready!"

He threw himself on her, and though she knew a wife's duty, she fought him with all her might.

In the cool dawn she felt weak and humiliated, and the memory of the way she had begged for a child sickened her. She had her horse saddled and rode through the luminous morning, dug in the iron-gray beach sand to uncover the pastel sail-shaped shellfish and watch them bury themselves again. Then she took a road up a mountain, beneath bamboo waving like enormous green ostrich feathers, until she came to a view of mornes sharp and shining as pieces of broken glass. She found peace nowhere. A kind of madness came over her as the day progressed.

She did not go back to the house at noontime, but instead found a tree that grew great orangelike fruit with a sweet, pink pulp. The natives called it the forbidden fruit and said it had grown on the fatal tree in the Garden of Eden. But Lily cut one down anyway and ate hungrily.

She knew she could not last the years until Acelie's debt was paid—if it were ever paid! She remembered Joe's assertion that the plantation would need saving many times and thought that it had the ring of truth. She admitted to herself that she would never love Edmond, only his brother, Joe. She would have run away with him if possible. It was not possible, of course. Even if she were to leave behind her heritage, her Acelie, Joe would not have her, not his brother's wife. Even a rogue like Joe would have scruples there. And he did not care for her. He cared only for Mimi, whose face he had never seen. It was a pain she would have to endure as long as she lived. She would give Edmond to Cyrillia; she would make that bargain. But first she must have the child to fill her life.

With the sudden plunging of the tropic sun, her madness grew. The breeze, sweet with the fragrance of grenadilla and roses, rippled the folds of the night as she dressed herself for bed. Her fingers were icy as she adjusted the ribbons of her gown. She did not allow herself to think that she had a plan.

He came into the room, lay beside her, took her into his arms. He sighed in contentment, as if he might have expected her to resist. He beat a rhythm inside her body as his passion rose. Her heart beat along with him, as wild and primitive as the plantation *ka*.

Faster and faster he moved. She felt the moment coming

when he would pull away, and she clutched him about the waist, clamped her thighs over him. She saw the panic on his face, the contortion of esctasy he could not delay. Through her triumph she felt the blow from his hand on her face.

"You are a demon, Lily! You are unnatural for a woman! I shall sleep elsewhere from now on."

"If you take another woman, perhaps I shall take another man!"

"Then I will kill him, of course."

Lily took little notice of the import of his words. She had captured his seed, and that had set her free of him.

9

She told Cyrillia the next morning. "I am done with him; make sure you get your pretties." The girl smiled and sang about her work.

As the weeks passed, Joe Beau Clair did not return to Martinique. The ship had returned a number of times, taking cargoes of bananas from elevations higher than Acelie's, where ripening came later. Each time the ship returned, Lily sent to know whether her brother-in-law was with it. Each time he was not, and she began to fear that he would never return. Somewhere some other girl had captured his heart; he had forgotten that he wanted Mimi. He had found some adventure halfway around the world. Would he really journey back for a night with a coaling girl? And what would she do if he did?

Edmond slept in another room now. Outwardly he was polite to her. She could easily give him all he needed in the outward appearance of a wife, and the arrangement was a relief. She knew there must be many marriages such as theirs about the island.

There came a terrible moment, though, when she knew she had not triumphed over Edmond. She was not with child, and so there would have to come another time when they must share a bed. Someday even he would insist upon his heir.

The cane grew and flourished, and every morning its quiet whispered presence in the breeze seemed to promise that all would be well. Surely the storm Lily had sensed had passed along with the nights of her marriage. She had no way of knowing whether Cyrillia had been successful in making her way into Edmond's bed, but the girl was cheerful and she wore a new bracelet of gold filigree when she went off to market at the village of Morne Rouge.

One afternoon as Lily sat languorously sipping rum punch on the veranda, she heard a commotion down among the thatched *ajoupas*. Angry voices echoed through the thin air, and before long Edmond came up the steps looking grim, wearing a wide-brimmed straw hat and carrying a riding quirt.

"What is wrong?" she asked.

"It's Pascal. I have had to dismiss him. I'm going to get his wages."

"Pascal! But he's always been a good worker!"

"Yes. It doesn't make it easier. But he has disobeyed my orders. Last night he went to St. Pierre to see his mother, who was dying of smallpox. So of course he must be dismissed before he infects all of Acelie."

"Of course. But poor Pascal! One can't blame him."

"Go inside, Lily. This will not be pleasant."

"No. I will stay to tell Pascal how sorry I am, and to wish him luck."

But Pascal was beyond accepting Lily's condolences. When he appeared in the drive to collect his wages, horrible curses sent Lily scurrying indoors to watch from behind the curtains, where her blushes could not be seen.

"Go, Pascal, or I shall have to drive you away!" Edmond warned. He flicked the riding quirt, and Lily realized why he had been carrying it. She gasped, for never had Edmond struck his workers.

The native lifted his arms to the sky and chanted. Lily felt a chill, though she could hardly make sense of what he was saying. Pascal took a stick and made a sign in the dirt, raising a cloud of dust, before he walked off down the palm-lined lane to the highroad.

Edmond rapped a command for the others to return to their work and punctuated it with a snap of the quirt. He came inside, slumped wearily, and called for Cyrillia to bring him a *cocoyage*.

"He's put a curse on us, hasn't he?" Lily asked.

"Indeed. He has entered into a pact with the devil that our cane shall not be harvested. He says there will be snakes in every row."

"But there are snakes in all harvests! He is only planning to take credit for any fatalities we have. Are our workers frightened?"

"Yes. We must see to it that they are not too frightened to work. Perhaps a priest to bless the fields . . ."

A storm roared in that night. Sheet lightning flashed, the wind whined soullessly beneath the eaves, and the night was filled with crashings and clatterings. Lily crept from her bed, closing the wooden shutters against the spanking rain. Even though she was French and secure behind Acelie's thick walls, the display frightened her. How much more it must seem that this was the beginning of the curse down in the workers' cottages. She took a lamp and tiptoed to Edmond's room. Always before, she had gone to her father on such occasions, and Edmond was her protector now. But then she heard the soft sounds of a woman's laughter beneath the beat of the storm, and feeling more utterly alone than she ever had before, she crept back to her room to lie shivering until dawn.

Morning routed the clouds from the sky. The horizon glowed with fawn tints and soft dove grays that merged into old gold. The leaves of the banana trees were shredded, hanging like streamers, shining with raindrops. The air had a sweetness that only the aftermath of a downpour could bring.

But the moaning of the wind seemed not to have stopped. It was strange. Lily thought as she lay looking out the reopened shutters. One could see that the air was still.

Then slowly it came to her that the moaning that last night had seemed so human was truly human now. She could discern many voices—those of men and women, the wails of children. She made the sign of the cross and rang for Cyrillia.

"What has happened, Rilla?"

"Oh, missy! It is the curse! The curse of Pascal!"

"The curse!" Lily was nearly as capable as Cyrillia of believing it.

"Everyone has trodden on a malefice. No one can walk. Come and see."

She went outside as soon as she had dressed. Everyone she saw lay in agony, clutching at horribly swollen legs. "What has happened, Edmond?" she cried, meeting her husband, also on a tour of inspection.

"Do you see the little prickly seeds lying all over the ground? Everyone has walked upon them barefoot."

"But it does not usually harm anyone to step on such seeds."

"These are different. Perhaps they have been soaked in a poison. Perhaps snake venom. Snakes were what Pascal threatened us with, after all. I will ride up the mountain and bring the witch doctor. There is no one else to send for. The French doctors have all they can manage in St. Pierre, and besides, the witch doctor will know better than they how to handle such a thing."

Days passed. The witch doctor came with his leeches and potions. The plantation rang with drums and chants. But the workers improved little. It became apparent that the cane could not be harvested, at least by Acelie's workers, and the cold fingers of the bank began to tighten around Acelie again.

"I will go across the island and see if I can find anyone who will come help harvest," Edmond decided one morning.

"No one will come," she answered despondently. "They will all be afraid of the curse."

"I must try. I cannot simply sit while Acelie is auctioned. I will be trying until the gavel falls."

She was touched by his determination. He was a good man, she thought. He was doing his best to keep the bargain he had made marrying her, even if she had not kept hers. "Of course I did not know what bargain it was I made, but I suppose I am a coward as a woman." She thought sadly of the laughter behind Edmond's door, and then got purposefully to her feet. She had failed him so much in their marriage, but perhaps there was one thing she could do to help.

There were certain things about the house that could be done without. All together they might bring enough, not for the next mortgage payment, but at least for extra wages to entice workers to Acelie. And they were her own things, basically, a woman's knickknacks. She could tell Edmond they were clutter and that she had been merely cleaning house. It would be a pleasant surprise for him when he returned. Calling Yzore and Cyrillia, she outlined her idea. Together they harnessed mules to a cart and brought it to the front door. Systematically they went through Acelie's rooms, stripping them of paintings, clocks, and other small pieces. Lily climbed onto the driver's seat and took inventory. She could not expect to get much for the jardinieres or the cameo glass, but that little desk of papier-mâché should bring a price, and the biscuit box was real silver.

She drove to St. Pierre alone, past the *savane* with its fountains and silk-cottons to the zinc-awninged furniture stores on Rue Victor Hugo. The pastel houses shone in the sunlight, and the water murmured in the stone gutters. The theater was open again, but still the ships hung uselessly in the quiet indigo water, and fewer than the usual number of laundresses worked with their feet in the icy water of the Roxelane. Each establishment at which Lily inquired told her the same story.

"We cannot buy; there is no business. *La vérette* . . ." Tired and discouraged, she climbed into the cart and flicked the reins, ready to head for home.

"Lily!"

She started at the sound of her name. "Joe!" The word she uttered seemed to pound in the beating of her heart. Oh, he was a thousand times handsomer than she had remembered! There was a spring in his step, an easiness in his smile, as though he had not a care in the world. How long since she had seen a man's face not etched in weariness! There seemed to hang about him an aroma, not of oranges and nutmegs of the marketplace, but of distant places, of the highroads of adventure and escape.

And she! She was caught, dusty and disheartened, plying her wares like a peddler woman!

"So! Acelie is in trouble again."

"Yes. We are in trouble. You shouldn't be surprised. It's what you predicted."

"It took no crystal ball. Trouble is the way of plantations. When Edmond has worked himself to death, he will have won only the right to be buried beneath her soil—if he is lucky."

"And I, Joe? What do you see in store for me?" she asked dully.

He studied her a long moment. "Do you wish to sell these things?"

"No one is buying."

"I am buying. I shall store them until the quarantine is lifted."

"I told you I would ask you to save Acelie only once," she declared, her eyes sparking.

"I am not interested in saving a plantation, only in making a good bargain," he said with a grin. "These things are cheaper while there is no market. In New Orleans I will make a tidy profit."

She cast a glare of resentment at him as he led her toward the bank, and he smiled down at the stone pavement. That was more like it. She had seemed different, somehow, this sister-in-law, and it had not pleased him. To his surprise, he had felt cheated at seeing her so spiritless. He had not realized that he had been looking forward to seeing her. It had piqued his adventurer's spirit to see what she would do next, and there she had been, drooping like a pink flamingo flower left too long in the sun. Thank heaven she had perked up. She had become more herself the moment he had suggested he was cheating her! He was not, of course. There were some good pieces in the cart, rare West Indian woods that would fetch a price. But more of the things were ordinary, and the glassware would not be worth all the packing to keep it from breaking on a voyage.

He looked sideways at her, seeing her chin lifted defiantly beneath the brim of her high-crowned hat. He would not have thought that one more disaster at Acelie would have defeated her. He had thought her stronger than that. It was something else. Maybe she was pregnant. She had looked quite peaked when he had spied her, though now the color had risen in her cheeks.

He sighed involuntarily as he thought of it. She had asked what he saw in her future. Pregnancy, of course. She would bear his brother child after child, and not more than half of them would live. She would be worn out producing children to fill Acelie's rooms, and if Edmond lost Acelie, then what? Edmond knew nothing but plantations. Edmond did not want to know anything else.

Joe did not understand why the matter bothered him. He had never been concerned about any French Creole woman before. They had been empty-headed pieces of fluff who deserved to lie in the beds they made for themselves. But none of them had ever been like his sister-in-law, Lily. He supposed that ever since she had bested him on the matter of Mimi, he had been rooting for her success.

He withdrew money for her in the gloomy interior of the bank and bid her good day on the glaring sidewalk outside.

"You have not forgotten the debt you owe me?"

"I have not forgotten, Joe."

"I shall come to Acelie to visit one day soon."

"We shall expect you."

As he lifted her onto the seat of the now-empty cart, he exercised his brotherly prerogative and kissed her on the cheek.

At last the sound of the *ka* was heard again at Acelie, and the harvest of the sugarcane was under way. Edmond had not been grateful for the surprise she had given him with the money from the furnishings. Indeed, she had made him inadequate by selling the things. He should have been the one to sell them, she saw. It would have been different if he had decided it must be done. She had unmanned him again, as she had in bed. She supposed she ought to have known better. It must have been that she had needed to be doing something. If only she had strength to behave as she should! It reminded her of the time she had cooked, and she did not dare tell him to whom she had sold the goods.

Her ploy had been of little help after all. Even by offering extra wages Edmond had recruited no more than half a dozen workers brave enough to come to Acelie. A few of the stricken workers had recovered, but none could yet stand long enough to do the full load of labor they had before. This harvest they would work with far from a complete *atelier*, and this time there was no question that Cyrillia and Yzore should go to the fields while Lily was left behind in charge of the house.

The cane cutters advanced like an army, the men naked to the waist, swinging great cutlasses in the sun. In the old days they had sometimes become an army in fact, repelling attacks of English corsairs along the coast. Lily always thought of these stories as the curved blades rose and fell, like silver shark fins in the topaz sugarcane sea.

Behind the cutters came the binders—the women securing the stalks into sheaves with cane leaves, carrying them away on their heads. And there were snakes. Each day the danger of the fer-de-lance grew greater, for as the cane was cut, the reptiles retreated, massing in the stalks left standing.

Each day Lily watched the horizon for the appearance of Joe Beau Clair. The kiss he had given her still burned on her cheek, and though she knew that when he came she would have to make the payment due him, she still anticipated his arrival. She had in her mind a plan, a desperate plan, but one that pleased her more than she wanted to admit. It was something she must do for Acelie, she would say to herself when her excitement became unseemly. But she was no longer the dispirited girl Joe had seen in St. Pierre, and the plan, more than anything, was the cause of it.

One noontime Edmond came angrily into the house. "Cyrillia is not in the field," he told her. "The binders are falling behind because of it."

"I will find her for you, Edmond," Lily said, and after he had left, she went through the empty house calling the girl's name. When all else failed she knocked at the door of Cyrillia's room. "Rilla? It's I." And a voice called permission to enter.

Lily had thought at first that Cyrillia had left the field out of humiliation at being made to help with the binding. Cyrillia was a house servant, almost like a member of the family. It would be natural for her to resent the rude work. But when she opened the door to the girl's room, all such thought vanished.

"Oh, Rilla! What is wrong? I will send for a doctor at once!"

"No, missy. A doctor could not help. Not even the witch doctor." Cyrillia lay weakly on her mat, which was elevated by two pieces of mattress stuffed with wood shavings. The room had no other furniture, only a trunk for her clothing, a pair of sandals with a leather band for the instep, and her tiny *chapelle* with a bouquet of flowers.

"It was not so bad in the house, missy. Then I could hide it. But in the fields, with the bending—it is three months now, I think."

Lily stared, not wanting to comprehend.

With a touch of triumph, Cyrillia smiled through her illness. "Yes, missy. I am going to have a baby. The child of your husband, Monsieur Beau Clair."

Lily reeled, and a sob burst from her throat. Cyrillia was to bear the child she would so gladly have borne herself! The child it had been her right to bear! Cyrillia had enjoyed herself in his bed, and he had been different with *her*. It had not mattered whether a native girl had one more child. It had not been worth interrupting his pleasure—never would he have to ask his brother's charity for that child! It would grow up as wildly and simply as a tamarind or calabash tree.

Her vision cleared as the first shock passed, and she gazed down at the girl who had been her dearest friend until a man had come between them. What had happened had been as much Lily's fault as Cyrillia's. It had been Lily who had not been content to lie beneath her husband while he did his will. It had been she who had undertaken to set his destiny and hers, and so doing, had driven him from her bed. Cyrillia had only taken the opportunity that was there. At least there would be a child in the house. She would love it like her own, Lily thought fiercely. It would give her existence meaning. She bathed Cyrillia's face in cool water and brought coconut milk for her to drink. Then she stripped herself to her chemise and opened the lid to Cyrillia's trunk.

"Missy, what are you doing?" said the astonished girl.

Lily lifted out a white muslin blouse, a calico skirt with

stripes of bright green and royal blue, and a painted yellow madras. "I am going to take your place, Rilla," she said.

"Missy, you cannot! Monsieur will never allow it! And there are many snakes now."

"I shall be careful of the snakes. Lie quiet and rest." She adjusted the clothing and turned for inspection. "How do I look, Rilla?"

"You look lovely. Almost as lovely as in your jupe dress." Lily flushed at the mention of her Carnival gown. As she turned to go, a thought came to her. "Rilla, when you find this Frenchman to marry you—this man who will make you more than his mistress—will your child be a problem then?"

"I am not thinking of a Frenchman to marry me any longer," said Cyrillia softly.

"You aren't? Why, Rilla? You were set on it!"

"I am in love with Monsieur—with Edmond," she said sadly. "There will never be anyone else."

10

Lily was not sure whether Edmond noticed that she, not Cyrillia, joined the binders in the canefield. He rode about tensely, his eye on the cane clumps. Two workers had been bitten this day. One seemed likely to recover, the other was already dead.

If Edmond were to notice her, he would have to send her away. It would be a matter of principle. But he needed her, and if he did not notice that she was not Cyrillia, in Cyrillia's clothes, then the problem did not arise. She was slower and clumsier than the other women, but she had watched cane bound all her life. She had played at gathering cane as a child, and before long she was binding as well as anyone.

She rather liked the work. Her body swung with unaccustomed freedom beneath the loose, corsetless clothing, and she lifted her eyes to the transparent blue mountains and sang with pure joy at being alive. Never had she felt so vital, and unknown to her, her face shone with the delight of it.

Death and danger were as near to her as the sound of the cutlass blades, and she who had always been protected reveled at her closeness to the essence of life. This is what natives have that Frenchmen have not, she told herself. And later she thought, "If a snake should get me, it would not be for nothing. Then Cyrillia should have her Creole to marry. And marry him she would, I wager!"

Perhaps it would have made as happy an ending as any Lily could foresee. But life was not to be so simple. He came to her room that night, where she lay exhausted in her thin *chinoise*. The sight of her in the fields had excited him, just as it had when she had helped to load bananas. She started in confusion at the touch of his lips, and hid her damaged hands beneath the flowing sleeves of her gown so that neither he nor she had to admit where she had been.

"Are you still angry with me, Lily?" he said thickly.

"It was you who were angry," she replied, trembling.

"Then may I lie here beside you?"

"Yes. It is your right."

He sank into the great bed and touched the silk of *her* bodice. In spite of her determination to comply, she went rigid. "Oh, Lily"—he sighed, as though troubled by something he did not understand—"I do not want to have it this way."

"Then don't," she said coolly.

"Things should not have gone so wrong between us," he said sadly. He left her, and for the first time she wept for a marriage that once had seemed promising.

Deep in the night there came a wail that set her upright in her bed with the knowledge that there would be only more weeping. It was a cry that could mean only one thing. Pascal had wreaked a deeper vengeance than the one of the poison seeds. Smallpox had come to Acelie.

It was two days later that Joe paid his call. Pots of tar smoldered against the blue sky among the workers' cottages, and Lily's face and hands had become well-tanned from her labors. As he rode past her on the way to the house, she unthinkingly dropped the cane she was binding and greeted him with a glad cry. He turned his horse and looked back at her, his expression too eager for a moment, as though he had seen someone else.

She held her breath in terror. Did he guess, seeing her in these native clothes? Indeed he had come too close to discerning the truth, and she ran away to the house, chattering inanely about not being presentable, while he looked after her with a mixture of amusement and appreciation.

She heard the two brothers enter the house together, and in a moment Cyrillia came up to her. "The gentlemen bid me tell you to wear something practical," she said. "You are going on a picnic."

"A picnic!" she could not believe her ears. It seemed to her that there had never been anything but wearying work and the interminable sound of the *ka*.

"Monsieur Joe has persuaded his brother. Monsieur Joe feels like having a picnic."

Lily could not help laughing, so well did Cyrillia's words describe Joe. "I can well believe that Monsieur Joe wishes to have a picnic. He would like all life to be a picnic. But Edmond!"

Cyrillia looked resentful. "It is because of you. Monsieur Joe says you must have a rest. He says you need an afternoon in the cool of the high woods or you will become ill from your work. He would take you himself, but of course that wouldn't be proper. So your husband has agreed to go, too." She paused and sighed, her hands unconsciously cradling her stomach. "Your husband still cares for you, missy."

Lily looked at her friend with pity. "Come, I will wear my shooting outfit. That will be perfect for climbing."

She created a sensation when she appeared before the men in her Norfolk jacket and checked knee-length skirt worn with knickers and gaiters. Her hair was done neatly in a looped catagan chignon, and a wide-brimmed hat offset the fine lines of her face, the roses that sun and excitement had kissed into her cheeks, and the dark eyes shining with golden light. She did not look at all in danger of becoming ill, as Joe had warned.

"Shall I have Rilla pack us a lunch?" she asked happily. What a joy to spend an afternoon with Joe! She hardly worried that in spite of Edmond's presence it might not turn out to be an entirely innocent afternoon. She knew she should be more frightened than she was, but her mood reminded her very much of the night she had slipped away to Carnival. If he asked her about Mimi...

"It is my invitation," he said in answer to her question. "I have brought everything we shall need. Pelee is clear today, so we will go up to the Crater of the Three Palmistes."

She clasped her hands in delight. "Oh! I have not been there since before Papa died!"

Once it had been a common treat. Groups of young people had ascended the slopes on Sundays after Mass to swim in the clear lake waters in the shadow of the volcano. How Lily had loved those times, filled with flirting and laughter. Edmond had often been her escort on such occasions, and it had given her quite a bit of status among her peers. Today her long absence from the mountain made the journey even more pleasurable than before.

They left the horses at the last plantation and began to climb the path through wild cane, guavas, guinea grass, and pink blossoms. Looking down, they could see canefields and narrow winding green valleys, and between an opening in the mountains, the sea appeared, looking itself like a strange azure cliff.

Then they entered a part of the island Lily especially loved, the primitive forest, the high woods. Among the great vine-wrapped trunks of acomats, silk-cotton trees, and ceibas they were plunged into a peaceful green twilight created by the leafy rigging of lianas and parasitic creepers above. The spaces between the great columns of the trees were occupied by vines, swinging like black ropes and cables in the dimness, and the acajous gave a rich smell of cedar. Here were trees that were rapidly becoming rare: the courbaril, with its dense chocolate-colored wood; the bois d'Inde; the gommiers, of which canoes were made. Once all Martinique furniture had been created from these woods, crafted by superb native cabinetmakers. But Martinique exported no lumber or furniture now, and only at such heights did the fantastic trees still grow.

The path had become a faint trace made by mountain-cabbage hunters who picked the tender young heads of palms to supply palm salad for the city markets. Now and then they passed one of these hunters carrying his wares wrapped in balisier leaves and tied with ropes of liana.

A cold dew fell, and unfamiliar insects sang as they climbed over the slippery roots and fern. Finally the trees became smaller, and beams of sunlight came again through the branches. They stopped to rest in a steep, open meadow. Far beneath them St. Pierre was a small red-and-yellow curve along the sea. Lily threw herself down to look at the dazzling sky and the line of knobby violet mountains that had moved so near.

"Oh, Joe, thank you for bringing us," she cried spontaneously.

"The climb is not too much for you, Lily?" He was absurdly pleased at having made her happy.

"Of course not! Why should it be?"

He shrugged and grinned across at his brother, who was glowering, as though he had discerned Joe's train of thought. So, she was not pregnant yet, after all. But Joe intuited that was not the source of Edmond's displeasure. He could not for the life of him discern why a man should be dissatisfied with such a wife. If she had married Edmond in the hopes of his salvaging Acelie, she had at least not sat on her bustle about it! When he had seen her there in the field, graceful and competent, she had risen another notch in his esteem.

But, yes, that was it. Edmond was thinking of her in the fields, too. That, too, was not too much for her, although, of course, it should have been. Joe had been away too long to know his brother well, but he did know how Creole men regarded their wives. What a blow to Edmond's pride her presence among the binders must be! And how desperate Acelie's position for him to allow it! Even if the harvest were successful, would he ever forgive her for having helped him?

They went on, passing deep gorges running with the cloud-fed rivers that supplied the island with its clear, cold water, and they entered the green twilight again in an upper belt of woods. Here the trees were smaller, dwarf palms and tall, fanlike arborescent ferns. There were blossoms of lobelia and plants with violet-red leaves, and then at last only low ferns and black, pointed volcanic stone. They arrived at the crater lake.

On a grassy bank between the water and the high green walls of the crater, Joe unloaded a meal of sausages and codfish pancakes, monkey oranges, little red dessert bananas, and white custard-like *corossol*. But though the climb had left Lily famished, her interest was not in the food. "I am going to swim," she announced, and going behind a huge mossy boulder, she emerged again in her bathing costume, a long tunic and drawers gathered at her slim ankles. Quickly she dived into the pool, which reflected mountain summits, and propelled herself down toward the bottom of yellow pumice-stone mud.

There were no fish to see here, nothing but mosquito larvae in the crystal water. Then she felt a percussion, and twisting to look up, saw Joe coming toward her, his clean, strong limbs in his bathing trousers looking as she had remembered them from Carnival night. She gasped, and losing her breath, swallowed a mouthful of sweet, dewy water as she crashed to the surface.

"What is wrong, Lily?" he teased, breaking from the water after her. "Did you think I was a shark? I know that you can swim very well. I remember it."

"You remember it! I do not recall that you have ever seen me swim."

"No, you would not remember. Nor did I until this afternoon. I have been thinking on this climb—I remember you from long ago. You were a little girl and your father let you run wild as a boy. Perhaps it is your becoming tan that makes me remember. You had a tan then, too. What do you remember of me, Lily?"

She laughed and splashed water on him in her confusion. "I remember that it was said that you were a rascal and would come to no good end. I did not know what was meant."

"And now you understand and you agree!" he accused gleefully.

"Oh, most certainly!"

"Then perhaps you would see things differently from the bottom of the lake," he threatened, and made as though to dunk her. She slipped away skillfully. A cloud settled over the water, covering them in mist. Her heart thudded with his nearness as she skimmed away to the bank.

It did not help her frame of mind that Edmond, exhausted from months of toil and worry, had fallen asleep beside the picnic lunch. Feeling suddenly exposed in her bathing attire, she changed hurriedly. When she exited her dressing spot, Joe had changed, too, and was holding out a piece of fruit he had chosen for her. She accepted it, glad even for Edmond's slumbering presence between them. Suddenly she was cold with the fear she should have felt before they had left Acelie. Now there was nothing to stop him from speaking to her of Mimi. And the disquiet of her heart told her that she was going to do the perfidious thing she had planned.

"Where did you go when you went with the ship from Grande Anse, Joe?" she asked. Any conversation would do, any delay.

"To Panama. And New Orleans. I visited Tobago. I did not go far."

He had not gone far—not far from Mimi, she thought with a shudder that was half horror, half joy.

"You have been everywhere, Joe," she prattled on, "I suppose you have been up there." She gazed up at the peak of the volcano.

"I have been there, Lily."

"Tell me what it's like."

"No one could. You must see for yourself. Would you like me to take you there?"

"Oh, yes! But what of Edmond?" She sat back on her knees and regarded her husband. "Poor Edmond. He will feel embarrassed at having slept here while we went on. I am forever shaming him. I sometimes don't make a proper wife." She did not know why she spoke so to him. There was something about the high altitude, some intimacy that the sharing of this beauty had brought.

To her surprise, he nodded with understanding. "When you sold the furnishings. When you work in the fields."

"Yes. It seems I cannot leave things alone. I suppose it is because I love Acelie so much."

"More than you love Edmond," Joe said easily.

She blushed and bristled. "Sir!"

"Oh, come, Lily, don't begin to 'sir' me again. I had thought we had at least got past that. I had begun to think you were an honest sort, too, though it is not usual with your kind. Admit that Acelie, not Edmond, is your passion. If he were your passion, you would do what he wished without questioning. You would be obsessed with his welfare instead of Acelie's."

She confounded him by smiling, a secretive little smile that gleamed as though it had escaped from her golden eyes in spite of her. "Women are not so simple as you think, mindless things to do nothing but traipse after a man. You would do well never to assume that a woman is honest."

She was thinking of the plan she had devised to trick him, but he could not know that. He did not know why she unnerved him so, sitting there with that smile, her jersey blouse bodice tucked carelessly, her hat beside her in the grass, and little tendrils of damp hair curling contentedly against her glowing cheeks. He felt an urge to lash out at her as he had on the beach at Grande Anse. Repressing it, he rose and looked at the blue-green summit of Pelee before them. "Edmond will sleep for hours. I am going up. And if you do not come, who knows when you will ever have another chance to see such a view?"

He struck off on a footpath that circled the lake. As he reached the far side, he thought he heard her little steps on the splintered stone. "Ah, Lily," he said to himself, "I have known many women, and it is simpler than you think. You will find out, should you ever fall truly in love."

Clouds swirled close to them as they struggled up through cushions of dark green fern, touched here and there with pale pinks and yellows. Suddenly the morne looked twice the height it had from the lake, and the lake itself vanished, covered by an opaque cloud. She was more alone with him than she had ever been with anyone, more entirely cut off from everything familiar than on her wedding night. She was suddenly dizzy with the sensation, and would have turned back, had she not needed him to lead her.

A natural ladder of lianas and roots led them over a chasm and onto a slanting surface of the peak, covered in lichen and brilliant mosslike green coral that was called bed of Jesus and used in Nativities at Christmas.

She saw crimson violets growing among the rocks, and bronze-green fireflies that would be spectacular at night. A hummingbird whizzed past, its sapphire head dark against the mother-of-pearl clouds that enclosed them on the mountaintop. She felt a pang of disappointment at the clouds. They had come for nothing. And then the ground rumbled beneath her, shaking her to the core with the knowledge of her utter vulnerability, her small, momentary spot in the universe. With a cry she flung herself into Joe's arms, felt them close around her. His hard chest quivered with laughter, and that pulsation seemed to merge with the mountain's.

"It is not going to erupt, you little goose!" he said. "It has never erupted!"

She lifted her head from his shoulder, stung at his tone. "Just because it has never happened doesn't mean it never will. It is still a volcano, Joe!"

"You are right; it is still a volcano." He had stopped laughing, but he had not let go of her. She looked into his eyes and was seized with a trembling as profound as that of the mountain. And then a cool breeze swept over them. The clouds parted, and they seemed to hang suspended in a blue void of sky and ocean.

"Oh, Joe!" she cried in wonder and gratitude. Valleys and forests, peaks and ravines were tossed weirdly below them like waves in a storm, and distant mountains seemed to rise from nowhere, resting only on the blueness. A band of pale light was all that marked the sea line, and there in the north rose an amethyst peak that was the wilderness island of Dominica. A perfect West Indian rainbow shimmered from horizon to horizon, passing over their heads so close that it seemed they might almost touch its great bands of ruby, lemon, and lavender.

Joe found himself thinking of Mimi, as though the coloring of the sky reminded him of the gold of her necklace and the purple of her gown, as though this ecstasy might be kin to the one he hoped for with her. But it was Lily, too, who had reminded him of Mimi for the second time today. First, when he had seen her in the fields, and just now when he had held her in his arms, he had remembered the sensations of Carnival. He glanced at the awed girl beside him and wondered if she would really keep her word. Strangely, she was thinking of Mimi, too.

"Joe," she said, "do you know the *case-à-vent* in the valley beyond Acelie?"

"Yes, of course, the hurricane house."

"Come tomorrow at midnight. Mimi will wait for you."

11

It cannot happen. The thought was with her all the next day as she worked the fields in the scorching sun. Beneath the yellow zenith of noon it seemed that night could never come again, and she took comfort in that, letting herself believe that there would never be anything but the beat of the *ka* and the mournful singing of workers as the sparkling cutlasses whacked the sturdy cane. Ahead of her in the row Edmond wielded one of the blades, and watching him, she admired his dedication, the single-minded purpose in the swing of his strong, sunburned arms.

Things should not have gone so wrong between us! Oh, Edmond!

The dusk gathered itself and rose from the valleys, and great bats flew up darkly over the last gold glow of the fields. Some things could not be stopped from happening, though they had never happened before. Pelee, though it had never really erupted, still seethed with steam and molten fire. And so it was with Lily as the sense of disbelief followed her into the night. Was it fear or excitement that made her unable to eat her dinner? Paleness or the fever of her cheeks that made her husband look at her with concern?

"I have been working too hard, after all, Edmond," she told him, and excused herself to go to bed early. In her room she sat by the open window, listening to the rustle of palm fronds in the warm breeze and the deepening concert of crickets and tree frogs. The night became fact, and still she sat and marked the passing hours on the hands of the watch with the silver letters JOE BEAU CLAIR.

When it was eleven she rose quietly, lighted the lamp, and opened the doors of her wardrobe. The violet jupe dress seemed to welcome her as she slipped into it; it seemed warm with the passions of Carnival, and when Lily looked at herself in the mirror, she no longer doubted what was to happen. Next, the vermilion foulard, the madras fastened with gold trembling pins, and simple native sandals for her feet. She had no need this time for the gloves with which she had disguised her soft white hands at Carnival. Her hands were brown and tough from the fields. She fastened her cloak over all, like night over sunset. Then, as a sudden last thought, she turned back, and removing her wedding ring, put it into a drawer so that it would not betray her.

The night was moonless. She felt her way to the stable, where she lighted a lantern to saddle her horse. Acelie was silent, the house utterly dark. From the *ajoupas* came a moan of the smallpox, and then there was silence.

She rode away from Acelie through the cut fields, down into a cool valley of fern and liana. She held her lantern out, inspecting the ground before dismounting. The stone hut, built half into the hillside, sat undisturbed in the blackness. She pulled on its heavy wooden door with both hands to force it open, and remembered once when she had been a child, it had taken twelve men to hold it closed against the force of a hurricane beyond its windowless walls.

Tonight nothing could keep the storm away. She lifted the light and looked about the place for danger. A centipede scurried across the floor, and with a shudder she seized a rock and killed it swiftly with a blow to its head. Removing her cloak, she dropped it on the dirt floor and took out her white Carnival mask and put it over her face. She blew out her light and waited.

She heard the sound of a horse moving cautiously through the vegetation. Then the soft thud of feet descending to the earth. The door squeaked open, and Joe's light came through. She caught her breath at the eagerness on his face.

"Mimi!"

"Monsieur!" she murmured softly.

"Mimi, why have you hidden from me? I looked everywhere." She felt a twinge of guilt at the longing in his voice.

"Monsieur knows why!" She managed to make her words accusing, as he touched the wire mask. "Monsieur wishes me to remove the mask. The scars have faded very little!"

"Upon my word, Mimi!" he cried. "I will not notice! Take it off now and let me see your beautiful eyes that I have dreamed so often of seeing. Let me kiss your pretty lips."

She moved behind him and pushed the door shut. He gave an exclamation of surprise as she bent and blew out his light. "Now, do as you will with me, monsieur. Only do not ask to see my face."

He seemed about to protest, but she was standing too close in the darkness, and with a moan of joy he pulled away the mask and covered her mouth with his. She swooned into the deepness of his kiss, meeting it with a free passion of her own. Her madras was gone, her hair tumbling down against his cheek. She did not resist at the touch of his hands on her buttons, but instead leaned weakly against him, her body alive with the desire of Carnival. Now she would know at last what it was to love a man! She could not have lived her life unknowing, gone to her grave demure and unfulfilled! It had been inevitable!

"My beloved, my darling!" His voice was in her ear. "Oh, I had begun to think this would never happen! I do not think I could have endured!"

"Nor I either, Joe . . ."

She knew more what was expected than she had that night at Carnival, and breaking from him, she spread her cloak and pulled him down beside her. Then he was kissing her again. She clung to him, her wanton need consuming her. Life might go on after this night, but she did not think she would even be aware of it. "Oh, Joe, love me!" she whispered.

Suddenly he gave a cry, and his arms no longer crushed her. He had discovered her identity, she thought dazedly. A curse, shockingly foul, reached her ears.

"Put on the lamp!" he commanded.

"Monsieur! The mask!"

Never mind that!"

She felt for it frantically in the blackness and clamped it across her face just as the room filled with light. A pistol appeared from his discarded jacket, and a shot rang out, shattering her senses as it reverberated from the stone walls. She sank to her knees, certain she had been killed.

On her cloak lay the writhing body of a fer-de-lance he had shot.

"It has bitten me!" he said, turning the gun on her now in fact. "It was not here when I came in. You brought it in a basket and hid it under your cloak! *She* paid you to do it! Lily Beau Clair!"

"No, no monsieur! It must have come in behind you! Or have been hiding in a crack between the stones. Madame Beau Clair—"

"Madame Beau Clair would do anything for Acelie! How convenient to have me dead! Her Edmond would have Beau Clair and enough money to keep them both forever! And you! Why didn't it bite you? You knew where it was! You were careful! Oh, Mimi, how much did she pay you to make you do this, when I loved you so much!"

In horror she saw him slide down almost unconscious with the effect of the dreadful poison. "Pretty Mimi," he whispered, "at least stay with me until I die!" And his head lolled back into oblivion.

She did the things she knew to do. She made a tourniquet, and wrapped the bitten leg in banana leaves. She did not stay to watch him die, but ran out to her horse, and covering herself with the cloak to hide the jupe dress, she galloped off for the closest help she knew, the witch doctor in his hut up the mountain. When she had got him, she went home and prayed at her ivory *chapelle*.

Her prayers were answered. He was still alive when they brought him to Acelie.

"What the deuce could he have been doing there?" Edmond wondered the next morning. "Tell me again how it happened."

"There was a girl, Edmond. I was not sleeping, and I heard her when she came to the door in the night. I went for the sorcerer myself. I was so frightened I did not think of waking anyone else."

He sighed. "Most frightened women would think of waking their husbands, Lily. But it is like you. And perhaps he has you to thank for his life. Time is important with such things."

"Do not expect him to be grateful, Edmond. Even if he lives."

Her husband gave a little laugh. "Why is it that you have such a low opinion of Joe? Ah, it is the girl! She explains what he was doing there, doesn't she? But why in the hurricane house, when St. Pierre has many nice beds? I will never fathom him, Lily. Was she pretty, this girl?"

"Perhaps," said Lily spitefully, "but I cannot see why any man would want her. She had had the pox."

She did not go to the fields that day or any of the following days. Cyrillia worked with the binders again, while Lily sat with Joe, using all the remedies the witch doctor had advised. She applied the leeches, so ugly that her flesh crawled at the sight of them on the skin of her beloved. She made poultices of herbs, orange leaves, cinnamon, and cloves. In her desperation she made a brew of rum and the head of the snake, which the sorcerer had roasted and pounded; and she forced it between his unknowing lips.

She nursed him both from choice and from necessity. He was never really rational, but sometimes he shouted strange accusations that she wanted no one to hear. He moaned after Mimi, telling her of his love, decrying his betrayal, and once he sat bolt upright and called out "Lily Beau Clair" in a voice like the thunder of doom.

She wondered what would happen if he recovered. Did he hate her enough to bring shame on them all? Would he bare everything to accuse her of plotting his murder? Would there be a trial, and would she perhaps be hanged? When no coaling girl could be found to protest innocence, it would seem that Mimi had run away in guilt.

How long ago it seemed that she had not been satisfied with Edmond! If only she could return to those days, secure in his devotion to her and and Acelie, with no more to worry about than bank payments and banana crops!

If only she had not had the cloak that night! There had been no place to put it except the floor. He, naturally, had inspected the room when he had entered, as she had herself. But both of them had been too hasty, too eager for their tryst. He had said it would be convenient for her to have him dead. How much more was that true now, that he might not live to accuse her!

It would be easy to let him die. She had only to fall wearily asleep at her duty—to fail to change the dressing or not to lift his head to help him as he gasped for breath. But Lily took great caution that these things did not happen. She splashed cool water onto her face from the red *dobanne* to keep herself awake. And when she nodded off anyway, the slightest shifting of her patient brought her to her feet with a start.

Cyrillia brought her pots of cocoa water and crab baked with lime juice and bananas. "Eat, missy. You must not get sick, too."

"I know, Rilla." The girl's waistline had rounded now. It was apparent that she would soon be a mother.

"I will watch for you while you sleep. I am not afraid to hear him speak of the ghost woman."

"The ghost woman!" said Lily tiredly.

"Yes, missy. This Mimi who has bewitched him. You remember that I told you once how he looked for her among the coaling girls."

"And everyone said she had put a spell on him that he could not rest until he found her," Lily said with a shiver. "The ghost woman who leads men over cliffs in the night."

"It seems that he has found her, missy. He had no chance against her. You can hear through the windows that he calls her a devil."

Lily slept, and let Cyrillia take a turn with Joe, and she dreamed she had become the *soucouyan*, the ghastly being that could shed its white skin at will by the road at night. She had discarded the pale shell of Lily and become Mimi, the dark *diablesse*, the ghost woman who destroyed men with their own desire.

The harvest was done. It was a relief to have Cyrillia helping her all the time. It was good to have the drum quiet, to hear the long sweet notes of the mountain whistler as it flew above the cassias and flamboyants. The smallpox was diminishing at St. Pierre, and it was rumored that the quarantine would soon be lifted. Sometimes when the breeze was right, she could smell the sweet, hazy smoke from the sugar mill, where Acelie's hard-won harvest was being processed along with the cane from Beau Clair and other plantations. Soon it would be shipped away to New Orleans, Boston, Canada. The sweet gold of cane would become the sweet gold of needed money.

Cyrillia did not come one morning. Instead it was Edmond who rapped on the door. "I will watch now, Lily," he said.

"Oh, no, Edmond . . ." She had no way of knowing what Joe might say in his delirium. If he implicated her as well as Mimi in a plot of murder, it would not be the first time.

"I will watch," he repeated, his face grim. "You have other things you must do. You must take care of Cyrillia."

"Rilla! Has she got the pox?"

He nodded. "Yes, and she is a *capresse*. You know it goes hard with them."

"But . . . I must stay here. Can't Yzore tend her?"

"Lily, Yzore is dead. It was the *vérette pouf*, the kind that strangles quickly."

"Yes, Edmond. It is what killed the priest who married us. I will go and see to Rilla."

Yzore was the only mother she had ever known, the only one to whom she might have confessed her crimes as Mimi, who might have advised her about Joe. Lily scarcely thought of that as she sat by Cyrillia. She thought instead that she would never again have that soft dark bosom to lean against, that no one would ever again candy breadfruit pods for her out of love or make her an amulet of blessed flowers to get her a baby.

Rilla's fevered eyes looked at her from the straw mattress of her bedroom. "Ah, missy, if I die you will have him on your hands again. Treat him gently, because he loves you."

"No. Do not talk nonsense, Rilla. You are not going to die."

"I hope not, missy. I am praying to the Good God that I will live. Even if I am too disfigured for him to want me again, I will have the child."

But Cyrillia did not keep her child. As the hours passed, she writhed in torment, and Lily saw the spread of blood. She was frightened enough this time to run for her husband. "Send for a doctor!" she demanded, and when he had written a note and dispatched it, she beat on his chest and said things to him that could not easily be retracted.

"Oh, it is all your fault! I should have been with child, not she! And my child would not be lost, though even if it were, I wish it were mine. She will die, too, and I loved her like a sister!"

He was horrified. Wives did not speak to husbands of their native mistresses, and when such a girl had a child, it had many fathers. It must be all the grief—her dead father and Yzore and the long nights and days of tending Joe. But it seemed to him that the longer he was married, the less he understood his wife.

Rilla did not die. And neither did Joe. He wakened from a long sleep and looked at her calmly.

"It went badly with the coaling girl, Lily," he said.

"Yes. I am sorry, Joe." She was trembling as though she had really been responsible for the snake. She had heard his accusations for so long she almost believed them. "Though if I had killed him it would not have been for Beau Clair, but because I could not stand loving him and knowing I could not have him," she thought.

"I loved her, Lily," he said softly.

"And what of me? You said dreadful things while you were ill."

"It doesn't matter about you. It was she who betrayed me. When the quarantine is lifted, I am going away from Martinique. I could never bear to return. And you shall have Beau Clair. I shall sign it over to Edmond, and everything will be as your father thought before he died. Your Acelie will be safe."

She had brought him into her power. She had extracted a higher price than she had dreamed, and it had not made her happy. What a joke that they called this island the land of comers-back!

Now that he was getting well, she spent as little time as possible in his room. She told herself that her presence there would be upsetting to him. More accurately, she could not bear to face the idea of his hate for her. And when she was near him, she could think only that soon she never would be again. Cyrillia, though weak from her own illness, saw to most of his needs. The disease had left its mark lightly; the *capresse* was still beautiful. Lily wondered if her face, with its few lingering scars, made him think of Mimi.

"Lily," he said one day when she had come into his room, "I have a strange memory of when I was sick. Everything was like a dream, but a dream with you in every part. Was it you who nursed me?"

"Yes, Joe." She had never pleaded her innocence to him, but now her heart leaped as she realized he was no longer certain that she had tried to kill him. She had nursed him, but he would be quick to see that it might have been from guilt, or from fear of becoming a murderess in fact. When he was strong enough, he rode away to Beau Clair, and she wondered if she would ever see him again.

He might come to say good-bye, but she thought it more likely that he wouldn't. Edmond went to St. Pierre for the formal transfer of the estate, and he brought Lily back a pair of tortoise-shell combs to celebrate the occasion. Once he had merely managed Beau Clair; now it was his entirely, as Joe, wealthy from other ventures, divested himself of his last ties to Martinique.

"Lily, it is time that we had an heir," he said, taking her hands gently in his as they sat together in the twilight on the veranda. He thought his words would make her happy, but she did not seem to hear him above the sound of tree frogs and wood crickets. She was beyond wanting the baby that she once had thought would fill her life.

"Are you worrying about Joe, Lily?" he asked.

"I suppose so. It does seem . . . wrong that his misfortunes should bring us security."

"Well, don't let it spoil your pleasure. Joe will be happier away from Martinique. Staying put debilitates him. If it had not been for that coaling girl, he'd have gone long ago. And *she* was not good for him, certainly. I cannot get over it! My brother and a coaling girl! It isn't like Joe to let a woman get him twisted up."

"He will forget her, won't he? Even though he loved her?"

"Of course. And our life will go on as it ought. It has been disrupted these months, Lily darling. We shall have peace now, my love, I promise."

But peace did not come. Instead, one cool morning she found Edmond seated again on the veranda with a table before him and a line of workers stretching down the steps and into the drive.

"Edmond! What is happening?"

"These workers are drawing their wages, Lily. They are leaving," he said grimly.

"Leaving? But why?" She was quick to see that the line was too long to be only Acelie's workers. There were many unfamiliar faces that must have come from Beau Clair. And there were no women among them, only men standing silently in their blue pantaloons and rough gray shirts.

"It is not that they think they have been treated unfairly. They are all going to Panama to work on the canal."

"The canal! That is Joe's doing, then. It is he who is forever dreaming about that impossible canal! What sort of brother is he—to give us Beau Clair and then take its entire *atelier* with him?"

"Lily . . ." He rose from his chair, embarrassed at the scene she was causing before his workers. She flounced into the house and waited for him to follow.

"I suppose you have not asked them to stay!" she cried when he walked into her trap. "I suppose that is beneath your dignity. You have not offered them more money!"

"I cannot offer money such as they will make in Panama!"

"If they survive. Not half of them will return. You know that, Edmond. You are sending them to their deaths!"

"I am not sending them. They are making their own choice. It isn't my decision, Lily. We don't have slavery anymore on Martinique, and I cannot tell free men what to do."

"They cannot go if Joe will not take them. You must talk to Joe."

Edmond turned and went back to the porch, leaving her gasping with anger in the hallway. "If he will do nothing, then I must!" she thought. Consumed by the moment, she did not think that this time when she took her destiny into her own hands the consequences might be a thousand times greater than when she had sold furnishings or lied to bankers, or even when she had promised Joe his Mimi.

She went into the library and took a pistol from the drawer of Edmond's desk. Then she went upstairs, and removing the jupe dress from her wardrobe, put it on, this time without the madras or the mask. If Joe did not believe she would kill him, then perhaps he would be convinced when he saw she was Mimi, who had nearly destroyed him with the snake. If she had to show him she was Mimi to have the workers put ashore, she would. She fastened the cloak over her, and slipping the pistol into her pocket, she rode for St. Pierre.

The quarantine had been lifted. In the roadstead sails rose above the sapphire sea, and pale clouds of gray smoke wafted from steamers. The coaling girls walked again along the landings below the basalt heights of Morne d'Orange—all those barefoot Mimis with their great trays destined for the fuel bins of ships.

She hired a canoe to take her out to Joe's beautiful square-rigger, *Sea Bird*. "Is your captain aboard?" she asked the startled crew. He was not, but he would be soon. With great courtesy they showed her to his quarters to wait for him. She laughed as she imagined the gossip she was causing, and took out the pistol and pointed it at the door.

She heard his footsteps coming. He opened the door and saw her. "Mimi did not kill you," she told him, "but I may kill you this time myself if you do not put my workers ashore."

He kicked the door shut behind him. "Come, little sister, give me the pistol. The passengers have paid their fare."

"You have infected them like the smallpox with your grand talk of Panama!"

"Perhaps. But I did not set out to do so. Some will die, but the others will never be plantation workers again. They will have money to buy land for themselves. It's a bold way to live, to have something one cares enough to die for."

"And you, Joe?" she said, her hand trembling on her weapon. "Do you want to die?" She loved him. She could never pull the trigger, but he did not know that. He thought she had already tried to kill him once. He thought she was capable, and if he seemed to have doubts, he would not when she showed him she was Mimi. Oh, if only she could show him who she was for another reason!

She felt her wrist twisted, and the gun fell away to the

floor. She tried to scramble after the pistol, but he held her, and even as she fought him, she gloried in his closeness. Suddenly came the thunder of a gun. She stared in disbelief at the pistol still on the floor.

"It is too late to put anyone ashore, Lily, even you. That was the farewell salute you heard. I gave the order to set sail when I came aboard."

"We have left Martinique!" She rushed to the porthole, to see the island becoming distant, the palms and banana trees merging into a solid sheet of green. "You must take me back, Joe!"

"No. I have sworn never to return. I will put you ashore elsewhere, but I will never go back to Martinique."

Suddenly heady freedom rushed over her, lifting her like the great green swells of the sea. "Or I either, Joe! I shall never return without you! You will need this watch to keep track of forever!" She took out the timepiece he had given her and watched his face go blank with amazement. And she flung aside her cloak and revealed herself to him.

"Oh, Joe! Take me with you! I am Mimi!"

A strange rapture swept over her as he held her fiercely against his hard, lean body. Sighs rose magically from the depths of her being. She was close to swooning, and yet never had she felt so joyously alive, so possessed by her senses. He had said that it was a bold way to live to have something to die for. Now she would live or die for him.

She could deny herself no longer. No matter that the fires of damnation might claim her soul, if only the fires of love might claim her now!

12

"I should have known long ago," he thought, touching her face in wonder. She was looking at him, half in ecstasy, half in terror, her dark eyes shining with the topaz glow of her love. He gathered her to him, kissing her deeply, feeling her respond in a way that left no doubt that she was Mimi, no doubt that she was incapable of wishing him harm.

She should have known, too, long ago—that no matter what she had vowed at her marriage only the vow she made now was sacred.

"I shall go wherever you go, Joe," she whispered when he released her at last. "You were right after all about women and their passions, but you were wrong that mine is Acelie. It has been only you, ever since that night we danced the *danse du pays*. Do you remember in the hurricane house when you asked Mimi to stay with you until you died? That is what I shall do, Joe. I shall stay with you until you die. And should I die before you, I shall turn into a black death's butterfly and put a spell on you that you still shall love no one but me."

"Oh, Lily, I love you, but I cannot take you!" He turned from her and sat with his face in his hands. "You are not Mimi. If only you were! I would marry you at once. Even in New Orleans, where such marriages are forbidden, I should mingle our blood together as others have done and declare us both Africans so that we might wed. But you are a wife already. My brother's wife! I have often been called a rascal, but I have a certain honor. I cannot take my brother's wife!

"I shall put you ashore tonight. We shall have today and then nothing more. I will keep my vow never to return to Martinique. If I were ever to see you again, I might not be able to control my need. Edmond loves you, Lily, but, oh, how wasted you shall be on him!"

She was afraid that he meant to set her aground at Roseau, the tiny capital of primitive Dominica, Martinique's nearest neighbor. But on they sailed, around its rugged green coastline, through cool mist so fine it could be seen only through backlighting from the sun.

Then they were out to sea again, the island fading to a spectral green against the water. She had never been so far before, and though she had lived all her life on an island, it was only now that she began to conceive of the hugeness of the ocean, to think of it as fraught with purpose and possibility.

And all this time he held her and kissed her, stroked her hair and studied her face as if to set it in memory. She took his hand and placed it beneath the swell of her breast, and felt a wild current race between them. But he did not venture further, as he trembled with restraint. She was his brother's wife, and to lie with her would be more than a simple sin of flesh. It would be against his deepest sense of honor.

On into the dusk they sailed, as though they would never stop. Then a dark, cloudlike shape appeared on the horizon. An island came out of the haze, pale slopes of blue and green with the sun fading over them. "Montserrat, Lily," said Joe with a sigh. The ship's gun fired a salute, and the boon of a reply echoed over the hills.

He took her ashore at Plymouth, a red-and-white town, half-hidden in the green fringe of mountains. The palms were slender and delicate as children; the streets, tiny with odd angles and curves and courtyards displaying candelabra cacti. He found her a neat, old-fashioned hotel of whitewashed stone.

"You will need money for passage back to Martinique," he told her, putting bank notes on the dresser. "And you must buy new clothes. Heaven knows you can't return to Edmond in a jupe dress. And this, Lily, my watch, to tell forever by, as you said. I shall keep the necklace."

"Near you always, Joe?"

"Yes, Lily." He kissed her once more. She closed her eyes at the touch of his lips, and when he was there no longer, she did not open them, as if refusing to admit that it was finished, that she was alone for the rest of her life. When she looked about her at last, a splendid orange sunset silhouetted the little palms, and hue of pink stained the walls beyond the sweet-smelling plume mattress. She rose wearily, let down her hair, and unfastened her jupe dress.

As she stood there in her thin, blue-ribboned chemise, the door burst open. She felt herself tossed back against the bed as a voice whispered, "Oh, my love, did I not tell you in the hurricane house that I could not endure?"

He took her greedily, striking beneath the white froth of her petticoat. Her body lifted to his as it had longed to since Carnival; her soul stretched toward that truth that had so long eluded her, and as darkness soaked up the last vermilion rays of sun, Lily Beau Clair finally knew what it was to love.

She lay floating on the pillow of his arm, her face pressed to his chest, her lips pursed in a kiss. She was happier than she had ever been in all her life. There was thunder somewhere far off. It was going to rain, and she should get up and close the windows. She would call Yzore. No, Yzore was dead; she would have to do it herself. She struggled toward consciousness and fell back. She was too happy, too content. The rain would not hurt this once, coming in the window.

Abruptly she was falling a thousand feet, as if from a summit. She waked with a little cry. Joe had sat up and spilled her from his shoulder. He put his finger against her lips for silence. The thunder became a terrible knocking at the door.

"Lily!"

"It's Edmond!" The words were in her eyes, though she was too terrified to utter them aloud. Joe kissed her quickly and reached for his trousers.

"I am going, Lily. I can't be found here." He vanished out the window, and she did not have the opportunity to see if he had found his way safely to the ground. The door flung open, and there was her husband.

"Why didn't you let me in?" he demanded angrily.

She floundered, and inadvertently told a truth. "I was frightened, Edmond."

"Well might you have been! What a laughingstock you have made of me! I suppose that brother of mine intended teaching you a lesson, sailing off with you! I hope he has succeeded."

"Oh, yes." She sighed. "I am so sorry, Edmond. I will never misbehave again." She was beginning to gather her senses about her, to realize what would happen if he guessed. Once she had threatened him with taking another man, and he had told her in so many words that he would kill him.

But as the realization came over her, so did it over him. He took in the tumbled covers, her unlaced chemise. Above all, he caught sight of a man's watch on the bureau, and seizing it, read the name of his brother there.

"No, Edmond, no!" she cried.

"Where is the pistol, Lily?"

"I do not have a pistol," she said, trembling.

"The one you took from Acelie. Never mind, I shall find it myself." He dug into the pocket of her cloak and drew it forth. "I shall teach that womanizer to seduce my wife!" The silver barrel glinted in the dimness, and before she could think what to do, he was gone.

She leaped up, fastened herself into her dress and cloak, and ran through the narrow, cobbled streets, trying to remember the way to the docks. Tears wasted her vision and made her way more difficult. One would kill the other, and though she had only a moment ago promised not to step out of her place again, she was doing it already. A duel was between men, and it was not for women to interfere.

A duel! Would it be that, at least? With swords, as was the French custom? Joe would have a chance. But suppose that she were a widow and free to wed? Would he even want her then? Could lying with him ever be the same as tonight? She did not want either of them to die. She must stop it somehow. The ocean shone darkly before her as she ran out onto the long wharf.

And then she stopped, weak with relief. The *Sea Bird* was no longer at its mooring. Far out to sea a light twinkled, and it seemed to her that he was telling her good-bye.

He had sworn not to return to Martinique. But suddenly she remembered that she had made that vow, too, when she had revealed herself to him. She would keep her vow, she thought.

She walked back to the hotel, and bolting the door against the possibility of Edmond's return, she fell into a troubled sleep and dreamed of Acelie that she so loved. The land of comers-back—she would never see it again.

In the morning she purchased a simple outfit of brown-and-green merino and one of gingham and a small beaded bag in which to stow Joe's watch and the remainder of his money. She had spent far less than she might have on the clothing, and the amount he had left her had been generous. She thought she would have enough for passage. But passage where? She could go anywhere as long as she did not go back to Martinique, to Edmond.

She went down to the docks, where a big steamer was coaling under the glaring sun. "Where bound?" she called up.

"New Orleans!" came the answer. And her spirit soared.

Part II

Babylon
(1889-1897)

1

The steam winch shuddered and whined, lifting the great anchor. Montserrat faded into the blue distance, and then the three tall craters of Nevis came through the haze.

Lily had managed to acquire a second-class cabin that suited her purposes well. The carpet was thin and the mattress too hard, but a few francs still jingled in her purse. She had waited two days for the ship to sail, and in that time she had not ventured from her cabin for fear that Edmond would come aboard looking for her. Was he finished with her so easily? She was still his wife! But Edmond did not appear, and she could only guess that he had sailed for Martinique by whatever means he had come. Now at sea, she was glad to come on deck for air and exercise. Excitement tugged at her, since she had surely left him behind. Freedom, rather than the fresh sea wind, gave her cheeks a special glow. She was afraid, of course, but the mixture of emotions was familiar to Lily. She was beginning to recognize that it would always be so when she followed the Carnival drums of her heart.

What would she do when she reached New Orleans? While part of her cried out in terror that she had no experience of foreign cities or of being on her own, another voice spoke with naive confidence of her untried abilities. Lily had no plan, only a simple, groundless faith in her survival.

Perhaps she would go to a priest. He would find her a convent in which she could wait until Joe came. How long would that be? And when he did arrive, what would he do with her, his brother's wife? She could not tell the priest the truth, of course, and the idea of lying to a priest unnerved her as much as the entire prospect of New Orleans.

The ship was bound by way of Cuba, and most of her passengers seemed to be businessmen who lounged about the decks in white linen suits and carried on earnest conversations on the price of sugar and cigars. Women were few, only three or four plump Spanish matrons traveling with their families, and the addition of Lily created a lively interest among the men. They watched her admiringly as the ship steamed by St. Martin's golden fog of sun and past the great shark-haunted harbor of Antigua.

They waited, unbelieving that no husband or protector lurked below, and finally, unable to deny themselves any longer, they began to talk to her, to vie with each other to sit beside her at meals or promenade with her on the deck. They were like a crowd of bashful schoolboys, she thought at first. Then they became more like a pack of wolves at bay. At night she lay sleepless behind the flimsy lock on her door, and she listened to every footstep that went past.

How long before one of the brutes broke from the others? How long until Cuba?

They had entered the Azure Stream, and the water was a brilliant cyanogen, matching a sky that paled to green at the horizon, flecked at evening with gold cloudlets like soft, earthly stars. She could not keep herself below. But indeed she was safer above—until one afternoon when she felt a touch in her hair that was not the sea wind, an arm close tightly about her waist. She twisted away frantically and sought the company of the matrons, who chattered on in Spanish, unable to understand her French or the English she had learned so well in school.

The next morning, to her relief, they spied the coast of Cuba with its undulating hills, so unlike the mountains and tropical forests of her girlhood. Cultivated fields and neat farmhouses gave way to the harbor of Havana, marked by the walls and towers of the Moro, the proud fort with its lighthouse and the Spanish flag fluttering from its angry bastions. Beyond was a deep lagoon and a rocky penninsula from which rose the domes and steeples and marble palaces of the fabled city.

The waters swarmed with hundreds of boats; she saw a dozen strange flags along with the more familiar ones that she had often seen in the roadstead of St. Pierre. And the Stars and Stripes of the country to which she journeyed made Joe seem suddenly near.

As the ship dropped anchor, it was boarded by hotel touters, customs-house officials, porters, and interpreters. Lily reeled with the temptation to go ashore, but the few francs that stood between her and destitution prevented it. Families of tourists began to board, and there were gentlemen with women who somehow did not seem to be their wives. Someone tapped Lily's arm, and she turned to see an elderly woman all done in black silk, her hands over the knob of an ivory-headed cane. Lily had noticed the old lady come aboard and had wondered if she were making passage.

"Madame Beau Clair..."

"Yes?" she replied in surprise.

"I am Blanche Drapeaux. The captain has told me you are traveling alone..."

"To meet my husband in New Orleans, madame."

"I hope you won't think me too forward, dear child, but I, too, am traveling alone. Cuba is a wonderful resort spot, and the climate improves my health, but now I'm on my way home to New Orleans, and my girl, my companion, has run off with some Spaniard. If you would like the position, I would require only conversation and fetching my heart medicine should I need it. I would pay you well, and I would be most grateful, for I'm sure the work is beneath you."

Lily was delighted with the opportunity. She moved her meager belongings into Madame Drapeaux's luxurious cabin, and soon her purse rattled with more money. An easy relationship bloomed between the two women, for Madame Drapeaux took a motherly interest in her new companion. In spite of her heart condition, she did not seem at all an invalid and spent most of her time above deck, where her hard look dispersed those men who sought familiarity with Lily.

"Tch, tch! In my day gentlemen never behaved so. Not in New Orleans." She had been a great belle, and had had many call-outs at Mardi Gras. Once she had been queen of the Mistick Krewe of Comus; on Mardi Gras night her king had drunk her health from a goblet made of gold.

"Poor New Orleans! What it has suffered since the Americans have taken it over! Thank heaven there are still a few of us left to uphold her standards. Your husband isn't an American, I hope?"

"He is French, madame."

"And he will be there waiting for you when we dock?"

Lily colored and dropped her eyes. "No... you see, he doesn't expect me. We had a plantation at Martinique. There was a worker, Pascal, who was dismissed. He put a curse on us, and because of it, our harvest failed. The plantation was auctioned, and I lost everything, except for these clothes. My husband was at sea, and he doesn't know what has happened. He had gone to Panama, but soon he will be in New Orleans, so I managed to find enough for my passage."

"But couldn't you wait with friends on Martinique?"

"I wanted only to see him as soon as possible, and it was too humiliating on Martinique. Acelie had been in my family for generations. And my husband! Who knows what he may do to those responsible if I cannot calm him first?"

"He is a swordsman, then, your husband?"

"Oh, yes! And I love him to distraction!" She shivered to punctuate this story, this strange mixture of twisted truths and lies that she had worked on from Montserrat to tell the priest. It was not so bad, telling it to Madame Drapeaux, who believed it all and patted her and made clucking sounds. How different she was from Yzore, and yet she was filling Yzore's place.

"And what will you do until he comes, Lily? New Orleans is a wicked city."

"I had thought of a convent."

Madame Drapeaux's laughter tinkled under the awning-shaded saloon deck, and two little greenish monkeys tied to the wheel hatch paused in their twittering to look down at her. "A convent! You would not last there, Lily Beau Clair, or I am no judge of character. You will continue as my companion when we reach New Orleans and save me the trouble of finding a new one. And you will hope he takes his time in coming, even though you love him so, because you were meant for gaiety; and that is what we shall have!"

It seemed to Lily that a merciful God had sent her Madame Drapeaux to save her from the mortal sin of lying to a priest. And she gave thanks in her prayers.

She was guilty of sins greater than lying to a priest, of course, but these she compartmentalized, speaking of them only in her devotions to the Virgin, who Yzore had said understood such things. Lily hoped it was true, for certainly no one else would, not even herself. "I did not give consent," she would think, searching desperately for exoneration. "When he came through that door in the hotel on Montserrat, he gave me not an instant to say no." But just as quickly, because she was honest, she would admit that she would not have uttered that word, that she had given consent the moment she had revealed herself as Mimi.

She tried to find remorse and penitence in her heart, but those emotions would not come. And she would find herself pleading that he would find her, so that she would have the opportunity to sin again.

They reached the muddy mouth of the Mississippi, and

Lily marveled at its rolling chocolate flood. She would never have identified this as a river. Rivers in her experience were swift and clear like the Roxelane, flowing from Pelee to the pure open waterways of St. Pierre. The gaseous odor of tidal flats stung her senses.

"At least I shall not have to drink it," she remarked to Madame Drapeaux.

"Oh, indeed you shall, Lily, unless you intend to make do with nothing but spirits. It looks much better when it has settled, and there's a lump of charcoal in the bottom of the keg that does wonders to purify it."

For the first time since leaving Montserrat, Lily's confidence was truly shattered. "I cannot!" she thought. "I would die!"

Madame had a carriage awaiting her beyond the docks, with their casks of sugar and their burlapped bales oozing white cotton. A postilion loaded their luggage, and soon they were riding along a wide boulevard lined with trees. Lily had never seen a street so wide and straight. And never had she imagined houses like these—great towers, windows of stained glass, massive front doors leading to marble steps, all set among plantings that were unknown to her.

Madame Drapeaux told her the low, spreading trees, with the graceful shape and small olive-green leaves were live oaks. Those with the heavy, waxy clusters were magnolias. In April the feathered mimosa would bloom, and in July the tall crape-myrtle hedges would be a lace of lavender and white, red and watermelon pink.

On St. Charles Avenue she was startled by the rattle of a trolley and craned her neck out of the carriage for a better look. Madame Drapeaux gave a crow of delight. "Well, Lily, what do you think?"

"It is . . . very strange, madame!"

"Never mind. You will feel more at home on Rue Royale."

The streets grew narrower and dirtier. Windows were boarded over, and drunkards staggered past stone walls and three-storied houses with balconies that reminded her of St. Pierre. There were palms, too, in a small park before a great cathedral. But did madame think the sight of this ruin would please her? She wished her employer had instructed the driver to go by another route.

"We are in a very bad section," she ventured.

"Yes, Lily. But it is the Americans who have done this. They and the war."

"The war, madame?"

"The War Between the States, Lily. Probably you don't know anything about it. You weren't born then, and Martinique is far away. It's hard for someone who lived through it to realize that another has never heard of it. The French Quarter, the Vieux Carré, was beautiful then. When I was a girl we sat on these balconies on summer evenings. And young men came to call. In groups, you know, so that no one of them should be considered too serious.

"But then the soldiers came and took quarters in these houses, and then, afterward, there was Reconstruction and the carpetbaggers moved in. It was simple, because almost no one was left."

"You were left, madame!" Lily had only partly grasped what the old woman had been telling her, but she read easily much that had not been said—the anger and determination, the refusal, even now, to be conquered, to give way to the decay of all she had loved. And Lily felt a certain kinship. It had been the same way in Martinique, the holding on to a way of life that seemed doomed.

"Yes, Lily. I was left. My husband was gone, killed by a Yankee bullet. My son was killed, too, and my daughter—gone, too. But I endured. My daughter was beautiful, and she was to have been married in a ceremony with Swiss Guards."

Madame's voice broke when she spoke of her daughter, and Lily did not dare to ask what had happened to her, as the carriage rolled under a great arched gate and into a little cobbled drive. "I have done everything necessary to remain where I belong," Madame Drapeaux said. "Here, we are home now."

The courtyard had a fountain around which grew caladiums and elephant ears. A fig tree hung over the walk, and clumps of bamboo grew against the walls. At the rear, ivy and rosebushes climbed the walls of a stone carriage house and a little balconied building madame said had been the slave quarters.

A small side entrance led them into the dining room, which opened through three large doors with fanlights, onto the courtyard. The furnishings of the house were dark and massive, and the drawing room, which madame called a parlor, had a high, medallioned ceiling and a fireplace of black marble. On the other side of the center hall was the ballroom, where girandoles twinkled as a breeze crept through the damask curtains.

"It's beautiful!" Lily cried. She could not keep astonishment from her voice.

"Yes, Lily. It is as it was. And there are others, too, who will not give up. Someday we shall have the quarter back again, though we shall never have our city from the Americans."

Life fell into a pattern. It was difficult for Lily to sleep at night amid the tinny piano sounds of a nearby concert house, where river water mixed with cresote passed for Irish whiskey. And it was difficult to get used to awakening in her small rosewood four-poster with only pale sunlight filtering through the mosquito netting to make do for Martinique's blazing sky.

At nine she prepared breakfast for her employer—coffee with chicory, and cream cheese with strawberries. Then the morning must be spent in dusting and cleaning, while madame, perching lithely on a stepladder, blamed the Americans for the dust. A black servant, Hetty, did the scrubbing and heavy work, and seemed strangely resentful of Lily, as though she thought a companion's duties should include scouring pots and waxing floors.

Hetty's dislike of her puzzled Lily, as did madame's hatred of Americans. Wasn't madame an American herself? But no, to madame, Americans were only those not of French descent, Lily discovered. Americans lived in the Garden District and had toilets and running water indoors. They were all beneath madame, having no breeding, manners, or family; and they were all the bane of New Orleans. The way madame spoke of them made Lily shudder at the idea that she might meet one someday.

"What a treasure you are, Lily!" she would say. "How fortunate I am to have a companion who was born under the fleur-de-lis!"

In the afternoon Lily was usually free to do as she pleased. Each day she rode the trolley to the docks to read the list of ship arrivals and ships that were expected. Returning before dark, she would pray at St. Louis Cathedral and perhaps sit in Jackson Square, where she could see people come and go to the French Market across the way and to the cotton warehouses at the edge of the river.

Already she was weary of being a companion. Her stomach ached often, from the water, she supposed. At first she had hoped that Joe had got her with child that one night, but it had not been that. She knew she should be relieved she was not pregnant, but when the possibility had gone, she was less happy than before.

She missed the fields of Acelie, the morning swims in cold mountain rivers. What of the gaiety madame had promised? But it must be coming, she thought dully. Madame had taken her to a dressmaker, and the garments she had ordered had been surprising things to order for one's companion.

There had been a tea gown of moss green on old gold, with a sash of mauve velvet, and even more elaborate evening gowns with long trains and trimmings of artificial pearls and butterflies. Madame had purchased day gloves and evening gloves, lace-edged white handkerchiefs, a fan ostrich feathers, a plush handbag with a gold clasp.

"It is too much, madame!" Lily had cried.

"Nonsense, Lily. I am not doing it just for you. I love buying beautiful clothes, and at my age it is ridiculous to buy them for myself. I should like you to do me credit. Perhaps there will even be a little gossip. When New Orleans marvels at my ravishing companion, I shall be imagining the time when I was young and had gentlemen by the dozens at my feet.

Her words made Lily uneasy. She did not want to be admired, especially not in public. She was, after all, a runaway, and there was always the chance that Edmond had sent a request to the police to look for her here. Lily wanted only to remain quietly hidden and wait for Joe. A little fun would not hurt, but it seemed to her that madame was arranging a spectacle.

"Are you fond of the theater, Lily?" Madame asked one morning.

"Oh, yes! In St. Pierre before the smallpox, Edmond used to take me almost every week."

"Edmond? But didn't you say that your husband's name was Joe?"

She flushed in confusion. She was still a novice at lying, and the idea of the theater had carried her back to that innocent time when she had been sweetly engaged, and the storm cloud that was Joe had not even formed on the horizon.

"Joe . . . did not like playacting, so his brother took me."

Madame nodded thoughtfully. "Joe will be angry with Edmond when he finds his brother cared so poorly for you and the plantation."

Lily wanted to scream with frustration. Was there no end

to this lying, once one had started? "Edmond died of the typhoid, and I shall weep if I speak of him more."

"Let's discuss the theater, then. That seemed to make you happy enough," said Madame Drapeaux; and Lily trembled with relief as her employer outlined the evening's entertainment.

They would see *Les Huguenots* at the French Opera House, the social center of New Orleans. Lily was not to take the trolley to the docks today and get herself covered with American dust. Instead she was to wash her hair in a tub in the courtyard, rinse it in lemon juice, and dry it in the sun. Madame's sullen servant, Hetty, helped her, pouring jug after jug of water over Lily's dark hair.

"Does madame go to the French Opera often, Hetty?" Lily asked, on her knees over the tub.

"Very often. She got a box, all fancy."

"Have you ever been there?"

"Yes. When madame has got nobody else to go with her, I goes. But I sits in the servants' balcony, and I doesn't wear fine clothes like you."

"That's too bad, Hetty." She thought of her jupe dress and wondered if Hetty might like to wear it to the black people's dances on Sunday afternoon on Dumaine Street. But she knew she must not make the girl a present of the dress. How would Lily ever explain what she was doing with such a garment?

"Hetty!" she cried suddenly. "This water! It's not muddy!"

"'Course not. That's rainwater. We catches it in a barrel under the eaves. Muddy water ain't no use to get your hair shining enough for the French Opera."

"But, Hetty, why don't we *drink* this?"

The girl looked at her in surprise. "Muddy water's for drinking. This is too good. Mud ain't gonna show in your stomach."

Lily pulled the jug from Hetty's hands and drank her fill. And when she had found the rain barrel at the back of the carriage house, life looked brighter than it had since she had come to New Orleans. She dried her hair in the sun and sang about the house until Madame Drapeaux insisted that she go to her room to rest, with cotton balls soaked in witch hazel pressed over her lids to make her eyes sparkle.

Hetty laced her into a dress of yellow crepe de chine with a shoulder-strap bodice and a skirt trimmed in layers of lace. Lily had objected when Madame had bought it, but madame had said such daring apparel was all the rage. Lily felt half-naked in it, her shoulders and arms exposed in the sleeveless low-necked gown. Hetty, surprisingly skillful as a hairdresser, twisted Lily's tresses into a graceful fall of curls at the back of her head and thrust a pair of yellow roses in the fastening.

With a mantle of spangled jet beads to offset the brilliant color of the dress, there was no doubt that she looked splendid as she entered the box at the theater. She saw heads crane in her direction, and her cheeks went a becoming pink. "Oh, Joe, if only I could wear these clothes for you!" she thought.

Lily wished madame had hidden her behind one of the latticed boxes, the *loges grilles,* from which the performance could be viewed in private. But these, madame explained, were for persons in mourning or for ladies who were near to giving birth. Below the horseshoe of boxes in which they were sitting was the orchestra section, occupied entirely by men, and above the boxes were the balconies for servants and others of African descent. Lily was surprised to see displays of silks and lace there, but madame told her that some of them were well off and even had plantations of their own.

But nothing in all the pre-performance activity could divert Lily from the idea of men's eyes on her, and it seemed forever until the lights of the glittering chandeliers were dimmed. The opera began at last, and Lily relaxed a little, letting herself be drawn into the music. Then gradually she became aware of a shadow behind their box. "Who is that, madame?" she whispered behind her fan.

"Sh, Lily! He is Jim Frey, an assistant to the commissioner of police."

Lily choked on a gasp. "What is he doing there?"

Madame Drapeaux chuckled. "You sound as though you thought we had broken a law, Lily. And we haven't—unless there is a law against looking as beautiful as you do. Perhaps there should be, but he is only waiting to pay his respects. He is an old friend."

"An old friend? But he's an American, isn't he? That is not a French name."

"There are some Americans one must acknowledge these days. We will receive him at intermission."

Jim Frey was a dark, swarthy man with a mustache and short side whiskers. His very glance seemed to crush her, as he might have crushed one of her roses by treading upon it. He was only one of a dozen they received, each clad in white waistcoats and straight black trousers and patent-leather buttoned boots. Some of them had French names and bowed with special warmth over Madame Drapeaux's hand. But more were Americans and seemed to have government positions.

It was Jim Frey who invited them to have coffee and éclairs with him after the entertainment. And to Lily's horror, madame accepted.

"Can't you make our excuses, madame?" she begged. "I am really very tired. And I don't like the way he looks at me. You remember I told you, my husband is a swordsman."

Madame Drapeaux's eyes glittered strangely. "Come, Lily, it is your duty to be my companion and go to coffee with me. I cannot help it if, except for you, we would not have been invited. It will be all right. You are quite properly chaperoned."

"Very well, but I do not like him. I wish at least some French gentleman had asked us."

"We shall have many invitations, Lily, but tonight it is better to accept his."

2

Madame Drapeaux was not wrong about the invitations. After that night it seemed that new ones arrived every day. She was forever busy now in the afternoons with bathing and curling for the evening ahead.

"I must go to the ship docks, madame," she would say.

"Don't fret, *ma petite*. You were there only Tuesday. He hasn't come yet."

Sometimes there were dinner parties beginning with cocktails in the courtyard and proceeding through oysters, shrimp, charlotte russe, and *café brulot* thick with cognac and spices and the aromas of orange and lemon. Other times, they were invited to simpler soirees instead, featuring backgammon and whist and great silver platters of chicken salad and sugared almonds. But no matter how large or small the gathering, there seemed always to be waltzing, whether to a single fiddle or an orchestra.

Here Lily excelled, and though she often did not care for her partners, she loved to dance and never refused. Madame seemed pleased with her liveliness and would sit smiling, her fingers keeping time to the music on the head of her cane. Often it would be dawn before they tumbled into the carriage to drive home. The mockingbird would sing as they crossed the courtyard, and they would lift their skirts to protect them from the heavy morning dew.

How pure and sweet the air would be then! And Lily would be elated from the night of dancing and admiration. On Martinique, even before *la vérette*, she had never had such a heyday. There the parties had been fewer, and it had been quickly assumed that she was Edmond's.

"Oh, madame! Is New Orleans always like this?" she would ask.

"Always. When one is young and beautiful and accomplished as you are, Lily. How wonderfully you danced tonight! Monsieur Gallier was quite smitten. He is a very wealthy cotton broker; we might do well to invite him to luncheon. And Monsieur Clairborne belongs to the Boston Club."

Lily felt a chill when Madame Drapeaux spoke this way. It was as though she were transported to some other time, as if she thought Lily were someone else. Madame would be as girlish and conspiratorial as though she had a belle of a daughter to marry off. What had happened to the daughter, after all? . . .

"I cannot forget that I have a husband, madame," she would say. "I wear a wedding ring, and I tell all my partners I am married."

Madame would sigh. "And you tell them your husband is a swordsman, I suppose."

"When it seems necessary."

Lily did not know of Joe's prowess at dueling, of course. She could only guess that he was accomplished. And he was not her husband! When she slipped away to go to the cathedral to pray, she often hurried back through the spooky gloom of Pirate's Alley and past the dueling ground of St. Anthony's Close. Each time she trembled and promised herself she would behave so that Joe would have no reason to fight anyone on her behalf. And perhaps when he came he would take her away from here at once, perhaps on the *Sea Bird*. And if he did not, what then?

Did he imagine that she had returned to Martinique with Edmond? Would he try to make her go back? She would not! The vow she had taken never to return was stronger than the sacred marriage vows. But she could not go on being madame's companion forever.

Lily's admirers were not all discouraged by her warning of her swordsman husband. Jim Frey, the assistant police commissioner, whose hand had wandered as they waltzed, had laughed aloud, as if at a charming jest. "I, an officer of the law, duel? But if I were to duel, it would be with pistols. Frenchmen are such fools when it comes to honor! Americans are always allowed to use pistols, since they have no expertise with swords. And I am very good with pistols. Would you like me to show you sometime? We might take a picnic to the Oaks, and I would shoot targets for you."

"Oh, no thank you. I am not interested in bloodshed, monsieur."

"Are you certain, Lily? You speak of it often enough. Wouldn't it excite you to have a man kill for you?"

She twisted away from him angrily and went to the courtyard to compose herself. The moon lay lazily in the sky, and a frog croaked monotonously beneath the perfumed gardenia bushes; but the breeze was too sharp for her low-cut dress. "Joe," she whispered into the darkness, "where are you? How long must I endure?"

The parties themselves had become wearying. So many of madame's friends were Americans, so many with government positions. Specials, she had heard them called, put into offices for which they had not the proper qualifications. One of her dancing partners had spent time in prison. And another had been indicted once for murder. These stories they had told each other in their jealousy. But nobody had told tales about Jim Frey. Was it because he was not corrupt? Or because they were afraid?

She felt a heavy hand on her shoulder and looked up into his thick face. "I'm sorry I upset you, Lily," he said. "It must be hard on you, being so far from your husband, with no one to protect you but Madame Drapeaux."

She sighed with relief as he moved his hand away. She had thought she had made a dangerous mistake coming out here. If he had tried to kiss her, and she had made a fuss! She felt almost drawn to him. He looked rather distinguished in the moonlight, fatherly, perhaps, since he was somewhat older than she.

"Madame does protect me well, monsieur."

"You must call me Jim, Lily. We are friends and should be on an equal footing. And even though you are working as a companion, it's easy to tell that you are a gentlewoman. Madame should not bandy you about at these soirees. You would like her to stop, wouldn't you?"

"Oh, yes, Jim. But she enjoys them so. She imagines she is living again as she did before the war." Lily all but choked on his name. Her antecedents were far better than his, she thought, but it did not seem wise to make an issue of it.

"I don't like to see you sad, Lily. Perhaps I can convince Madame Drapeaux to make your life easier. I will explain to her that you cannot fend off all these admirers forever. You would be grateful for that, wouldn't you?"

"Oh, yes!" He had a kindly streak that she had not guessed. And all that evening when he asked her to dance, she turned to him with a special eagerness and a brilliant smile. She saw at last that he was talking to Madame Drapeaux as they sat together on a velvet-covered lyre sofa, half-hidden by a large pink jardiniere of palms. Peering from behind her fan, Lily saw that Madame Drapeaux seemed agitated, and then she could observe no more, as she was swept away to dance.

She was at the refreshment table, sampling one of her favorites, fried oyster patties, when Madame Drapeaux sought her out. "Come, Lily. It's time to go home."

"So early!" said Lily, startled. "It's hardly past midnight!"

"Go and get your cloak, Lily. These old bones are tired. The party is over for us."

"Yes, madame." She fairly flew up the carpeted stairs to the room where the ladies' outer gear had been laid on a bed with a lacy *ciel*. What a wonder was Jim Frey! His talk with Madame Drapeaux had borne fruit already.

Most nights when they returned home the Vieux Carré was quiet. The gaming houses had closed, and the ladies of the street had already snared their prey. But tonight, women walked about with their hair loose to their shoulders, and toughs carrying slingshots meandered on the sidewalks. Raucous laughter and cheap music blotted away the sound of the horses' hooves.

Madame Drapeaux sat weakly back in her seat, her eyes closed. Lily felt pity for her employer. How easy it was to forget all this when one partied all night and came home to sleep peacefully all day! Lily had almost forgotten herself how foul the place could be.

Lily began to feel disquiet. What had Jim Frey said to Madame Drapeaux to make her change? Undoubtedly he was a man of power, with sanctions he could use. All for her gratitude? When she thought of that, she almost wished she had not allowed him to take her part. It had seemed a simple thing then.

But for the moment Lily was content not to borrow trouble. She smiled to herself, thinking that she would not be exhausted in the morning. She would arise at the time she usually went to bed, and take the trolley to the docks before Madame Drapeaux was even awake.

Madame opened her bag as they alighted and gave the big iron key to Lily to unlock the door. Inside she clung to Lily's arm. "Help me upstairs. I am not well."

In the dimness Lily peered at her employer's pale face and was filled with alarm. "It was Jim Frey, wasn't it?" she cried. "He upset you! Oh, I shall never forgive him!"

"It is . . . my illness. My heart. Help me up to bed at once."

Lily half-carried the old woman up the stairs and laid her on the huge half-tester Seignouret bed. "I'll get your medicine," she said as she turned to the bureau.

It's no use to look for it, Lily," the old woman interrupted as Lily frantically scattered the contents of the drawers. "It's all gone."

"Gone!"

"I've used it all and forgotten to send for more. Loosen my stays and fetch me a cup of brandy. That is all you can do."

Lily jerked at the silk dress and unlaced the fastenings beneath it. Running down to the drawing room, she reached for a decanter of golden liquor. The darkness was relieved only by a tawdry blue glow from a barroom across the way as she raced back up. "The driver must still be here, madame," she cried. "I'll send him to rouse the pharmacists!"

"No, no, Lily. It's no use sending him. He will only drink up the money in a saloon or bet it on a rat fight." Madame's face had a blue tinge. Lily thought that certainly she would die without the medicine.

"I will go!" she cried. Hetty had long since gone home. There was no one else.

"No, Lily! Not you! You can't go out there. Not alone!"

But there was nothing else for it. Madame Drapeaux was unable to protest further, as she gasped for breath and whimpered as though suppressing a ghastly agony. Lily changed her spangled cloak for her plain one and pulled it close to hide her gown of rose-colored satin.

"I'll be back as soon as I can," she promised, and dared not ask if madame would be all right until then.

A sob rose in Madame Drapeaux's throat. "Oh, Lily," she whispered, "I'm sorry! I'm sorry!"

Lily slipped out into the darkness, too frightened at first to step away from the shadows of the doorway. Then with a deep breath of resignation she walked out onto the banquette, her pace purposeful, her head held high. Perhaps, after all, it would be all right; for the first sailor who stumbled drunkenly toward her reeled away again, doffing his round cap with a startled, "Good evening, ma'am," as though he thought her a vision of his insobriety.

Six blocks to the pharmacist. It seemed so far. But one block was past already. Her confidence grew. Ahead of her was the door of a barrel house, where men lounged with foaming mugs and their detachable celluloid collars unfastened. She hurried across the street and scuttered along the wall, as dark and clandestine in her black cloak as a New Orleans cockroach. On the far side a girl went past in a knee-length calico skirt, and men in the doorway called to her loudly.

"Hey, Meg! Will you dance for us tonight?"

"How's business? How about a kiss before I buy?"

Nobody noticed Lily. Her heart thudded as a trombone slithered over a melody, as lascivious as a man's hand stroking a woman's flesh. Behind her footsteps came, sharp and crisp. Then they slowed, the sound so soft she might have thought it was only the whispering of old papers blowing in the gutter. *Someone is following me!* she thought.

Three blocks now. That was her strength. Her sanctuary lay so close! And yet, he had time. She would have to turn onto a side street, away from the glowing oil lamps. She would run then, she thought. It would take him by surprise. She would be at the pharmacist's house before he had time to catch her. And she gathered her skirts, ready to hitch them up to flee when the moment came.

The corner approached, dark and confined beneath the overhanging galleries. If only there were lights behind the heavy green doors of the houses. But the lower floors were mostly boarded up. A law had prevented prostitutes from inhabiting the ground level in this area, and since the upper two stories were cribs, the first floors were mostly vacant. Only one door stood ajar, a light filtering from the stairs to show torn wallpaper and a broken mahogany railing. Lily could see that once this had been a fine residence. It was as though there were some special force in this place that delighted in destroying all that was lovely, she thought. A *diable*, Cyrillia might have said, and Lily did not doubt that this devil's lust for destruction included her, too.

The corner was upon her. Lifting her petticoats, she dashed headlong toward safety. She had not been wrong about the person behind her, she thought as a cry rang out like that of a hunter whose quarry was breaking cover. The sound froze her heart and set fire to her feet. Then, too late, she saw the body of the man sprawled inert with liquor on the banquette before her. Even as she tried to draw up short and change direction, she was falling. Landing atop the drunkard's unthinkably dirty body, she felt the coarse hair of his chest against her cheek. He lurched and closed his arms around her. "Easy, lass. I'll give ye what ye need," he muttered, his terrible breath choking her nostrils.

But the man behind her had not given up his quest. He seized her now, his arms crushing her breasts. The man on the banquette staggered to his feet, clutching at her skirts as she struggled to get away. They were fighting over her like two dogs over a tasty bone! Her cloak fell away, and then parts of her dress began to rip. Little bits of pink feathers that adorned it fluttered away like pluckings from a bird.

She fought back with all her ineffectual strength. She could scream, but would that only bring others? More to share in the degradation she knew must be coming. She felt light-headed, and the faces above her spun. She must not faint, she thought. If they had her, it must not be that easy for them! And yet, surely it was nature's way that she should swoon to save herself from the unbearable memory of what was to happen.

Then came the sound of horses. Carriage lights swung over the banquette, and a man's voice was shouting. She felt herself dropped against the cobbles. They were gone! Someone lifted her, and weakly she began to struggle again.

"Lily," he said gently, "dear Lily."

She raised her eyes and looked at her rescuer. "Oh, Jim!"

She laid her head against his fine worsted frock coat, and her arms reached up around his neck. He set her in the carriage, arranging her next to him against the plush cushions, and he took out his handkerchief to wipe the grime and tears from her face. She whiffed a strange perfume close to her nose. It seemed to choke her breath away. She reached out to move his hand, and then she knew no more.

3

The pillows beneath her head were deep and soft, with cool silk cases. Above her a blue canopy swam into focus, dripping with lace hangings. She sighed, and her body, clad only in her chemise, sank deeper into the feather bed. She remembered suddenly and began to try to sit up. Jim Frey's face shone in the yellow gleam of the oil lamp.

"There, Lily. You are all right now. You are with me."

"It is not all right, Jim! Madame is ill! I was sent to get the medicine!"

"Sh, little one. Madame is all right. I took care of it all when I sent to let her know where you were. I could not take you home in such a state. It would have killed her to see you."

"You are very thoughtful, Jim." She lay back, letting her gaze travel around the room. Near the bed was a carved table of marble and rosewood, and across the way was an armoire with glass doors and several chairs in rep and damask with *tête-à-têtes* to match. If she had had to faint, she could not have found a better place than in his carriage! Strange to think how she had disliked him at first. In her confused state it did not occur to her to ask who had undressed her. She was quite content to believe it had been his maid. But there was something strange about this place. It seemed to shift with a motion that was not caused by her lingering dizziness.

"Jim, where am I? Is this your house?" He had a mansion in the Garden District, she knew.

"Not my house, my boat," he said with a chuckle.

She grabbed the covers around her and leaped up to peer from the window. Beyond was a railing, white in the moonlight, a trimming of gingerbread over the deck, and after that only the blackness of the Mississippi, the froth of water over the paddle wheel.

"We are under way!" she cried.

"I had planned a little trip to Natchez, Lily, and I thought you might come with me. You shall have a vacation away from madame and all those parties. Aren't you pleased?"

"But . . . I must go home!" Her head spun wildly, and she knew she was still unwell. "I cannot go with you unchaperoned! And madame—"

"Madame Drapeaux has given her consent."

Lily was aghast. "Her consent! But my husband!"

"You have no husband, Lily!"

She stared at him. The kindly face now held an evil leer. Yes, this was as she had perceived him the night at the French Opera. But now she saw him a thousand times more clearly.

"Are you calling me a liar?" She stood indignantly before him, the blankets pulled angrily tight.

He laughed with pleasure at the sight she made, so outraged and proud and desirable. "Was his name Joe or Edmond? Madame says there has been some confusion."

She extended her left hand. "Look, sir, do you think this means nothing?"

He lifted her hand and kissed her fingers, ignoring the wedding ring she meant him to see. "Indeed, Lily, it does not mean nothing. This palm of yours tells me all I need to know, and I am not a gypsy fortune-teller. This hand is not soft as the hand of a lady should be. And these little pink traces. They are barely noticeable, but anyone who has spent his life about the Mississippi would know they were once the cuts of cane leaves.

"And your skin! Don't tell me that its pretty color comes from the sun! No, Lily, a tarbrush painted that complexion! You were a field girl on Martinique or wherever you really come from. And you got into some trouble, with a fine gentleman, of course. Was it he who taught you your manners. You had to flee—"

"Get my clothes! Put me ashore at once!" she cried, her voice hoarse with fear.

"Come, Lily, you have had your fun. You did not find me so objectionable a while ago when I rescued you from those devils. Shall I give you back to them? I can, you know. They were my men. Think what I am offering you! All the money you can possibly need—a pretty house where you shall live and raise the children you bear me like a proper quadroon mistress. Perhaps you would like a place on Ramparts Street, as the custom was before the war."

"You are unthinkable, monsieur!"

"Now, Lily, you said you'd be grateful. There'll be no more parties and no more men looking at you. I have paid Madame Drapeaux a pretty price for you. Of course, if you reject me, madame will find it necessary to let you go. You will have no reference and no husband. What will you do then? Shall I tell you? Or do you already know what happens to unprotected girls like you in New Orleans? You will find yourself in a bordello on Basin Street. That will not be too bad, with its walnut woodwork and oriental rugs, but as you are used up, the price of you will go down. But never mind, you aren't going to reject me. You see how lucky you are that I have a passion for you."

He made to embrace her, and the blankets dropped away as she tried to stop him. She felt his lips pressed against her bare shoulder, and repugnance filled her with a great power. She wrenched free and ran for the door, out onto the moonlit deck.

"Don't be foolish, my girl. There's no place you can go."

But there was one place she could go, and go she would rather than have his hands on her body.

The river rose to her vision, dark and treacherous. She had seen great logs spin in its whirlpools, but if she were to be consumed, let it be by the river. She stripped off her last petticoat and climbed to the railing, a strange sight, poised there in her lacy chemisette and pantaloons. "I choose the alligators over you, Jim Frey!" she said. And she jumped.

She seemed to fall forever, his anguished cry echoing in her ears. She felt bound for hell, so long did the descent unfold, but she had the satisfaction of thinking she had dealt him a blow that would diminish him, an insult that would follow him to his very grave. Then the river splashed around her, and she forgot everything else.

She could not believe that water could be so heavy. It wrapped about her sluggishly, and she could do nothing but drift with the current, using all her energy to keep her head above the surface, as she was swept back toward New Orleans. Her arms tired; she swallowed great gulps of the dreadful water. Her body chilled, and her mind fogged.

She dreamed of the Roxelane, thought of the laundresses she had seen afflicted with the water disease from standing in its icy current, their feet and stomachs swollen horribly, their faces fleshless. She thought at times she shared their fate. Or she would believe that a torrent had washed down from Pelee to drown her in its sudden flood, and in her ears she heard the roar of the foaming confluence, the crashing of bridges and the rolling of great boulders.

Then again would come the solitary toot of a riverboat whistle. She would remember where she was and try to call for help. But always the water weighed against her mouth as the river skillfully gagged her.

Once she had been Mimi and thought it a lark to be a coaling girl. Once she had only been in fear that someone would penetrate her disguise, spoil her fun, and expose her to her father's wrath. Once she had worked in the fields, delighting in her closeness to the earth, even to the danger of the fer-de-lance that lurked in the cane clumps. She had thought girls like Cyrillia were fortunate in their freedom.

But never before had she really known what it was like. Now she was really Mimi, she thought. There was no disguise to be stripped away to reveal Lily Beau Clair of Acelie, whom everyone had known since her birth, tan or no. Jim Frey had offered her pretties—lace fans with carved ivory sticks, silver earrings with amber sets, even a gold necklace like Cyrillia's. Jim Frey would have given her anything. Better to die, she thought wearily, wondering if Joe would ever learn what had become of her.

And then he seemed to be beside her in the water. She could almost reach out and touch his springy cinnamon-colored hair, and he wore his bathing gear as he had when they had swum in the Crater of the Three Palmistes.

What is wrong, Lily? Did you think I was a shark? I know you can swim very well! I remember it.

It was said that you were a rascal and would come to no good end. I did not know what was meant.

And now?

Now I know, Joe, that those words were meant for me, too!

She was sinking, but she was not frightened. She was only angry that it should be Joe who was pulling her down. *Let go of me, Joe! Enough is enough! I cannot breathe!*

Perhaps you would see things differently from the bottom of the lake!

The heavy water grew leaden, and its motion ceased. And Joe was gone.

4

"Sure, she's a pitiful sight, Etienne. It's a wonder she didn't go off the hooks. Bring me a bit of that broth, there's a lad. I think she may be coming around."

Lily stirred and moaned. Somewhere she had been hearing that voice with a trace of Irish brogue for a long time, a girl's voice, sometimes petulant, sometimes soothing, but always demanding with its insistence that she awaken.

"Come on, sis," the voice said. "I've got other fish to fry. More things to do than nurse the likes of you!"

"Speak to her gently, Susan. Don't call her 'sis.' Use her name." The man spoke English, but French obviously would have been more natural to him.

"Her name, Etienne! Who's to know? Half the time she raves that she is Mimi, and the rest she bellows that her name is Lily!"

"Ah, it's the delirium. It's peculiar. There she was lying there in the mud on the riverbank without anything but her pretty underthings—near dead, and would have died if we hadn't happened along. I wonder—"

"Less wonder is she had been stark naked!" the girl said. "I don't like it."

"It was you who insisted on bringing her home."

"I know. If she'd been a man, I'd have stepped over with never a by-your-leave. But she is a woman, and it gets my dander up when a woman is treated too rough."

"Your dander is always up, Susan. Come here and give me a kiss."

"Stop it, Etienne! I'm not in the mood for that, what with worrying about her. What if there's trouble because of her? What if the police—?"

Police! The word struck Lily like a dash of cold water. Fear rushed over her, and she cried out and struggled for consciousness. Colors edged into view. She saw a clear sorrel red, almost the color of a *capresse*'s skin. Cyrillia, she thought confusedly.

Then the red shifted, and she perceived that it was hair, not skin. It flowed to the shoulders of a girl with gray-green eyes and a milky skin with a sprinkling of tiny freckles across the nose. Hers was not an earthy beauty like Cyrillia's nor was it cool and rarefied like Lily's. Hers was a practical sort of good looks. She had a look of warmth about her like a brick from a hearth, and Lily sensed a sultriness used with the care and calculation of a Sunday bonnet.

"Are you in trouble with the police, sis?" she inquired as she saw Lily's eyes focus on her face.

"He thinks I'm dead," she murmured, taking in the simple room, the double bed on which she lay, its thin, sagging mattress supported by an iron bedstead. In one corner was a kerosene cookstove, and on the greasy, flowered wallpaper, a cheaply framed print of the Virgin Mary, with her red valentine's heart dripping blood from her chest.

Etienne was lithe and slender and far too elegant for the stained wing chair in which he sat gracefully polishing lint from his narrow, pointed boots. "Who thinks you are dead?" he asked her.

"Him. The police—Jim Frey."

"Jim Frey—the assistant commissioner. Did he try to kill you?"

"He abducted me and took me aboard his boat. And I jumped rather than let him have me."

"You did that? And to Jim Frey! You won't want to meet up with him again!"

"But how shall I help it? I must go back to my employer. I have clothes there—and money." Lily sat up in agitation, and immediately darkness closed over, sending her once more into oblivion. When she waked again, an oil lamp was burning in the dark and Etienne had gone. Susan brought a steaming bowl and urged a spoonful of amber liquid to her lips.

"It's not gumbo, sis. I can't abide those French concoctions. It's only made from a soupbone. I hope you're not finicky."

The broth slid comfortably down Lily's throat, making a welcome current of heat, and she smiled gratefully at her benefactress.

"Now, who is this employer you must return to?" Susan asked. "Is it your madame? Perhaps Etienne can arrange for you to have another, if you keep quiet about Jim Frey."

"It was not a madame," Lily said stiffly. "I was a lady's companion."

"No need to get huffy. One just assumes—especially when a girl is found half-naked in the river. It's next to impossible for a girl to be anything but a harlot around here, but I am not a harlot either, and determined not to be, and plenty have made the same mistake about me. You said there was money..."

"A little. Enough to pay you for your kindness. But..." Lily turned her head on the pillow and gave a little sob as she thought of Madame Drapeaux.

"But what?"

"My employer may be dead!"

"The rat killed her?" said Susan incredulously. "Jim Frey murdered an old lady?"

Lily shook her head. "She was very ill. I was sent for medicine at night, and he caught me. When he had me, he told me she had given her consent. He said he had paid her. That is impossible. She was always careful about me. She was like a mother."

Susan's eyes had taken on a knowing look. "Her name?"

"Madame Drapeaux."

"And she lives on Rue Royale? Ha!"

"What is it? Why did you laugh like that?"

"Because, you poor innocent, everyone knows about Madame Drapeaux. And you said you had no madame!"

Lily sat up angrily, fighting waves of dizziness. "You know nothing about it! She is a fine old lady whose life was destroyed by the war. Her husband and children gone, and nothing left but her house that she clings to and tries to pretend that none of it happened!"

Susan sighed. "That is all true, but there is more. Where does she get money to keep her house and her carriage? And her cruises to Cuba? Who pays for those?"

"Who?" said Lily, quietly now, for she recognized a ring of truth. Hadn't *she* met Madame Drapeaux in Cuba?

"It is the likes of Jim Frey and his friends. Madame Drapeaux is an institution, and rich gents who have tired of New Orleans types can't pay her tribute enough! In Havana she finds girls who need positions, and once she's engaged them and brought them to the Vieux Carré, they can't escape. They haven't got enough money to go home, nowhere to turn. Madame Drapeaux has the knack of picking just what the customers will buy, but for a while she forgets about that.

The girl becomes almost a daughter, like her Evaleen, whose ghost haunts Gravier Street, where her mother saw her hanged as a Confederate spy."

"Hanged!"

Susan shrugged. "The Yankees weren't usually as bad as that, but it was some of Beast Butler's favorite crew. It was a lynching, without a trial."

"Was she really a spy?"

"Me dad said so. That was the year he came over from County Clare to escape the potato famine. And she was a great beauty, with an eighteen-inch waist, and the sky turned dark the moment she died."

"Might I have another cup of that broth?" Lily was feeling stronger now, beginning to take calm stock of her situation. "Now, tell me what happens to Madame Drapeaux's companions. No, that's silly. I am better qualified to tell *you*. She takes them to the French Opera House for all the men to see . . ."

"And because she's of such a fine family, everyone pretends not to know," Susan put in. "It would reflect on them all to admit it."

"Madame Drapeaux and her companion are invited to parties, where her victim meets all her 'old friends.' Madame has a lovely time and forgets, but then the friends become insistent, and the companion is expected to grant favors—trips to Natchez on riverboats. And I thought he lied when he said madame had agreed! Madame wasn't sick at all. It was simply her way so that she would not have to know. I have much to learn about New Orleans, Susan. Madame did tell me it was a wicked city."

"And you have not learned half. But never mind, I'll teach you. What's your name, anyway, sis? Shall I call you Lily or Mimi?"

"Lily. Please, Lily. I have had enough of Mimi! She was a girl of color, and I dreamed I was she. I had a tan, and Jim Frey thought—"

"You must take care to avoid that problem in New Orleans, Lily. But you have a fine pallor now," said Susan with a laugh.

"It is so wrong, Susan."

"What is wrong, sis?"

"To treat a woman differently because of the tint of her skin. I never realized what it was like before," said Lily wearily.

"Maybe. But any woman will be treated like a queen if she has a good protector. That is what really matters, to any woman. Tell me about yourself. Where do you come from, and did you have a protector there?"

"I come from Martinique, and I had a protector, but now it is hard to say."

"Martinique." Susan's pretty brow knitted. "I never heard of it. Is that some town upriver?"

They spent long hours talking together during the days of Lily's convalescence. Susan, alone in the world since the death of her father, nevertheless had large ambitions. She had a beautiful voice, and she was determined that someday she would sing at the French Opera. "I will be a legend, like Adelina Patti or Jenny Lind," she would declare, her eyes shining. As she went about her work, her voice would lift into old Irish airs, and Lily would see that Susan no longer scrubbed dirty pots, but stood on a gilded stage with flowers at her feet. And when she made the walls ring with the splendid notes of "Rose of Tralee," it seemed even to Lily that the little room was showered with a dust of gold.

Susan would make Lily tell again and again about her home on Martinique. "It does sound grand. I never saw a mountain," she would say as Lily tried to describe the green heights of Pelee. "Someday when I'm rich I'll go there and see it. Oh, Lily, how could you have made a vow not to return to such a place? How much you must love this Joe!"

And Lily would think of the passing days and her inability to go to the docks. She had been sick a long while. The delirium had lasted almost a week, Susan had said, and even now when she tried to walk more than a few steps, she grew faint. He might have come and gone! But she would not have wanted him to see her this way, destitute, without even a gown to her name. She did not want to burden him with pity. That must not become mixed with his love. And in her pride she did not ask Susan to check the notices for her, but risked losing him instead.

It was obvious anyway that Susan could not really spare even the trolley fare. She had a job singing in a concert saloon, and whenever she collected a little extra money she immediately spent it for a lesson in opera. The room would reverberate with Italian arias, roundly sung but strangely pronounced.

"I cannot get it for the life of me!" Susan would cry, and defeat would show in her gray-green eyes.

"Let me help you, Susan. It will be good to have some use for my schooling."

"And manners, too, Lily. I cannot use them now, in this pigsty, but when I am a lady, I will need them."

Etienne had been teaching her French, much of it vulgarized, Lily found. "A lady would not say it that way, Susan!" Lily would say, and Susan, frustrated, would storm out of the house. But later she would be back. And if she said, "It's only me Irish impatience," she corrected "me" to "my" herself.

The nights were lonely with Susan away at the concert saloon, and Lily, though used to retiring early on Martinique, never slept easy until she returned. She would fall to thinking that here on Chartres Street, she was only a few blocks from the spot where she had been abducted. What if Jim Frey discovered that she was not dead? Some nights Susan did not return at all, and Lily understood that she passed these nights with Etienne in the rooms above his establishment on Exchange Street.

"Are you in love with Etienne?" Lily asked once.

"He is nice enough, but if I were to settle for marriage, it would not be to him."

"Then why . . . ?"

"He is my protector, and I could not have a better one. He's a fencing master, and nobody tampers with the sweetheart of a fencing master. It's the saving of me! I wouldn't part from Etienne for the world! I would do that only if I were certain I was past needing him. And Etienne doesn't care to marry, of course. Fencing masters have all the girls they want."

"What about Americans? I thought *they* dueled with pistols."

"Yes, but Etienne is a marksman, too. He keeps up with the times, that one. Not the worst thug or finest gentleman wants to deal with Etienne, whether it'd be a call-out under the Oaks or a knife in the stomach on Gallatin Street."

Lily grew stronger, and with her strength came resolve. It would be dangerous, but she would have to return to Madame Drapeaux's for clothes, and hopefully, her money.

One day while Susan was gone, she put on Susan's gingham dress, and thrusting a butcher knife into the pocket, set out on her risky errand. Lily wore her hair down so that she would look the part of a cheap strumpet and so that her lack of petticoats would not draw attention. Susan had not possessed any extra ones, and neither had there been a second pair of shoes. But the length of the dress hid her feet as she made her way barefoot over the dirty cobblestones.

The house was just as she had remembered. Wisteria and bridal wreath were in bloom, twining with the tulip pattern of the ironwork railings. She watched the house carefully for a time, and then, crossing the street, she slipped around into the alley and let herself into the courtyard by a gate near the carriage house. Lily opened its creaking wooden door and peered into the murk. The carriage was gone. Then she was in luck, and Madame Drapeaux was not at home.

More boldly now she crossed the courtyard beneath a low mimosa with big powderpuff blossoms. She glimpsed the scarlet flash of fat goldfish in the pond beneath the fountain, and the sighing of spring leaves in the warm breeze mingled with the splash of the water. The serenity of the place hit her sharply after the squalor to which she had become accustomed. She remembered thinking that there seemed a force in the Vieux Carré bent on the destruction of everything beautiful. Now, strangely, she had become part of that force, an intruder in what had once been sanctuary. She felt the handle of the knife in her pocket, and closing her fingers around it, hoped she would not have to use it.

Madame was gone, but someone was inside, she thought as the side entrance door swung out at her touch. They would never go away and leave the house empty and open. She crept inside, and hearing a noise, sank to her knees beside the walnut sugar chest where Madame Drapeaux still kept coffee and spices locked away, as in earlier times. A shadowy form flitted by. Hetty! Hetty mustn't see her! Hetty had never been her friend. The shadow went away, and Lily heard the girl's voice singing in the kitchen.

Lily darted for the entrance hall, smelling lemon from the polished banisters as she ran up the carpeted stairs. In her old room she threw open the doors of the armoire. Everything seemed as she had left it. The fine gowns were well-pressed and hung with precision; and the shoes were all still in place—the evening slippers with the low Louis heels and the rosettes on the toes, the bronze kid pair that laced up the front, and the "Cromwell" shoes with the high-cut tops and large bows. In the drawers of the bow-front chest the pretty underthings lay untouched, along with the fans and gloves and pins for her hair.

Underneath everything was the jupe dress and Joe's watch.

She gave a sigh of delight as she held the timepiece against her cheek and kissed it. It had seemed more important to find these things than to find the money. But she needed money above all, and opening one of two shallow drawers on top of the chest, she found it safe, too, all the wages she had managed to save since Cuba. She laid the purse down, and finding a brocade valise, turned back to the armoire. The jupe dress would go in, of course, and the two poor gowns she had purchased in Plymouth on Montserrat. No one could accuse her of stealing those, and they would not draw attention to her in her present circumstances. Shoes—two pair, no, four! She and Susan must have a pair each for day and evening, and if they did not fit Susan, Lily had no doubt that on occasion her friend would gladly make do.

And now a parasol, to avoid the tan that had added so much to her woe. And tea gowns—the ruby plush for herself, and for Susan the green crepe de chine. She stuffed the clothing recklessly into the bag, which bulged with her loot, and then she began to rearrange the armoire so that madame would not be likely to miss what she had taken.

She had become as absorbed and elated as any sneak thief as she made her haul. But suddenly she became aware that the door of the room had opened. She jerked her head around, and there was Hetty. The two women looked at each other in horror.

"You's dead!" said Hetty, her eyes wide. "Mr. Frey, he say ol' river got you!"

Lily's hand went to her pocket, felt the knife there. "I was in the river, Hetty. Perhaps I am a ghost. You had better keep clear of me!"

She saw Hetty consider the possibility of her being an apparition. She was a superstitious girl and not inclined to regard it lightly, any more than Lily herself, had the situation been reversed. At last the girl's eyes flicked to the beaded purse on the bureau. "Ghost wouldn't need money. You's stealin', Miss Lily."

"I'm not! I earned this!"

The girl's mouth twisted with cunning. "It's yours, then. I didn't know it was there before. You gives it to me, and I'se not gonna tell madame 'bout how you ain't no ghost."

"I can't give it to you, Hetty. I need it too much."

Hetty smirked. "Then I guess I'll just hafta—"

She broke off as Lily's knife glimmered between them. Lily trembled, not wanting to have to hurt Hetty, but hoping she could kill her if she had to. One way or the other, Hetty must not tell tales. "If I kill her, I will be a murderess at last!" she thought, remembering the way Joe had accused her from what she had thought was his deathbed.

"I must not let Hetty get the knife! She will have more skill than I." She understood better now the girl's antagonism toward her. She had thought Lily a field worker, putting on the airs of a lady, going to parties, wearing beautiful clothes. How gladly would Hetty have changed places with her, though she knew a "companion's" fate! Lily would be more unsafe than ever in New Orleans if she killed Hetty, but how could she leave her alive? Would the money really silence her?

"Please, miss! If madame finds that money gone, that's gonna be one thing. She gonna say I took it and make it up from my wages. But dem dresses! One of dem's worth two-three times what you gots in that purse. What's she gonna do to Hetty then?"

Lily shivered with relief. She had been mistaken to think that Hetty would tell Madame Drapeaux. Madame would never believe her—not if all these dresses were gone. She opened the bureau again with one hand and flung the ivory fan and the gloves into the valise. "Do you know what the fan is worth, Hetty? You will have to arrange this room very carefully, so that madame won't notice anything. Move away from the door, Hetty. I am going now."

To Lily's satisfaction, the girl moved as she was told. It was not until Lily was halfway down the stairs that Hetty found her voice. "Anything happen to me cause of this, I gonna buy a gris-gris for you! Ol' gris-gris'll take care of you, even if ol' river didn't. You'll see!"

Feeling a chill, Lily ran faster, dragging her bundle out into the sunshine.

5

She spread the beautiful gowns in a glorious mountain on the sagging bedstead, and changing into her merino dress, she took Susan's reed shopping basket and went to the French Market. There, beneath the long arcade, she purchased sweet pineapples and two loaves of French bread to scoop out and fill with hot fried oysters. For dessert she bought pralines of the fancy-date-and-cream variety. When she returned, Susan was in their room staring with disbelief at the bed.

"Are these yours, Lily? You actually wore these things?"

"I wore them, but only half are mine. The rest are for you."

"Lily! Oh, dear Mother Mary! It's like a dream!"

Lily laughed, enjoying Susan's perplexity. "You will need them when you sing in some fine place, Susan. Come, let's eat." And she uncovered her basket to show what she had brought.

They feasted together in the light of a candle set on the small round table. Lily spilled open her purse and divided the coins that shone on its scarred surface. "Half of this shall be yours, too, Susan."

"Oh, no, not that! You have given me enough."

"Take it, Susan. You are still stuck with me. It will pay my share of the rent until Joe comes."

Susan scooped up the coins and put them into a jar, which she secreted at the back of a cabinet. "I've always paid the rent before, Lily. This'll be our emergency fund. It'll be for either that needs it. And neither will touch it unless it's the last ditch. Agreed?"

"Agreed!" Lily said happily, flushing with food and success. "We're a team, then, aren't we? Neither of us is alone anymore."

"And each of us shall help the other whenever she needs it."

"Yes. Always."

Lily felt more comforted that night than at any time since she had left Martinique. The friendship that had grown between her and Susan had become a thing of strength. From now on she would have one person in the world she could count on. She fell asleep even before Susan left for her night of work at the concert saloon.

At first her sleep was dreamless, and then the nightmares came, so many nightmares to tumble one after another. There was Joe, lying on the floor of the *case-à-vent*, bitten by the snake. And Edmond in the doorway of the hotel in Plymouth. She felt his hands on her; he was using her horribly. She thought at first it was in the wagon on the beach in Martinique, but it had never been that dreadful, and she looked and saw that the face above her was Jim Frey's. She screamed then, bringing all her force to bear against him. She was falling, and the river was below her. Then with a thud she waked to find herself in a tangle of covers and mosquito netting on the floor.

Susan was frying pancakes for breakfast, and the morning breeze was already hot and humid and filled with rancid smells as it blew in the window. "Screaming like that is no way to keep the police off, sis! Lucky that peeler on the corner there has still got a gutful from last night."

Lily picked herself up and peered out at the policeman standing drunkenly by the lamppost. "Oh, Lily, don't get in a stew," Susan went on. "I was only joking. You're safe as long as Jim Frey doesn't know you're alive. But what a promotion he'd give old Jack down there if he found you! Here you are, his fortune, not a block away, and he doesn't know it. Poor Jack!"

Lily sighed and did not rise to Susan's jests. Life had looked better last night than it did this morning. "What is it, Lily?" Susan said. "You're not usually like this. Are you still worried that Hetty will tell on you?"

"No."

"What is it, then? Something you didn't let on about that happened at Madame Drapeaux's?"

"Yes, but it was nothing, really. Only that Hetty threatened me with a gris-gris."

"Gris-gris. Well, *that* is nothing. A little bag of pepper and powdered brick and maybe a bit of snakeskin. You can't believe in such things, Lily!"

"Oh, Susan! You do not know! When someone starts to work black magic on you, anything can happen. On our plantation there was a worker who was dismissed, and he almost wrecked our cane harvest by spreading the ground with poison seeds."

"Well, there is nothing you can do about Hetty. Come and eat."

"You are right, Susan. I have enough real problems, haven't I? I will not worry about voodoo anymore until it comes."

Exhausted from the long night, Susan fell into bed. Lily fastened herself again into her merino dress, and having stashed all the bounty of the previous day away in the armoire, took coins from her hoard and went out to catch the trolley.

The ride to the docks was pleasant. Lily delighted in the speed and the clatter, at the hot wind blowing in her face. It was easy to forget about voodoo here. She was cheerful as she made her way among the bustle of cranes and stevedores and the fluffy debris from the towers of cotton bales. She would find good news in the listings today, she was certain. But as always, there was nothing.

She was in a sober mood on the way back. She would have to get employment somehow. She supposed she was fit to be a governess or a companion. Perhaps she could work in a shop. But how would she find such a position? She bought a copy of the *Picayune* and read the advertisements over a cup of *café au lait* on the little gallery that opened from their room. To her delight, there were a number of possibilities. One required a responsible young French lady as governess for children aged four and six. The section was distant Metaire, and she would not be likely to meet Jim Frey there. If she went right away, she might apply and be back before dark.

Susan waked as Lily was putting the finishing touches on her hair, humming "Little Feathered Lovers" as she prepared to leave.

"Where are you going, Lily? To the docks?"

"I have already been."

Susan sat up excitedly. "Has he come? Is that why your mood has changed? I never heard you sing."

"No, he hasn't come. But I have discovered the solution to my problem. It's so simple, Susan. There are advertisements in the newspaper. Someone needs a French girl for a governess, and I am certain to suit."

She groaned. "Indeed you are! Oh, Lily, have you learned

nothing yet about New Orleans? If you answer that ad, you'll be carried off, quick as anyone can lay feet to the ground! You'll be lucky if you're not shipped to a brothel in Galveston, I shouldn't wonder!"

Lily put the paper down. "What should I do without you, Susan? I do not believe I will ever learn. Tell me, how does a girl get a position, then?"

"She knows someone who knows someone. A family friend has a friend . . ."

"But I don't know anyone!"

"No."

She remembered Jim Frey's prediction. She would wind up in a Basin Street bordello. At first she would command a price, the furnishings would be fine. But then the cost of her would go down. "What can I do?" she asked.

"I know what I would do," Susan said. "I would sell what I had and buy a ticket back the way I came. Edmond is still your husband. He will have to take care of you."

"I would never see Joe again!"

Susan, brushing out her sorrel hair, shook her head at Lily. "I have never loved a man the way you do Joe, and I can't imagine it. I'm not sure I want to be in love, seeing what it's done to you."

Lily took the trolley again the next morning, this time to Canal Street, where she began to make the rounds of stores and shops, asking for employment. She found nothing, and the next day she went again to the docks. And so it went, one day the shops, the next the docks. She was surprised at how fast the money disappeared. She had never handled money before. Her father had done it, and then Edmond. And every time she bought a bowl of *gumbo filé* from an old black woman at the French Market, her purse grew lighter. She would have to economize. But how? By not going to the docks as often? She could not bear that, and she began to skip her supper instead. Still the purse grew empty. She sold the ivory fan at a pawn shop, taking half its value. The days dragged on, and jasmine and hibiscus bloomed. The air became almost sweet from the scent of magnolias in decayed courtyards, and disreputable-looking children splashed in the muddy river water down past the French Market and Jackson Square.

Lily ceased to look for employment. Better to save the trolley fare and the leather of her scuffed patent shoes. She sold her wedding ring, thinking she could live for weeks on the proceeds.

"Lily, Lily, go home!" Susan begged. "Soon you'll have nothing. It'll be bagnio for you! Acelie is your inheritance. He'll have to accept you there. Oh, how quickly I would go if I were you!"

Always another woman would gladly do what Lily could not. Cyrillia would have made Edmond a good wife; Hetty would have been delighted to be Jim Frey's mistress, and Susan—even Susan! "Joe will come. He must," she would whisper. He would come; there was no other way.

It was Etienne who suggested a solution. "You could do art poses at the French Pigeon," he said one evening when he had treated both girls to dinner at Tujare's across from the French Market.

"Oh, Etienne, don't be ridiculous! She would never get home the first night. She is prettier than any of the girls, and you know she refuses to have any man but her precious Joe. Who is to keep her safe?"

Etienne smiled, showing his perfect teeth, and gave a lovely Gallic shrug. "You know, Susan, her voice is not good enough to sing, and being a beer jerker is worse than art poses. What else is she to do? I shouldn't mind offering my services to escort her home afterward. It would soon be known that I took an interest in what happened to her."

"Oh, Etienne, thank you!" Lily cried.

"I don't know, Lily." Susan was still skeptical. "You're too much the fine lady for such things."

"I am too much the fine lady to starve!" Lily said. "Please, Susan. I know I can do it!"

"Oh, all right, then. I'll speak to someone tonight about getting you on."

Art poses—to stand about and look like a pretty picture and let the customers ogle all they liked. It was not something she would have chosen, but after all, how bad could it be? She was delighted when Susan came in the next morning and announced wearily, "It's all set. Ten a week, and you go tonight."

Ten a week. It sounded like a fortune. And best of all, Susan had assured her that men such as Jim Frey were not apt to patronize the lowly likes of the French Pigeon.

"Do I need a costume, Susan?" she asked when it was almost time to leave.

"Wear your merino. You will get your working clothes at the Pigeon. You could not go through the streets in them."

She felt a flutter of fear in her stomach at that. It grew to a hard, icy knot as they strolled the racketing streets with Etienne to the concert saloon. The French Piegon stood with its doors open to the street, but inside it was as if the murk and odor of stale bodies and cigars had been locked there for a hundred years.

Men with loosened ties and bowlers pushed back on their heads sat drinking at little round tables, while women in knee-length skirts and low bodices hung over them—the beer jerkers who waited the tables and tried to turn tips with flirtation and kisses. Here a girl sat on a man's lap, and there another lifted her leg to a chair to tie her shoe, seemingly oblivious of the head of a drunk against her thigh. And some of the women were smoking!

Lily peered through the gloom and saw the models on the little stage, ghostly in nothing but white cotton leotards that reached to their ankles and fastened with false modesty high about their necks. The costumes left little to be guessed at, molding every faint curve of their bodies for the customers' eyes; but it was not the costumes that made Lily suddenly feel faint.

Never could she have imagined such postures of lust, such expressions of frozen invitation. There came a crash of drums and cymbals, and the girls straightened. Faces went blank. Lily had only a second's relief before they struck new poses, stances they must have developed carefully, each trying to outdo the others in her salacity.

Susan had her by the elbow. "Come on, now. Upstairs with you to change."

She followed in a daze up the dimly lighted stairs to a tiny room where costuming of all sorts hung about on hooks and pegs and lines, mingling with cheap street clothing. Susan was holding out a model's outfit. "What's wrong, Lily? Shall I tell them you can't do it?"

Lily shook her head wordlessly, unable to speak. It seemed her only hope. She must try.

"Well, you're to go to the next set, then. Remember, sis, it's not quite so bad as it seems. They can look but they can't touch. You're well off being a model. I've got to go now."

Lily sat alone, quivering in the little room. Her hands were cold despite the sultry night, and currents of icy perspiration ran between her breasts. Downstairs she heard Susan's beautiful voice singing. How wasted it was with that untuned piano and that husky dissipated clarinet! But her audience gave her a warm round of applause. Lily heard light steps running upstairs. "It's time!"

But for Susan leading her by the hand she would not have made it to the stage, and mercifully she was too blind with fear to see the naked craving on the faces of the men, or the resentment her young, unspoiled figure brought to the eyes of her sister performers. The crash of cymbals seemed to deal her a physical blow that would send her groveling to her knees to cover herself. Instead she gave a gasp of uncertainty, and throwing out an arm in a graceful position, pursed her lips like a maiden about to be kissed.

The reaction of the audience was immediate. There were catcalls, booings, stomping on the floor. The man with the cymbals frowned and hit them together again. Sobs started in Lily's throat. She was aware that she had been completely inadequate, and now she tried to copy the pose of the girl next to her. Her efforts brought her a kick in the shin from the person emulated, an angry "Get your own, sis!"

Lily could endure no more. Surrendering to her sensitivities, she let her feet take flight up the stairs, and a storm of laughter followed her as she went. She leaned out the window of the dressing room and was sick to her stomach, depositing her dinner on the banquette below. And then she wept, too desolate and humiliated even to change into her merino dress.

"Oh, Joe," she whispered, "why couldn't you have come?" She saw as never before that she could not survive in New Orleans. And if it came to a bordello, she could not survive that even for a night. Susan had been right. She would have to hope she could sell her gowns for enough for a ticket back to Martinique and Edmond. And though Joe would never know she had come looking for him, she would think of him every day until she died.

Exhausted from weeping, she fell into a doze, waiting for Susan. Below she heard the coarse strains of the cancan. She loved to dance, but she could never dance to that. Then the music changed; she lifted her head to a tune she had heard on Martinique in the ballroom when she and Joe had done the *danse du pays*. She crept out and peered downstairs. The musicians were playing more or less to amuse themselves, and nobody was dancing. The customers were all drinking, not giving the music much of their attention.

Suddenly she knew that there was one thing she did do well. One thing she might turn to a marketable skill. She did not let herself think further as she ran back to the dressing room and stripped off her cotton leotard in favor of a long red gown.

Dance! But she could not face them again! They might laugh her down before she had even reached the stage. Even as she moaned in frustration, she found a domino, and slipping it over her head, she swept down the steps and onto the stage so quickly they hardly had time to see her come.

Then they were aware only that something magnificent had begun to happen. The French Pigeon grew quiet as Lily danced, and the cheapness of the cancan was replaced by a primitive purity. Her body spoke of the beauty of passion in a way it could not have on Martinique, when she had not experienced it, and she spun almost into a trance as the drums beat louder and exuberant voices began to call to her, "Dance! Dance, caleinda!"

With a final wild thunder of drums it was over. She was aware of men storming the stage, of hands reaching for her.

"Let's see who you are, lass!"

"It must be that little prig of a model!"

"Go on with yer, it could never!"

She evaded them somehow and found the stairs. Would they follow? But no, even among these dissolutes there were rules, and they only raged below at the foot of the staircase like dogs that had treed a cat. She sank down on the little wooden chair, her breath coming in gasps, her heart banging away like a shutter in a storm.

"You've a trick or two about you, Lily! And I thought you a helpless lady!" Susan was looking at her in astonishment, her gray-green eyes alight with excitement. "You've got a job! He says he'll pay you fifteen a week!"

And Lily, scarcely able to believe her good fortune, offered a prayer of thanks to the Virgin.

6

She danced every night after that, often wearing her jupe dress and always a carnival mask or domino. Business was brisk at the French Pigeon, and Lily knew she had become the new gossip of the Vieux Carré. Stories about her identity were rife. She was a Bulgarian countess, a murderess escaped from prison. Nobody believed that an ordinary girl danced behind the mask. And the proprietor of the French Pigeon credited Lily with the ingenuity of her disguise. She had had trouble convincing him at first, but she had insisted that she would not dance without it. She had been too afraid she would freeze with shame out there with her face open to the customers' voracious gaze. And when she danced, she thought of Joe and of Carnival, and she danced only for that.

After closing they would always go to the open-air café at the end of the French Market for coffee and square doughnuts rolled in powdered sugar. Life had become almost gay. Lily was contributing to the rent now, and Susan was able to take her singing lessons with more regularity. On Sunday afternoons Etienne would hire a carriage and drive them to Lake Pontchartrain for a picnic or a swim or a game of croquet or lawn tennis. Such times helped Lily to forget the tawdriness of the French Pigeon.

She was learning the ways of the concert saloon. She had become accustomed to the art poses and the cancan and a similar dance, the clodoche. She had learned that brandy was made by mixing a pound of burnt sugar, a half-ounce of sulfuric acid, and a plug of chewing tobacco into half a barrel of water. The tobacco was for bead and sparkle, and olive oil provided the tawny taste for port. Worst of all were the knockout drops that frequently found their way into the drinks. And in the alley behind the saloon the French Pigeon maintained its own crew of sneak thieves who systematically rolled the sodden, doped customers who were dragged there.

The girls had come to accept her now. There was an element of jealousy, of course, for she made more money and commanded more attention. But in a way they were proud of her. They sensed she was not like them, and protecting and petting her seemed to make them feel better about their own womanhood. She was the lone flower in a barren garden, and if any man reached to grab her skirts as she danced, he found his hand pulled away by an indignant beer jerker.

And then came Henry Wickersham. Susan was riding the trolley back from the docks one day with Lily, and it was she, ever alert to the nuances of her surroundings, who noticed him first. It was a beautiful day, but blistering hot, and Susan had come along for the ride, mostly to get away from the closeness of the Vieux Carré. They had been sitting near the windows, enjoying the breeze, nibbling ices they had bought from a vendor, when Susan whispered, "Don't look now!"

"Look where? Why?"

"Behind you, silly. There's a man staring at you. He has been ever since we got on."

"Men are always looking at us, Susan."

"This one is different. He is rich, you can tell. He's quite the swell."

Lily felt a chill. "Is it Jim Frey? Would you know his face?"

"I would, and it's not him. This fellow's got more class."

She looked in spite of Susan's admonition. He saw her and gave a nod of greeting. Not acknowledging it, she swung her head quickly back to the front of the car. He had been quite handsome and very distinguished in his cheviot coat and his jockey vest. He had had an amused expression, as though he had known that by staring at her he could make her turn around.

"He is getting off, Susan! Thank heaven!"

But as he went past, he bent and whispered something in her ear. Uncomprehending, she gave him a startled look.

"What did he say?" Susan asked eagerly.

"He said 'personal.'"

"Personal!" said Susan with a giggle. "Oh, Lily!"

"What does it mean?"

"It means that in the personals column of tomorrow's newspaper there will be an advertisement asking you to contact him and telling you how."

"Advertisements! Well, I have learned about that at least!"

"No, no, Lily. This is different. Lots of gentlemen use the

papers to become acquainted with ladies. Perhaps he's married. And even if he weren't, he'd need a formal introduction. The personals do away with problems like those. It's such a private way for men and women to get together."

"Well, I certainly don't want to get together with him. I know what he wants! It is the same thing as Jim Frey."

"Oh, no, it's not the same at all. Jim Frey paid for you, and he threatened you. With this gentleman it would be of your own free will. It would be a friendship, and if you should find yourself in bed with him and him giving you presents and money, so much the better. You have all the luck, Lily, and you don't even want it! You could say goodbye to the French Pigeon within a week if you answered his advertisement."

"Let us forget it, Susan! I'm not even going to buy a newspaper tomorrow."

But Susan did not forget it.

"Here it is," she cried, brandishing the *Picayune*. " 'Would the lady in the yellow dress on the trolley yesterday meet me at Alexander's for supper at eight.' " Susan's voice rose over the sound of a steam calliope driving past the balcony where Lily sat fanning herself and drinking pink lemonade.

"He has a nerve!"

"I suppose you're not going."

"Of course not!"

"Oh, why don't you face up to it? Your Joe isn't coming to New Orleans. Maybe he's sailing around the world or maybe yellow fever got him in Panama. Have supper with the gentleman! What can it hurt? You would have a fancy meal, that's sure. It's an expensive place."

"I shall have a nice stew of red snapper for my supper."

Susan threw down the paper in disgust and thoughtfully adjusted a loose hairpin in her chignon. "Well, if you're not going, then I am! He's too good to waste."

"Susan! He didn't ask you. And what about Etienne?"

"Etienne won't know. And I'll make the gentleman happy enough to have me for a dinner companion."

As evening came Susan dressed herself in the green crepe de chine that Lily had stolen from Madame Drapeaux and took off grandly in a hack. She missed her first set at the French Pigeon, and Lily worried. But at midnight she rushed in, already having changed from the lavish gown, but with the telltale little evening slippers still on her feet. "I have so much to tell you!" she whispered eagerly as she brushed past

Lily on her way to the stage. Then her fine voice rang out exuberantly on a silly little ditty that was almost obscene. It suited the customers perfectly, and the French Pigeon rang with applause. A momentary grimace crossed Susan's face as she jumped down and pulled Lily upstairs with her.

"Oh, Lily!" She clasped her hands in an uncharacteristic gesture of transport. "Oh, he is the answer to all my prayers! And he owns a dozen sugar mills among other things."

"A dozen sugar mills? Are you sure?"

"Oh, yes. You have only to see how he spends money to know that he's full feather! I won't have to sing in this heap much longer. And he will pay for all the lessons I need. I shall have a grand piano to practice, and silk dresses to wear while I do it."

"Susan! This is all arranged over one supper?"

"No. Not exactly. But tomorrow afternoon we are to see a matinee at the St. Charles Theater, and after that, supper again."

"Well, that is good. I'm glad he traded me for you without any trouble."

"He didn't, exactly."

"What do you mean, not exactly?" Lily was suddenly wary.

Susan's gray-green eyes looked an appeal. "Well, you see, the appointment is for the three of us."

"The three of us?"

"I explained to him how shy you are. I said I had come in your place, to size him up, so to speak. To make sure of him. I told him how you'd been stranded in New Orleans, and that you had had a bad experience that had made you afraid of men."

"That's true, at least about the bad experience. I suppose you did not tell him that I am waiting for Joe?"

"Of course not. You've been a widow for over a year, but you're still daffy with grief. And that helps account for your reluctance, too. What luck we've some good clothes, hey? Oh, Lily, please go! I know I can snare him. It's the only chance like this I'm likely to get. He's not even married!"

"Susan—"

"We're a team, remember?"

Lily sighed. But for Susan she would be dead in the river. What could she do?

The play at the St. Charles Theater was *Galatea*, wherein a cold marble statue was brought to life by love. Here beneath the twenty-three thousand cut-glass girandoles of the chandelier, Lily was enrapt, hardly noticing Henry Wickersham beside her, smelling of cool masculine cologne. He put a hand on her knee; almost absently she removed it. They went to supper, where he ordered delicious papabotte game birds, turtle soup, mirliton squash stuffed with oysters and shrimp, a fine claret, and pastries for dessert. She had not had such fare since the days of Madame Drapeaux, and she ate healthily and danced with him and told him quite honestly that she was enjoying herself. The languor of the meal came over her, and she wished she might go home and sleep. Instead she must dance later at the French Pigeon, but he did not know that. He did not guess at her station in life, she saw. Susan had done a job on him which her own manners and bearing were not likely to betray.

"Beau Clair, Beau Clair," he mused as they danced. "I haven't heard of a family of that name here."

"But why should you, sir? You are American."

He chuckled. "I move in both societies. Business doesn't know nationality, Madame Beau Clair. May I call you Lily?"

"Indeed you may not!"

"You are hard, Madame Beau Clair. But I shall think of you as Lily. The Lily is a lovely flower; it's too bad that you put it to shame with your beauty. You couldn't be related to Joe Beau Clair?"

She stared at him, hoping he did not feel the jolt that shot through her at the mention of Joe's name. "We are distantly related, monsieur."

His arm tightened around her with satisfaction, as if this mutual acquaintance were a bond between them. "That rascal has had the better of me in many a game of faro, and now and then he has bested me on other dealings, too. We'll have a surprise for him when he's in port, eh, Lily? We'll have dinner, the three of us."

Lily almost fainted. "You are forgetting my friend Susan," she managed to say.

He looked over at Susan, her hair glimmering coral in the candlelight. "You're quite right. We'll ask Susan. Joe would like her, I think, but I am surprised that you even know her. She is straight from Irish Channel."

"Susan is an extraordinary woman, monsieur. She has a wonderful voice and is studying opera. She will sing at the French Opera one day."

"How very interesting. Well, she must sing for me, then.

Tomorrow night I'll arrange for a private room upstairs . . . Oh, there is Archer, and I must speak to him."

The man who had stopped beside their table was very tall and well-built, with an aristocratic elegance and a thatch of blond hair. His blue eyes gleamed with a seriousness that was almost a fever, and she was fascinated at once. What could he be, with that sensuous mouth and those long exquisite fingers? Was he a gambler?

"Madame Beau Clair, may I present Archer Snow, the distinguished architect. All New Orleans clamors for his services, but I have been among the fortunate. He's building me a house in Coliseum Square."

"It will be a showplace, I am sure," said Lily as she offered him her hand.

"Would you care to dance, Madame Beau Clair?"

"I should like it," she said, delighted at the opportunity to be away from Henry, but disconcerted at the same time by the way Archer Snow was looking at her, as if he saw past her white skin and dark eyes to attributes that other men missed. There was something desperate and haunted about him, she thought, as if he were searching for something he was afraid he would never find. But he was pleasant to dance with. His hand at her waist was matter-of-fact, and though he had not Joe's musculature, his lean hips reminded her of her lover.

"It will be very gaudy," he said suddenly as they whirled in a waltz.

"I beg your pardon?"

"The house. It will be very gaudy. Henry Wickersham has no taste."

"Then why are you building it, if you are displeased? Monsieur Wickersham said you were sought after."

Archer Snow grimaced. "I am sought after by rich people, none of whom have any more taste than Henry Wickersham. Do you like Italian Renaissance? There will be imitation towers and black onyx mantels and scads of statues in the gardens, which will have artificial ponds and hills."

"And there will be marble bathrooms and carpeted halls, I imagine. It doesn't sound so bad."

"Henry will be glad to know that you approve. Perhaps you will be its mistress."

"Its mistress? Not I!"

"Don't be too sure. Do you know why I am here tonight?"

She shook her head in bewilderment.

"Because Henry wanted me to see you. I am to alter the plans to set off your looks, and the colors in the bedroom must complement your eyes!"

7

"Susan, I will not be a party to supper in a private room. I will not go. This idea of yours is not going to work. Henry Wickersham wants me for his wife. And I couldn't marry him, even if I wanted to. I am married already."

Susan tilted her head and ran her hands underneath her luxuriant red hair. "Henry Wickersham will just have to change the colors of his bedroom again. This is going to be even better than I thought. I am going to marry him!"

"He wants a woman of quality, Susan. And he said you were straight from Irish Channel."

"Henry Wickersham has a new house, and he wants a wife for it. He's shopping for her just like a new suit. But it's not just the cloth of the coat that'll make him buy it. It'll be the cut as well. Henry Wickersham doesn't know what he wants. He's a man. How should he know?"

"You have a very low opinion of men, haven't you?"

"Certainly. Can you give me a reason why I shouldn't?"

She stood with her hands arrogantly on her hips, her eyes blazing with a green fire and her hair flowing.

"No," said Lily, and thought of the customers of the French Pigeon. "Your father, perhaps?"

"An old drunk who did nothing but pine for Ireland and die of the sauce when I was sixteen. Even Etienne wouldn't care a fig for me if I didn't warm his bed now and again. A woman must get what she can, Lily. That is what you have to learn."

Lily sighed. "You remind me of another friend I had. Her name was Cyrillia, and she was determined that she should marry a Creole of Martinique."

And did she?"

"No. She fell in love."

"Well, it won't happen to me. I've seen what it's done to you. I am going to be an opera singer. And Henry will be my way."

"And if he doesn't want his wife to sing?"

"I'll find a way to deal with that. We are very much alike, Henry and I. We are both selfish. Just this one night, Lily. Please come. Then I won't ask anymore."

Susan had her way. Then went to supper in the private room Henry had arranged at a restaurant on Bourbon Street. Obviously Henry had not spared expense. The room contained a baby grand piano, a pair of brocade Louis XV sofas—a kind that had been made in New Orleans and shipped up the river until the war—and a massive Chippendale dining table, its eight legs ending in bold ball-and-claw feet. Velvet draperies, imported French wallpaper, oil lamps glowing softly through hand-painted shades—all of this for a pair of entertainers from the French Pigeon!

Susan sang before supper, not the lyrical Irish melodies Lily loved to hear, but opera, arias from *Rigoletto, Il Trovatore,* and *Les Huguenots.* Henry sat with Lily on a sofa, unfastening her ruby gown with his eyes. There would be a problem soon about these gowns if things went on this way. She and Susan would not have enough. But Susan had said she would not ask another such favor. It would be tonight!

How? Henry was giving very little attention to Susan, even when she sang so wonderfully, her face glowing with concentration, alight with the joy of her song. She was a sight any man should fall in love with, but Henry was not even looking.

"Susan is a veritable Jenny Lind!" she exclaimed, to draw his admiration to her friend.

"If you say so, Lily. I am not much of a connoisseur of music. But I am a connoisseur of women."

He left no doubt about his meaning, and she fanned herself vigorously, hiding her face behind ostrich feathers. "Sir! You are much too forward."

"And you are much too timid. Can't we be alone? I fell in love with you the instant I saw you, and my intentions are honorable. There is no use being coy. I intend to have you, my dear."

"Don't talk so. I shall leave," she whispered. And then, thankfully, the meal was served.

The fare was, if anything, more elaborate than before. He had ordered broiled pompano, leg of mutton in caper sauce, lobster salad, fried parsnips, champagne jelly, a basket of nougats. Lily was relieved as they chatted inconsequentially about the food and the theater. But as the evening wore on,

Susan grew strangely silent. It was not like Susan at all. Before her coffee was brought she retired to one of the couches, her head lolling against the carved flowers and foliage of its crested rail.

Lily grew frightened. She had expected Henry to make a move to have her to himself, but she had not reckoned with this. Lily understood exactly what had happened to Susan. Lily had not done her stint at the French Pigeon for nothing. She knew the effect of drugs in a drink.

"What luck," cried Henry. "Your friend has fallen asleep. Come, Lily, give me a kiss!" She felt his hands on her shoulders, and his lips sought hers. She jerked away in repugnance. Perhaps it would have been better to submit, for her resistance angered him.

"Don't play the innocent, Lily!" he cried. "I have told you my intentions. I know you are a lady, but you have been married. You have known men's ways."

"I know too much of men's way," she said, drawing a deep breath of decision. "It's you who are innocent of women— you think I am a lady. Susan told you that, when in fact I am nothing but a dancer in a concert saloon. So you see, I would not do for your house in Coliseum Square."

"I don't believe you, Lily. But if what you say is true, then there is a price on you. A hundred dollars to take off that dress and let me have you. Don't worry about Susan. I have dosed her so that she will not stir." His hand slipped into her bodice and kneaded her breast, and when he released her, she felt something rough he had left there—money, burning against her bosom!

"I am a dancer, but there is no price on me!" she cried wildly. "I am . . . I am . . . Jim Frey's woman. You will answer to him if you touch me."

Her words had an instant effect. It was not something a lady would have thought to say. He flung her from him, sent her crashing against the scrolled knee of a table leg. The look on his face was horrible to see. Rage, desolation, betrayal, fear—all mingled on features that a moment before had been hot with passion. Had he cared for her that much?

He was a man who was used to having what he wanted. As Susan had said, he had gone shopping for a wife like a suit of clothes, and he had expected his order to be filled. He was a powerful man, but not as powerful as Jim Frey. No end to what sanctions Jim Frey might take against a man in New Orleans! And a rich man had so much more to lose. Especially if that rich man were engaged in shady enterprises, as Henry might be.

"Get out of here, you filthy wench!" he shouted. She stumbled to her feet and ran, hailing a cab to take her back to the Vieux Carré.

The French Quarter seemed almost safe after her trial with Henry Wickersham. It was familiar now, a known quantity. She wished nothing more than to lose herself again beneath its garish cloak. But what of Susan? She should not have left her there, she thought. But what could she have done? She could not have carried Susan. Would he vent his wrath on *her?*

Lily danced with a terrible nervous energy, and her audience applauded her and urged her on. The hours passed, and knowing it was impossible, Lily still hoped Susan would come. When Etienne arrived to escort them home, she told him that Susan was ill. "I would like to go and see to her, Etienne," she said. "I don't want to go for coffee tonight."

He acceded easily to her wishes. "Should I send for a doctor?" he asked worriedly.

"No, no! It's only . . . a female complaint," she said, and blushed.

"Are you certain? You look very pale yourself. There was a rumor of cholera last week. I would like the doctor to check."

"Please, Etienne, you're embarrassing me!" she pleaded, and spun away from him up the steps to their room.

How bleak the place was in the predawn! She lighted a lamp, although it was nearly sunrise, and sat sleepless, her mind whirling while the first noises of day filtered up to her—the scraping of chunks of ice being dragged from the ice wagon, the rustling of magnolia leaves in a breeze from the river, the insolent crow of a rooster in some once-grand courtyard.

Perhaps she should have told Etienne the truth. *He* would have found Susan, and he would have made Henry Wickersham pay for what he had done. But could she tell the story so that he would not be angry with Susan? She had a good idea of Etienne's importance in Susan's life. He was the reason that both of them could walk unmolested through the Vieux Carré.

She took out the hundred-dollar bill Henry had pressed into her bosom and wondered what to do with it. She had not earned it—thank heaven! But neither did she feel compelled to return it, and at length she stood on a chair, reaching up to the jar that held their emergency fund and putting the money inside. Then, without undressing, she fell into a fitful sleep.

Footsteps hurried up the stairs. She wakened groggily, aware that it was midday and the oil lamp was still burning. Lily stared as Susan burst in. "Oh, I was so frightened!" she cried, finding her voice at last.

"Frightened, were you, sis? Do you mean you didn't guess that I had all the aces? Think of it, and Henry dealt the hand himself!"

"What do you mean, all the aces? You were drugged—"

"Drugged!" Susan's pert nose wrinkled with disdain. "Do you really think it is possible for anyone to drug a girl from the French Pigeon? I whiffed the drops the instant I lifted the glass. Henry will have a bill from the establishment for the spot beneath the table where I dumped it."

"You pretended!" Lily cried in astonishment. "You left me to his mercy! Oh, Susan, I trusted you! And how I worried!"

"Take it easy, sis. I knew you'd get out of it. I'd have regained my senses quick enough if he had tried to collect on his money. But I knew, Lily. You have the common sense of a tramp, even though you are highborn! To threaten him with Jim Frey! It was perfect!"

"And then?" asked Lily wearily.

"And then I had him where I wanted him. All in a dither and soured on you. I had only to moan and flutter my eyelids and let my bodice slip. What a night I've had! I've spent the hours between silk sheets, and how he wants me! But I've told him he can't have me again without a wedding ring on my finger."

"And he agreed? Do you mean you are engaged to him?"

"I shall be. He's taking me to show me the house he's building today. I told you it would be the cut as well as the cloth!" And stripping off her clothes, she dropped them on the floor and fell into bed.

Within a week Susan left the Vieux Carré for a fancy uptown apartment. Lily took a trolley to see it, and Susan delighted in displaying the deep rose-patterned carpets, the mahogany card tables, the velvet armchairs. In the bedroom there was a huge Creole-styled bed carved with birds and garlands of flowers.

"Isn't it lush!" Susan declared of the bed. "You can see

why the French say 'always room for one more.' I've measured it—it's eight feet wide."

"Birds on a bed are bad luck," Lily said fearfully. "Madame Drapeaux always said so."

"Oh, pooh, Lily! I can't believe you're jealous. You certainly had your chance."

"Susan, don't marry him! Don't marry without love. Think of what happened to me when I wed Edmond to save Acelie."

Susan smiled wisely as she ran her hand over the cool marble top of her duchesse dressing table. "I am not you. I am not squeamish about bedding Henry, quite the opposite. We understand each other, Henry and I."

"I don't think you understand him or yourself either! What does he say about your singing?"

Susan giggled and rang for her maid to bring them cakes and orange-flower fizzes. Then she smoothed her new delaine gown and said happily, "You'll never guess! Henry's already telling everyone that I've just arrived from New York and that I've had small roles at the new Metropolitan. I'm to have the finest coach to teach me. Oh, it's ever so much nicer than the French Pigeon, and I've nothing to do but pet Henry and mind my Irish brogue. But Henry will get me a speech teacher too. And as for the birds, look, they are in the wallpaper, too. Strawberry thief, it's called."

Lily gazed at the colorful design, the shades of orange and green, the two little larks, beak to beak, pecking away at forbidden fruit. "You must name one of these birds Susan and the other Henry." She sighed. "I can't think of anything that would describe the pair of you better!"

Susan wore a gold ring with a large oval-cut diamond and a crusting of emeralds. She shopped for her trousseau at all the finest shops.

Lily went on dancing at the French Pigeon. And Etienne went on escorting her home afterward. She had been afraid at first that he would desert her. After all, his protection of her had been only a favor to Susan. But he had been in love with Susan, and he was desolate. Now he needed someone for company in the early-morning hours, someone to sit with him over coffee and square doughnuts in the French Market. He had taken the news philosophically when he had seen that Henry had intended matrimony. He had not made a fuss.

"Henry Wickersham will be in trouble with me if he does wrong by her!" Etienne would declare almost every night.

"Would you have liked to marry her?"

"Yes, but I never asked. She had her sights set high. And maybe she didn't know how I felt. Fencing masters don't need to marry young. It's just as well we didn't marry, she would never have been satisfied."

"You will find someone," she comforted.

All the French Quarter thought he already had, and Lily walked as safely through the streets of the Vieux-Carré as across the verandas of Acelie. Nobody dared to bother Lily. Nobody except one.

Lily was shopping in the French Market one morning, having braved the odor of the fish stalls to purchase red snapper. She came out onto the arcade, holding her breath, her eyes watering, and there was Hetty, seeming to jump at her from behind a columned post.

"I'se found you, Miss Lily!" she cried in a cackle of triumph. "I knows where you live. Madame Drapeaux's got another companion, and when she went to have them dresses altered, she found out 'bout what you took. I tol' her how you came back like a ghost from the river, but it wasn't no use. Now I'se living in the Swamp, hidin' from the police, and I'se lucky to git me a crayfish or two if I finds fish heads for the lines. It's all your fault. When I gets money, I'm gonna buy you a gris-gris. I'm gonna buy it before I buys me a griddlecake." She shook her thin black finger in Lily's face. "Ol' gris-gris gonna get you! You got any money, you best buy you a tomb, so they won't be sticking you in an oven in the graveyard wall."

Hetty vanished into the crowd, her plaid tignon lost among dozens like it, and except that her heart was beating so fast, Lily would not have believed she had been there at all.

"I must find another room," she told Etienne that night.

"Why, Lily? What's the trouble?" He didn't laugh as Susan had when she related the problem of Hetty and the gris-gris. He was as superstitious as she. The next day he found her a place in the Pontalba Apartments on Jackson Square.

A baroness had built them with the idea of elegant shops on the ground floor and grand living quarters above. Jenny Lind had stayed there, behind a door that locked with a special golden key, and had looked out at this same view of the tiled roofs of the French Market and flatboats on the Mississippi. But now the cockroaches had taken over. Lily set the legs of her kitchen table in buckets of water in hopes of creating a moat the insects couldn't cross, and each time she dressed she shook her clothes, just as she had done because of centipedes on Martinique.

Now and then a rat scuttered across the fine hardwood floor, but she was safe again from Hetty and the gris-gris. And madame had not believed Hetty, which meant that the incident had not set Jim Frey upon her trail.

Susan and Henry were planning an elaborate Catholic wedding, and Susan wanted Lily to attend her. Lily was hesitant. What would Henry think of it? And might not someone recognize her?

"Oh, Lily! Who would recognize you?" Susan urged. "Jim Frey is powerful, but he's only an uncouth, uneducated policeman. Henry would not invite him or any of his friends to our wedding. Henry moves among a different set—stockbrokers and lawyers and such. And I must have someone cultured, too. Even Henry knows that. It's bad enough I haven't even my old father to give me in marriage."

So Lily remembered again all she owed Susan—her life, her job at the French Pigeon, her protector, Etienne—and she allowed herself to be fitted for a trained gown with a drapery of yellow faille over carnation silk. There were teas to attend and shopping for china and crystal and linen; and Lily fell into the mood of luxury, almost forgetting that the bounty came from Henry Wickersham.

Now and then he went with them, driving his big brougham instead of the little two-seater buggy he had provided for Susan. He treated Lily indifferently, as if nothing had ever passed between them, but when Henry was along, the purchases were even more lavish than when they were by themselves. If Susan ordered a dozen lacework pillowcases, he promptly made it two dozen. Was he trying to impress Lily with what she had missed? He had scarcely a word for her these days, and he and Susan laughed together buying silver goblets and carpeting and even a watercolor that Henry swore was an original Audubon. If love of spending and ostentation could be a bond between people, then surely it was a strong one between Henry and Susan. They were alike, Susan had said. And in this natural habitat of wealth and ambition, perhaps they were.

Now and then Lily took a night off from the French Pigeon and stayed overnight, luxuriating in hot baths in the huge tub and a roachless night in the bed with the carved birds. Soon Henry would take her place in the bed, but not yet, for Susan had been careful to keep her word that he should not have her again until they were married.

And then, returning to her apartment on the morning of the wedding eve, she found what she had been dreading—a little cotton bag, lying at her door. She trembled and pulled back her skirts. Gris-gris!

8

She turned and ran to the open-air café at the end of the French Market, where Etienne sat moodily over *café noir*. "Hetty has bought the gris-gris, Etienne! She found me and put it on my doorstep in the dark of the moon!"

"Sit down and calm yourself, Lily. There are ways to counteract a charm."

"But I don't know New Orleans ways!"

"Have some coffee. Then we'll go get the gris-gris and see what is in it."

She stifled a scream when he dumped out the bag and she saw the bloodstained lock of hair and the head of the lizard mingled with the magic yellow dust. Etienne blew out a deep breath. "It's a very strong charm, Lily. Come, we'll go see Annie Gould."

"Who's Annie Gould?"

"She's the best voodoo doctor in New Orleans. Do you have money?"

"Yes."

"Let's go then. It's on Monroe Street near Royal."

It was strange to be walking through a sunlit morning on such an errand. The air was warm and sweet, and the odor of jasmine and roses already baked in the breeze. But when they stopped before the little plastered cottage, Lily was feeling cold and sick. Etienne rapped on the door with his walking stick.

"Nobody's home, Etienne," Lily said.

"There's eyes behind that lace curtain, Lily. They're trying to decide about us."

Lily was almost hoping they would not be admitted, when a head appeared around the door. Lily jumped, and then was abashed. It was only a barefoot little black girl.

"What do you want?"

"To see Annie Gould," said Etienne.

"What for?"

"A voodoo charm. We've got money." He took Lily's beaded purse and shook it to prove the fact.

"You wait." The child vanished, and the door went shut. Lily would have fled if it had not been for Etienne. He grinned encouragingly at her. "She'll be a voodoo herself someday, that one!"

Then the door opened again, and an old woman in a calico dress and an orange tignon ushered them inside. The little room was musty and dark, with all the windows shuttered except the little front one that had been used for peeping out. A blanket had been thrown over that now, and the only light flickered from a candle on a plain square table. The cypress floor was sprinkled with crumbs of soft brick, a custom of good housekeeping.

The voodoo doctor took a seat behind the candle and indicated two rickety chairs for her guests. "Now, tell Annie Gould," she said almost cajolingly. The soft singsong voice, the candlelight gleaming from her eyes, made her almost hypnotic.

Etienne took out the gris-gris and passed it across the table. The old woman dumped it out and studied its contents. "Ah. Not one of mine. Dr. James done this. Very strong gris-gris, this, but never you mind. Annie Gould's got better magic. You got five dollars?"

"Five dollars!" Lily said involuntarily.

Annie Gould fixed her with a glare. "Five dollars or you gonna be dead, pretty lady, if this gris-gris was for you!"

Lily shuddered and put five dollars on the table. Quickly it disappeared beneath the old woman's hand. "You's lucky you got five dollars. Now I tells you what to do. You gonna need goofer dust."

"Goofer dust? What's that?"

"That's dust off a grave. Got to get it yourself tonight after midnight. But this gris-gris is very strong. Not just any ol' goofer dust gonna do. Got to be from the grave of Marie Laveau. You know 'bout her?"

Lily nodded. She had not been in New Orleans too long a time, but the first thing anyone was likely to hear about voodoo would be about Marie Laveau, the famed voodoo queen who had reigned until a few years ago.

"Go after midnight to St. Louis Cemetery Number One. The grave that says 'Family of the Widow Paris.' Not to the grave with the red crosses in St. Louis Number Two. That one's phony voodoo. You trust Annie Gould; she tells you right."

"And what do we do with the goofer dust?" Lily breathed.

"Put it in this gris-gris bag. Take it along to the house of the person who brought you the gris gris. And then you pour it in your palm and blow it in their face. And do it before the rooster crows."

"But . . . she lives in the Swamp!" cried Lily.

"That's your trouble. That's all Annie Gould can say." And she ushered them out.

"Oh, Etienne, who can find anyone in the Swamp? Even the police can't!"

In the sunlight, Etienne looked grim. "Maybe the police can't, but maybe I can. Give me money and I'll use it to buy information. What's her last name, this Hetty?"

She raided the fund in the jar, and on Etienne's instructions she stayed in her room all day so that nothing could happen to her. She had intended riding to the docks to check the ship arrivals again, but now she could not risk it. She had not been to the docks in several days. It seemed that more and more she put off the trip, finding other things she needed to do. Could it be that she was giving up hope?

Etienne brought her fried chicken from the braziers of the French Market for her supper, and they ate together in her rooms. "How shall I ever be able to thank you, Etienne? You are doing so much more for me than you ever bargained."

"I'm only doing what I want to do, Lily. Otherwise I would only drink myself into a stupor thinking of Susan's wedding tomorrow. I would wind up in the alley behind the French Pigeon."

But she thought that he drank more wine than he should with his meal anyway, as he talked incessantly of his love for Susan.

He walked her to the concert saloon, promising that when he returned he would have news of Hetty. It was a little past two in the morning, and she was dancing her last time when she looked up and saw him in the doorway. He made a circle with his fingers to indicate success, and handed her a paper bag as she ran offstage. "Put these on," he said.

Inside she found a boy's clothing. Cheap trousers, a shirt, a loose-fitting tweedy jacket, and a soft hat with a bill to hide her long hair. She did as he had instructed and met him in the street.

Babylon 165

"You look a proper lad, Lily," he told her, and she noticed that his breath reeked of liquor.

"Why must I dress like this?"

"Because we are going to the Swamp, and it will make the Vieux Carré look tame. A girl wouldn't be safe there, not even with me. I would do the deed for you if I could. But you know Annie Gould said it must be you."

"You've found where Hetty lives?"

"I think so. But first we must find another residence—in St. Louis Number One."

They entered the cemetery from Basin Street, across the way from the three-story turreted bordello called Mahogany Hall, leaving the laughter and music of the Viex Carré behind as they walked into little streets lined with the whitewashed houses of the dead.

In the glow of the moon, crickets chirped, and a lizard slithered in front of them. Ivy climbed the walls of the tombs, and ferns grew in the crevices. Here and there a candle guttered in a red or blue container, and on most of the tombs, even the ovens in the wall, there was a shelf containing cut-glass vases filled with lilies or gladioli.

The tombs of the rich had porches railed in wrought iron, with chairs where mourners could sit and think of the dead, but Marie Laveau's tomb wasn't one of these. They found the inscription that Annie Gould had told them on a weedy, tiered grave. There were coins in the chinks in its surface, and Etienne told Lily that people put them there to pay Marie Laveau's spirit for answering their prayers.

The grave was heavy with dust. Lily was grateful that it had not rained lately. And she was grateful to Americans, remembering that Madame Drapeaux had always attributed New Orleans dust to them. Carefully she scraped as much as she could into the tiny gris-gris bag and put it into the pocket of her unfamiliar clothing.

"What now?" she asked.

"Can you ride a horse?"

"Of course. Can you? You are a bit unsteady, Etienne."

"Oh, come. I needed the liquor to fortify me and make me able to stand my grief. I have a man waiting with the horses on Dumaine Street."

They mounted the horses in the abandoned lot where on Sunday afternoon blacks still danced the Congo dances from the time of slavery, and they rode out of town on an oak-lined shell road behind the levee. At the edge of a bayou Etienne reined in and gave a whistle. The ghostly waters, laced with muskrat trails in the green confetti moss, remained silent. And then there came the unearthly cry of an owl in flight.

"What is it, Etienne?"

"I hired a guide to meet us here. I offered the scoundrel enough that he should not have forgotten." He was walking along the bank, exploring it with his lantern. "Ah, here is a pirogue. It must be his. He's only late." They waited beneath a great oak hung with gray Spanish moss, and the owl kept up its disembodied shrieking as it sallied endlessly among the cypress.

Etienne put an arm around her as she drew close to him, shivering in her cheap coat. "It's cold here, not like in the city," she whispered.

"Yes, and the bird makes a terrible sound. But it is the little sounds that are more dangerous. The little splashings that are alligators and water moccasins."

"It's another bird that frightens me most. The rooster. Your guide isn't coming. Did he tell you directions?"

"Down the bayou to a big cypress with six knees, and take the third channel past it. But, Lily, you aren't thinking—"

"I'm going. You don't have to come with me. It's dangerous, and you don't owe it to me."

"It's more dangerous than gris-gris," he snorted drunkenly. "Let's go back to New Orleans."

"You can. Will you give me your pistol before you go?"

He rose with a groan and went down the steep bank to the pirogue. "A fool would go with you; a coward wouldn't. I suppose, like a good Frenchman, I will choose being a fool. What a shame it's not you I'm in love with, at least. Come, help me push the boat off."

They slid quietly into the brooding waters, into the den of the worst of thieves and murderers. Pirates, renegades of every sort had found refuge here—everyone who like Hetty, was hiding from the police. They should not have been surprised when Etienne's guide appeared after all, waiting with a gun and two comrades on the hummock behind the six-kneed cypress.

The boat was jerked rudely up onto the knoll, and with a howl Etienne rose from its bottom, where he had been slumped, half in a daze. His pistol cracked and one of their assailants fell back wounded into the water. A second shot followed the first, and Etienne cursed as his weapon dropped from his maimed hand. The man who had shot the gun away was rifling Etienne's pockets. The other was doing the same to Lily, who forgot to be a boy and fought against him with the indignation of a girl.

"Let me go!"

"Maybe. When I have got your money." Her hat suddenly fell away, and her attacker gave a whistle of surprise. "Hey! Hey, Jean! We've hit it rich tonight. This one's a woman."

She knew what they meant. They would take their pleasure, and then they would sell her. Hetty had won. The gris-gris had got her, she thought as they pulled back her jacket and opened her shirt to gaze at her breasts in her camisole beneath.

They emptied her pockets. "No, not that!" she cried instinctively when they found the gris-gris bag.

"Ah! You got something special in here, little gal? Gold maybe? A diamond?"

"Goofer dust! Don't spill it!"

But they already had. She felt herself pushed rudely back. Her head hit dizzily. Then she was aware of silence, of water purling gently around the cypress.

"Lily?" Etienne was shaking her.

"I'm all right," she whispered.

"It was the goofer dust. They would sooner find a girl who doesn't carry that in her pockets."

"Yes, but it's gone," she mourned.

"Maybe not. Give me the lantern. Careful, now." They found a minuscule mound beneath the bag and managed to work part of it back inside.

"There's very little, Etienne. And it's mixed now with other things."

"We have nothing to lose," he returned with an attempt at a grin.

The gaunt cypress trees stood silhouetted against the graying of dawn when they found the proper channel. Even in the growing light Lily nearly missed seeing the weathered shack, it's bowed floor hanging like a hammock between stilts at the edge of the water. She left Etienne to hold the pirogue, and clambering up the ladder, she rapped at the door.

Hetty's evil face appeared, and Lily blew the thin film of dust with all her might.

And somewhere a rooster crowed.

9

Had it been enough to break the charm? She went to Etienne's rooms on Esplanade Avenue and helped him to bed, oblivious of the strain on decorum. "Your poor hand! It's all my fault!" she grieved.

"Not all your fault," he said. "I shouldn't have been so careless. I should have guessed they were waiting there and got all three of them instead of only one. You were right. I shouldn't have drunk so much. If it is anyone's fault but mine, it's Susan's. Go along with you, now. Don't worry. This hand will hold a sword again. And the doctor will give me a draft so that I will sleep for hours. It suits me perfectly to remember nothing about Susan's wedding day."

She went straight from Esplanade Avenue to Susan's apartment, where she knocked at a back door and had to remove her hat before the maid recognized her and let her in.

"Lily Beau Clair! You're incredible!" cried Susan when she saw her. "You've missed the wedding breakfast. And I shall have to burn those clothes, or Henry will think I have a lover already."

"I've been to the Swamp, Susan," Lily said.

"The Swamp? Oh, you'd never! Even I wouldn't dare go there."

"I went last night with Etienne. I had to find Hetty. She'd bought me a gris-gris."

"Oh, that nonsense. You went to the Swamp over that? It would have served you right if you'd been murdered."

"I nearly was. And Etienne—his hand was injured by a bullet when we were waylaid by robbers. He says it will be all right and that he'll be able to shoot and fence again, but . . . Oh Susan! A man like Etienne must have dozens of enemies ready to pounce on such a weakness."

"It's a shame, Lily. Come, you've got to hurry. Shall I have rose water put in your bath? It won't do for the matron of honor to stink like the Swamp."

Babylon

"Susan! Did you hear what I said? Don't you care a bit? It wouldn't have happened if he had not been drinking so because of his love for you."

"Of course I care, Lily. But what would you have me do? I'm to have a husband now. I can't go running to pet Etienne. Hurry, now!"

Lily pulled off her boy's clothes and sank into the sweet-smelling bath, trying to forget the night and her sense of guilt and her lingering fear that Hetty's charm might not have been counteracted.

A strong charm, Annie Gould had said. How much goofer dust had she needed? Had her dust been too impure?

Susan's gown of white Ottoman silk had a high, lacy neckline and elbow sleeves. Her shining red hair glowed brightly beneath her crisp floor-length veil, and her bouquet of blue dahlias accented the luminous glow of her gray-green eyes. Henry had almost filled the big church, and as Lily and Susan half-stepped down the aisle in their embroidered satin slippers, it seemed impossible that such a short time ago Susan had had only one set of petticoats and one pair of shoes.

It seemed impossible that tomorrow night Lily would dance again at the French Pigeon, impossible that only hours before a bit of dust from a tomb had prevented her being sold into white slavery. This was her natural milieu, the mode of life she would have known if she had stayed where she belonged with Edmond; and she reacted happily, charming all the guests at the reception buffet at Henry's club.

She thought she had danced a hundred waltzes before the evening buffet was brought out: turkeys, roasts, and hams, glass bowls of salad, a nougat piece in the shape of a wedding bell, sherbets and ice cream in baskets carved from orange peel and decorated with candy roses and violets.

Once or twice she was close to Susan, who was beautifully flushed with triumph. "Isn't it grand!" she whispered. "I could never have done it without you." And then Susan was whisked away to dance again, lying gaily to her partners about her operatic career in New York.

"I shall give it all up now that I've found Henry, of course," Lily heard her say.

"Oh, but you mustn't! What a waste! I shall have a word with your bridegroom myself if he doesn't agree to it." And soon she was prevailed upon to sing.

"Oh, goodness! On my wedding day?"

"But what better time for singing?" someone cried, and a clamor went up. So Susan, displayed to great advantage beside the flower-garlanded piano, sang and sang, and her audience was spellbound by her lively beauty and her magnificent voice.

"You *must* sing in New Orleans . . . My wife knows someone . . ." Lily heard snatches as she moved away in search of a cup of punch. So Susan would have her dream, it seemed. And the dapper Henry would not object to his wife's singing in public as some stiff Creole gentleman would. Already Henry was glowing with pride. Perhaps after all it would be a good marriage, she thought. And she thought how lucky it was that he had got over his early obsession with her.

But suddenly he was beside her, and his eyes had a queer, glittery look. "Lily, here is someone with whom I believe you are well-acquainted."

She turned with a pretty smile and looked straight into the swarthy, evil face of Jim Frey!

"Madame Beau Clair," he said with a bow, "we meet again!"

He swept her out to dance before she could gather the wits to resist. Over her shoulder she saw Henry watching them speculatively, his glass in his hand. And above her the twinkling girandoles spun into a thousand little stars in a swirling, inky sky.

She must not faint! The expression on Henry's face left no doubt that he knew about her and the assistant police commissioner. She had used Jim Frey to frighten him away from her, and now Jim Frey was his revenge. His eyes told her he understood the disaster he had dealt her. She thought of the night in the Swamp and the spilled goofer dust. She had not had enough! Annie Gould's remedy had not worked. She saw Hetty's face—the black finger wagging at her: "Ol gris-gris gonna get you!"

"So, Lily, you did not make a meal for the alligators when you jumped into the river. Perhaps you'll make *me* a tasty morsel yet! Or do you still find me so distasteful?" His arm tightened about her unpleasantly.

"Sir!" she quavered with all the indignation she could muster.

"Still the lady, eh, Lily? I suppose you are going to tell me again about your swordsman husband?"

"I am still a married woman."

"Perhaps you are. You no longer have that tan. You told

the truth about that. But you will pay for the insult you dealt me. Your husband, who cares for you so poorly, will find my mark on you when he sees you again."

She twisted away from him and ran up the polished staircase. She was safe for the moment. He would not force himself on her here. She found another way down, half-supposing that she was playing into his hands and that he would be waiting there for her. But the way was clear, and she took a hack back to her apartment on Jackson Square, causing a stir of interest as she alighted in her gown of silk and yellow faille.

Bolting the door, she stacked the furniture against it, sitting watchful through the night. Finally, not having slept the night before, she fell into a fitful doze. When she awoke, sunlight was gleaming on the roofs of the French Market, a blue jay was calling in the palmettos around Andrew Jackson's statue, and she was still safe.

She bought croissants and took them to Etienne. He was still in bed, propped up white-faced on his pillows. "Did you bring a newspaper, Lily?" he said. "I want to read about Susan's wedding."

"I brought it, Etienne. The wedding got a big play. Henry is an important man."

"Tell me everything. Was Susan a beautiful bride?"

"I've never seen her look so wonderful. And she sang, and everyone was impressed. When they return from their honeymoon to Europe, she'll have a chance to sing at the French Opera. I'm sure of it!"

He sighed and let his head drop back. "That is good. It's a compensation for losing her."

"Poor Etienne! How is your hand? What did the doctor say?"

"It hurts a great deal, but the doctor says it will mend."

"I'm glad for that!" She turned away to the stove to make coffee, and he began to read the account of Susan's wedding.

"Lily!" His voice was a cry of concern, and she twirled to see him sitting upright in his nightshirt. "This says that that police commissioner, Jim Frey, was among the guests. That was the man who tried to buy your favors from Madame Drapeaux. The one you jumped into the river to avoid. He could not have helped but see you."

She pushed him back in the bed. "I waltzed with him. Nothing happened. Don't exert yourself."

"Something *will* happen. He won't let it go at that."

"Perhaps he has other things to do," Lily said, trying to hide her trembling. "There are other girls in New Orleans. And Madame Drapeaux has a new companion."

"No, no. Don't fool yourself," he said in agitation. "Perhaps it's the gris-gris! If only I had protected you better last night! What did he say to you? Tell me the truth."

"He said my husband would find his mark on me," she said softly.

"Then he will come for you. It will be easy enough for him to find where you live and where you dance."

"Yes. Henry will tell him," she said bitterly.

"You will have to leave New Orleans. Do you have enough in your jar for a ticket to Martinique?"

"I don't think so."

"It doesn't matter. You must go somewhere. Anywhere will be better than here. Oh damn this hand of mine!"

"I will go, Etienne. Jim Frey is not your battle."

She did not say this time, "But if I go, I will never see Joe again." This time she had already known what she must do. Tomorrow she would buy a ticket on any boat that was sailing, just as in Montserrat. Joe would be out there somewhere on the ocean, and somehow, sometime, their paths would cross. She must believe that and try to survive.

Tonight she would go to the French Pigeon and collect her earnings. Tomorrow she would be gone. She did not want to risk involving Etienne, in his condition. That could mean only more calamity.

"I wish I could have said good-bye to Susan," she mused. "I wish I could be here when she sings at the French Opera. I'll write to you and tell you where I am, and you will send me the reviews."

"Yes. I'll do that. Take this pistol with you. You may need it, and it will be little good to me for a while. Why are you smiling like that?"

"I was only thinking that I took a pistol when I left Martinique, too. It did me little good!"

"I will come with you tonight when you go to get your wages, Lily."

"Don't."

"Yes. It's a matter of honor. I did not do right by you in the Swamp, so if the gris-gris brought Jim Frey, it's because of me."

She packed her clothes into her valise that afternoon. And she counted the money in the jar. It was too bad that she could not find a ship without waiting until the next day. But she needed the money from the French Pigeon, and she could not get it until evening, when the place opened for business. She knew she should have done the errand the night before, after she had left Susan's wedding, but she had been too disconcerted, too frightened. Now at least she had the pistol.

Etienne did not come to escort her, and she wondered if he had reconsidered. She tried to seem nonchalant as she made her way through the streets. Reaching the French Pigeon, she collected her due. The proprietor was sorry to see her go. So were the girls, the art models and cancan dancers, who had at first made her life so miserable. "We will lose class with you gone," they said. "The tips won't be half as much."

And: "So, you're on the run, are you? It's no surprise. At least tell us before you go if you are the murderess or the countess or what!"

"It's nothing as exciting as all that," she said with a smile. "I am only looking for the man I love."

"Aren't we all!" they said. "Good luck, sis!"

It was less than a block beyond the French Pigeon that Jim Frey's men found her. They must have been waiting, some of them sitting in the concert saloon to see her departure. They threw her to the banquette fully in the glow of a streetlamp. There were people nearby; she heard shouts and screams. She struggled for the pistol in her skirt pocket and heard it discharge as it fell away. Then there was only the grunting of her attackers as they labored to hold her. Everyone else had gone away; no one would help her. Etienne, she thought dimly as she gritted her teeth and waited for the ripping of her clothes.

"Jim Frey said to leave his mark on you," one said.

His mark. Then surely whatever was to happen would not be here in the street. They would take her to him, at least. But something glittered close to her face. A ring on the finger of one of her assailants—a special ring with blades around it, a footpad's knife for cutting the bottoms of pockets. She gave a terrible scream as she felt its coldness against her face. And she fainted before she even felt the pain of its slicing.

10

Her friends from the French Pigeon found her and carried her inside when the men had gone. The doctor who came and sewed stitches in her forehead told her she was lucky. There would be a scar, but it would be high. "You'll be able to cover it with a fashionable fringe, young lady."

She had never thought that fringes suited her, but there was no other way. She spent several days in a room above the French Pigeon, and when the bandages were removed she saw that the cut had a curve and a cross mark to it. Had it been meant to be the letter F? His mark upon her! She would carry it to the end of her life. He could not have thought of a better way to humiliate her. Unlike the memory of a night in his bed, this could never fade, never be forgotten.

But she was not as unhappy as Jim Frey might have hoped. He was finished with her now. She had no more reason to be afraid of him, and for the second time she was saved from having to leave New Orleans. Within a week she was dancing again and making her excursions to the docks. She missed Susan and Etienne intensely. Etienne had not come to the French Pigeon since before the attack. His hand could not have kept him away for long, certainly. If he had decided to stop being her protector, she could not blame him. For all his heartbreak over Susan, had he found another woman already? And now he no longer needed Lily's friendly company?

At least she must go and see him. She called twice at his rooms on Esplanade Avenue, but he was never home. The third time a man went past as she knocked. He was much the same cut as Etienne, slender, lithe, and elegant. "Are you looking for Etienne?"

"Yes, and I can never seem to catch him at home."

"It's no wonder. He's dead these two weeks."

"Dead!"

"A shame, mademoiselle! He was the finest swordsman in

the Quarter, and bested me at many a competition. And he did not even have the luck to die in a fair fight."

"How did he die?" she asked, horror swimming inside her.

"Knifed in the back. And nobody seems to know exactly why. They do say it was the doing of Jim Frey. Are you a sister or a sweetheart?"

She shook her head blindly and asked where he was buried. She took flowers to his grave in St. Louis Number One and sat weeping for hours. It had been a long while since she had allowed herself such a luxury of tears. New Orleans had become unbearably bleak, and when she could cry no more, she closed her eyes and let herself think of Acelie in a way she had not for months. She saw the morning sunlight on the yellow stone of its walls, remembered the flow of its irregular roofline like the crests of green island mornes. She heard the cry of the mountain whistler, breathed the bougainvillea in the piazza. Acelie, the one place on earth she loved and to which she belonged. Was she doomed forever to wander? It seemed so.

A few days later, as she came offstage, a man in a well-tailored shepherd's-check suit handed her a card. "I am with the Manhattan Ballet. Can we talk?"

She bade him wait while she changed, and took him out to the French Market, where she had so often gone with Etienne. "I will come right to the point, Madame Beau Clair," he said. "I had been told of you, and now that I've seen you dance, I would like you to dance with us."

She had become too canny to be easily lured. "But why, monsieur? I know nothing of ballet."

"You don't need to. You will dance a specialty number. No one in New York has seen anything like what you do."

"New York!"

"Yes, of course. That is our home base. Wouldn't you like that? It's the most exciting city in the world, and you would have money to enjoy it. And next season we expect to tour the Continent."

"Ah! What guarantee that you will not simply ship me off to some house of prostitution?"

He gave a roar of laughter. "Madame Beau Clair, I do not take you for a fool. Check my credentials at the theater. I'm sure you'll decide to accept. You can't go on forever dancing at the French Pigeon for fifteen dollars a week."

He was right, she thought. She couldn't go on forever dancing at the French Pigeon. It was her chance, and if she didn't take it, when might she have another? Jim Frey would not bother her again, but now she had no protector with Etienne dead. Soon they would sniff her out, and she would no longer be safe in the Quarter. She checked his credentials, as he had suggested, and satisfied he had been telling the truth, she accepted the offer. Her salary tripled and she moved out of the French Quarter to a pleasant little flat farther uptown.

Life assumed a new routine. She was up by eight and at the theater by nine to rehearse. Perhaps there would be a matinee, and always there was an evening performance. When the ballet girls had washed the paint from their faces and folded their costumes, there was little time to sit over coffee. Straight home to bed most of them went, and were hollow-eyed anyway in the morning.

"It is a hard way to live," Lily complained.

"Oh, but it's exciting and all for art," came the reply. "And it'll be something to remember when you are too old for it and surrounded by screaming children."

"It's a good way to find a husband to get you the children," another would say, laughing. And they told her she would love New York and invited her to lodge with them in their boardinghouse on Bleecker Street. "There are all sorts of artists and writers there," they said.

Soon they would leave New Orleans. Lily tried not to think of it. But she was secure now, and, still dancing in the jupe dress and domino, she created a sensation at every performance. Gentlemen sent flowers to her dressing room and requested she dine with them, but Lily rejected them all. She wanted no man but Joe. But without a man she would have to support herself, and to do that she would have to leave New Orleans. It was a dreadful logic she could not refute.

"There's a gentleman asking to see you," one of the girls told her after a performance one night. He's handsome and he's left his lady cooling her heels in the lobby. A fancy lady she is, too—Jenny Van Artsdalen, the daughter of a banker!"

"I have no wish to see any gentleman."

"But he's very insistent."

"Then I shall have to lock my dressing-room door."

The next night he was back again in the front row, alone this time, she was told, but she did not bother to look.

"The gentleman is here again," someone whispered as she came offstage at the end of the performance.

"Then shoo him away."

But suddenly she felt herself lifted in two strong arms,

carried away outside, and a well-remembered voice murmured, "I will not shoo. Oh, little Mimi, I cannot believe I have found you. I would know that jupe dress and that dancing anywhere. And now that I have you, I will never let you go!"

11

"Joe! Oh, Joe!" She turned her face into his kisses, clinging to him with a fierceness that told of the long months she had been deprived of him.

"Tell the driver where to go," he said. She was only vaguely aware that he had climbed into a carriage, still with her in his arms.

"But . . . I am not properly dressed . . ." She pulled back with the thought that she must return to the theater.

"You are dressed the way I like you best, my magnificent little coaling girl. All the bustles and drapery and kilting in the world could not improve on that jupe dress. But tell the driver where you live, and soon you shall not need even that."

She gave her address and sank back against the seat, riding through the warm New Orleans night in the wonder of his embrace. Moonlight spilled into her bedroom as he watched her move barefoot across the cypress floor. The air was rich with the warm summer scent of jasmine, and Lily herself seemed to shine with a fine purple fire, sending sparks back against the moonglow as she walked. Oh, how he had yearned for her! He had been spoiled for other women after her, had tried to lose himself in the jungle of Panama, had tried to submerge himself in adventure larger than himself, the dream of continents divided.

But none of it had been any good anymore. He had not cared about the Panama Canal, nor about excitement or glory. The only adventure he had wanted had been in her arms, and the harder he had worked at arranging equipment transport or helping to survey the way through the festering wilderness, the worse his longing became. He could not bury it, and when there had been epidemics of yellow fever, Joe had tended the sick without fear, for if he succumbed, he might at least hope to see Lily again in his delirium.

The delirium of rapture that flooded him now was finer

than any he might have dreamed. She turned with a soft, graceful motion for him to unfasten the buttons of her dress, and her dark eyes gleamed golden lights of love as he pushed the garments to the floor, his hands lingering on the smooth wonder of her breasts and hips. The gesture she made of opening herself to him was frank but not bold; there was almost disbelief that he was here, that he wanted her, that he would fill the need that quivered undeniably through her body.

He lost himself in her then, utterly, in a way he had never been able to lose himself in the jungle, and surprisingly, he found himself, too, as though she emerged as the North Star to guide his life. He saw that she was crying, and he drew back, afraid he had been hurting her. But she tightened her grip on him, her tears only happiness, her slender, delicate body shuddering as though it would break with ecstasy.

They lay together afterward in an all-but-tangible sweetness that made a deep, solid barrier against the world around them. Lily had forgotten Madame Drapeaux and Jim Frey, the French Pigeon, Hetty and gris-gris. Joe forgot the murderous roughness of Panama.

"Joe, oh, Joe, what took you so long?" she whispered, kissing him.

"My dearest love, if I had known you were here!"

"Oh, didn't you know in your heart that I must be? That I would follow you forever?"

He laughed gently. "Lily, you must remember that you are unlike any woman in my experience. And in my experience, even a woman who has a fling at Carnival goes back to her husband as she ought."

"And you thought that I ought?"

"Yes, of course." He gave her a puzzled look. "Wives ought to stay with husbands. That is what all society says. I had no reason to think you had not gone back."

"No reason! When I had only that moment tasted love! I could not put the bottle back on the shelf. I could not waste my life and live it all a lie. I had only to take my choice of sins, Joe. A lie is a sin as well."

"Then we shall live the happy sin, Lily, forever. But what happened there on Montserrat when Edmond came?"

"He guessed that we were lovers," she said with a shiver. "And he swore to kill you! He took the pistol—I was so frightened! But you were gone."

Joe sighed. "It doesn't please me to take what belongs to another man, especially when the man is my brother, Lily."

"I do not belong to him like a table or a chair!"

"That is an idea that will take some getting used to. And he loves you."

"He did, once. But even before I left, he had taken my *bonne*, Cyrillia, to his bed."

"The pretty *capresse*? I remember her."

"I did not make him happy, Joe. Even on the night of our marriage, my heart belonged to you. But I did not understand then, and thought I could give my love wherever I chose. I didn't know that love has a will of its own. I will make you happy, Joe!"

"And I you," he whispered as she drifted asleep in his arms.

She awoke with a start. Outside, the sun was already bright and hot. She struggled out of Joe's grasp. Already past eight! She put the coffee to boil and ran water in the bath. She was absorbed in sudsing herself when a faint sound made her look up.

"Joe! How long have you been watching me?" she said, and blushed.

He laughed happily. "I have not been watching you for as long as I want to. Pray do not reach for a towel. Oh, Lily, you did not blush so last night!"

She stumbled out of the tub, silvery rivulets streaming down her fine body, all rosy from the steam of the bath. But he held the towel away, catching her against him, wet as she was.

"Joe, please, I have not the time," she said with an attempt at stern dignity.

"What do you mean you haven't time? Didn't I tell you last night I would never let you go? It's a vow I intend to keep. You have nothing to do with the rest of your life but to make love to me."

"Oh, come, don't be silly. You're going to make me late!"

"Late! What could you possibly be late for?"

"Rehearsal. I'm supposed to be at the theater by nine."

He gave her the towel. "Oh, is that all? Well, dry off and come back to bed. You are not going to rehearsal, of course. That is all over for you."

"Over?"

"You don't have to do that sort of thing now. And I don't want my woman dancing for a lot of men to see."

"Last night you didn't object! You were in the front row, so I was told."

"You were wonderful. But that was before I had claimed you. Now I shall provide all the money, of course, and you shall dance only for me."

She sighed and let him lead her back to bed. A wave of relief washed over her. She need never bother again about her own welfare. All would be taken care of—her food, her clothing, her entertainments—just as they had been in her childhood. She would lead the life of a lady with Joe.

No, not quite the lady, for she would always be an outcast, never accepted into society as Joe's mistress. Long ago on Martinique he had told her that no lady would ever have chains on him. And now she did, and she supposed it made her no longer a lady. But now did he want her to be one?

She had left her husband—a lady might do that, she supposed. But could a lady dance at the French Pigeon, do all the things that Lily had done in the business of surviving in New Orleans alone? She had an idea it would be better not to tell Joe any of it. Better to let him think it had been the ballet from the first! Leave out Madame Drapeaux, the squalid Vieux Carré apartment, all the rest.

She lay back in the luxury of his arms and enjoyed his love, but later, when he slept, she paced restlessly. It had become a habit, this surviving on her own. She had begun as a helpless novice, but she had been quick to learn. She had become as skilled in street wisdom as Susan herself, and she suddenly realized that she had begun to take pride in the fact. And she had been proud of her dancing at the ballet, proud of the acclaim, the applause, and of the style in which it had supported her.

"Something to remember," the ballet girls had said. Yes, it was that. But would she ever be as content now as if she had married Joe from her father's house?

By the time he awakened at noon, she had banished such thoughts. She had spent the morning making a hearty jambalaya, frying ham and sausage, browning flour and spices for a roux, cooking all with tomatoes and boiled rice in a heavy iron pot. When he had a steaming plate in front of him, she remembered to ask him a question that had been nagging at her.

"Joe, who was the woman you brought to the theater that first night?"

"Do you mean Jenny Van Artsdalen?"

"Yes. The ballet girls seemed to think she was someone important."

"Her father is important. He's invested heavily in a shipbuilding concern and wants to experiment with the new clipper-ship designs. I've put money in myself, but mostly my part of the bargain is in my knowledge of sailing."

"But aren't clipper ships passé? I thought that steamships were the only kind being built."

"Steamships have the advantage of short voyages and along the coast, but for those long reaches across the sea, where the wind seldom changes, the clipper is still faster. It's building ships for the grain race to Australia we're primarily interested in."

"And Jenny? Is *she* primarily interested in *you*?"

He gave a shout of laughter. "If she is, that's her problem, not mine—or yours. It would not be the first time a woman has had me in her sights and lost."

"She is very rich. She will expect to have you if she wants you."

"Oh, very well. Shall I go and marry her so that she won't be disappointed?"

She flung herself into his arms. "Oh, Joe, don't even joke about such a thing."

He covered her face with playful little kisses. "Jenny Van Artsdalen is nothing to me, Lily. We shall hear no more about her."

Since Joe found Lily's quarters cramped, they began to look for a house within a day or so. She wished for something Creole, with galleries and long windows, but outside the Vieux Carré they could not find such a residence available. There were plenty of fine new houses with gingerbread and turrets, but Lily did not like them.

"We are looking for a home, Joe," she told him, "and such a place would never be home to me. I will always need a touch of the French, because that is what I am." The thought of Madame Drapeaux came to mind unbidden, and she felt something like sympathy for the woman, who had gone mad rather than leave the place where she belonged.

"But we can't go on living like this!" Joe would complain. "I've no place to put my clothes, or even a shelf for my shaving mug." And one day, having been gone all morning, he told her he had a surprise and took her to see the house he had bought.

It was a fine construction of pink granite with a grand

doorway framed with stained-glass side lights. But the walnut staircase, the marble bathroom, the bay windows did not impress Lily. It was a tight place, full of claustrophobic nooks and crannies, unbearably confining after the sweep of Acelie's airy rooms and great sashless windows. How could she accept this place as home?

But Joe was eager and led her to the back to show her that at least it had a beautiful walled courtyard with a fountain, and there were crape myrtles in bloom, irises, plumbago, and periwinkle. He had been thinking of her wishes after all!

"Can you make do here, Lily? It's the best we are likely to find."

She looked into his face and suddenly knew how lucky she was that he loved her and that they were together. He would live here with her, and here she would shut away the world to make a sanctuary of love. "Wherever you are, Joe, I can always make do," she said.

They began to shop for furnishings. Joe was amused that Lily already knew the best place to make every purchase. But he was less amused when all the shopkeepers seemed to know Lily and treated her like the best of customers.

"How did this happen, Lily?" he wanted to know. There was a tenseness about him as he began to wonder about those days she had spent in New Orleans without him. Could it possibly have been as simple as she had said? Or had she had a lover she had not told him about? Someone she had visited these shops with to set up housekeeping.

"Oh, it was Henry and Susan," she answered. "Susan was my friend, and we were shopping for her wedding. They are building a house in Coliseum Square."

He relaxed a bit. "I should like to meet these friends of yours."

"I did not say friends. Only Susan is my friend. I don't like Henry at all." She stopped in the middle of examining a set of china cups and felt suddenly atremble. "Joe, let us go and have some refreshment. I am tired."

"Are you ill?" he asked in concern, as they sat over tea.

"No . . . it was just that I remembered that this Henry already knows you. Henry Wickersham is his name, and he says he plays faro with you."

"Oh, that Henry. It's no wonder you don't like him. Lucky for you he had his eye on marriage, or he'd have given you trouble for sure. He's a demon with women."

"Joe . . . I've no wish to meet up with him again. You see, I told him we were only distantly related . . ."

"And he will know you're not my wife? All right. New Orleans is a big place. We will simply avoid him."

She felt a little better then. But could Henry really be avoided? Jim Frey was finished with her. His revenge had been swift and violent. But Henry had a different turn of mind. Henry preferred to toy with his prey, and she feared that, like a cat playing with a mouse, he would never truly let her go as long as she squirmed, as long as there was more damage he could do.

Henry had revealed her to Jim Frey. Would that be enough? What if he discovered she and Joe were lovers? Would it delight him to tell Joe about Jim Frey? And then, Joe being a proper Frenchman, he would go after Frey—and perhaps wind up in St. Louis Number One, like Etienne!

They bought a huge French bed, and the day it was moved into the house, they moved in themselves, though the place was only half-furnished. She was vaguely depressed that day, without knowing why.

"Is it the house, Lily?" he asked, quick to notice. "Does that still bother you?"

"No. It's not the house."

"Maybe it is that today is the last performance of the ballet, and they are leaving in the morning."

She stared at him, amazed at his perception.

He grinned. "I have tickets for tonight's performance, and afterward we are giving a party for all your friends."

"A party here? Oh, Joe!" She flung herself at him, suddenly elated. "But everyone will have to sit on the floor, because there aren't any chairs, and what will the neighbors think! A whole ballet company! And on our very first day!"

Joe smiled mischievously. "It will be quite bohemian, my love. And we will make a scandal. But you've no qualms about that, have you? It will not be our first, or our last, I trust."

All afternoon the refreshments came—a case of champagne and two dozen bottles of wine, little sandwiches and petit fours, oysters and shrimp, and a nougat piece. And when the last curtain call was over, they all arrived, some with their gentlemen, whom they must leave behind when the train pulled out in the morning, some still with dancing tights beneath their cloaks and stage paint on their faces.

There had never been a party like it. For all it was the first night in months they had not had to face a rehearsal the next day, and though they had been dancing all evening, the bare, uncarpeted floors intrigued them. They danced through the parlors and the dining room, and even upstairs, in and out of the bedrooms. Now and then one of those bedroom doors would slam shut, and Lily, hearing it over the din, would say to Joe, "Thank heaven we hung curtains up there, at least!"

Downstairs there was nothing to block the view of peculiar people sitting Indian-style on the floor with bottles propped on their laps and others dancing above them. Someone had brought a guitar and a drum, and before long they struck up a caleinda.

"Dance, Lily!" came the cry.

She felt the beat in her blood, but she hesitated and looked at Joe. Was *this* public dancing, the kind of thing he wanted her never to do? But he called to her, "Dance with me, Lily!" And she was carried away into the ecstasy of the music.

How long it had been since she had danced with Joe Beau Clair! Not since the night of Carnival, when she had ridden away from him—forever, she had thought. How much had changed since then—she more than anything! She was no longer a girl, but a woman; and her vision, once bounded by the lavender joining of sky and sea beyond Martinique, had not stretched wide. And she watched his eyes as he danced with her and thought that he approved the difference. What a life they would have together, she and her Joe!

Then, because she was generous, she allowed others to share him, and they danced with him one after another, presenting themselves to him without invitation. Joe loved it all, admiring each one in a friendly way that Lily did not mind, and all the girls adored him. He was a rare being, this man with the compelling blue eyes, who danced on and on, unafraid to feel the music and explore it. Something about his mien seemed to say that he approached all of life with the same fearless enthusiasm.

They understood Lily better now, too. He was a man who had been worth waiting for. How lucky she was, they thought. They looked at the house and the big new bed and told her with sighs of envy how fortunate she was to be sharing both with Joe. "For us it will only be drafty rehearsal halls that always smell of gas. But we will think of you here with all the magnolias and him."

The sun was up before most of them left, having drunk

café noir from the new china and consumed an impromptu breakfast of waffles from the pristine plates.

The place was littered with bottles and dishes and the butts of cigarettes. Lily, disheveled from the dancing, surveyed the mess, arms akimbo. "Perhaps we had better find all the silver and count it, Joe. I am not too certain about some of those gentlemen."

"If it's gone, my dear, then it's too late to count it. Come along. The party isn't done."

"It isn't? Everyone's gone."

"*We* are not gone." He lifted her suddenly in his arms and carried her upstairs. He tossed her lightly onto the big bed. "Take off all your clothes, Lily Beau Clair, every stitch. We have christened the house properly, but not the bed."

He went out, and she struggled with the fastening of her silk gown, tore open the laces of her chemise. It would not do for him to return and not find her ready. She started to crawl naked beneath the sheet, but then she felt the warm morning breeze on her skin, and opening the shutters to the courtyard, she unfastened her hair and lay boldly uncovered for him to see.

He caught his breath at the golden sunlight on her white skin, at the round breasts trembling from the shadowed rivers of her tresses. He stripped himself and sat beside her while she marveled at the promise of his strong thighs. "Thank goodness I've found one bottle of champagne left," he said, and popped the cork.

He poured two glasses and proposed a toast. "To this bed. To all the love we shall know together here." The glasses clinked, and before she had even time to set hers aside, he was kissing her, and as he pinned her against the pillows, it spilled and beads of champagne stood in the soft brown curls of his chest.

Afterward she slept on and on, aware of his arms about her, aware of the sweet heat of the day, of mockingbirds singing in the courtyard and the scent of flowers drifting in. "I shall be here forever with him and all the magnolias," she thought, awash in the earthly paradise of her longings.

But Joe would not stay in New Orleans forever. The thought intruded and would not be turned away. It was an idea she had pushed back as long as possible. Joe would go again, and there would be nothing to do but sit and wait.

She put on a robe and cleaned up the house. Then she bathed, and dressing in crisp gingham with fresh pink ribbons in her hair, she looked as innocent and appealing as a little girl. He opened his eyes and smiled at her as she brought him coffee on a tray. "Oh, Lily, there will never be a match for you anywhere!"

"Then you must keep me with you always."

"Always. Of course. What is on your mind? I can tell by that look of yours."

"When you leave New Orleans, may I come with you on the *Sea Bird*?"

"What!" He sat up, fully awake now, though he had not yet sipped his coffee.

"I want to come with you, Joe. Please! I don't get seasick. You said you would keep me with you always."

He ran his hand over his cinnamon hair and stared at her, perplexed. "But, Lily . . . you are a woman! A man may keep a woman always, but that cannot mean all the time. Do you see the difference? Men and women are meant to do different things in life. I shouldn't think I would have to explain it."

"Most women have children. That is what they are meant to do. It is what I once thought I was meant for, too. But we shall not have children, shall we, Joe?" The golden lights faded as she fought not to cry. He pulled her to him gently, laid her head against his shoulder.

Children! It was a matter he had not given thought to, but she was right. Neither of them would want to have children who could have no name. He felt her slender body shake with sobs, and he felt an utter lout. He had been so happy with her that he had never considered what it would mean to her not to have this fulfillment so necessary to a woman. Had he not sinned enough in taking her from his brother? He scowled, displeased with himself, but now she raised her face to him, sensing his mood.

"I am not complaining, Joe. Oh, I complained bitterly to Edmond when he wouldn't let me have a baby until Acelie's debts were paid. But then I didn't have love. It will be enough to be with you, and what Edmond didn't tell me about preventing babies, Susan has. Any method you choose will suit me. I am willing to pay the price."

"My angel," he murmured, and covered her cheeks and lips with grateful kisses.

"But, Joe . . . you mustn't expect me to be like other women, then. I'll want to share your life with you, all of it. It was you who made me feel how big and exciting the world could be, you who made me dissatisfied on Martinique. Say you will take me with you, Joe!"

"I will take you, Lily," he promised, amazed at himself. Strangely, the idea of her sharing his cabin as the *Sea Bird* frothed across the seas filled him only with delight. Oh, how he loved her, as he had never expected to love a woman, and part of the reason was this disability of hers to stay where she belonged, this compulsion to go chasing after what she wanted.

"It's a bargain, then," she said, and gave him her wonderful smile.

12

He began at once to keep his agreement to share his life with her. He took her with him on his rambles about the docks and shipyards, showed her the new designs under consideration for the clippers. She listened to everything he had to say and asked questions. Never once did she protest that it was too much for her to understand. Being her teacher gave him a new feeling of importance, and he began to enjoy her in ways he had not known a woman could be enjoyed.

"I am off to play faro," he told her one night. "I suppose you don't want to come *there*." It was odd how he did not want to be parted from her, even for the most manly of pursuits.

"I should find it exciting," she answered. "Are women allowed in a faro club?"

"A few come to supper, but I've never seen any in the gaming rooms. Do you want to find out?"

"Why not?" she answered. She was a game one, his Lily, he thought, and he went off whistling to make his toilette.

The supper room of the faro club was elegant, deeply carpeted in velvet, replete with gilded mirrors, mantels of Vermont marble, and a finely frescoed ceiling. Lily made quite a stir in her Empire tea gown of ruby plush with a rose-cut diamond brooch, a gift from Joe, pinned at the center of her bodice. They ordered mock-turtle soup, broiled rockfish with Hollandaise sauce, cauliflower baked with cheese, a good Madiera, and vanilla meringues for dessert. There was no charge for any of it, since the management expected to make its profit at the gaming tables.

"The butler will not admit anyone who is not a regular," Joe explained. "Nobody can play here who cannot lose with ease. Men who go broke cause too much trouble."

"Are you that rich, Joe?"

"No. I couldn't afford to lose like most of these gentlemen. But I am a skillful player."

"Well, then. Am I to see you play?"

"That is what we came for."

He rose deliberately and ushered her into the gaming room. Something of a gasp went up, but nobody said anything. He had made the move too boldly, with too much self-assurance. Nobody wanted to challenge him on the score. She must be someone of importance for him to bring her here, and she had sailed in beside him as if the idea of expulsion had never occurred to her.

The haze of cigar smoke stung Lily's eyes as she looked about. At one side of the room was a sideboard supplied with liquor, and in the center of the room was the faro table, which resembled an ordinary dining table with rounded corners. The thirteen suit cards of a whist deck were laid upon its tight green cloth, and at the head of the table the dealer sat with an open-faced silver box.

"The box contains a full deck," Joe explained. "And the dealer will pull out the cards one by one. The first wins, the second loses, and the third wins, and so on. You can bet on any card to win by putting money on a card on the table."

She kept her face calm while he bought five hundred dollars in checks, though the amount astonished her. He bet on the queen in her honor and won twenty-five dollars and winked at her. "What next, Lily?"

The bright blue check Joe collected from the dealer gave Lily a little thrill. Twenty-five dollars, as easy as that. She once would have worked nearly two weeks for as much. But gambling wasn't new to her. She had seen many a crooked round of keno in her days at the French Pigeon, and the game of craps had been named for a French Quarter street. It was easier to lose than to win—or wasn't it, if you were Joe?

"Bucking the tiger." That was what she had heard playing faro called. And she had heard that tricky riverboat gamblers lost fortunes to "the tiger" when they were ashore. She smiled innocently and suggested a red five-dollar check on the eight.

"Oh, that's not enough to have any fun. Let's bet fifty." She grasped his arm in dismay as the eight fell into the losing pile.

Joe only grinned. "Shall we stick with eight, Lily?"

"I don't want to pick any more. I haven't the touch," she murmured. Suddenly she hated the place and wanted to go home, but she had not the nerve to tell him. She had asked to share his life, and he was allowing it. Gambling was a part of him, she saw. It was as natural for him to play faro as it was to invest in the Panama Canal or in a ship to break records on the Australian grain runs. Danger and imagination—he needed those elements in everything, she thought, remembering the way in which he had chosen to help Acelie, not by a loan of money, but by risking a ship to collect bananas at Grand Anse.

Danger—he would find no lack of that in his relationship with her, she thought, wondering if he were enjoying his audacity in bringing her here. She did not like the secret looks the men gave her. Would there be trouble, even in this swank place? Had Joe been right, that "always" shouldn't mean all the time?

He was beginning to bet more inventively now. Twenty-five dollars for an ace to follow a jack. Fifty said the second queen to show would be the queen of diamonds. And he was betting not only with the bank but with others at the table. Her stomach tightened as he bought another five hundred dollars' worth of checks.

But he was winning. How did he manage it? She herself could hardly keep the bets straight; she hardly knew which cards to cheer as they appeared in the silver box. The game had become lively. Everyone was drinking heavily, as bourbon, gin, and brandy moved from the sideboard to the table in tumblers of pressed glass. And Joe kept winning and winning.

Suddenly, across the table a man stood up, his pile of checks gone. He tossed a last purple hundred-dollar check in Joe's direction and bellowed, "You are cheating, sir, to have that woman here. She is a distraction. Remove her at once!"

A general commotion erupted, agreement and disagreement, champions for Lily, defenders of male privacy. "Please, Joe, I am ready to go!" she cried. But it wasn't that easy.

"If she goes, he will go with her, and so will all his winnings," someone pointed out.

"Sit down and play, Monsieur Beau Clair!" Hands reached for him and shoved him down in the rod-back Windsor chair. Joe laid about him with a pair of steely fists, and one customer stumbled back and another fell beneath the table.

"I shall decide for myself when I want to stay and when I want to go!" he shouted. His eyes shot blue smoke, his lip quivered with menace, and Lily shivered. So this was how he was when he was angry!

"Please, Joe, let's go," she said, putting a hand on his arm.

He shook her off as roughly as though she had been one of the men. "I have decided to stay, Lily. Sit down."

"A good decision, sir. It would be a shame to lose the company of your lovely lady."

The room grew suddenly quiet, and there was no more discussion about whether Lily should stay. No more hands reached for Joe, as if a final authority had decreed it. And indeed that voice had been chilling. "How pleasant to see you again, Madame Beau Clair," said Jim Frey. He was florid with drink, and he seemed to be searching her face—for the scar, she thought, hidden behind the fringe.

"The new hair style is becoming," he told her after a moment. "And this is your husband, the swordsman whom we have all heard so much about. Introduce us, please."

She gritted her teeth and tried not to glare at Jim Frey. It would not do for Joe to see that she wanted to kill him. Frey did not seem angry with her. On the contrary, he was truly pleased to see her. He had conquered her, and the sight gave him satisfaction. She made the introduction, trying not to notice Joe's discomfort at the remark about his swordsmanship.

But Jim Frey noticed and was quick to probe deeper. "Have you dueled often, sir?"

"I try never to."

"But an expert like you can't avoid challenges. How many have you killed?"

"Three," said Joe, and fixed Jim Frey with a cold stare. Lily could have fainted. She had not known.

"Ah, when one has such a beautiful wife to defend! But she tells me she does not like to have men kill for her. I suppose it's because three is plenty to die over one woman."

"It was not over a woman," said Joe shortly. "Would you care to play a hand with me?"

Lily tugged urgently at his arm. "Joe. I don't feel well. The commotion has upset me."

"We will go when I am ready," he said, scarcely looking at her. In this world of men, he could hardly hear her. She saw that he had decided to prove himself against Jim Frey, but at least he had chosen only cards. Cards would be bad enough, she thought. "Joe, please!" But he was already placing bets.

"Shall we bet that two sevens will come one after the other?"

"A long shot, sir. Five hundred dollars says they won't."

"Done," said Joe. It seemed impossible, but he won. And after that, he won again. Jim Frey did not seem disconcerted.

"Really wise of you to forgo dueling," he went on conversationally. "So many of these young Creoles, you know, are all for honor. And sometimes even perfection isn't enough. You remember, Lily, that fencing master in the Quarter who was knifed a time ago."

So, he was telling her he was responsible for that, too! As if she had not known! "I don't remember it, monsieur. But I hope the police will find whoever is responsible. Finding murderers is your job, is it not?"

"I'm doing my best. It's not easy sometimes." And he chuckled with appreciation at her gibe. "I did think you knew him, though. Ah . . . there are four cards left. Shall we bet on the exact order they'll appear?"

"Jack, deuce, ten, king," said Joe, and put down ten purple hundred-dollar checks.

"No, no. Ten, king, jack, deuce," guessed Frey. She prayed that neither would be right, but Frey was, and he collected Joe's thousand dollars.

The hours wore on. Everybody began to stop playing to watch Joe and Jim Frey. They sat across from each other, jaws tight, and there was no more conversation. Like Joe, Jim Frey seemed to have forgotten Lily, seemed to have forgotten that she was the reason he had gotten into this game in the first place.

Jim Frey was confident and skilled, but Joe was more so. It was three in the morning when Frey folded. Almost nobody was there to see his defeat, and Lily was grateful for that at least. Even the attendant was dozing, his head against a roulette table.

"Shall I have your draft this afternoon?" Joe asked.

The commissioner shrugged. "You have the right. But you're a sporting man. I've lost a great deal. Would you care for another wager?"

"Perhaps. If it's amusing."

"Oh, I think you would find it so. I have a boat. And I understand you are a seagoing man. Shall we see how well you fare on the river? Double the amount I owe you—my boat against any boat you choose."

"New Orleans to Cairo?"

"Very well. Next week? We'll arrange the details later."

Home at last. The little Louis heels of her evening slippers clattered over the still-uncarpeted floor as she made for the bedroom. While Joe was tending to the horse and carriage, she undressed and tumbled into bed. She had put on a nightdress of blue silk that Joe especially liked, but she wasn't thinking of sex. The blue had only been the top garment in the drawer, and more than anything Lily wanted to pull the covers over her head and forget the awful face of Jim Frey, as muddy and treacherous as the Mississippi River bottom.

A chill shook her as she relaxed the self-control she had exercised all evening. Jim Frey! But he was finished with her. There was no reason to be frightened. Jim Frey had nothing against Joe. Or had had nothing against him until Joe had beaten him so badly. Suddenly she was furious, and she realized with surprise that it was Joe at whom she was angry.

Joe, and not Jim Frey! Joe picked that moment to come into the room, and uncovering her as she lay facedown, he caressed the small of her back. She responded, but not the way he had expected. She sat up, clutching the covers around her. "None of that tonight, Joe Beau Clair!"

He grinned at her feminine whim and stripped away his coat and his cambric shirt. "Why not? You can't expect me to sleep beside you without it! It would drive me mad, and you too, since I shall make you want it quick enough. I always do."

"Not tonight! Why didn't you come away when I asked you to? Why did you play cards with Jim Frey? Do you know what he is?"

"A very crooked policeman," said Joe, absorbed in removing his stockings. "I'm surprised you know him, and socially, too, it seems." His voice was hard with warning.

"I . . . met him at Susan's wedding. I had to waltz with him, and he trod clumsily on my toes."

"Henry Wickersham's wedding. Well, Henry should be above associating with his ilk, but I suppose it's to be expected. Henry's no paragon of honor himself. But are your toes all Jim Frey trod on, Lily? You must tell me the truth."

She drew a deep, shuddering breath. "That is all, Joe. But I don't like him. Why didn't you come away?"

"Because I would have seemed a coward. He tried to bother you, and you told him how dangerous I was. That much is clear. So it was necessary at least to trounce him at faro. Did you boast of me to every man in New Orleans, Lily? Shall I have many others?"

"Oh, did you have to beat him so badly?" she cried.

"Yes. That was necessary too. I showed him I was not to be taken lightly."

"Then why didn't you take his draft and put an end to it?"

"Because that would have been cowardly, too. A man must always grant another a return match if it is asked. And he would not have asked if he had twenty-five thousand dollars."

Her eyes grew wide. "Twenty-five thousand dollars! Is that how much . . . ? Joe, it will be twice that now! Jim Frey would kill for less!"

"Frey expects to beat me in the race, Lily. He will not send his henchmen after me."

"And will he beat you?" she asked breathlessly.

Joe smiled. "Who's to say? He has a very fast boat."

"And if you win . . ."

"We will worry about that when the time comes. Frey's methods may do for a fencing master, but not for the likes of me. Did the fencing master die because of you, Lily?"

"He wasn't in love with me," she evaded. "He was . . . a friend of Susan's. But you are like him, Joe. You and your honor! Jim Frey has nothing of honor."

"True. But I am better than he. Come and find out, you mix!" He dived skillfully beneath the mosquito netting, reached for her bodice, and jerked at its strings.

She clutched at her gown as her white breasts tumbled out and his lips claimed his prize. "Men and their honor! It doesn't make sense!"

"It's not supposed to, to you," he murmured. "You are a woman, and you are supposed to understand *this* better."

She groaned in arousal, still fighting his hands, and she managed one more question. "Joe, the three you killed . . . ?"

"Pirates. Once off Africa. Twice in the China Seas."

And then, as he had promised, he drove her mad with desire. She clung to him helplessly, begging his entry to her body, and she lost her train of thought in a storm of rapture.

13

The morning light seemed to glare with the harshness of reality. She felt cold without Joe's heat beside her. She could think clearly now. Joe would not be in this fix if not for her. It would not have happened if she had not mixed where she should not. She should not have gone to the faro club, and then Frey would never have known Joe. Joe had been right, when he had said that some things were only for men. He came in at noon, and she told him her decision.

"Do you mean you won't go to the shipyard with me anymore?"

"No, I won't."

"And you won't be coming with me when I sail?"

"No."

"All because of this Frey matter! Dammit, Lily, I have dealt with such things before!"

"But not encumbered by a woman. Who knows what trouble I might lead you to."

"You have led me to trouble enough already!" he cried. "Haven't I betrayed my brother because of you? But there are things more important to me than staying out of trouble, Lily. You *are* my trouble. My torment and my joy. I, at least, am willing to keep our bargain. Come with me."

But she would not be moved. "What will you do with your life, Lily?" he asked. "Shall I find you an entreé to fine society and shall you give tea parties and make shellwork baskets?"

"I would always be an imposter in society, even if it suited me. But I will be your mistress always and live only for love."

He went out without touching the sponge cake she had made for his dessert. When he came back, it was past midnight, and she whiffed the aroma of a delicate perfume beneath the liquor of his breath. "Where have you been, Joe? I was lonely."

"To a business dinner, Lily. It wouldn't have interested you. A matter for me, you would say."

"But some lady was there. She had fine taste in cologne."

"Jenny Van Artsdalen. She was my dinner partner. It could hardly be helped, since the affair was at her father's house. Come with me next time, if you're jealous."

"As your wife?"

"Of course."

"Jenny's father won't be as interested in doing business with you if you confront him suddenly with a wife."

"I don't care a fig!"

"I will stay in the background and give you less problems."

"Then don't complain about Jenny's cologne." He muttered a curse and fell into bed. For the first night since he had come to New Orleans, he did not make love to her. She clutched her pillow tightly to stop herself from reaching out to him with her longing, and she asked herself why, why was he treating her so, just when she was being noble!

She had determined to stay out of his affairs, but it was a resolve she could not keep long. The wheels were already moving, and she could not help it that she was home when Jim Frey came to call. She could not help it that her new little Irish maid was still untrained.

"There is a gentleman, madame. A Mr. Frey."

She jumped up from the velvet cushion of a violet ebony chair. "But he will be wanting monsieur, and he is not here. Send him away, Margaret!"

"But he says since monsieur is not at home, he wishes to see you."

"Tell him I am not at home either."

"Madame, I have already . . ." She was frightened, this sixth of ten children of a millhand. She had been so proud of her crisp uniform and her wages, and now she had made a mistake.

But Margaret was not half so frightened as Lily when the dark face of Jim Frey appeared in the archway of the parlor.

She was alone with him for the first time since the night she had leaped from his bed into the river. He crossed his burly arms over the slope of his chest, and the muscles of his thick neck twitched, as if betraying an emotion that would soon burst him loose from the confines of his collar. His eyes fastened again on the fringe over her forehead. He wanted to see the scar, and it was almost more than he could manage not to push back her hair to see it.

Lily backed against the fireplace. Behind her skirts she took up a fire iron. If he tried to look, it would be the last thing he saw, at least for a while. She was too furious to care that an unconscious Jim Frey in the parlor would be difficult to explain to Joe. But Frey did not take the few steps across the room that would have earned him the blow.

"I've come to ask a favor, Lily."

"I'm not in the habit of granting favors, monsieur!"

A laugh bellowed up, shook his great chest. It was not without true humor. The joke had been on him that night, and now that he had evened things, he could laugh at himself. "So I found out. And the lesson cost me three hundred dollars."

"So that is how much you paid for the privilege of abducting me and chloroforming me."

"I hope you are flattered. But there is much more at stake now. And a night, even with you, is not worth fifty thousand dollars."

"Fifty thousand dollars is a matter between you and my husband."

He smiled at her, a long, slow smile that spread like a spill of raw, black molasses up into the turn of his mustache. His lips parted, showing a golden tooth, canted in his lower jaw like a glittering little tombstone. Etienne's tombstone—and how many others'? How many others had he been responsible for?

A tremor went through her as though someone had stepped on *her* grave, and her gold-filigreed butterfly earrings shook, giving away her agitation.

"Has he seen it yet?" asked Jim Frey.

Had Joe seen the scar? That was what he meant, of course. And he knew the answer. Joe had not seen the scar, or else she had managed to explain it somehow. Otherwise there would have been trouble.

"You do not want him to know, Lily."

"Perhaps I do! He would see you dead!"

"Or I him. You don't want to take the chance, or you'd have told him already. I am always being amazed at finding that everything you say is the truth. Were you honest, too, when you said you hated bloodshed? Fifty thousand dollars is a matter between you and me, or someone's blood will flow. It won't be mine, I'll wager!"

"Please don't make any more bets, sir. You have lost enough already."

"But it's hard to cheat at faro. Are you willing to wager that I won't turn and fire at nine paces instead of ten? Who would dare to testify that your husband had been shot in the back. Or there might be some distraction at the crucial moment. It's you who'll be gambling if you don't deal with me, Lily, and the odds are not very good, once your Joe learns about you and me."

She knew he had her beaten, and an awful calm came over her. "What do you want me to do?" she said.

"All you need to do is find a way to make him lose the race." He had a pleased grin of triumph now. "Maybe you can ax a blade or two of the paddle wheel when he puts ashore to fuel. Whatever, it's up to you."

"But I'm not going on the race."

"Yes, you are. Otherwise I'll see that he knows about that decoration of yours. Your husband will ship a fighting crew, and he'll keep watch. But he'll not be watching you, lass. Is it agreed, then? I am in a hurry. I'm afraid I cannot stay to tea."

"Indeed you can't." She rang a bell for the maid to show him out, and after he had safely gone, she sent a porcelain posy holder crashing after him.

Fifty thousand dollars! Could Joe lose that much?

"Of course not," he told her when she asked. "But don't worry. I have acquired a very fine boat, one of Van Artsdalen's, and I'm having it stripped of everything extra. All the upper parts that catch the wind are being taken down, and I've arranged with coalyards to have flatboats waiting to be taken in tow."

"You mean you're not going to stop for fuel, Joe?"

"No. Isn't that clever?"

"Does Jim Frey know that trick, too?"

"Well, I hope not. There is betting all up the river, and I'm told the odds are in my favor. Do you want to come along and see me win?"

If only she could obliterate that awful, telltale scar! She pushed back the fringe and stared at it in the mirror, tried ineffectually to cover it with rice powder, then, in a frenzy, beat at it with her hands. The hysteria passed finally, and she was only frightened, feeling herself a viper as she lay in bed at night with Joe. How could she sabotage the boat if he didn't stop? And if she did manage, and he caught her, would he love her still? Would he think her his joy as well as his torment? And she hadn't known he couldn't afford to lose!

And then she would think that none of it would have happened if she had not run away from Martinique. Just as he would not have been bitten by the fer-de-lance in the hurricane house if she had not been playing at being Mimi. She had caused him such harm, when she wanted just the opposite. Would he survive this as he had survived the snake? Would it have been better for Joe if he had not found her? And a new wildness came into the way she loved him. She threw her soul into each night as though it might be the last, knowing that soon, one way or the other, she would lose him.

She bought a new gable hat and an elegant serge dress to wear on the trip. She might at least make Joe proud of her as she tripped up the gangplank in view of the crowds that had gathered to watch the race begin. She caught a glimpse of Jim Frey, a dark contrast to his lacy white boat, pretty as the hyacinths that floated in the bayous of the Swamp.

The boat was too pretty, she thought. Jim Frey had not taken down any of its ornamentation to make it go faster, and it sat lower in the chocolate water than Joe's boat. Jim Frey had a crowd of partiers with him, and he was carrying food and liquor and a fiddle player. Jim Frey did not expect to have to try to win.

The starting pistol cracked. Frey tipped his homburg to her as the boats began to move. An hour out, and Joe exulted, "By God, Lily, it is as easy as plucking a dead chicken! What a fool that Frey, with all his extra weight. I do believe he thinks I am afraid to beat him."

By the time they took the first barges in tow, they were ten minutes ahead. Now and then they lost sight of Frey's boat altogether as they rounded a bend in the great river. All along the shore, at every village, people waved and cheered, and even little boys fishing under the willows called encouragement. Joe's face shone with joy, and the boat's whistle gave forth long blasts of satisfaction.

The sun drifted down against the river, and cool water odors rose into the twilight. In the distance they could see the lights of Jim Frey's boat and hear the sounds of music and laughter. Frey had stopped for fuel, and Joe's boat had increased its lead. On Joe's boat it was quiet. There was only the splash and purl of water, the crunch of shovels against coal. She stood on the deck, her domed parasol folded now, and watched the moonlight turn the foam of the paddle wheel to a dazzling circle of fire. Joe came up and stood beside her, his shirt unbuttoned and rolled to his elbows, his face smeared with coal dust.

"How beautiful you look there, Lily. It reminds me of some other time, but I can't think when."

"The night you swam away from me to your ship, from the beach at Grande Anse," she supplied. He had looked the same way then, stripped half-naked, every inch of him charged with vitality, with the triumph of successful adventure.

"Yes, I suppose that's it. But tonight I shall not swim away from you. Go and make ready for me."

She went into the bedroom he had given her, changed into a sheer white nightgown with pink ribbons, and lay on the bed in the river breeze. She did not really like night on the river. It reminded her of Jim Frey, and she could not forget that he was on this river tonight, as he had been on the night she had jumped. Then he had nearly cost her her life; now he might cost her Joe's. If she could not think of some way to make Joe lose. She heard his footsteps on the gray deck planking, and then he was inside, dripping water onto the rose-patterned carpet.

"Have you been for a swim?"

"Only a dunking. A few buckets of the river over my head to make me fresh for you."

"Van Artsdalen may mind the water marks on his carpet. Take care!"

"He won't notice, Lily. He'll be too busy being richer than he is now. He's bet a wad on me. He can buy a new steamboat or two or three."

"If you lost, he'd be furious!" she said, scenting new peril.

"No doubt. But, Lily, I am winning!" He dropped his wet trousers carelessly onto the rug and threw himself blithely atop her.

She loved him ravenously, trying to absorb him into her with every pore of her body. When would she ever know him again like this? So charged with the glory and satisfaction of manhood, its essence seeming to tingle even in his arms and in his fingertips as they caressed her. She fought to make the moment last, and the cry she gave was as much of defeat that it was finished as of esctasy at fulfillment. From the crown of passion she slid into a dark oblivion, as though, if she could have love no longer, she would have nothing at all.

But even the oblivion did not last. Faces drifted into it. Jim Frey with his awful smile. Madame Drapeaux. Hetty and her long finger pointing. And Joe—Joe lying dead beneath the oaks.

And she turned him over and saw the spread of blood at the back of his coat.

A noise awakened her. She was alone in bed, and beyond the railing there were lanterns. They were taking on more barges of coal. If only Joe were not so clever. If only he would stop just once.

But suddenly she understood what she had to do. She put on a dressing gown and went down into the gallery, acquiring a butcher knife without putting on a light. Barefoot, she went onto the deck, and hanging over the stern railing, she cut the tow lines apart. Shouts of disbelief came to her ears as she backed into the shadows. The barges parted company with the boat, carrying the stoking crew with them.

She could not believe it had been so simple.

The mishap cost them over an hour. Jim Frey's boat won handily, and Joe was moody on the trip home.

"How will you pay the money?" she dared to ask.

"Don't worry. I'll find a way." But his confidence in himself was damaged. "I don't understand it. The line was cut, Lily. It was someone on my boat. Someone was working for Frey. That was why he was so cocky. But they were all men I trusted. I don't know where I went wrong."

She could have told him where. It had been the night he had danced with a coaling girl named Mimi. But she kept still and wondered what would happen next.

14

"Dearest Lily, I'm home!" The visiting card was waiting for her in the silver dish in the hallway when they returned to New Orleans. She ran her hand over the finely engraved letters that read "Mrs. Henry Wickersham," and her heart lifted.

She rushed to the new telephone Joe had just had installed and asked Central to put her through to the Wickersham residence. Less than an hour later Susan pranced up in her shiny two-seater.

"This is swank!" she cried as they embraced. "I thought I'd got the wrong address! But how . . . ? Did Joe . . . ?"

Lily nodded, blushing happily. "He came back! And, oh, Susan, it has been worth every day of waiting! And you . . . you look wonderful!"

"Don't I, though!" She twirled for Lily to admire her new hopsack skirt and her frilled blouse.

"I've never seen an outfit like that!" Lily marveled.

"Of course not. The skirt came from London, where women are all clamoring for more freedom, and the blouse is from Paris. The sleeves are called gigots, but in England they already call them 'leg of mutton.' That is like the British, don't you think? Utterly unromantic. They say such clothes will be all the rage here before long."

"I should like my dressmaker to copy the skirt. It must be wonderful to go without any bustle. But what else has happened? More is different about you than your clothes. Would you like coffee?"

"Orange-flower fizz, if you've got it. And pralines, Lily. Have you any made with cream and dates? I've craved those for months. It's good to be home."

When the refreshments had been brought, they curled up on a lyre couch like two schoolgirls sharing confidences. "What would your little maid think, Lily, if she knew that six months ago neither of us was any better off than she?" said Susan with a giggle.

"She reminds me of you sometimes—with her Irish singing. Perhaps that's why I keep her. She's very clumsy."

Susan's blue eyes widened, and she put a hand on Lily's arm. "I haven't told you the most important thing of all. Singing! I am to sing in two weeks at the French Opera."

"Oh, Susan! You shall have your dream!"

"It's only the beginning! And you must be there, Lily, no matter what!"

"I will!" Lily promised.

"It could never have happened without you," Susan said, suddenly serious.

"Without *me*? You did it all yourself."

"I did those things that had to be done, the things you would never have done if you'd been me. But I'll never forget, Lily, how you shared the clothes you took from Madame Drapeaux's, and how you taught me French and manners, and most of all how you went along about Henry."

Going along about Henry! That had been a terrible mistake. It had been through Henry that Jim Frey had found her again. The very thought made her pale.

"Lily? What's wrong?"

She shook her head and tried to smile. "Nothing. Do you know I still have our emergency fund in a jar in a cabinet? I don't feel safe without it there."

"Ha! We must go and put it in the poor box. We'll never need that again. Lily, you look ill. Has Joe got you pregnant?"

"No . . . it's that I haven't told you something important. And I don't want to when you're so happy. Etienne is dead."

"Dead! How could that be? Did he catch a fever?"

"He was killed, a friend of his told me."

"Oh, come, Lily. No one would fight Etienne. He was too sharp to tamper with."

"No *one*, maybe. But three or four. And his poor hand was injured, too, a thing you didn't seem to care about when I tried to tell you."

"On my wedding day, you told me!"

"Yes, on your wedding day. Even so, you might have cared. He was crazy with grief over that or he'd never have got hurt in the first place."

"Wait a minute. Are you blaming me? It was you who took him on that wild-goose chase to the Swamp!"

Lily went over to the window, smelling the newness of the damask curtains as she looked out at the gardens of marigolds and moss rose.

"Oh, I didn't mean . . . Yes I did, too. I think we're both to blame. We used him, you and I. But mostly it was my fault. It was because he was my protector he was killed."

"Huh! You aren't thinking straight at all, sis!" Lily turned to see Susan, hands on her elegant hips. "It's a man's world, and they make the rules. How else should we have got along? And Etienne was one of them, pleasing though he was, and he took his use of *me* when he liked. It's the ones that wielded the knives that are to blame. And the one that paid them, for I imagine it was like that. It sounds like the work of Jim Frey. Was it?"

Lily hesitated, but there was no use trying to fool Susan. "Yes, it was Jim Frey."

"He found you!" Susan whispered, her eyes gleaming with anger. She got up and purposefully closed the heavy oak doors to the parlor. "What happened when he found you? Did he make good the bargain he made for you with Madame Drapeaux?"

"No. Frey is vile, but he's not a rapist. It was a matter of his pride, I suppose. He swore he'd leave his mark on me."

"His mark?" Susan frowned, puzzled.

"He had Etienne murdered to clear the way, and then . . ." Lily lifted her fringe, and Susan gasped as she saw the scar.

"He did that? The beast! I'd like to mark *him*!"

"Don't talk so. It's over, and I don't have to be afraid of him anymore. It's all I want. That and for Joe not to discover it."

"He's bound to look beneath that fringe someday!"

"I pray that when he does he'll believe it was the result of an accident—a fall while carrying glass. And I've already caused Joe to lose fifty thousand dollars to Frey in a boat race. Frey said he'd tell if I didn't make Joe lose."

"Fifty thousand! A fortune! But how did Frey find you?"

"I don't know," Lily murmured. "He did, that's all." She had hoped Susan wouldn't ask.

"Was it Henry?" said Susan, her fingers closing over the scrolled arms of her rosewood chair.

"Yes, if you insist on knowing. It was at the wedding. Frey was there, and Henry brought us together to waltz. Henry's a coward, Susan. I rejected him, as I did Frey, but Henry hadn't even the manhood to take his revenge himself."

"Now, hold on, sis! You told him you were Frey's woman! Why shouldn't he have thought you wanted to see him?"

"He knew! And he was delighted. He'd planned it all. You could see it in his eyes."

"You're guessing, Lily. You imagined it that way. Remember, it's my husband you're talking about now."

"I'm not imagining it. Oh, Susan, how can you be so blind!" Tears tumbled down Lily's cheeks as all the grief she had been holding back burst forth. She had needed comfort from her best friend, and this was what she was getting instead. Susan seemed to be on Henry's side. Was that what marriage did to a woman, even when there was no love?

"Susan, he may be your husband, but you know what he is. He is the sort of man who will drug a girl to get her friend to bed. You knew from the start. Oh, he's a monster! He is filthier than Jim Frey, though he does move in such grand company."

"Are you trying to destroy our friendship, Lily?" Susan cried. "He's the man I share a bed with. He's no saint, but he's only a man. And all of them are rotten some way!"

Lily knew she should draw back and try to soothe Susan, but she was nearly hysterical, and the truth, pent up so long, was a flood that could not be controlled. "That is how you stand to be married to him, Susan! You imagine all men are bad and he is no worse than the rest! It cannot work, because he is, he is!"

Susan's face had an awful look that Lily could not interpret. Was it simple anger? Or did she know that Lily was right? Was she already questioning the arrangement she had worked so hard to make? Susan left, and Lily feared she had lost her dearest friend.

In the days that followed, when Susan did not come to visit again, she told herself that Susan was busy rehearsing and having her gown fitted for the opera. She was lonely, because Joe was not home much, either. In unguarded moments he looked worn, but as soon as he saw her watching him, he would flash her a grin and like as not pull her down for a kiss. Rarely did his attentions end with the kiss. He would love her deeply, not with the abandon that he had before, but as though his need for her had grown, as though he sought peace in the sanctuary of her body.

He was in trouble, she thought, and sometimes after he slept, she would weep in the pillow.

"Have you found a way to pay the money, Joe?" she asked at last.

"I told you. Don't worry."

"But I'm to blame. It was because of me you gambled with Jim Frey."

"The one who cut that tow line is the one I'd like to get my hands on, Lily. Then I should have a fine revenge!"

He came in late one night, and she smelled Jenny's light, flowery perfume. "Did you go to supper again at the Van Artsdalen's?" she asked.

"No. I took Jenny to the theater."

"Oh," she said in a small voice.

He gave his trousers an exasperated kick. "I was only taking your advice."

"*My* advice!"

"Van Artsdalen may lend me the money to cover my debt if he thinks I'm interested in Jenny. At least he hasn't tried to end our business arrangement, though he lost money on the race. I could pay back everything from my part of our Australian venture."

"And Jenny? What sort of person is she?"

Spoiled, stupid, silly—those were the descriptions she wanted to hear. Anything to reassure her. Instead he said only, "She does not deserve to be used as I am using her." And Lily knew that this was another cause of his dissatisfaction.

She tried to forget all her problems on the night of Susan's first performance at the French Opera. She tried to forget that the last time she had sat beneath these chandeliers, it had been as Madame Drapeaux's companion. And here she had first seen Jim Frey, a sinister shadow behind their box. But tonight she had Joe beside her, handsome in his embroidered waistcoat, and onstage her friend was creating a tremendous success. She looked sidewise at Joe, and she was delighted to see that he was applauding heartily as the lights came on at intermission.

"She's wonderful, Lily. And you say she sang in the Vieux Carré and saved her money for lessons?"

"Yes, but you mustn't tell anyone that story. She is supposed to be from New York. Joe, who is that girl who is looking at you so?"

He glanced where she indicated, into a box nearby, and the

girl with soft auburn curls hid her blush behind her brisé fan. Joe stood and bowed. "That's Jenny. I must go and pay my respects."

She watched unhappily as Jenny Van Artsdalen greeted him with simple pleasure. She was a pretty girl, but no great beauty; and her Empire gown with its rounded yoke and sash suited her perfectly. She was not one to wear clothes with flair, but the eagerness of her smile would have melted many a man. She was in love with Joe, and if she were capable of dissembling, she did not bother.

Jenny spoke to Joe earnestly, while Lily sat stiffly, wishing he would come back. Suddenly she could not keep her eyes from the box she had occupied with Madame Drapeaux. There sat the elegant old woman in her best black silk with a necklace of shell cameo, and Lily clutched the railing, dizzy at seeing her old employer again. Before she could look away, Madame Drapeaux saw her and acknowledged her with a nod and a puzzled expression.

"She doesn't remember me! She is trying to remember where we have met! That is how insane she is!" Lily thought, and then Joe was back.

"Did you enjoy your visit?"

He gave her a grimace of a smile. "We will see how *you* enjoy yours."

"Mine?"

"She asked who you were, and being a truthful cuss, I told her."

"You didn't! Oh!"

"I did. I came right out with it. I said you were my sister-in-law. You can't imagine how delighted she was that Edmond had such a beautiful wife. She's coming to call on you tomorrow, if it's convenient."

"Oh, but it isn't!" cried Lily in horror.

He grinned maliciously. "Face up, Lily. Remember, you wanted her not to know about us."

Before she could answer, the theater lights blinked and went dark for the second half of the program. She tried to put Jenny out of her mind until finally Susan took her last curtain call in a gown of blue Genoa velvet. In the orchestra seats below the boxes, the gentlemen were on their feet, giving her an ovation, and there were baskets of roses and camellias.

Lily was in a daze as they walked out of the theater. It couldn't be that she envied Susan! Susan, who had had to marry a man like Henry to get where she wanted to be. But she sighed as they rode away into the soft night.

"What are you thinking of, Lily?"

"Of the days when I danced, I suppose. And I had applause and flowers."

"You don't miss that, do you?" He looked at her quizzically.

"Of course not. How could I when I have you? But, Joe . . . why is it that you object to my being onstage, and Henry doesn't object to Susan's doing it?"

He slid an arm around her and pulled her against him. "It's very simple, Lily. Henry is rich and likes things garish—like that house of his—and he isn't in love with Susan. She's just something to flaunt to make him feel more important. When a man loves a woman as I do you, he must keep her all to himself and know that her every passion is only for him."

"You need not worry on that score, Joe," she told him as she lifted her lips for his kiss. "You are everything to me, my entire life!"

Everything! Her entire life! How she would like to tell that to Jenny!

Jenny sat nervously in the drawing room, balancing a cup of tea on her lap. "I hope you don't mind, Madame Beau Clair, I couldn't resist coming. I hadn't known that Joe had family in New Orleans."

"I have only recently come from Martinique."

"Martinique! Oh, with its mountains and cold rivers and fine sand beaches! Joe has told me, and I hope he will take me there when . . ."

She stopped herself suddenly, her teacup clattering and the flowers on her straw hat bobbing uncertainly. *When we are married!* Even unspoken, the words were stunning. Was it the ploy of a crafty woman announcing her intentions, or only what it appeared to be, hope running far ahead of actuality?

"Miss Van Artsdalen . . . Jenny, you mustn't count on marrying Joe." The words came out sympathetically. Whichever was the case, she didn't doubt that Jenny loved Joe. How could she not feel for a woman who loved him and who was to know the exquisite pain of not having him?

"I do not count on it, of course . . . but I think it is quite possible!" Jenny's voice was determined, but her face was very red, and she didn't notice at all as Lily took her cup and put it in a place of safety on a cock-beaded pier table.

"My dear, I am sure that he finds you amusing," Lily said, feeling cruel, "but Joe . . . well, Joe is not to be tied down. When Joe wants a woman, he finds a different sort than you. He told me once no lady would ever lay claim to him."

Parts of Jenny's face had become alarmingly pale, leaving large blotches of red like strawberries floating on cream. Lily took out a gauze fan and waved it in her face.

"I love him, Madame Beau Clair. But you aren't really his sister-in-law. You love him, too. I saw the way you looked at each other at the theater."

She had guessed it. Joyfully Lily admitted the truth. "I am his sister-in-law, but my marriage to his brother is over. If you look in the bedroom, you will find Joe's things in the armoire next to mine. He loves me, Jenny, and he always will. He would have told you before now if I had allowed it."

Jenny swayed, and Lily fanned her harder, wondering if she should run to look for her smelling salts. Then Jenny spoke as if from a great distance. "At least you'll never be his wife!" The idea seemed to do her good, and she began to regain herself, reviving with a fluffing of skirts and hair like a wilted flower put into a vase of water. "It's all as I suspected," she said. "He can't marry you, can he? Because of his brother. You must give him up for his own sake, Madame Beau Clair. That is what I came to tell you."

"Give him up? Why should I?" Lily was taken aback.

"Because a man must have a family, of course. That is why every man like Joe eventually marries a woman like me."

"Joe is not interested in children," said Lily with a laugh. "Think of it—when would he have time for them? Can't you just see him with an infant on his knee!"

"I have seen him with four on his knee. How little you know him, and you his mistress. There's more to a man than what he does in bed."

Lily looked at Jenny blankly, and a quiver of fear started in her stomach. Whatever was Jenny talking about? It occurred to her for the first time that Jenny might have known Joe longer than she, on his other trips to New Orleans. And perhaps she had been in love with him even before Lily had danced with him as Mimi.

"Would you like to see what I mean, Madame Beau Clair?"

"Indeed I would."

"Then I will send you an invitation. You won't mind that most of the guests will be under four feet tall? And come as Joe's sister-in-law, please. It will save embarrassment."

"All right. If you like," Lily said.

When Jenny had gone, Lily paced the floor. What sort of disaster might this interview bring? She had expected Jenny to be crushed. And she hadn't been!

Lily felt secure in Joe's love, and yet, he was a bachelor. If any woman were clever enough . . . It amazed her how clever love made a woman. Jenny was not clever by nature, and yet she had become wily in only a few minutes. "It can't be that I'm afraid I'll lose him to that insignificant creature!" Lily thought.

But she felt on the verge of hysteria when she whiffed Jenny's perfume again that night. "Did you take Jenny to the theater?" she asked.

He kissed her gaily. "No, my love. I only went to dinner again. And Van Artsdalen has lent me ten thousand dollars to help with my debt to Jim Frey. And I'll repay him handsomely when I take his ship on the grain route. I'll have no Judas aboard then to spoil my time."

"I'm so glad, Joe!"

But she didn't know whether to be really happy. Jim Frey must be paid, of course, but she knew that Jenny had arranged the loan. Jenny knew the competition was hard, but she wasn't giving up. Lily shivered and sought the comfort of Joe's arms.

Jenny wore a dress of sprigged lawn, which made her look like a stem of the bridal wreath that grew in the luxuriant hedges of her Garden District mansion. The gingerbreaded house rose from the center of the grounds like an ornate teacake on a platter of roses, jasmine, and lantana; and all about the green expanse children ran, playing tag around the pineapple palms, live oaks, and magnolias.

"I'm delighted you could come," Jenny said to Lily, and turned a look of unfeigned adoration on Joe. "Would you care for punch?"

Joe did not have time to answer. The children saw him suddenly and came running with whoops of joy. He squatted to take them in his arms, and quickly they bowled him over in the grass, climbing over him familarly with no fear of retribution. Little boys with freckles and frayed reefer suits.

Little girls with Irish faces, standing over him, more careful not to muss their starched smocked-yoke dresses.

The Van Artsdalens' picnic for orphans!

Joe challenged the boys to a game of ball, and dropping his coat and his octagon tie on a white wrought-iron chair, he streaked off. The little girls gathered around her, looking at her clothes and smiled shyly. "Are you married to him?" one asked at last.

"No, I am his sister-in-law, Lily. And who are you?"

"I'm Mary," said the sprite. "I'd marry him myself if I could."

There was a burst of giggles. And then another said, "I'm Sarah, and I'd rather have him for a father. He brought us a baby house."

"And kitchen dolls!"

"And toy soldiers for the boys."

"Do you see him often?" Lily asked.

"Oh, yes. Every time he's in New Orleans."

It went on all afternoon—games of croquet, singsongs, trips to feed the ducks in the artificial pond. There was a huge meal of baked chicken and salads and pecan pies, and afterward an unprogrammed contest at throwing watermelon rind. To Jenny's horror, even the girls could not refrain from entering the juicy proceeding. Clothing was forgotten, and even Joe did not emerge unscathed. As Lily came toward him with a handkerchief with which to clean his shirt, he let fly a hunk that caught her hat and sent it groundward, dragging hair and pinnings as it went.

There she was, disarrayed in such fine company, and without thinking, she seized a quarter melon and charged him, skirts flying up around her calves. He stood stock-still for a moment, horrified at what he had accidentally done, and even more astonished at the consequences. As she reached him, he took a step backward and stumbled over a hummock. Lily fell on top of him, and squashing the melon between them, they rolled downhill together, Joe's arms about her and the warm male scent of him mixing with the smell of the grass. But then the ground leveled, and she had a large pink stain on her bosom and a shoe missing. Joe was breathless with laughter.

"Oh, Joe, we have made a scandal!"

"Of course. Making scandals is the thing you do best. Come, let's make another." And there in the sweet grass he owned her with a kiss.

"Oh, Jenny, you asked me here today to show me something, and instead I've shown you what you did not bargain to see!" she thought. But that night she could not sleep, and she could only hope that Jenny had been as disconcerted by this kiss as she had been by the sight of Joe happy and boyish with the children.

"Joe, are you asleep?" she whispered.

"No."

"I didn't know you loved children so." She rested her cheek on his naked chest, her fingers toying lovingly with the springy curls above its hardness.

"Oh, Lily," he sighed in exasperation.

"What is it? What have I done?"

"It's not anything you've done. It's what I know you're thinking. You're wishing to give me a baby."

"Yes." She sat up in bed and saw his eyes take in the swing of her breasts in the low bodice of her gown. "But I can't, can I? Though everything in nature demands I do. You need children, Joe."

"You might go back and have a child with Edmond, Lily. He needs children more than I. He needs a son to continue his line . . . and yours at Acelie."

"Oh, no, I wouldn't!"

"You are still willing to give that up altogether to stay with me?"

"Oh, yes!"

"Then if you have no doubts, why should I? Children are more important to a woman than to a man. Be quiet now and go to sleep, or I will love you again to keep you still."

"Joe . . ." He did not wait to hear what she had to say, but carried out his threat immediately, jerking her gown above her hips. She tried to resist, but no lock on her body could defy the key of his mastery, and she opened her body at his first touch. She gave herself to loving him, grasping his broad back to pull him to her until the crash of her climax sent her drifting into a downy cloud of sleep.

Vaguely she knew that he was stirring beside her. Then she was alone in bed. She opened her eyes and watched him putting on his trousers. "Where are you going?" she asked.

"Just out. I'll be back soon."

"Do hurry, darling."

The hours slid on. Crickets droned in the hot night, and beyond the mosquito netting, insects buzzed, insistent to be admitted. She heard footsteps downstairs. "Joe's home," she thought in a murmur of contentment.

Then the door slammed back. A light flared suddenly, hurting her eyes, and a voice, cold with anger, said, "Wake up, Lily!"

His face was terrible to see. The blue heat of his eyes on her like hellfire, and the menace of his mouth struck her mute with fear. "Come here," he said; and when she hesitated, he bellowed with rage and jerked down the netting so that she floundered beneath it like a caught fish. He pulled her toward him over the sheets, yanking the netting as if she were a pack to shoulder. She found her voice and screamed for him to stop, as she hit the floor with a thump.

"Get up, Lily. Get out from under there!" He turned away from her and rummaged in a drawer. She saw the glint of silver as he took something out and slid it into his pocket.

"Your pistol! Joe! What are you going to do with that?" She was half out from under the mosquito netting now, and he jerked her the rest, hurting her arm with his grip.

"I am not going to shoot *you*, though maybe I should. I have been to see Henry Wickersham to try to arrange a loan to help pay the rest of my debt. And Henry tells me I have a debt that cannot be paid with money."

"Oh, Joe, no . . ."

"Why is it you wear your hair in that new way, Lily?" he said dangerously.

"It's fashionable—" Her neck snapped back as he pushed savagely at the fringe. She felt she could almost see the livid scar branded onto his pupils as he beheld it.

"Damn!" was all he said, but the earth shook. He let go of her, and she fell helplessly to the floor.

He is going to fight Jim Frey! She could not stop him. She could not even walk. Sobs racked her weak frame, and her breath came in awful gulps. The room receded toward darkness, then spun again to light as she struggled for a grip on herself. She lay still, trying to contain her grief, trying to marshal her strength for some sort of defense. What could she do? At last she stood dizzily and phoned for a hack.

Jim Frey's rococo mansion was not far from the Van Artsdalen's in the Garden District. Despite the strange hour, the butler who answered her ring only looked at her sadly and did not seem surprised to see her. Mr. Frey had gone. He had gone with a tall gentleman with curly hair. Joe and his honor! What would Frey have taken not to fight Joe? *Her* honor? It would have been all she had to offer.

She sat her *chappelle* in the window and prayed as the sun came up with angry, bloody hues and the first rattle of trolleys cracked like guns, waking her from a daze of exhaustion. There was a sound in the room, and she lifted her head.

"Joe!"

He looked at her coldly. "Jim Frey is dead."

She gave a sob of joy. "But how—?"

"How is it possible for an honorable man to win a duel with a dastard who fires on the count of nine? It is simply that I am not too proud to duck what I know is coming."

15

She was all alone in the pink granite house. She moved about restlessly, reading a book or trying her hand at a piece of needlepoint. There was still decorating to be done, but none of it was fun without Joe. Was she supposed to wait here the rest of her life to see if he would forgive her? Growing angry at him, she would hurl a pillow across the room or slam a cabinet door so hard the glass panes shook. How insolent of him to leave her here as if she were no more than one of the chairs! She had not belonged to Edmond like a piece of furniture, but it had been because she had refused to. She did belong to Joe that way, and it was her own choice. She loved him and she would wait forever, just as a lamp or sofa would wait for its owner to move it. And sometimes she was furious at herself for caring so much.

The ballet was in town again, and some of her friends came to visit her. "You could dance again," they told her when they discovered her predicament.

"Joe doesn't want me to dance," she said.

"Joe's not here!" they said.

But it didn't matter where he was. He was her lord all the same. She went to every performance, and even knowing that the neighbors would gossip, she had several of the girls stay with her during the engagement. The bright stage chatter, the dining-room carpet thrown back for the practicing of dance steps, made her life bearable. She practiced with them and was happy, almost forgetting she did not really belong.

Then they were gone again. She realized for the first time how much the stage had become part of her. She left the carpet rolled back and perfected her steps for hours every day. It was a small protection against the emptiness.

Then Susan came back. She sat in the same rosewood chair, stared at the teacakes Margaret the maid had set out, and said, "You were right, Lily. He's worse than the rest. He's a monster."

Lily said nothing and waited, noticing how listless Susan seemed, without the appetite for life she had had when they had lived in the Vieux Carré.

Susan sighed and toyed with the huge bow of mousseline de soie at the throat of the empire dress. Her gray-green eyes were bewildered, as if all the tenets she had built her life on had proved untrue. "I'm not happy, Lily. And that's awful, isn't it, when I have everything I was after. I am to sing in Europe in the spring, but even that isn't enough. I suppose the dream didn't measure up to the reality. Sometimes I think I'd have gladly stayed in Irish Channel to be as much in love as you."

"*That* has not worked out so well. He's gone, you notice."

"And I know why, that's the worst of it! You don't have to tell me this time that it was Henry. He's a jealous brute, too! He got drunk one night, imagining I'd paid too much attention to some man, and he bragged how careful my admirers ought to be. Maybe he'd get them killed, as he had Jim Frey. He'd told Joe about it, and not, as I first thought, because men stick together, but just because he saw he could do damage! Now that he's seen that it bothers me, he talks and talks about it. Especially about how he expected Frey to win the duel, because he and Frey were thick."

"Thick because Henry'd done Frey a favor leading him to me," said Lily.

"To think I doubted you! I closed my eyes on purpose!"

"It's understandable, Susan. You had married him."

"That's what I can't stand! The idea that I must live with him forever! Do you know why I am excited about singing in Europe? Not because I may stand on the stage of Albert Hall like Sarah Bernhardt, but because business will keep Henry away."

"Leave him, Susan. It's no way to live."

"I can't. I have a career, but people don't pay a hundred dollars a seat to see me as though I were Jenny Lind! Not yet, that is."

Lily smiled. "You haven't changed, Susan. You aren't ready to settle for a loving husband and his babies."

"Humph! Where should I get that, any more than you? Maybe we'd both settle for that if we could. But I'll take next best. I'll ride in a carriage overflowing with roses, and gentlemen will drink wine from my slipper."

"And then you'll leave him." Lily laughed.

"Then," said Susan with a sigh of longing.

Susan came often after that. They shopped together, trying to muster enthusiasm for buying bric-a-brac for Susan's Italian villa or for Lily's pink Gothic house. They bought clothes and lunched wickedly on chocolate éclairs. But nothing really made them happy. Only when Susan sang did she seem like the girl Lily had first known. And her singing had become even more compelling than before. Was it the expensive coaching she had had? Or was it that Susan poured even more of herself into it, making up with her music for something indefinable she had lost?

When they had finished shopping, they would often drive to St. Louis Cathedral to light candles to add to the tiers of flickering red glasses. As Lily knelt at the altar to pray for Joe's return, she wondered what Susan prayed for. Susan's face had a rapt expression when she turned it up to the Virgin, and Lily knew she was not asking forgiveness or pleading for an understanding heart. And one day Lily could hold her curiosity no longer.

"What do you ask God, Susan?" she said as they drove away. "I can tell there is something you believe would make you happy."

"Oh, certainly. I pray that Henry will give me cause."

"Cause?"

"To divorce him. Something I can show in court. That he beats me or commits adultery."

"But you can't divorce him. You're Catholic."

"Oh, I don't mean divorce him to be free to marry again. I would just like to be legally free. I would get a share of his money then. But's he's a fox. Careful to the core. I hired a detective to spy on him."

"And?"

"Nothing."

The enormity of it hit Lily all at once. "Susan, you are praying for a man to sin! You must never do that again!"

"Men sin. Especially men like Henry, sis. I'm only praying I'll catch him," said Susan, and the next time they were at the cathedral, Susan's prayerful expression was unchanged. Lily, on her knees, added to her devotions a plea for Susan's soul.

"Blessed Mary, show me a way I can help Susan, so that she can give her life to singing as God meant, and not hate him anymore!"

The idea came to her in a dream. She awoke bathed in perspiration beneath her mosquito netting. At first she thought it was her prayer that had been answered. Then she realized it was Susan's.

She could help Susan. She could free her from Henry forever!

"No," said Susan when Lily told her. "Remember how you scolded me simply for wishing that a man would sin. And now you want to cause him to."

"But he won't, don't you see? He will only seem to. You will be free, and Henry won't have to commit adultery or beat you. A divorce! You'll get your share of his money."

"Henry would fight a divorce," said Susan with a shudder. "I don't think I've got the nerve."

"But it's what you've been dreaming of!"

"Yes, but that was dreaming! A scandal'd bring out my days at the French Pigeon, and it might ruin my career. I'd end up where I started."

The matter was stalemated. But only for so long. Lily stumbled from bed one morning to answer the insistent ringing of the phone. "It's Susan," whispered a voice. "I've got to see you right now!"

"Come ahead, then." Lily yawned, and she was still in her wrapper when Susan arrived a few minutes later. "What is it, Susan?" she asked. "Shall I fix us coffee? Margaret hasn't arrived yet."

"No coffee. Nothing," Susan said urgently. "Come upstairs in your bedroom before anyone's about." She dragged Lily by the hand, and when they were behind the bedroom door, Lily sat among the rumpled bedclothes and stared at her friend's flushed face.

"Last night Henry went out to play and I drove to see the detective."

"He's got the goods on Henry?"

"No, not that. But there's a way. A way I can divorce Henry without his even knowing it!"

"Good heavens!"

"All I need is a crooked lawyer, and the detective will get me that. The lawyer and the witnesses."

"Witnesses to what?" Lily breathed.

"To his assaulting you."

It was Lily's plan, the thing she had dreamed, but the words on Susan's lips chilled her. In the dream she had been with Henry in the parlor. He had put his hands on her, and she had screamed and run for the door. As she reached the knob, he had ripped the bodice of her gown trying to stop her, his face livid now with fear, not passion. In the hall outside were people brought by her screams, and she collapsed in their arms, pointing an accusing finger back at Henry. Joe had settled with Jim Frey, and she had resented the satisfaction it must have given him. Women could not duel, but there were other ways, and she had not yet had revenge on Henry for his part in that. It would be sweet. . . .

"Lily? You don't have to do it. It could be dangerous."

She drew a deep breath. "I want to, Susan."

"Then I will send you word when it's arranged."

The plan was ingenious. The lawyer would have a divorce hearing set, and there would be a subpoena. Then the innocent messenger would be sent to deliver the document to Henry at the Boston Club. But when the messenger arrived, the butler there would point out another person as Henry Wickersham. The fake Henry, well-paid for his work, would accept the document, and the messenger would swear it had been delivered. The hearing would take place with no defense from Henry. And the divorce would be granted! Lovely!

"But he'll be furious, Susan!" Lily said. "And he's capable of anything!"

"I'll leave New Orleans as soon as the legal work is done. When he finds out I've divorced him, I'll be away in Europe. It'll be too late. I'll have my settlement and my career, and whatever scandal he wants to whip up won't be heard in Paris!"

The days slipped past. It was almost Christmas. Lily had decorated the parlor with holly and mistletoe the day the invitation came to tell her that Mr. and Mrs. Henry Wickersham requested the honor of her presence at a dinner party on Friday night. Her heart thudded in a way quite inappropriate to news of a simple holiday gathering. She knew it meant Susan had everything ready. She dressed for the occasion in the spirit of the season in a red plush gown and wore a filigree "dog collar" about her throat. Even with her silk evening gloves her hands were cold as she rode through the chill night to Coliseum Square.

Coliseum Square was not really a square, but a long, triangular park laid out in the 1830's to be a center of classical culture. The dream had collapsed with the war, but many of the rich had built homes here, Greek Revival-style mansions with fluted Corinthian columns and simple detail. Henry's, looking more garish than it might have in a different setting, dripped with scrollwork and towers and oddly shaped wings.

Inside there were double parlors with great chandeliers and eighteen-foot ceilings.

"Good evening, Madame Beau Clair." She turned to see a cryptic aristocratic face beneath a thatch of blond hair. Where had she seen it before?

"How do you like my creation? Do you imagine it's as lovely as the fee I received for designing it? And now Wickersham insists on my dining here so he can show me off as well as this monstrosity."

"It is . . . dramatic, Mr. Snow," she said, remembering. He had the same haunted look he had had before. He hated the house, an emotion most men would not have entertained, when building it had paid them so well. He had a feeling for beauty, she thought, and the constant thwarting of it pained him. She was glad when he told her they were partners for dinner.

"I'm glad I didn't have to design this house for you, Madame Beau Clair," he said. "Mrs. Wickersham is better suited, with that flashing red hair. I could never have begun to accommodate your delicate looks here."

"If I ever build a house, I shall call on you, Mr. Snow. I would trust you to make it beautiful."

Lily could hardly eat any of the excellent supper. The roast goose went untouched, and she drank rather more than she should of the claret; and though she looked often at Susan, she was afraid for their eyes to meet.

No one would have guessed that Susan was nervous. Her gown of lavender bengaline brought a depth to her eyes and caught the rosy tones of her cheeks. Silver earrings shaped like spiders dangled beneath her glowing hair as she called wifely remarks to Henry at the foot of the Duncan Phyfe table. Susan was playing her part perfectly. But hers was easier than Lily's. *Come into my web.* Was that the reason Susan had worn the earrings? It would have been like her. Lily shivered and was glad that their intended victim was almost hidden from her view by an enormous candelabrum.

Never had a dinner seemed to go more quickly. The gentlemen withdrew for cigars, and Lily, rising dizzily, went upstairs to find a bathroom where she could dab cold water on her cheeks. As she came out onto the Indian cashmere carpeting, she came face to face with Henry in the hall.

"Would you like me to show you the mirror room, Lily? You haven't seen much of the house."

It wasn't exactly as they had planned it; it was better! Let

Henry walk into the trap without anyone to lead him! She took a deep breath and thought comfortingly of the extra maids Susan had hired, who had agreed to swear to whatever they saw.

As she came downstairs on Henry's arm, she saw that most of the guests were leaving. Archer Snow looked back at her and tipped his hat as he went out. She was sorry to see him go, but relieved, too. She would have hated for him to witness the tawdry scene that was to come.

Susan breezed past. "Lily, dear, I've a terrible headache. You don't mind if Henry shows you out?"

"I have promised to show her the mirror room first, my love," said Henry with a smug glitter in his eyes.

"Do, by all means. All New Orleans is talking of it, Lily." Then she was gone, and there was only the clatter of cleaning going on in the dining room.

"Come, Lily."

He led her off into another wing into a spectacular six-sided room with great mantels of black onyx. Three of the walls had huge windows, and the other three had large gold-leaf mirrors, so that wherever she stood or sat she could see in six directions and was surrounded by an eerie reflection of lamps and milky starlight.

In spite of her fear, Lily was distracted and blew out a breath of admiration. Henry laughed with genuine pleasure. "Do you like it, Lily? What a pity it couldn't have been yours. I wanted it to be your house."

"I am sure it suits Susan better. Archer Snow says so."

"Come and sit here beside me and let me see how you would have looked here," he said. She fought down her repugnance and sat gingerly on the velvet-tufted seat of the ornate oval-backed sofa. "Archer Snow is wrong, Lily. No one could look better in this room than you."

She gritted her teeth and let her hand lie on the sofa. He took it at once, covering it with his own soft-skinned fingers. She controlled a tremor as she remembered that those fingers were deceptively strong. The minutes ticked away on the globe clock on the mantel, and she felt hysteria growing.

She swallowed hard and lifted his hand toward her breast. Her eyes closed, but the awful feel of his touch upon her did not come. Instead he pulled his hand away. And she heard his vicious, gloating laugh.

"So, you're hot, are you, you minx! That is what happens to you when you see what you could have had. Joe's pink house is not much beside it! You're a little whore, Lily; you've proved that tonight. Come, out you go!"

The room spun in a haze of mirrors and lights as he moved toward the door. This was not like her dream at all! They were all waiting for her screams—the maids, the lawyer, the fake Henry—it all depended on her. It defied everything in Henry's character that he should not try to make love to her. Rage welled in her that the one time she needed the advances of a lecher this should happen, and before she knew it, her anger poured out in a scream. She jerked the doorknob away from him, tore wildly at her dress, pulled at her hair. She raced out screaming, hearing echoes of her voice reverberate from the ceilings and walls of the great house. "Help! Help! Rape!"

But this was not her dream, either. The hall outside was empty. She whirled about, searching for her rescuers, her witnesses, the secure arms about her.

There was no one. Nothing but Henry's laughter floating above her screams, bouncing from wall to wall as if there had been a dozen of him. "Who are you looking for, Lily? I pay better than Susan, you see. And I have paid her conspirators to go home to bed."

"Susan!" she screamed.

"Susan can't help you. I paid to have her locked in her room. And now let's not make a liar out of you. You cried rape, and rape you shall have!"

They were near the top of a mahogany staircase. She stepped backward as he reached for her, tripped over her gown, and fell, her body banging painfully on the polished steps. She hit bottom dazed, her skirts askew, her body bruised and hurting. "Get me a doctor, Henry," she moaned, as his face appeared over her.

"Perhaps, but not until I've had my fill of you. I have wanted you for too long."

She was too weak to move. Her body convulsed as she felt his hands intimately beneath her petticoats. And then came worse. Her stomach contracted at the sight of his unbuttoned trousers, and she somehow gained strength. As her vision cleared, she perceived a suit of armor, standing like a strange, impassive person at the foot of the stairs. Reaching up with both arms, she pulled a lance from its mailed grip and struck him insensible.

16

She remembered little of what happened after that. The sight of blood on his forehead remained in her memory, but nothing of how she had struggled back up the stairs and found Susan's room to unbolt the lock. She remembered how they had wept in each other's arms, and there was a vague impression of a carriage ride back to her own house. Then she had been lying in the big French bed she had shared with Joe. There had been a doctor telling Susan that she had suffered only a pair of broken ribs. She had been made to swallow a draft, and then she had slept.

Unwilling to leave her to Margaret, Susan had come every day to look after her. Lily had been unable to eat for days. When she slept, she had the same nightmare over and over, and she begged Susan to help her into bath after bath, as though she would never be clean. But now she was beginning to be better. She had come downstairs to lie on a chaise longue in front of the fire. Susan had told her it was Christmas Day, and the aroma of plum pudding had given her an appetite.

"What will you do now, Susan?" she asked her friend. "He knows."

"I am not going to leave him, sis! I am going to stick in and get my share. He has got my Irish up, and no one can stick like the Irish!"

"You will be going to the Continent, and you'll be away from him at least."

"I won't be going. He's managed to cancel that at least. But I might have canceled it myself to stay with you."

"Don't be silly. I am all right now."

But she wasn't. It was more than the fact that she had no energy and spent whole afternoons in bed imagining that the air pressed on her like great weights. The nausea she had experienced at Henry's touch had seemed to stay with her like a permanent fixture of her life.

A fear grew with every day and came to haunt every moment. How did a woman know if she were pregnant? Back at school on Martinique there had been whisperings and speculation. Someone had said that a lady always fainted at the moment of conception. Another suggestion, largely supported, had been that the skin of her stomach became a different color. And then, they had argued until a girl with an older sister had put forth this odd signal Lily was now experiencing.

"You've missed the curse twice!" Susan cried when Lily timidly told her in the bleakness of February. "It's a sure sign. A baby. It won't do!"

"But it will have to do, won't it?" Lily said thinly. "It's there."

"It doesn't have to do at all! Oh, Lily! You're still innocent after all this time! You've got money, and when you've got money, you don't have to have a baby if you don't want to."

"You don't?" she asked, puzzled.

"We can get you an abortionist."

Vaguely she knew what Susan meant. She had heard talk in the quarter, and now and then thugs from the Pigeon had been paid to go and dump someone's body in the river from one of those establishments. "It would be terrible doing that!" She shuddered.

"But I know a good place. Women die in childbirth, too, you know. And what will you do if Joe comes back? Will he want it?"

"I don't know. But I am going to have it."

"Think how things may turn out. Especially if Joe doesn't come back. Sooner or later there would be no money in the bank. Your child would grow up to a footpad or worse, and if it's a girl, well, you know what can happen to a woman without funds."

"Susan! Watch your tongue! Margaret will hear you. And she thinks I'm married to Joe."

But Susan kept up her plea, day after day, and Lily was forever closing doors to protect her secret from the maid.

"Make up your mind quickly, Lily. It is easier done early."

"I will never do such a thing, Susan." But how would she handle Joe?

She began to go to the docks again, not because she was so eager to have him return now, but because she could not bear to be surprised. She had an idea he might come soon. It was

Carnival season, and Joe was not one to miss such a show—if he were coming back at all.

"The *Sea Bird* is docking tomorrow," she heard someone say as she stepped down from the trolley. She had been expecting it, but somehow she wasn't prepared.

"With a fine load of spice, I hear," came the answer, seeming to spin around and down, as if poured through a funnel. *A fine load of spice,* and then the trolley seemed to be turning, too, and she caught at a metal rail that twisted away from her grip. She heard a great roar, as if a hurricane had struck at once, its whirlwinds responsible for the unnatural gyrations of the words and the trolley. She felt annoyed as she fell, unable to keep her footing.

This trolley doesn't work correctly. I must speak to the management. And a distant clatter was all she heard as the horses pulled it over her.

She thought she was home at Acelie. She wept at the sight of its yellow stone against the crumbled mountains. The air was fresh as it never was in New Orleans. She could hold the lemon sunshine in her hand, and on the veranda she saw her father holding out his arms. She ran to him, begging his forgiveness.

"Oh, Papa! How I've failed you! I did not keep Acelie for our family. I did not even have a family. I didn't bear Edmond a son. And I loved Acelie so." The cool vistas of bananas and cacao received her. She was free as she had never been in the pink granite house, and her heart soared over the expanse with the joy of a mountain whistler. There was Yzore, gathering her to her soft bosom and telling her she had candied breadfruit pods for her.

"But, Papa. Where is Edmond?"

And he smiled at her and patted her cheek. *It still can be, Lily. It still can be.*

Then there were other voices. She fought them back. "Be quiet! I can't hear what my papa is saying!" But they kept on and on, getting louder and louder.

"There, now, I can feel a pulse again. And me about to call the dead cart."

"When she finds she's lost the baby, you may need to. Some women are like that."

She opened her eyes and was aware of a great whiteness. "Is this a hospital?" she wondered.

"Yes. Tell us where to send for your husband. We didn't know."

"My husband!"

"Yes, of course. You need him now."

"My husband is . . . at sea." How could she send them for Joe? Perhaps he had not come back to the pink house at all, but if he had, how could she face his disapproval? He had not wanted her to be pregnant, and she couldn't bear it if he blamed her or failed to share her grief.

She was still unsteady a week later when she was driven home to the pink house. She noticed its oddly bleak look even before she had been handed down. She did not understand at first, and then she saw that the curtains were gone from the windows. When her key did not turn in the lock, she was filled with panic. She fought to keep her voice even as she returned to the carriage and gave the driver another address.

The Gothic houses were built close here, made of frame construction, some built in pairs with joining walls, like Tweedledee and Tweedledum. Others were connected one after the other like chains of paper dolls.

When the driver stopped, she picked her way over the broken slate walks to the door she wanted.

"May I speak to Margaret, please?"

"My Margaret's done nothing wrong!" said the spare, lean-faced woman who had answered her knock.

"No, no. But I must speak to her!"

"There's a lady, Margaret," the woman called. "She looks about to faint." And then there was her maid, ushering her into a shabby parlor, pressing a glass of water to her lips.

Roughly she pushed it away. "Muddy! From the river. I never could drink that! Margaret! Were you there when Joe came? What happened?"

Margaret looked as though she might faint herself. "I . . . told him the truth, madame. He made me tell. I thought he'd kill me if I didn't. And then I thought he'd kill me when I did."

"What did you tell him, Margaret?"

"Why, that you'd gone to the abortionist, of course. I knew what must have happened when you didn't come back that day. Oh, madame, how could you do it? Your husband's own little baby! He waited there three days, and never a one but he didn't break the crockery. Terrified, I was! He went to those places looking, and when he came back, he looked like he'd been in a dozen fights. And then he paid my wages and had wagons come to take the furniture to the auction house."

"And my clothes?"

"Sold, too. He didn't think you were coming back. Dead or gone forever, he said, and he didn't seem to care much which it was."

"My account at the bank will be closed too, then," Lily said, dazed. "I have nothing, Margaret. Nothing at all."

The girl looked at her with something not quite like pity. "I'll take you in for the night, though you don't deserve it. It's my Christian duty. I'm a good Catholic girl, and I'd never do the thing you did. You'll have to answer for it on Judgment Day."

The bed she slept in that night had a holelike sag, and she kept falling into it as if into a grave. The mildewed pillows stung her nostrils, and a single shaft of moonlight cast shadows of weird beings up the stained wallpaper of the high, narrow room, which had been meant for dining but which the crowded family used for sleeping instead. How many had given up their places for her to have this bed? She guessed that more than one slept here. She could not ask the favor again. Where would she go tomorrow? It was that, and not the final judgment, that worried her. She could dance again, but not in the French Quarter with no protector, and the ballet wasn't in town.

She agonized even more over how she would account to Joe. Would Joe ever believe she hadn't had his child aborted? Was she meant to return to Acelie now, take up her duties as Edmond's wife? Had that been what the dream had been telling her? *It still can be, Lily. It still can be.*

She thought longingly of home as she drifted to sleep, and in the morning she walked until she found a church. She went in and knelt at the altar and prayed that the Virgin would give her a sign. "Shall I give up Joe forever? Shall I borrow money from Susan and go to Martinique to beg Edmond to have me back? Spend my life in penitence for what I've done?"

She came out into the sunlight again, and a child in a starched pinafore called to her from a perch on a fence. "Lily, hello!" The little girl from the Van Artsdalens' picnic who had wished she could marry Joe.

"Is this where you live, Mary?"

"It's the orphanage, yes."

Lily thanked the Virgin for the sign and went inside.

17

"Ring the bell now, Lily, and call the children in."

"Oh, but it's still light, and the ball game is tied."

The nun smiled ruefully at the beautiful young woman in the simple dress of wash dimity, her cheeks flushed and her dark hair curling unabashedly around her lively face. How she had changed since she had come here! If only the peace Lily seemed to have found could last. But the sister had her doubts. Lily was too beautiful, and she had about her an aura that was foreign to convent life.

"Ring the bell, Lily," she ordered again. "It's you who want to stay out, as much as the children. It's time for vespers and then bed. They mustn't fall asleep at their morning prayers."

"Yes, Sister." She pulled the stout rope, and the big black bell echoed over the grounds, reverberating from the stone walls that cast long shadows into the twilight. The children came running as the sound blotted out the sweet drone of locusts. They formed a line and smiled at Lily as she passed down the row straightening a smock, tying a shoe, giving each an affectionate pat before the line moved off to the chapel.

"Life agrees with you here," the sister said.

"Yes. I find much satisfaction."

"And the children all love you. You are what we have needed here. You are meant for children."

"Perhaps I wasn't. I have none of my own, nor expect to."

"But God sent you to us. These are all your children. Wouldn't you like to become a novice, Lily? Haven't you prayed to know if you have a vocation?"

"No. I am too much in sin."

"Sin can be forgiven."

"Only if the sinner is repentant. And I am not. There is a man in my heart who will keep me forever from being a bride of Christ."

"If you are not to be married to him, then you must pray for strength to put him aside."

But the sister saw how miserable Lily looked at the mere thought of putting him aside. And she knew what man was in the girl's heart. Hadn't she mentioned her relative Joe Beau Clair when she had come asking to be taken in? And the sister had heard of this Lily Beau Clair before. She had been at the Van Artsdalens' picnic—his sister-in-law, they had said. But the sister didn't believe that. Why should a sister-in-law turn up penniless and in need of everything, as Lily had?

She had been his mistress, and something had happened, something very tangled, perhaps more unpleasant than a nun's sheltered mind could grasp. Something about Lily's very appreciation of the convent indicated that she had known too much of life. And now, what was to happen?

Joe Beau Clair would pay the orphanage a visit someday. Lily knew that. No doubt she hoped for it. And then? When the nun knelt for vespers, she remembered Lily in her prayers.

In the dusky chapel Lily tried to keep her devotions pure. She asked the Virgin to help her in her teaching, and she begged for release from the pain of her love for Joe. She prayed for release, but she did not repent of loving him. She could not be sorry for a one of those golden days she had spent with him, and the memory of his naked body intruded on her prayers with a shocking, wanton beauty.

It had been several days after she had taken up residence in the barren convent room before it had occurred to her that she had chosen the one place in the world where she would be certain of crossing paths with Joe again. It might be years, of course. But even if it were, she was afraid it would be too soon for her to face, with equanimity, even then. A century might not be long enough.

"I hate him!" she declared to herself. "I hate him, and I shall tell him so the instant I see him. How could he believe that I would destroy our baby? How could he think it of me? And when he knew I wanted a baby so much!"

That was what hurt most of all. Not losing him, but the manner of her losing him. She would never stoop to explain to him that she would never have willingly parted with his child.

But in another way she felt she deserved any punishment he gave her, for degrading herself in the plot against Henry. Confession was what was needed. Every week, as Lily sat in the cubicle next to the priest, she planned to tell the sordid tale. But each time she was unable to face the memory, and a tight fist seemed to jam the words back into her throat, choking off her salvation.

"What is it, child? Tell me and be absolved," the kindly priest would say. And with a sob she would whisper, "Nothing. Nothing more, Father."

Perhaps with years of dedication, release might come. But even then there would be the matter of Joe. And surely that unconsecrated love was enough to doom her soul. It didn't seem fair that if she were to suffer in the afterlife, she could not at least have heaven on earth. But she hated him. In the unlikely event that Joe wanted her again, she would never forgive him. Never.

She rose with the sun each morning, and after helping to herd the children to the cold chapel for prayers, she passed bowls of smoking cornmeal mush down the long wooden breakfast table. Then came the lessons. Lily had supposed when she applied for work that her fine lady's education would be put to use. But the nuns weren't interested in teaching music, language, and history.

"There's no use in their knowing those things," they told Lily. "Reading, writing, catechism—that's enough of books." The boys often went from the convent straight to dock work at the age of fourteen, and the girls took places as kitchen maids. But a fine hand with a needle might win a girl a favored place as a seamstress, so it was sewing that Lily taught, showing the little girls the niceties of fashion that the nuns didn't know. She could teach them to bake, too, to help them on their way to becoming cooks in fine households. How lucky it was that Yzore had not kept Lily to the pursuits of a lady. She was determined to spend the rest of her life in the convent, unless God gave her some other sign.

Then one afternoon she was told she had a guest. "Tell the gentleman to go away," she said, wondering who had come to torment her.

"But it's a lady. A fine-looking lady with beautiful red hair."

She flew down to the visitors' alcove to Susan.

"Let me look at you, sis! A person would think you were an orphan yourself in that gown! Why didn't you tell me where you'd landed? I searched all New Orleans."

Lily flushed. "I'm sorry, Susan. I would have, in time. I needed to sort things out—"

"Don't try to explain. I wouldn't blame you if you'd had enough of me. But when Joe came, what a scene there was!"

"You saw him?"

"Indeed I did. He guessed the abortionist was my idea, and he frightened me more than any man ever has. He had murder in his eye!"

"What did you tell him?" Lily whispered.

"I told him you hadn't had an abortion, of course. Did you? What else could I say? But it wasn't any use. He tore apart every such place in New Orleans looking for you. Probably he thinks you are dead. I did. Then finally I remembered you'd had this thing about convents, how you'd intended to wait for Joe in a convent when you first came to New Orleans. And after I'd checked all the others, I thought of the orphanage. Oh, Lily, I am happy to see you!"

"And I you, Susan! I have been so alone—except for the children."

"They're a consolation, I suppose."

"Oh, yes! For all the children I wanted of my own."

"What are you going to do now, Lily? You can't stay here forever."

"Yes, I can."

Susan sighed and straightened her serge jacket. "I guess I expected you to say that." She sighed. "I don't see how you can stand it to let life pass you by."

"It's easy enough, considering what I have seen of life. I had much sooner live in a convent than with Henry, as you do."

Susan's mouth turned up in a happy little smile, and her eyes danced. "Henry has gone away for six months, Lily. I do believe he's tired of me and the house. I'm having a lovely time. I'm singing again at the opera, and I am not without admirers."

"He'll come back sometime."

"Yes, but meanwhile there's no reason not to have fun. Tomorrow night I'm giving a party. You're to come, of course."

"Me! But I don't want to go to a party. And if I wanted to, it would be out of the question. The convent doors are closed at dark."

"Pshaw, Lily! It's no problem. You're to spend the night with me. I've already arranged it with the nuns. They think it will be good for you."

It was no use trying to weasel out. "Please, Sister, I don't want to go," she begged.

The nun shook her head sternly. "You have hidden long enough, Lily. You must go and face the world before you can find true contentment here."

"Pray for me, if I go. It has always been dangerous for me out there."

"I always pray for you, Lily. See if you can bring back cakes. The children are so excited."

Lily was not in the mood for a party. The great towered house had only one memory for her, and the very gardens seemed to breathe, not the sent of honeysuckle and lantana, but the evil miasma of Henry Wickersham. The gathering was a large one, for Susan wasn't one to have a simple get-together when she could have a grand affair.

Huge platters of food, silver bowls of flowers, men in frock coats and ladies in sleeveless, low-necked gowns with trained skirts and cascades of lace. Lily wore a gown of apricot bengaline provided by Susan, and her dark hair was caught up in an elegant Greek-style knot.

"No one would know you were a convent teacher now, Lily," cried Susan as she fastened a moonstone collar about Lily's slender throat. "There! You can't tell me it's not pleasant to look so magnificent."

Lily tried to remain glum as she gazed at her reflection, but instead a little smile broke free, making her beauty perfect.

"Oh, Lily, all the men will be in love with you tonight!"

"That's the problem. I don't want men to be in love with me."

"Don't worry, my little recluse. Nothing will come of it, and tomorrow you'll be safely back in your convent. But have fun tonight."

Madame Drapeaux had always said that she would not last in a convent, that she was meant for gaiety. And the strains of a waltz below excited her. What if Madame Drapeaux's perceptions proved true? What then? But Susan was right, of course. One night of fun, and then back to the convent with a whole plateful of goodies for the children, Lily thought as she went down the great staircase.

The carpeting was new, but suddenly she seemed to see the stains where Henry had bled from the blow she had dealt him. She began to tremble as she realized she was standing right where he had almost raped her. From the ballroom came the lilt of "The Southern Rose Waltz," and the suit of armor stood impassive as ever, the lance she had used replaced in its fist.

"Madame Beau Clair!"

Startled, she looked up into the face of Archer Snow. He looked happier than when she had seen him last. The haunted expression was still in his eyes, but something else shone there, too. Perhaps he had had the good fortune to fall in love, and she found herself hoping that the lady deserved him and understood him, for there was something fine and easily damaged in his nature.

"I've been waiting for your call," he said.

"My call?"

"Have you forgotten you promised to engage me if you ever had a house to be built? It was an assignment I looked forward to. You haven't given the job to another?"

His blue eyes were sparkling, and suddenly she felt in good spirits. Blue eyes like Joe's, and yet not like Joe's. Eyes that did not remind her of stormy oceans; eyes that did not pull her into them like rushing tides. But eyes that instead seemed to speak of the sky, of deep calamine atmospheres she might float into, like a gull soaring above a turbulent sea.

She laughed and tapped his frock coat playfully with her fan. "Indeed, no one but you shall build my house, Mr. Snow."

"I am relieved to hear it. Would you like to dance?"

"With pleasure. They are playing one of my favorite waltzes."

All her troubles fell away from her as they whirled out onto the floor. He was a skillful dancer with a good sense of rhythm, and she gave herself up to him, delighted to let him guide and master. How long it had been since she had experienced the luxury of such surrender to a man! Not since Joe had gone. . . .

"But tell me, Mr. Snow, whatever are you doing here? You don't like the house, and I have the idea you don't care much for Mrs. Wickersham, either."

"In truth, I dreaded coming. But I've a friend who's interested in theater people who shanghaied me here."

A friend. He was telling her that he had a lady. It irritated her that she felt a pang of disappointment. Then the music stopped, and Susan was at the orchestra stand calling for everyone's attention.

"I'll have the grandest treat for you all in a few minutes,"

Babylon

she promised gaily. "A young lady is going to entertain us with native West Indian dances."

"Goodness! How extraordinary, Madame Beau Clair," Archer Snow said, but Lily had slipped from his side as the crowd greeted the announcement with applause.

So that was why Susan had insisted she come!

When Susan found her, she was upstairs already stripping off the evening gown, looking for the convent dress, which seemed to have vanished. "Oh, good, you're getting ready," Susan said, deliberately misunderstanding. "It's a shame we don't have the jupe dress, but I've had one made that is almost like it. I hope it fits, since there wasn't time to try it."

"It's no matter whether it fits or not, Susan. I'm not going to dance. And you knew I'd say no. Otherwise, you'd have told me before. We had plenty of time this afternoon to try the gown."

"Oh, Lily, why not dance?" Susan pouted. "It would make the party! And I've already announced it. You wouldn't make me look a fool!"

"That's what you're counting on, Susan—that I won't make you a fool. But there are limits to friendship. This is a scrape of your own making, and you'll have to get out of it alone. I know you well enough to know it's more than a novelty for your party you're interested in. It's me. You can't stand the idea that I am happy in the convent. You are scheming to get me out. That's the main thing about you, Susan! You are always scheming. And you should have learned by now that your schemes don't always work."

"Prove to me my schemes don't work!" Susan smiled and held out a dress of gold embroidered satin, showed Lily the scarlet petticoats beneath.

"The sleeves are all wrong," Lily said scornfully, though the very sight of the garment stirred her desire to dance.

"I know. The seamstress couldn't quite imagine, and they turned out almost leg-of-mutton. Are you really going to make a fool of me before all my guests? Please dance, Lily. Then I'll let you go back to the convent. I won't scheme anymore."

"Oh, very well, if you promise." Lily sighed. "Hand me the petticoats." Already she could hear the drums in her ears; her pulse was pounding the beat. Dance. She knew the savage emotions it would stir. She knew it would make her long for excitement, for love, for Joe. When would she have this opportunity again? And if she were overcome by it, she could quench the fire with her morning prayers.

"The mask, Susan. You know I can't dance without it."

Susan handed her a white wire mask. "I knew you wouldn't let me down, sis," she said.

A primitive beat had replaced the waltzes as Lily stood poised on the stairs. She was aware vaguely that she was not thinking clearly, that Susan's scheme must somehow go deeper than she saw. Susan must have some plan beyond a simple desire to break her resolve to spend the rest of her life at the convent. She thought of the sisters who had thought the evening would do her good and was glad they couldn't see her as she danced down to the ballroom, where the center of the floor had been cleared for her.

The red petticoats swirled. The gold spun fire, and as always, she imagined Joe beside her as she danced. The drums seemed to call his name, and she danced to fight him away, her movements wilder than ever before as she struggled in the grip of passion. The music seemed to caress her, like Joe's hands on her thighs. She twisted away, shook free, only to be reminded of his lips on hers, the burning wonder of his eyes devouring her.

As the drums beat a crescendo, she fell to the floor, her hair streaming, her arms and throat shining with perspiration. She could have stayed there forever, sinking into a black depth of oblivion, but she became aware that the drums had stopped, that the spell had broken and people were moving toward her. She staggered to her feet and ran upstairs on quivering legs.

Alone, she sobbed and beat her fists against the brocade-papered walls. She had not danced since Joe had left her, and all the defenses she had mustered against his loss had been destroyed. But gradually she began to be calm. She knew she must go back to the party, lest guests notice her absence and speculate it had been she.

She wanted to find Archer Snow. Somehow she trusted his presence would bring her the comfort she needed. He was the one person who seemed to have no demands to make of her, she thought as she changed to the apricot gown. Though she had known him only slightly, he had always put her at ease. He did not flirt or hint, and he did not squeeze her waist when they waltzed. It was an experience that intrigued her, one she had not had with other men. She must find Archer

Snow... But he had said he had come with a friend, and she must be claiming his attentions.

She saw him almost at once. His tall form, topped by its wild thatch of blond hair, was difficult to miss. He was not with a lady at all, but deep in conversation with another man, much shorter than himself, who was making commanding gestures to animate the strength of his feeling about whatever he was saying.

She went over and stood beside Archer, smiling up at him. "Dear me!" he said when he saw her. "Where have you been? You've missed the most wonderful dancing."

"I felt a bit faint."

"Are you better now? But I haven't introduced you to Giles Benton, the friend who brought me here. Giles, this is Madame Beau Clair."

"A pleasure," said Giles, but he scarcely spared her a glance as he continued his harangue. "I tell you we must find that woman, Archer!" he declared.

"Oh, I agree completely that she was marvelous, Giles. But I've already asked Mrs. Wickersham, and she won't tell. She is some society lady, most likely. That is why she danced in the mask. It would be a hopeless matter."

They were talking about her! She tugged at Archer's arm to make him notice her again, for he seemed almost as preoccupied as Giles Benton. "What would be hopeless, Archer?"

"Giles wants to find that girl who danced."

"Yes, but why?"

"You haven't heard? Giles is a well-known theatrical director I met on a trip to New York. He's agreed to do a play at the French Opera, and I'm backing the venture. But now Giles has decided he must have that girl for the part. And it's impossible, naturally. Her husband would never allow it."

"What part, Archer?"

"Salome. We are doing Oscar Wilde's *Salome*. It couldn't get past the censors in London, you know, but in Paris it was a sensation. Sarah Bernhardt was to do it in New York, but there were complications. And now Giles thinks that no one but Mrs. Wickersham's dancer must be the Princess Salome."

"I shall find her, Archer, if I have to tear New Orleans apart!" Giles said. "And nobody who sees it will ever forget my *Salome*!"

"Will you give her half your kingdom, Giles?" Archer teased.

"Like Herod, I will give her what she asks," he answered.

Salome. The Dance of the Seven Veils! The part was made for her, of course! And that had been Susan's real scheme. The reason she had had the gold-embroidered jupe dress made, the reason she had made Lily dance. But now Susan had drawn back.

"Why didn't you just finish the business and tell Giles Benton who your dancer was?" she asked when the guests had left.

"That is your decision, Lily. There is another life waiting for you. Giles Benton will make you a star. You would be rich and never have to depend on anyone again for the rest of your life. You can have fame and wealth, or you can go back to the convent. Which will it be?"

"The convent."

"Very well. You've proved me wrong, then. But I shan't feel guilty about you anymore. And I did, you know. I owed you something, because, after all, it was I who got you into the mess with Henry, and but for that you'd be with Joe again now."

"Joe. Joe wouldn't like it if I went onstage," she mused.

"Oh, there you go with that muddled thinking of yours. You're done with him, remember, and he with you. What would *you* like? That's what's important."

"But I've never acted, Susan."

"Let Giles Benton worry about that. He's a genius."

She went back to the convent, passed out tea cakes, and was distracted all day. She remembered how she had missed dancing with the ballet, how she had been almost jealous of Susan's debut at the French Opera. And yet, dancing was painful. She told herself to deny temptation, and spent half the afternoon in the chapel. It was no use. The convent that had seemed peaceful and pleasant was now dreary. It was all spoiled, she thought with a sigh. Her demon was leading her again, and she was helpless before it. She packed a valise, and hailing a cab, asked the driver if he could help her find the residence of Giles Benton.

"Whom shall I say is calling?" the butler asked, dubious of this girl, a waif in a dimity convent dress.

Lily drew a deep breath. "Say that it is Salome."

18

"Did you ever love a man, Lily?"

"I did, Giles."

"And he made you hate him."

"Yes. How did you know?"

Giles Benton, stretched lazily on a chaise longue, made a desultory gesture with his mint julep. Moisture trickled down the glass in the hot afternoon, and gathering at the bottom, fell in a single grand drop to the cypress floor. Overhead a mahogany ceiling fan stirred the air, drawing a torrid breeze past the white lace curtains of the parlor. Lily's feet were bare for dancing, and now she lifted her skirts a daring inch and whished them for coolness. "Please let me stop, Giles. We've been working all day. Everyone else is napping or sitting on a quilt drinking lemonade. I'm the only woman in New Orleans working like this."

"You are the only woman in New Orleans who is going to be Salome. Come, now, think of this man. He made you hate him. It doesn't matter why. He did, or you'd be with him still. You are that sort of woman. And yet you love him! You can't stop loving him." Giles Benton wore thick reading glasses, and his powerful eyes were large behind them, their hypnotic quality increased tenfold.

"I don't want to think of him!" she cried, but the voice could not be shut away; the voice went on, a great emotional shovel digging endlessly for feelings she would sooner keep hidden safely away. Giles Benton made actresses from pain and torment. He was an artist, a sculptor, paring away everything to a fine, raw edge, all the trappings, the cushions of civilization. And there was left only the molten current of human sensibility, a pure torrent of agony and passion.

"Read it again, Lily. Think of this lover when you have the head of John the Baptist on a platter. You loved him, and you destroyed him."

She shuddered and lifted her eyes to the spinning fan.

There was nothing to do but obey. She had learned that over the weeks she had been working with him. He would have his way.

"Perhaps it is you I shall think of, Giles. You I hate. You I want to destroy."

Giles Benton chuckled, tasted his julep, wriggled his thin lips. "Come, now: 'Thy body was a column of ivory set on feet of silver . . .'"

"'It was a tower of silver decked with shields of ivory . . .'" Lily's trancelike voice took up the lines of the play, and Joe rose to her mind. She saw the magnificence of his slender commanding body, felt her helplessness before his kisses. She tried to disregard the vision. Instead, it became stronger, dazzling her senses. "'Thy voice was a censer that scattered strange perfumes, and when I looked on thee, I heard strange music—'"

Giles's voice was an intruding whisper. "Ah, yes. And now the head. The head, Salome!"

The terrible thing done in plaster of paris lay on the lid of the grand piano. Swaying, she approached it, seized it by its mane of coarse black hair. It swung like a heavy pendulum as she lifted it. Her throat constricted, and for a moment she was not able to speak. Speak—address this severed head.

The first time she had seen it, she had screamed. And though she had mastered most of the play to Giles's satisfaction, this last scene was far from perfect. How many times had Giles exhorted her to think of the head as a symbol of womanly triumph! How many times had he urged her to hate it as she would a lover who had scorned her!

"'I will kiss thy mouth . . .'" she whispered. Her hand shook and the head wavered and she wondered if it could not have been made lighter. It was so heavy to hold, as if it had been real. That was the way Giles liked it, of course. She put out a hand to catch herself as she went faint, and then someone removed the head from her grasp and put a steadying arm around her waist.

"Giles, you're a beast!" She leaned back against Archer as he spoke, and heard the thunk of the plaster head as he hurled it across the room into a leather-covered chair.

"You're interrupting, Mr. Snow!" Giles snapped.

"Nonsense. Lily is finished for the day. She's going for a drive with me."

Lily was afraid to look up, afraid to see Giles's livid face, and she clung to the safety of Archer's arm as he led her out of the room. Archer had a way with Giles. Giles might bluster, he might threaten, but before Archer his menace subsided. The mad dog became a gentle puppy. Such, perhaps, was the power of money. Even Giles Benton did not dare risk the wrath of a wealthy angel. Or was it more than that? He was an unusual man, this Archer Snow. She had never met anyone like him. And she was glad to see him for other reasons than that he had freed her from the rehearsal.

He came nearly every day, and they would have dinner together, the three of them. She knew that over the candlelit table he drank his fill of her as much as of the wine, and the idea did not upset her as it would have with another man. There was something in the reverence of his gaze, as if the prism of his soul refracted her beauty into rainbows, separating hue from hue. And it was this same understanding of Giles Benton's genius, she thought, that made Giles turn mild in Archer's presence. It was the reason Archer could peremptorily call Giles a beast and haul her away from rehearsal and the hideous head of Jokanaan.

"We are going for a ride, Lily."

"Thank heaven! I need the air."

"You're not going to faint now? I could take you back to the house."

"No."

"You've forgotten your shoes. Wait here. I'll go back for them."

She sighed and rested against the seat of his fine brougham, listening to the mimosa and palms rustling against the hot wind. She had been living here in Giles Benton's rented Garden District mansion for more than a month. She had been certain at first that she knew what would happen, and she had insisted on inside bolts for her third-floor apartment. But never once had she heard Giles Benton's feet on the stairs. He had abused her, desecrated her in every way but one. Even when he had come upon her practicing the Dance of the Seven Veils in tights, her body taut and glowing, he had merely given her an appraising glance before going on about his business.

She was not Lily Beau Clair to him. She was Salome, Princess of Judea, a mere instrument of his greatness. Or was she? Archer Snow was in love with her, and Giles did not like it. Was he jealous? Why didn't he make a move himself, then? She supposed it had something to do with his molding her to the role of Salome—to her destiny, he would tell her grandly. Archer had not declared himself either. But could there be a storm building over her head—both of them in love with her?

He came back with her shoes, lifted her foot in his palm, kissed its dainty arch as he put the slipper on. They drove along the river to feel the coolness coming off the water. "Oh, Archer, I'll never be able to do it." She sighed.

"Yes, you will, Lily."

"Why are you so sure?"

"Because Giles says so."

"Giles is insane."

"I know," said Archer, "but he's a genius. He's a wonderful director, and someday he'll write a marvelous play himself."

"Why doesn't he do that now and forget *Salome*? I wish I could!"

"I think he hasn't found his subject. Giles is peculiar that way."

"He's peculiar every way. I . . . am afraid of him."

The afternoon sunlight shimmered on the water, and the carriage wheels crunched over the white shell road. She had not realized what a relief it would be to be away from the house. "It's because he's bothered you?" Archer asked.

"No."

"Then it's because he makes you think of this man you loved."

"I suppose so."

"I shall speak to him, Lily."

"Please . . . don't. I don't want a quarrel between you. It's something I must face for myself."

"You will be rich and famous and all of New Orleans will be as much in love with you as I am, Lily."

"Oh, Archer, please don't say you love me!"

"But I do!"

"There is no hope for it!"

"You don't know that. Let me kiss you, dearest." Before she could say no, he reined in beneath an oak and took her in his arms. His kiss quivered with a sweet warmth that was as much unlike any kiss she had known as he was unlike any man. If only she could be in love with him! Was she wrong about its being impossible?

Giles Benton came to her room that night. Incredibly, after all these weeks she heard him mount the stairs and clutched the covers with tense hands as his knock sounded on the door.

"Who is it?" she called. Anything to delay, to give her time to think.

"It's Giles. Let me in."

"But . . . I am in bed, Giles."

The mild tone of request left his voice, and she heard the command of her teacher. "Open the door, Salome!"

She parted the mosquito netting and slipped out of the bed, glided across the murky floor, her gown of sprigged lawn glowing with ghostly starshine as she pulled the bolt. Her heart thudded, reminding her of the deep rhythm of a Martinique bullfrog in the Rose d'Inde.

She had become conditioned to obeying him. She had become his thing, his creation. She had lost her will before him, and as his eyes gleamed on the creamy curves of her breasts above her low bodice, she wished that she had stayed in the convent, serving a proper God.

He put his hands on her shoulders, and the touch repulsed her. They were small hands, softer and with a feel of more decadence than even those of Henry Wickersham. A yellow glare exploded in her brain like a flash of powder for a photograph, and she saw suddenly that she had not yet lost all her innocence, that Giles could show her degradations beyond what Henry had. His eyes fastened on hers, and she waited, cringing.

"Lily, you went driving with Archer Snow today."

"Yes, Giles, I did."

"You are never to do that again," he said. His mouth twisted in a menacing grimace, and his hands pressed down upon her shoulders.

"But, Giles—"

"Archer Snow is in love with you. Suppose you fell in love with him, too? Then you would no longer grieve for this man who hurt you. You would be stupidly happy, and you would no longer be Salome. You are not a natural actress, Lily. You can't evoke what isn't in you. You must hate your lover, Lily!"

"You know I hate you, Giles. Won't that do?"

He smiled. "No. But it shouldn't surprise you that I don't care much for you either. You are a silly whore, a girl who lets her heart run away with her. That is the type I must always work with; it's the only kind that does well on the stage."

"I am not that sort of woman, Giles!" She found strength of her own, somewhere deep inside where he had not conquered her, and she moved to slam the door against him.

He blocked it, and the awful smile did not leave his face. "You are a whore, Lily. It's your nature. You gave yourself to a man you did not marry, but I do not need to know that to know you are a whore. It breathes from every pore of your lovely body that you are mistress to love—rapture's mistress, I might call you! You are never to go driving with Archer again, Lily. I do not want you alone with him!"

"And if I am?" she cried.

"Then I will make you sorry. I will teach you things men do with women that your other lovers never will." He left and closed the door behind him.

In the morning he gave her her costume. Layers of gauze dripped from its jeweled headdress, the bodice glittered with imitation emeralds and diamonds, and her wrists and arms were decked in bracelets. But the bodice ended too soon, just beneath the breasts, and the skirt began beneath her navel, its many layers of flimsy material set with tiny bells that jingled enticingly with her every move.

"Giles, I can't appear in public in this!"

"Of course you can. It's what Salome would have worn."

"But this is not ancient Judea! It's New Orleans!"

"So much the better. It will be more appreciated. It will drive men wild. That is the thing you are good for—to drive men wild, as Salome did Herod. You are the evil of womanhood personified in that getup!"

She did not doubt that he hated her. She wondered how many of his actresses had suffered his wrath and whether any had felt the horror of the desecration he had threatened.

"Dance, Salome!"

She danced amid the veils, her bracelets jangling, her bare torso gyrating. She thought of the love she had given Joe and of how he had condemned her without even seeing her, had passed judgment and executed sentence. Tears she had pent up for months streaked her cheeks as she thought of how he had believed her capable of killing their unborn child, of behaving as though their love affair had been only the casual arrangement of a strumpet. And his voice seemed to blend with Giles's as he called her a whore, a mistress of love.

Revenge sang through her as she seized the severed head and felt it swing from her hand with its grisly weight. " 'Thou didst bear thyself toward me as to a harlot—to me, Salome, daughter of Herodias, Princess of Judea! Thou art dead, and thy head belongs to me!' "

She heard the sound of applause and turned to see satisfaction at last on Giles Benton's face.

She opened at the French Opera, and the sound grew to thunder. The roar of it frightened her as the curtain dropped. The trance in which the role had held her broke, and no longer the lustful Salome, but Lily again, she would have run away had Giles not grabbed her and sent her back for her curtain calls. She lost track of how many times she bowed before the glare of the lights. It might have been ten times or a hundred, but somewhere along the way she lost her fear and began to relish the adulation, to smile and catch the roses that were tossed to her, kissing the petals and throwing them back to her admirers.

Somehow she found herself out of the theater, and dressed in a gown of duchesse satin with deep falls of lace over the sleeves, she was being handed into a carriage pulled by white horses. But oddly, the horses were being unhitched. She gasped as the carriage tilted and eager young men in frock coats and silk evening shirts fell to the shafts to draw her along the streets. She gripped the seat and smiled at them all, fighting down panic as they arrived at the hotel ballroom that had been engaged for the opening-night celebration. There was a mob in front of the place, and she heard the whistles of police as hands reached for her hand, her dress, any part of her that could be touched.

Suddenly Archer was beside her, clearing a way into the ballroom, and everyone stood back as he danced the first waltz with her. "Oh, Lily, you were more marvelous than I ever dreamed," he whispered.

She was only just beginning to realize what it all meant. The play was a success. And she would really be wealthy. Never again would she dance at the French Pigeon or teach children in an orphanage. Never again would she have to depend on any man for her support as she had Joe. She had a power, a freedom that was unknown to most of her sex, she thought as she danced with Archer.

And then Giles came forward to claim his turn, and she thought of all she owed him. It was he who had insisted that she do the play. He who had made her Salome.

"Oh, Giles, thank you," she whispered.

His smile was a trifle unpleasant as he answered, "No

doubt it is the last time you will do so. You will forget quickly enough. You will soon believe all you read and hear about yourself, and you'll forget who created you. No matter. I did not create Salome for your benefit. I shall reap my fame and my percentage, and you'll always belong to me."

She was glad when the waltz was over, gladder still when she had done with other dignitaries and Archer claimed her again. "Come, Lily, there's something I want to show you," he said. He danced her close to a door that opened into the kitchen, and pulling her inside, put a cloak around her, covering even her hair. Before the pack of admirers could follow, he whisked her out to a carriage.

"It's pleasant to ride in the ordinary way again." She sighed as the horses clopped along the dark streets. "Where are we going, Archer?"

"I want you to see a little triumph of mine, now that I've seen yours." On the outskirts of the city, he turned the horses into a narrow lane lined with oaks. Long gray banners of Spanish moss streamed in the moonlight as they approached a house.

"Oh, Archer," she breathed. She did not have to be told that the house itself was what he had brought her to see. The odor of raw lumber mingled in the air with the scent of newly planted bushes of jasmine and bridal wreath. Simple white columns rose gracefully over the wide veranda, and a flight of steps swept majestically to a shell walk. It was a classic design in which new ideas had been strikingly melded with old. The fanlight above the door had a swirling design that reminded her of peacock's feathers, and inside mantels and archways moved in flowing curves, supported by elongated Art Nouveau statues of women with flowing hair. The lighting fixtures were not chandeliers but squares of translucent glass painted with delicate Oriental-looking designs.

Everything was airy and open; it had the feeling of openness Lily had missed since leaving Acelie. But she could never confuse this house with Acelie. That house had been comforting, furnished with the possessions of generations. And this house was exciting, modern, and fresh as a new morning. It appealed to her sense of adventure, and she ran about to look at everything, stopping only to exclaim over some discovery and to cry, "Oh, Archer, I love it! Oh, I think it must be your masterpiece!"

The furnishings themselves were as modern as the design, and obviously were selected to complement it—great oak sideboards with inlays of bleached mahogany; tall ladder-backed chairs that matched the long sweep of walls and windows. Even the vases had lone, sinuous lines.

"Oh, it's perfectly wonderful! How I wish it were mine!"

"It is."

She stopped short and stared at him. "Archer, whatever do you mean?"

He drew her back to the main hall and showed her something she had missed in her hurry—a great painting in a silver frame. "Do you know what it represents, Lily?"

"It's a print of Aubrey Beardsley's illustration for *Salome*," she said, looking at the bold black-and-white study of a woman.

"Long ago you promised I might build your house, Lily, so I've done it. It's a statement of my love. Say you will live in it for me."

"For you?" she said, puzzled. "Do you mean with you?"

"With me? Oh, Lily, could you ever? Would you marry me?" He took her in his arms and kissed her. The power of his great love mingled with the success of *Salome*, and overcome, she swooned away.

She saw his face over hers as she lay on a bed; his eyes were anxious as he fanned her cheeks, eager as he hoped for his answer. "Oh, Archer, I cannot marry you. . . ."

The light dropped out of his expression, but he did not miss a beat as he waved the fan above her. "It is that lover of yours, then. You still love him more than you hate him?"

"No!"

"What then?"

"I . . . have a husband already—on Martinique."

"A husband! I do have such beastly luck! I thought you were a widow."

"A widow? Oh . . . that was the story that Susan told Henry Wickersham when he was interested in me. I suppose you heard it then, that first night we met, when Henry wanted you to change that monstrosity of a house to suit me. I was married to a man on Martinique, and I ran away with his brother. That is the simple truth of it."

Archer sighed. "I am glad that you told me, Lily."

"Archer, I am sorry. I deceived you without even meaning to do so. I let you fall in love with me. I did not think. I was thinking instead of *Salome*, and it was so pleasant to have your company."

"Don't worry, Lily. It can't be helped. And anyway, you have told me what I longed to hear."

"What, Archer?"

"That you like my house and my company. You shall live here, Lily. You must. This house is meant for you. Here you shall be free of Giles Benton." His hands were working on the fastenings of her dress. "Come, we must get you to bed."

"Archer . . . I cannot!" she cried, pushing him away.

He laughed. "I did not mean like that. I meant to sleep, of course. Tomorrow night, you dance again. I shall be watching, Salome!" He blew her a kiss and left her alone.

19

When she awoke, her public had found her already. There were carriages in the lane, and she saw police forming a cordon across the lawn. An awed little maid served her a breakfast of cream cheese and waffles, and when she went downstairs, she found a haughty butler guarding the door. At ten Giles Benton blew in, personally bringing her clothing and rave notices from all the newspapers.

"It will give you a swelled head to read these," he muttered. "I suppose there's no help for it."

"I will try to remain humble, Giles."

"Never mind. Humility is alien to women, and all that applause night after night is not going to help. Ah, this is a beautiful house! Archer Snow is a genius!"

"Yes, and he thinks the same of you."

"And the two of us both in the clutches of women. I, who must take snippets like you and turn them into objects of public adulation, and Archer, who is moved to build masterpieces so that snippets like you can live in them. I did think Archer had better sense. I thought he was different."

"All men are alike where women are concerned," said Lily wisely.

"You aren't going to marry him, are you?"

"No."

"I thought not. God save me from a lovesick actress!"

He did not seem to mind her living in Archer's house. In fact, Giles seemed to have forgotten his prohibitions about Archer. Everything was all right so long as she was not in love with Archer. She called the place Snowdown in honor of its designer, and in a matter of weeks it became a landmark. Archer had a high fence built around it and hired guards to patrol its gates.

He himself was there every morning. She came to look forward to the sight of him puttering in the gardens beneath her window, happily in his element. Always she would send the maid to invite him in to breakfast, and they would sip *café noir* on the patio together, reading the newspapers and discussing events of the day. He was as interested in the management of the household as she, always asking who their dinner guests would be and suggesting what should be included on the menu.

One would have thought him the master of the establishment, to see them together. There was little to indicate that at night he hung his trousers elsewhere, and indeed all New Orleans thought they were lovers. Had he not sponsored her play and built Snowdown for her? When one of them was invited to a supper or party, it was always expected the other would come too. They were always together, always affectionate, gay, and companionable.

They had received an offer to take *Salome* to New York, but Archer didn't want them to go yet. They were happy in New Orleans at Snowdown.

It was a pleasant life—an exciting life. "Oh, if I could have met him first!" she would often think. "Then I would not have married Edmond. I would not have fallen prey to Joe."

He was gentle and fun to be with. He was intelligent and witty—he knew every *bon mot* of the day. He was handsome, elegant, and he adored her. But he adored her in a different way than Edmond or Joe. He was more civilized than most men. He did not have that animal drive just beneath the surface, that gnawing, uncontrollable need for her body that Joe and Edmond had had, each in his own way. Now and then he kissed her and touched her breasts and told her he would like to bed her. Each time she laughed and told him no, and he went away with that gentle smile of his.

But did she really like it that way? How many times at night did she awaken dreaming of the glory she had known with Joe! And then it was she who was consumed by that terrible craving that nothing could fulfill. Nothing—unless it was the lover who had scorned and rejected her, left her penniless and alone. In those awful hours before dawn, she admitted to herself that the fame of *Salome*, the companionship of Archer Snow, had not cured her of her love for Joe Beau Clair. It was a disease, and she wondered if at last it would destroy her.

The problem grew, and Lily could no longer sleep at night. She lay restless, tossing on the silken pillows, her mind and body consumed with need for her lover.

"Take Archer to bed," Susan said when Lily confessed her problem.

"I don't love Archer!"

"But you like him. Go ahead. It'll soothe the itch. It's what I do. You don't think I let Henry near me anymore after what he tried to do to you?"

"How many lovers have you taken?" Lily asked, intrigued.

"Oh, dear me. I didn't keep count. One is about like another, you know. Interestingly different in detail, but in sum about the same."

Lily sighed. "It's not at all that way with me."

"But you don't really know. You've only had two men."

For once Lily did not listen to Susan. She did not have to try other men to know that no other could ever move her as Joe had. She began to stay later and later at parties, dancing until sunrise, when she returned to Snowdown so exhausted she could fall into a stupor of sleep.

Then one cool dawn, there was no need for sleep. As she opened the door of her bedroom, a shadow moved across. Naked arms grasped her; she breathed heady, masculine aromas as her breasts were crushed against the crisp, springy hair of a strong chest. She swayed in bliss as her lips were commandingly covered. She felt she had slid into a dream, waking. Then he drew back and looked at her, and she remembered she hated him.

"Joe! Let me go!"

There was nothing gentle in those hurricane eyes of his as she struggled to free herself. She saw that he hated her, too. But he needed her just as she needed him.

"Ah, Lily, that's right, fight me. That's the way it should be. That's the way I want it."

She felt her dress rip as he threw her to the bed. Her breasts were bare to his ravenous gaze, and then his rough hands tore again at her clothes, and her stomach and thighs were exposed. He put an arm beneath the small of her back, forcing her to arch toward him as he stripped the skirts away from her legs. She made use of this new freedom of her lower limbs to try to kick him, but her struggle only fired his passion, and the thought wandered through her head that she had known what would happen, that indeed that had been her intention.

She beat at him as his entry drew from her a long, wondrous moan; and, tears streaming from her eyes, she bit his cheek as he tried to kiss her.

"Why don't you scream, Lily? That would bring the maid, and she could bring the police. You're being raped, aren't you? Is it the scandal you're afraid of? Everyone would be on your side, and I would be lynched. Wouldn't that please you?"

Lily did not answer. She had all she could do to fight back the sounds of ecstasy that would convince him that nothing could please her more than what was happening. But he knew already. He knew her so well he could tell just how close she was to her climax. He felt her strain toward it, and he drew back, gazing at her with leering blue eyes as if to require her to acknowledge that he had mastered her utterly and completely. She gasped for breath, hating him as she never had before. Was he going to humiliate her entirely, refusing to grant her her release by scorning to take his own pleasure?

He hovered above her as she gritted her teeth, determined not to beg him to return to her body, but somehow her hand betrayed her and pressed against his buttocks. He plunged back against her with a terrible force, and his body convulsed with her, as they were both buffeted in gales of transport.

"You knew it would happen, didn't you, Salome?" he said when he could breathe again. "You knew that I would come back to New Orleans and find you the toast of the town. And you knew I couldn't help going to see you perform. Did you think every night as you did the Dance of the Seven Veils that I might be in the audience? Is that why you are so marvelous in the role?"

"I am wonderful because Giles Benton made me so. It's a miracle he does, making actresses of silly girls like me." She delighted in giving him an answer other than the one he sought, but she saw, too, that there was truth in what he said. Hadn't she known that he would find her as Salome? Hadn't this encounter been inevitable?

"How did you get in, Joe?"

"I came over the wall and climbed up the trellis. Oh, and there is a guard you had better give a bonus. He got himself clouted trying to defend you."

"You ought to leave now that you've had your fun," she said. "He may wake and raise a hue and cry." She spoke haughtily, her voice a challenge as she hoped that he would insist on driving his conquest home by telling her she was his and he would never let her go.

Instead he reached for his trousers. "You're right. I should go. And I hope I find the strength not to come back again. God help me, I still love you! I have slept with others, trying to forget you, but you are my *diablesse* in every incarnation—Lily, Mimi, Salome! Oh, how I rue the day I went to Carnival!"

"No more than I, Joe Beau Clair!" she cried after him. "No more than I!"

"So he came back, did he?" Susan asked. "I hope you gave him a piece of your mind for leaving you!"

"It was a piece of *me* he wanted!" Lily sighed.

"Of course you put a stick through his wheel about that?"

"No."

"No!" Susan put down her teacup and stared at her friend. "I always thought you were the one of us that had principle. What are you coming to, Lily?"

"I suppose I'm what I've always been. Giles said I would always be rapture's mistress."

"Joe will be at the theater tonight," Susan said suddenly.

Lily felt her heart jump. "He won't! Why should he be?"

"For the same reason he couldn't stay away last night, sis, when he came here. I'm right, I'll wager."

That night Joe Beau Clair told himself he was only going for a stroll. But his feet wandered toward Toulouse and Bourbon streets, to the area of the French Opera. She would be dancing again soon, his Lily. No, not his anymore. Was she anybody's Lily? Did she belong to this Giles Benton of whom she had spoken? Or to Archer Snow, who had backed her debut?

He had spent the early part of the evening with Henry Wickersham at a faro club. Henry had been pleased to fill Joe in on what was common gossip. Archer Snow had built Snowdown especially for Lily. Everyone assumed they were lovers. But Henry, being Henry, had heard gossip that was not so common, and he chuckled at the discomfort he knew he was causing Joe as he told it.

There had been a certain rumor about Giles Benton and Archer Snow. It had been said that there was more than a business relationship between them, if Joe got his meaning. And now Archer Snow had fallen insanely in love with Lily, the creation of his old paramour. Giles Benton had them both in his power, so the story went. Giles was at the center of this queer triangle, and scenes in the bedroom were as much under his direction as those on the stage.

One could imagine no end of depravity with this trio, and Joe ought to be glad to be rid of Lily, Henry said. Henry supposed Joe was grateful to him for putting him onto her ways—for having told about that scar under her fringe. What could you expect of a girl who got mixed up with the likes of Jim Frey?

But Henry had pushed his story too far. Joe might have believed Lily the mistress of Archer Snow, but the rest of it went beyond credibility. Henry was fortunate that Joe had so much on his mind. What Henry had said was plenty of reason for Joe to give Frey Henry for company in St. Louis Cemetery Number One. The two of them would be a fine pair to poison the worms!

Joe had been so preoccupied he'd hardly noticed Henry more than a flea. Grateful to Henry Wickersham indeed! What a fool Joe thought he had been when he'd listened to him about Frey. If Henry Wickersham hadn't told him about Frey, he'd never have known that she had been protecting him, that she had cut the towrope when he and Frey had been racing.

And he would have had her still. He would have been with her when she'd found herself pregnant, and he would have had his child, too, by now. She would never have had it aborted if he had been with her—he'd have seen to that.

The idea bothered him more than he wanted to admit. He tried to force it back as he had so many times, the idea that it had been his fault as well as hers. No, no, he told himself. He had been justified in doing what he had. He had left her money in the bank, and she had known it. And she had been able to pass as his wife, if she had needed. No, she had no excuse for what she had done!

Perhaps she had thought he didn't want a child. The thought slipped in as it had before. True, he had agreed they should have none, but what she had done was revolting, unnatural for a woman!

He wouldn't go and see her dance again tonight! No, he must go on trying to regain himself as he had these past months. He had sailed. He had had adventures. The daughter of Samoan royalty had rubbed his hair with coconut oil and allowed him to remove her dress of native cloth of mulberry bark, but all had been sour without Lily.

Babylon

"Men and their honor!" she always said. Part of him was close to agreeing with her. If he had not been so quick about his honor, if he had not been so worried about his freedom . . . And now none of it seemed any good. How simple the world had seemed before he'd met her.

When he found himself in front of the theater, he knew he had no willpower left. And then, when she danced, he grew angry again. Who was she to make him feel that he would give his soul for one more hour in her bed? Could it be that the dance was more frenzied than it had been the night before? That there was some special message of defiance in it for him? When she sank to the stage at the end of her dance, she seemed unable to rise, and King Herod had to take her by the hand and lift her to her feet.

"What would thou have, Salome?"

She trembled so that the little bells on her skirt jingled again. "The head of Jo . . . kanaan!"

Her lover felt ice in the pit of his stomach. He knew that when she had faltered she had almost said, "The head of Joe Beau Clair!"

20

"Giles, I am tired of being Salome. Couldn't we do another play?"

"Don't be impatient, Lily. You are better than ever in *Salome*. These past weeks there has been something extra added—some new dimension. It would be foolish to quit now. You shall have another role in time, when this one wears thin."

"It is I who am wearing thin, Giles. It's the role that will last and I who will give."

"She does look tired, Giles," Archer put in, as the three of them sat over dinner at Snowdown. "Perhaps a small vacation would be in order. Somewhere cool, I think. You have seen very little of this country, Lily. Perhaps the mountains of North Carolina. I know an excellent lodge near Asheville. I would be glad to take you."

She put her hand over his gratefully. "Oh, yes, mountains! It has been so long since I have seen any. I miss the mountains of Martinique."

"No!"

She whirled to see Giles's livid face.

"Only a few days, Giles," Archer protested.

"She will get out of character. She's not a natural actress, I tell you!" He brought down his fist and made the silver jump.

"Giles!" Archer cried, but the director stalked off, banging his way out to his brougham without waiting for dessert.

"Why does he act that way, Archer?" Lily said with a shudder. "It's almost as though he's afraid that I'll get out of his grip some way—and why? It's not the money he cares about. He's got enough already."

"Never mind, Lily. I'll bring him around."

"What is the matter with him, Archer?"

"It's between him and me. Don't fret about it. Remember, we know he's insane."

"Do you think you could persuade him to close *Salome* while you're at it?"

"If that's really what you want, then I'll get it done, my love."

"Oh, yes, Archer."

She never knew how he managed it, but Giles's attitude changed. "You shall have a vacation, Lily, and then, when you are rested, we'll talk about a new role."

"Something without dancing, please."

Giles rubbed his hands through his graying hair. "Yes, without dancing. You mustn't become stereotyped. I shall give you some of Ibsen's work to take with you. We might try *Hedda Gabler*. It's an ambitious role, but your public would love it."

One change had been made in the plans that Lily did not like. Archer was no longer to go with her to the lodge in the mountains. "It's business, Lily." He shrugged. "It can't be helped. I should have liked to go more than anything."

"It will be lonely without you."

"But I must go to Europe and see after some investments instead."

"Will you be going to France?"

"Yes, it's possible."

"Maybe you'd see about an investment for me. I am interested in that new Panama Canal Company they are forming."

He looked at her agape. He had had his brokers carefully manage her earnings, but this was the first time she had shown a desire for any particular venture. "It would not be wise, Lily," he said. "There will never be a canal. Even Ferdinand de Lesseps has failed."

"Nevertheless, buy me a few shares."

"Very well. It's your money."

It gave her a sense of reckless release to invest in the Panama Canal, though she was hard put to know why she had done it. Joe once had. It was a sentimental gesture to the past, and one that was likely to cost her. No wonder women were considered incompetent to handle their own money, but she could afford the loss.

How quickly precious things slipped into the past! Acelie . . . Joe . . . and now *Salome*. Snowdown's airy look had shifted subtly to one of vacancy, and boxes and portmanteaus in its hallways gave it an unsettled feel that her homey touches of wicker and bright cushions and impressionistic paintings did nothing to quell. On the closing night of *Salome* she felt she was preparing to go to the funeral of someone she had murdered.

What would this vacation solve, after all? When she returned, Joe would be gone, most likely. She would no longer wonder if he were there every night watching her dance. Instead of that torment, there would be the torment of knowing he was not. The mountains would not cure her of the pain of loving him.

"There is a gentleman to see you, madame."

"Very well, I'll come." She felt a slight annoyance. It was less than an hour before she had to leave for the theater, and she was supposed to be resting. The maid should have told the gentleman she could not see him. But Lily couldn't rest; she might as well take care of whatever it was. It must be the man come for the luggage, she thought with no interest as she went downstairs.

"Lily!"

She almost fainted at the sight of Joe Beau Clair in her parlor. Swiftly she closed the heavy wooden doors, and then, leaning against them, she studied him. He seemed a bit thinner than when she had seen him last. His curly brown hair was cut shorter, and in those blue eyes a look she hadn't seen before mingled with an eagerness that she was afraid might be reflected from her own.

"Lily, I've come to ask you to forgive me. I should have known you wouldn't destroy our baby."

She tilted her chin warily. "You thought so once. You sold the house and all my clothes and left me to the mercy of New Orleans. What has changed your mind? Is it only that you don't want the inconvenience of raping me again?"

"Oh, Lily. When I sold the house, I was mad with grief. I thought you were probably dead. I had torn apart the Vieux Carré looking for you. I thought you had bled to death, and they had thrown you in the river, like so many girls. Then I found you alive and I was furious again. But now Susan has told me that you lost the child in a fall from a trolley. Forgive me and put an end to this hell I've been living in!"

She hesitated, searching his face. Clever Susan. She had seen how much Lily needed Joe, and she had made things right. But could she forgive a man who had thought that of her?

"What about *your* forgiving *me*?" she stalled. "I cut the towrope and made you lose the race. I interfered, and you said you couldn't bear living so."

He sensed success and grinned at her. "I have found I can't bear living any other way than with you!"

"I do not intend to give up acting the way I did dancing with the ballet."

"I will accept that, too, Lily. Perhaps it will keep you from interfering. Say you forgive me."

She trembled and shook her head. "I must think, Joe."

"Then think tonight while you are dancing. And when you have finished, come to the train station and I'll be waiting for you. We'll take your vacation together." And confidently he blew her a kiss on his way out.

The theater was jammed for the final performance. Every seat was filled, and people stood in the aisles. She danced for the last time, wondering what she would do when the curtain fell. It was really not a difficult decision, and the dance that was supposed to be permeated with scorn and revenge instead had a quality of innocent joy. She would go with Joe, of course. Joe had had good reason for his confidence, she thought, unable to keep from smiling, even as she addressed the hideous plaster head.

"'They say love hath a bitter taste. But what matter? I have kissed thy mouth.'" She spoke her last lines, and soldiers rushed forward to crush her beneath their shields. The curtain dropped, its heavy velvet muting the torrent of applause, the shouts of "bravo."

Giles Benton came out to take the final curtain call with her. "It's a good thing we're quitting, Lily," he muttered. "You behaved very strangely tonight."

"Don't be so picky, Giles. Smile. No one else is displeased. Oh, and Giles, I won't be staying long at the party tonight. I'm frightfully tired."

He wouldn't like it, but he couldn't yell at her onstage; and when the curtain fell, she darted away to her dressing room to change, pausing only for words of farewell to members of her cast and crew.

"Monsieur Beau Clair is waiting in your dressing room," said her maid. "Was I right to let him in?"

"Yes. It's all right." Her spirit soared. How like Joe not to be able to wait, even for her to come to the station! Would he make a show of it and carry her off in her scanty costume, as he once had in her jupe dress when she had danced with the ballet? Or would something else happen behind the locked door of her dressing room? Something that could not be delayed for the rocking berth of the Pullman car clacking away into the mountains in the night.

In an ecstasy of expectation she threw open the door of her dressing room. And there before her stood a ghost, the specter that had haunted her ever since she had left Martinique, the man she had wronged more deeply than she could ever wrong anyone else.

"Edmond!"

"What is it, Lily? Didn't you expect me? I told your maid my name. Imagine seeing you dancing on a stage like that! Like some common native girl! But that's all over. You are going back where you belong. Back to Martinique."

His words were crisp and matter-of-fact, though she saw desire in his eyes as he looked at her bare torso, the rise of her breasts in the short, tight bodice.

"I am not going, Edmond. It's absurd to think I will. There's nothing between us. I don't love you, and I have been your brother's mistress."

"My brother! That is still it, isn't it? Is that who you thought was waiting here? Is that why you were smiling so when you came through that door? He's in New Orleans, all right. I saw the *Sea Bird* at the docks. I suppose *he* doesn't mind the way you flaunt yourself! I swore to kill him, and I will, if I find him."

Her mind whirled. He would kill Joe! She must get away—get away with Joe. "Edmond, there's a party. They are waiting for me. Afterward, you can come to my house. Snowdown is the name of it. Then we'll talk."

He saw through the suggestion at once and shook his head sadly. "No, Lily. I know that if I let you out of my sight, you will run away again. You are still my wife; that is what matters. It took me a while to sort things out. I was so shocked the night I found you in Joe's bed. I loathed you then; I never wanted to see you again. But now I have had time to think. You belong to me, and I am going to make you do what's right. You'll be a wife and bear me children. What use is everything I have done without children?

"Oh, Lily, if you could see how beautiful Acelie is now— how the cane and cacao are flourishing. I have paid the debt as I promised you the night we married. I have kept my promises. Keep yours."

He looked so fierce she was afraid of him. How odd to be afraid of gentle Edmond. She would never have imagined it possible in the days when he had been her suitor and she had been able to manipulate him as she pleased. But even then she had known he was a man of principle.

"I am in love with Joe," she said bravely.

"I am not concerned with love, Lily. I have not come to beg you to care for me instead of him. I have not come to throw myself at your feet. I have come only to take what is mine. And if you love Joe, all the more reason you must come with me. If I find Joe, there will be bloodshed. Perhaps it would be I who would die, but you would be responsible, either way, for fratricide."

Looking at his determined face, she knew he was right. She cursed the fame she knew must have drifted on some ship to Martinique to bring him here, and she understood that she had become the crossroads at which one brother would murder the other. Unless... unless she did as he asked.

"If I go with you, will you promise not to fight Joe?"

His lips turned in a wry smile. "I will not fight Joe, so long as you do your part. But if you run away again..."

She sighed. "I will not run away, Edmond, ever again." Tears streaked her cheeks as she left the theater, and those who saw her were touched that the closing of the play should so affect her. The *Picayune* reported the next day that there had been something strangely profound in the way Lily Beau Clair had repeated the last line of the play as she departed: "'They say love hath a bitter taste. But what matter? I have kissed thy mouth.'"

21

She wept again when she saw Acelie gleaming with a new roof and a new coat of yellow wash. She had thought it lost forever, and she wanted to gather it to her with its memories and its ghosts. The great green banana trees, the golden cane, seemed to lean toward her with rustling welcome, and far off in the *ajoupas* she heard the soft sound of a banjo drifting on the breeze.

The house, the island, she so loved. If only the people she had loved could be here too! But better that Papa was in his grave than to know the disgrace she had brought him. Even Yzore would tell Lily she had been wrong to run away with Joe. Yzore would not understand a Creole lady having a heart like anyone else. And then, as she made her way toward the kitchen, toward the part of the house where she had always been most comforted, she found the one person who linked her girlhood to her present.

A sob caught in Lily's throat as she saw Cyrillia swaying gracefully as the cane in a great balata-wood rocker. She was singing, and in her lap was the most beautiful baby Lily had ever seen. Curly brown locks reminded her of Joe; huge dark eyes shone from a soft, plump face just tinged with the clear red of its mother's skin.

"Oh, Rilla," she whispered. "It's a boy, isn't it?"

The baby gave a startled cry as Rilla jumped up, gathering her child against her calico bodice, and Lily saw that she was already pregnant again, her breasts swollen from nursing, her stomach already large for another birth.

"Yes, missy," she said with a touch of defiance.

"Oh, do let me hold him!"

Rilla did not release the baby. "You will have your own soon enough now."

"Yes, and the same man shall father it. But, Rilla, I didn't want to come back. And now that I have, I don't want to spoil things for you."

Babylon

"He will sleep only with you. He told me."

Lily shuddered, remembering. "You know I don't wish it."

"It doesn't matter. In this world it is not what women want that counts." And suddenly she wept and thrust the baby to Lily to hold.

Night came. The lilac clouds went dark behind the banana trees and palmistes. The breeze rustled, still warm and sweet with the scent of woodsmoke and sugar as she went upstairs where the huge form of the bateau bed waited for her. She stood gazing at it, remembering the loss of her virginity and how she had put the blessed palm leaves from the Corpus Christi procession above it to get her a child.

Tonight if she were to put such a charm there, Edmond would not tear it down! He had not touched her all the way to Martinique, and she had known he was waiting. Waiting for her to reconcile herself to it, waiting so that his son would be conceived here, as it should be. And after she had borne it, he would not be content. He wanted a dozen children. This he had told her as they stood together at the rail of the ship that was bringing them home. Their sons would be a bond between them, she would see. "You will be content someday, Lily," he had promised.

Content! Could she ever be? She had tried not to think of anything at all during the trip. Even when they had passed Montserrat and she had glimpsed the palm-curtained town of Plymouth where she had lain first with Joe, she had tried not to think how she had left him waiting for her in New Orleans. She had fought against picturing him as he waited, forced to concede defeat. Her heart ached at the thought of his certainty that she would forgive him.

What did Archer think? And Giles Benton? She had left no word for anyone for fear Joe might trace her and decide to come after her. She had left New Orleans with as little fanfare as she had entered it. Giles would be furious. And Archer—what would he do with Snowdown now? How far away New Orleans seemed as she heard her husband's footsteps coming. It was as if this had been the only reality always, the thing that everything must return to. How little it mattered what women wanted.

She dropped on her knees before her little *chapelle* and began to plead that somehow she would find it possible to receive him. She did not ask to understand why the world must be arranged as it was; she did not ask for a miracle of passion to see her through. She asked that she might become resigned like other women and do the duty to Edmond that she had pledged before God.

She was still on her knees when he entered. Her eyes closed shut in prayer, she heard his shoes drop, heard the soft descent of his trousers to the wooden floor. He sighed with impatience as he waited for her to finish her devotions.

But she was not praying anymore. She had become too distracted, and yet she could not rise from her knees. Then she felt his arms around her matter-of-factly, lifting her up. "Come, Lily, I know you're not praying. Don't you think that's sacrilege, using your altar to avoid me? I will save you from that sin at least, though I have been so ineffectual at saving you from all your others."

He laid her on the great bed. "Think, Lily, the sooner it is done, the sooner we shall have our heir. And while you carry the child, I will let you alone."

"Yes, Edmond," she said. She must try to be grateful for that at least, but as he lowered his body to hers, she was suddenly reminded of other men who had tried to take her against her will. And suddenly this was no different from Henry Wickersham or Jim Frey. Suddenly she could not help fighting him, she knew she was winning over him. He was not the cad that Henry had been. He could not bring himself to violence. She escaped and shut herself into another room, to weep until dawn.

She was always weeping since she had come back. It seemed to her and to Edmond, too, that it would go on forever. It hurt him because he loved her still. He listened all night to her sobbing, sitting with his head in his hands. What had he ever done that he should be treated so? Why couldn't she love him instead of his brother?

He was not the madcap his brother was, but Joe could not have loved her with any more fervor than he. He was not an adventurer in the same sense as Joe, but he was a strong man who could rise to a challenge. He was competent and determined, a man who, having set a goal, would go on trying when all seemed impossible, when all others would have given up. It was those qualities that must give Acelie its heir. She must let him into her bed, and it must not be by force that she surrendered herself. He would settle for duty; that was all he had ever really expected.

As the sun laid its first warm glimmers on the shadowed cane, he watched her slender figure cross the veranda and take the earth path lined with logwood bushes and calabash trees as she went to the river to bathe. A few minutes later Cyrillia came out carrying their son, the sunlight polishing her skin like a rare jewel. As he gazed on her ripe body, he thought of the unbridled nights he had known with her, and a rush of heat surged within him.

He valued Cyrillia, but it did not occur to him to think that he loved her or that he should be grateful to her for all she had given him. He had never acknowledged that the child in her arms and the one in her belly were his, though he knew it, of course, if he bothered to think of it. Anyone could see the family resemblance in the baby, but no one expected him to acknowledge this son. Indeed, it would only have embarrassed everyone. He had come to her room the day after the birth and had congratulated her on a handsome child. She had given him her worshiping smile and been satisfied.

She seemed especially desirable to him this morning, after his frustrating night with Lily. The fruitlike roundness of her body enticed him, and he knew that even now, this close to her time, she would not deny him. But it was not Cyrillia he must lie with. The bounty of Cyrillia would never get him an heir. She was a mere appendage to his life, and it was Lily he must get with child. The sooner his seed took hold in her, the sooner he could seek release again in the willing arms of Cyrillia. He went downstairs and followed Lily to the river.

Unhesitatingly Lily scrambled over the rocks and into the crystal current of the Roxelane. For the moment she forgot the night that had passed, splashing the cold water onto her face to ease the burning of her eyes. Overhead a mountain whistler sang in a silk-cotton tree as she swam in the swirling rapids. How she had missed the Roxelane! She had expected to have to be content with sluggish bayous and the muddy width of the Mississippi and to imagine the whistler's song in the trills of the mockingbird. And here she was home again, like a dream. She struck out into the water delightedly, feeling hampered by her bathing costume. It seemed old-fashioned to her now, giving her little of the freedom she had had in the black serge bloomer-type suit she had bought in New Orleans. That was symbolic, she supposed, of all the freedom she had had there and would never have again. She had worn this outfit when she had swum with Joe in the crater of the Three Palmistes. His presence had made her feel naked in it, she remembered, and in spite of herself she looked up toward the high woods, toward the source of the rushing currents, to the cloud-shrouded mountaintop where she had once stood above the world with Joe Beau Clair.

"Lily!"

She gave a start as she saw Edmond standing on a boulder above her on the bank.

"G-good morning, Edmond." The cold water that had been so pleasant was suddenly chilling. But perhaps it would be as always. He had never spoken to her in the daylight of anything that had happened during the night. Why did she sense that this time would be different? He had something important to say or he would not have followed her, and she knew that there was only one such matter between them.

"Lily, do you remember the agreement we made in New Orleans? You would come here to live as my wife, and I would not go looking for Joe to kill him, as honor says I should?"

"I remember, Edmond."

"You aren't keeping your part of the bargain. You will give me no choice."

"I'm trying; it's all I can do," she said with a shiver.

He glared at her, and she was reminded of the time that Joe had been so angry with her when he'd found that she had cut the towrope. They were alike in some ways, these brothers, she thought fearfully. "Are you threatening me, Edmond?" she asked.

"No. I would never do that. I am telling you a truth. If my home has been damaged beyond repair, I must deal with the man who destroyed it, even if he is my brother. It will be better for everyone if you simply do what is right. Come back to the house when you have finished here and behave as you should to me. I will be waiting."

"Now?" she gasped. "In the daytime?"

He smiled at her ruefully. "It's possible to do such a deed even in the daylight, Lily. I suspect you know as much. You are far from the innocent girl I married."

When he had gone, she clambered out of the water and tried to warm herself against the heating rocks. She had tried to force herself, and she had not been successful. What was to prevent its happening this time, too? Her stomach churned at the thought of going into that room with him. She felt she could not take the first step back to Acelie. But what he had said about Joe had been clear enough. Finally she got to her feet and set out along the path. The mountain whistler seemed to follow her, flitting from tree to tree as she walked back to the house.

Edmond sighed with satisfaction when he heard her in the hallway. He would be gentle with her, he thought—as gentle as she allowed. But he must be firm, too. He remembered how willingly she had submitted to him on their wedding night, and how lost he had been in the glory of possessing her. He was not thinking of Cyrillia now. If only it could be like that again, he would forget the native girl forever. It was Lily he loved, Lily, his wife, whom he had worked so hard to marry.

Was he wrong not to duel Joe? Would only Joe's death erase him from her heart? She would hate him at first, of course. But then, as the years passed, she would mellow. She would understand that it had been necessary. . . .

But he did not relish bloodshed. Perhaps she would run away again to that strange life where people called her name, applauded, and threw flowers at her feet. She might go back to the stage, back to New Orleans. It galled him to think that she was home not because of him, but because of Joe.

She opened the door, and he saw with astonishment that she wore not a *chinoise* or a negligee, but a riding habit. "Lily, where do you think you are going?" he demanded.

"I have decided to go and consult a priest. Perhaps he can help me find a way to accept my duty. It is all I can think of to do."

He let her go with a sigh. He could not say that she wasn't trying to keep her bargain now. He could only hope and wait for her return.

The city of St. Pierre was unchanged. The yellow and red of its buildings made a bright twisting ribbon beneath the tropical sky, and water gurgled everywhere, cold and pure in open conduits. Looking toward the sea from Rue Victor Hugo, she saw boats seemingly suspended in the blue mix of sky and sea, and she breathed in the garlic-sugar aromas that permeated the town, drifting through the bluish-gray slatted shutters of the sashless windows. She heard the cries of street vendors, hawking alligator pears, snails, creole roots and herbs, cakes of codfish, and beans.

Crossing the Roxelane, where the rocks were white with wash and laundresses stood in the numbing currents, she went down to the central marketplace. It was out of her way, but she felt a need to see all the things there that had been familiar to her from childhood—ivory heads of palm, shaped like elephant's tusks; brown sapota fruit; cans of worms, which natives were frying alive to eat as a delicacy that tasted like almonds. As she stood transfixed by boats of blue, lilac, green, and scarlet fish pulled up into the middle of the paved square, the city suddenly quivered to the sound of great bells, the carillon from the cathedral. With a pang of apprehension Lily felt that the chimes rang for her alone, drawing her to the errand from which she had been wandering.

She turned at once and ran past stalls of sea needles and swordfish and sharks hung to sell, up little mossy, mosaic steps toward the church. But before going inside, she thought of another pilgrimage to make, to the Cimetière du Mouillage behind the church at the foot of Morne d'Orange. The air was sleepy with the scent of jasmine and white lilies; and the palms, the emblem of immortality, rose a hundred feet above the graves. She found that Edmond had set her father's with black-and-white chessboard tiles, like most of the others, and a black cross stood at its foot, bearing his name on a white plaque.

"Oh, Papa," she cried as she knelt beside it. He could never have imagined all that had happened to her. She skipped over it and went back to what had concerned him most when he had been dying. "Acelie is safe, Papa," she whispered. She did not add, "if only I can bear it a son," but as if he had heard her, the tall hot grasses seemed to answer, "It still can be, Lily! It still can be!"

Everything her father had dreamed of for her and for generations to come could still happen. It was the same message she had heard in her delirium in New Orleans when she had fallen from the trolley and lost Joe's child.

She could have sat for hours in the grass of the cemetery, where even death seemed unfrightening, a soft, vaporous presence rising into the bright air. She laid her head against her father's stone and almost wished she might sleep here beside him forever as she had once used to sleep in his lap. To sleep here beside him forever and have her duty done. She looked with near-envy at the peaceful white chapels and white Madonnas and angels. But she was still among the living, with much to be accomplished, and at last she walked back between the great twin palmistes that guarded the gate and went into the cathedral.

The coolness welcomed her; the flames of votive candles

flickered out of darkness. Then, as her eyes adjusted, statues of saints moved from the murk like a company of old friends, and she saw the arches and columns she had always loved. She dropped to her knees, and tears streamed down her cheeks as she prayed, "Let there be a way! Let it be possible for me to do my duty and to be content!"

She heard the soft swish of the priest's robes as he came to stand near her, waiting for her to finish her devotions. "Can I be of service, my child?" he asked as she lifted her head.

"I hope so, Father. You see, there is . . . a problem with my marriage." How she wished he were Father Jacques, whom she had always trusted.

"Come to my office, where it is more private," he suggested, and she followed him away from the sanctuary to a small room with a balata-wood desk and big rattan chairs. "Would you like a cocoyage?" he asked.

"Yes, please. I'm thirsty. I've ridden a long way."

He rang a little bell and told a servant girl who came to bring the refreshments. He folded his hands across the desk and looked at her complacently. "Now, this problem. Have you discovered that your husband has a native mistress?" It was the complaint he heard most, and women were always relieved to have him guess the trouble. "You must be patient. Such a woman means little to a man, and perhaps it is better—"

"Father that is not my problem!"

"Well . . . what, then?"

She lowered her head, and through her shame fought unsuccessfully to find the words.

"Perhaps it would be better for you to talk to the priest that married you," he said gently. "That is sometimes easier. What was his name?"

"Father Jacques."

"I don't know him."

"No, you wouldn't. He died during the smallpox epidemic. *La vérette pouf* killed him the day after he married us, and he had spent all night giving last sacraments in the lazaretto."

"That is a sad story. I have heard many sad stories of *la vérette*, which was before my time here. Come, you must tell me, then."

Still Lily choked over the words. "I should never have married him!" she cried at last.

The priest chuckled. "There is probably not a single young

lady in the world who doesn't think that at one time or another."

"No! You don't understand! I mean, when I took the marriage vows, they were lies. Oh, I didn't understand it all then, but I was already in love with another man. I married him because my father was dying and wanted it. And now I do not know how to turn lies into truths. I do not know how I can be his wife."

The priest blinked at her, taken aback by her outburst. He was young, and in his limited experience he had never heard such a passionate complaint against a husband as Lily Beau Clair's. He was glad when the door opened and the servant girl brought the *cocoyages*. The interruption gave him a chance to collect himself.

Dismayed, he watched her reach for hers and take three large gulps of the coconut milk and gin. She would make herself giddy that way, he thought. "What is your name?" he asked. "And the date of your marriage? I will look in the records. Perhaps Father Jacques wrote something there that may be of help."

She told him her name and the date—the same one she had just read on her father's grave. "I cannot imagine that there would be anything."

"Nevertheless, I will look."

She finished the *cocoyage* and waited for him to thumb through the files. He was going to be no help to her, she feared. He would end by simply telling her to do her duty and give her no idea how to make her reluctant body comply with the necessity. And whatever could this record of her marriage yield? Father Jacques couldn't have guessed there was anything wrong.

"Were you married in this church?" the priest asked.

"No. At home. Because of my father. The name of our plantation is Acelie."

Still he thumbed the files. "I cannot find it," he said at last. "There is no record."

She did not grasp the enormity of his words. "But of course it's there," she said impatiently, wanting him to get on with her problem.

"It is not."

"But I was married."

"The priest did not record it. I can't understand it." He shook his head in confusion, then drew in his breath as an explanation occurred to him. "You said the priest died. It must be that he died before he could record the marriage. He had spent the night in the lazaretto. You must see if your husband has a copy of the certificate. Do it at once!"

The urgency in his voice surprised her. Beginning to comprehend, she stared at his horrified face. "If you cannot prove the marriage, you are living in sin," he said. "In the eyes of the church you are not married."

She raced wildly back to Acelie over the limestone highroad, urging her mare on, heedless of the heat and the dazzle of the midday sun. She rode up mountainsides, along ravines, through villages, never pausing even to drink from the bamboo pipes of drinking fountains along the way. Flushed and disheveled, she burst in on an amazed Edmond.

"Lily, have you seen the priest? What can he have told you to make you so happy?"

She was not happy yet. It was only a wonderful hope that he mistook for happiness. And now she began to go cold with dread at the question she must ask. "Edmond, do you have a copy of our marriage certificate?"

"Why, no, I don't think so. That is at the church."

The coldness dissolved as she cried joyfully, "Oh, Edmond, it is not! Edmond, we are not married!"

He did not share her elation. His face went dark as he cried, "We shall see about this!"

"Edmond, where are you going?"

"To St. Pierre. And they shall turn all their records upside down to find it!"

"But it isn't there. Father Jacques died before he could write it down. It's good fortune for both of us, Edmond! Can't you see it that way? I don't love you, and now you'll be free to marry someone else. Someone who will give you children easily."

"And you will marry Joe."

"Yes!"

"It cannot be! We will soon clear this matter away. You are my wife, Lily."

He thundered out, and Lily, feeling a presence behind her, turned to see Cyrillia standing there, her eyes wide. "Oh, missy, what will happen?"

"It's a miracle, Rilla! The Virgin has heard my prayers and yours. I am free of him, and you shall have him."

"Unless he finds the certificate."

"Yes."

Night fell, and a storm blew up. The banana trees

thrashed, and a palm tree took fire from lightning and burned like a giant torch. They closed the shutters against the buffeting wind and waited.

"He will not come tonight, Rilla," Lily said as the hours passed. "He won't come in the storm. We will have to wait until morning to know which of us will be his."

"You think it will be as easy as that for me to have him, missy?"

"Why not? He loves you. It is just that he doesn't realize it. He has only thought of me."

"I am only a servant girl. He will want another Creole for a wife."

"Oh, Cyrillia, don't lose heart now. Your grandmother didn't lose heart when she made Monsieur Bon free her. He loves you, and you will arrange for him to understand he must marry you."

The girl gave a strange moan and clutched at her stomach. "We must talk of it later, missy."

Lily ran to the *ajoupas* for the native midwife, and sat with her friend through the night as Cyrillia labored to give birth to Edmond's child. And when Cyrillia's son cried with terror at the racketing storm, it was Lily who rocked him back to sleep.

As the ragged clouds were swept away into the lavender morning sky, the baby gave its first vigorous cry. "It's a girl, Rilla!" Lily whispered.

"A girl!"

"Yes, and she is as new and beautiful as the day, and the pink of her skin is like sunrise."

"She will not grow up to be a servant girl, missy!"

"No. She is the great-granddaughter of Monsieur Bon, and her name shall be Beau Clair."

The hoofbeats were slow and tired as Lily heard Edmond returning to Acelie. She went into the sitting room to wait for him. She knew as soon as she saw him that he had failed, and her face lighted.

"Oh, Lily, how can you look so happy when I am miserable!" he cried. "I still love you. And you loved me once! Lily, come with me to the cathedral and take the vows again."

"I never loved you, Edmond," she said gently. "I was a young girl and I was told I should love you."

She felt warmer toward him than she had in years as he sat there so crushed and bereft. She had been his so long, and before that, her father's. Now she belonged to herself, and back in New Orleans wealth waited for her. Even Acelie, her dowry, would be hers again. She smoothed his hair and kissed him, as aware of her power over him as she had been the night she had married him. "You have a new daughter. Come and look at her. You will feel better."

"A daughter?" he said blankly. "Whatever do you mean?"

He acknowledged the second baby no more than the first. Indeed, he was too preoccupied even to admire her. But while the attention of the household centered on the new arrival, the neglected older brother climbed onto Edmond's knee to seek affection, and Lily noted with satisfaction the fondness between father and son. Edmond loved this boy. He had not planned to, but it had been a natural thing.

"It will be a disaster for you if you marry Joe," Edmond told her. "This love affair is very romantic, but it will be different when you tie him down."

"I am not going to do that."

"You can't help it, Lily. That's what marriage is about. Think it over in New Orleans. Then come back to me. I'll be waiting."

She moaned in frustration. How long would it take him to see what was right before his eyes? How long before he would see that he loved Cyrillia and that he already had his heir?

Edmond did not give up hope. He moved his belongings from Acelie back to Beau Clair, but he agreed to manage her plantation for her as he always had. It would be a way of showing her that he would love her, and only her, forever. When her dowry, Acelie, was legally transferred to her again, she packed carefully, collecting all the treasure she had had to leave behind when she had left so abruptly with Joe. The day before her departure, she shopped in St. Pierre, buying bolts of calendared madras, huge gold earrings and bracelets, and *chinoises*. For Archer she purchased long thin Martinique cigars, and for Joe, a more intimate gift, long, loose pantaloons of indienne with designs of lizards and birds.

The farewell gun echoed, and she watched the city become a reddish streak against the mass of green mountains as Martinique faded to a shadowy gloom. She had engaged the finest cabin, and since she had been quickly recognized as Salome, she was an instant celebrity. She sat every night at the captain's table, and one evening, because she was in such a generous mood, she performed the Dance of the Seven Veils in the ship's salon. At Havana she indulged herself and went ashore for a drive along the wide, tree-lined boulevards. The shining domes, the deep colonnades, the magnificent houses with windows grated to the street caught her fancy. She told herself that she would have Joe bring her here sometime after they were married. She took a drive past bookstalls, out of the older section of town, into an alameda lined with statues, fountains, theaters, and gaming establishments; and she passed a night at an American hotel with rooms built around a quadrangle garden. In the morning she gave a thought to Madame Drapeaux as she boarded the ship again for New Orleans. Was there a procurer on board today? And was some other girl about to meet the fate Lily had so narrowly missed? She saw girls who she felt certain were destined, knowingly or not, for brothels; and she wanted to do something about it. But what?

She shuddered, thinking how lucky it was that she had been saved both from the fate of Madame Drapeaux's companions and from a loveless marriage. Life rose ahead as perfect and sparkling as the azure waves, and she lost herself in dreams of Joe.

22

She had scarcely finished unpacking at Snowdown when the maid told her that Archer Snow was waiting in the parlor. She ran down at once, and as happy to see him as he was to see her, she let him crush her in a bear hug.

"Lily! Where have you been? What a fuss there was! Giles was beside himself, and that man Joe Beau Clair—"

"Did Joe come here?"

"Did he come here! I have seen no fury like his. Said he was to go away with you, and accused Giles and me of spiriting you off to prevent it. He and Giles would have come to blows if I hadn't calmed them down. I don't know which of them has the fiercer temper. And then, of course, when Beau Clair was convinced we didn't have you, we all thought of kidnapping. So did half the thugs in New Orleans. We received half a dozen ransom notes when the press found out you were gone.

"Beau Clair insisted on checking out every one himself, never mind that every man on the police force was running the leather off his shoes to have the glory of finding you. He sent a couple of rogues to their graves along the way, and he took a bullet through the shoulder himself. You've turned up at a lucky time. I don't think the wound would have kept that lunatic from the chase more than another day."

"He is still in New Orleans!" she cried, her golden eyes suffused with joy.

"He is that! Down at the docks recuperating in his cabin on the *Sea Bird*. He is that lover of yours that pained you so, isn't he? I knew it the moment he came in here accusing *me* of being your lover and of having secreted you somewhere. Would that I could have told him he was right and put that bullet in his shoulder myself."

"Dear Archer! You would have made a fine champion. I am going to the *Sea Bird* now, and when I come back I will tell you where I have been and the news I have brought. Oh, Archer, I am so happy!"

Her happiness was overshadowed by another emotion as she arrived at the pier where *Sea Bird* was docked and saw a two-seater with blue silk upholstery hitched there. Somehow Lily did not doubt what lady the carriage belonged to; and a rage swept her, like a bird returning to find a cat near its nest. How could she possibly see sweet little Jenny Van Artsdalen as a menace? Joe would have no use for a woman like her!

And then Jenny walked onto the deck, looking perfectly delightful in a chiffon bodice and a bell skirt gored to fit her tiny waist. Her fair hair gleamed in the sunshine, and cherubs might have floated above her like an illustration on the cover of *Godey's Ladies' Book* as she bent to look into the water, a smile of contentment playing at her mouth.

"Miss Van Artsdalen!" cried Lily. "I'm surprised to see you here. Does your father know where you are?"

Jenny's expression turned to dismay as she saw Lily, and gratifyingly she flushed. "I . . . have been taking care of Joe," she said. "He has been injured and needs someone to nurse him."

"How kind of you! But I'll take over now."

"You must not go in there, Madame Beau Clair! You will make him exert himself, and the wound will open again. Haven't you caused enough trouble? He was shot because of you."

"Move away from the door, Jenny, unless you wish him to have the sight of us pulling each other's hair."

"He's sleeping. Have the decency to leave him alone."

"He will be happier awake when he hears what I have to tell him. I am free to marry him!"

She saw the devastation her words brought. But Jenny did not crumple. A tide of honey flowed out of her face, leaving bare the rock of her love beneath her demureness. And as always at such moments, Lily was impressed. Jenny seemed a quiet, unassuming child, a tender flower to be blown away at the mere hint of a wind; yet, beneath the facade there was strength.

"You! Marry him? You haven't the stuff of a proper wife. It will be a disaster."

A disaster. Hadn't Edmond said exactly that? But Lily paid Jenny's words no more heed than his. She supposed she should feel sorry for Jenny as the fancy carriage went off down the cobblestones, but something warned her against pity.

She opened the cabin door and went inside. How beautiful he looked lying there, a slightly troubled expression on his features as he slept. She knelt beside him, studied the strong lines of his face, smoothed his hair behind the curve of his ear.

"Oh, Joe, how I love you!" she thought. She smiled knowingly and kissed his lips to watch him awaken to paradise.

The blue eyes flicked open and looked at her coolly, then with a burst of excitement. "Lily!"

"Yes, Joe. I have sent Jenny packing, and I am not part of your dream!"

He sat up suddenly and pulled her into his arms. "Be careful, now," she said. "You must get well. There will be time for that later."

"Now is the time for it! I am well enough."

"Are you well enough for a wedding? I should like you to marry me as soon as possible, Joe Beau Clair!"

He stared. "Lily, do not tell me you are not a dream. How can you be anything else, sitting there asking me to marry you?"

"I am not a dream, Joe," she said, trembling with rapture. "I have been to Martinique and returned a free woman!"

"Is my brother dead?" he cried.

"Nothing so unhappy. It's only that a priest who died years ago from smallpox did not record the marriage. I have never been married in the eyes of the church, Joe. I shall be a wife for the very first time when I am yours."

"Lily! Oh, my treasure! I cannot believe it. Come here and let me show you what is in store for you when we are married. Let me show you what you have to contend with for a lifetime." He jerked her across him, her petticoats flouncing up over her calves.

"Joe, stop! It's indecent not to undress me first. I am getting all rumpled."

"I am a sick man, Lily. Sick with impatience. I can't be bothered with all these buttons and plackets." He was kissing her, his hand deep beneath her gown, pulling at the only part of her attire it was necessary to remove. She struggled halfheartedly, the patent-leather toe caps of her doeskin shoes kicking as her lacy muslin drawers descended. Then the sensation of his hands on her body overcame her, and she lay helpless, her body open to him, her merino skirt crumpled about her white hips.

"Let me undress, Joe; you are destroying my clothes," she murmured as his lips moved over her. "Everyone will know what has happened to me here."

"Never mind, Lily. They will know by the look in your eyes when I have finished with you."

She thought that they all did know—the butler who opened the door for them at Snowdown, and Archer and Giles, who were having supper inside together.

"Archer, Giles, I am to be married!" she cried.

Archer looked at her oddly, and then he smiled, and flourishing his napkin onto the table, came to kiss her cheek. Archer had always been a good friend, and she wished with a rush of affection that she could tell him how much she valued him.

"I wish I were in your place, old man," Archer told Joe, shaking his hand. "When's it to be?"

"Immediately!" Joe's tone left no room for doubt.

But Giles had other ideas. "No, no, no," he declared. "If you're going to marry Lily, it must be done right. Women like Salome should not be married in a priest's office or in some musty room in City Hall"

"Life is not always like a play, Giles!" Archer laughed. "You are forever trying to put on a show."

"Why not? It's my genius. Would you doubt Shakespeare? 'All the world's a stage!' " He was not angry, as she had thought he would be, at the idea of her marriage, and she wondered why. She thought he even seemed pleased. It had been quite different when he'd thought she might be in love with Archer. Lily could not make sense of it, but she was relieved anyway.

"Giles, I don't want a display—"

"Wait a minute, Lily. I think Giles is right." She looked with amazement at a grinning Joe. "I have waited long enough to claim you. I should enjoy having everyone watch me pluck the finest flower of New Orleans womanhood."

"I thought men did not like such things."

"I do. What do you say, Lily? It would be fun! You'll wear a dress of white satin and a coronet of roses to hold your veil."

"Roses are not fashionable," she protested.

"You will make them so. And the horses of our wedding carriage will be festooned in roses, too."

Lily laughed and clapped her hands in delight. "Do you really mean it, Joe? Oh, I should love a wedding! It was all so horrid before when I was married."

"You were never married before," he reminded her in a tone that promised her a wondrous new bliss.

As the days passed, she was surprised to find that he had as much flair for the dramatic as Giles Benton. He was forever thinking of something new to add to the wedding festivities. He suggested that a shipload of tropical fruit be imported from Martinique and that dozens of birds of paradise should be released as Lily descended the stairs.

"I suppose you'll want me to do the Dance of the Seven Veils in my wedding dress," she declared in amusement.

"No, but you may ask Susan to sing at the reception. What do you say to that song 'Little Feathered Lovers'?"

"Of course that," she said with satisfaction. "It has been a long time since we danced to that tune."

"Since you were Mimi the coaling girl."

"I was afraid you had come to St. Pierre for your wedding, but you said you would never be caught by a lady in a crinolette."

"And now I have been, haven't I?" He nuzzled her neck fondly. "It was a long time ago, but it seems I have been dancing to that song ever since. Perhaps it would be better to release the birds when Susan begins to sing."

"Whatever you like, Joe. Are you certain you don't want to send to China for a shipload of spiders to spin their webs in the oaks so that we will have a canopy of silver to drive beneath with our rose-covered horses?"

He did not rise to the gibe. "It's been done, Lily," he answered seriously. "We must think of something else."

He was buying Snowdown from Archer for their home after they were married. Archer had made him a bargain price, but he would sell only under one condition. "I built the house for Lily," Archer had said. "I would like it to be in her name."

Joe did not care much for the arrangement. "I will feel silly with my wife owning my house."

"Suppose you gave me Snowdown as a wedding present? That would be all right, wouldn't it?"

He thought it over. It matched the grandness of the wedding that he should give his bride a mansion. "Very well,

I will give you Snowdown, but do not expect any other trinkets!"

"I shall be satisfied, darling. I won't ask you for anyone's head on a platter."

She had invited him to move into Snowdown at once, but he had declined, preferring to remain in his bachelor quarters on his ship. "We will observe the proprieties for once," he said. But he came often to the house, and while he was there, he forgot proprieties and filled her days and nights with love.

After he had gone, she would lie in bed listening to the sound of tree frogs and cicadas droning in the grass and in the curly gray Spanish moss of the oaks. Her happiness was marred only by the thought that it was too great for one human being. Sometimes it seemed to her that she could not even contain it all, that it flowed out of her soul and mingled with the moonlight, forming a molten alloy that shone in warm, magic pools on the cypress floor. And sometimes she slipped from bed and danced in those fantastic ponds, to bathe herself in the glowing enchantment of love.

Giles Benton oversaw the fitting of her wedding dress. He was used to dealing with beautiful women and their apparel, and dressing Lily for her wedding was no different from dressing her for the part of Salome. He was expert at knowing just what draping of fabric would exhibit Lily best, and he drove both her and the dressmaker wild with frustration. Lily gasped the first time he jerked a piece of the bodice loose from its basting, exposing her in her chemise, but she soon grew used to this peremptory rearranging of her garments.

"The sleeve must go this way!" he would exhort the seamstress. "The leg of mutton must stand out as if it is proud of the privilege of covering her arm. Put horsehair in it!" And Lily thought he made her walk a mile before he was satisfied that her skirt made the correct rustle.

"The waist is too tight, Giles," she complained when the final stitches were sewn.

"No, Lily. It's just right—nineteen inches."

"But, Giles, I can't breathe!"

"Then you must lose weight. You are perfection, and a woman who is perfection has a nineteen-inch waist. The papers will want to know."

"Giles, why is it you don't object to this marriage?"

"I? Why should I object? He is the sort of man you should marry. You will never grow dull and complacent while you are his wife. He will keep the juices flowing. But no doubt a man like Joe Beau Clair will always make you miserable, too. I am counting on it. You will always be walking a tightrope between love and despair, and the depth of your love and suffering will show in every role you play."

"You'll be disappointed, Giles. Joe will never make me suffer."

"Won't he? I suppose he never has before!"

He had, of course. He was a man who loved and hated passionately and who took retribution at the first sign of betrayal. She shivered as she thought that Jim Frey had not lived another day when Joe had determined revenge. He was as swift and powerful in war as in love. Giles was right that a man like that could never be a tame and gentle lover. But Lily had experienced that kind of marriage, and she was eager to try the other.

Then, even before the wedding, Joe began to fulfill Giles's prophecy. He was late one evening when he came into the parlor at Snowdown. She had been waiting for him, wearing a bengaline skirt with a fall of scarlet chiffon. A moonstone comb held the twist of her hair, and she had arranged little dangling kiss curls to emphasize the delicate line of her high cheeks and slender throat. The air breathed of the jasmine she had put in all the vases as she stood up noiselessly to meet him and waited for him to close her in his arms. She sighed as he kissed her with firm expertise, and thrilled to the touch of his strong hands lifting her chin.

"Oh, Lily, you are so beautiful!" The words were wistful; his tone was different than on other nights.

"Joe, what's wrong?" she cried in alarm.

"I've got to make a voyage, Lily."

"A voyage? You can't mean now!"

"Now. Tonight."

"But we are to be married!"

"It can't be helped. One of Van Artsdalen's customers, a company in South Africa, demands the ship it has ordered immediately. And it seems there is no one that can be trusted to sail it there but me. It's a fast and tricky vessel—it must be. It will have to outrun pirates with cargoes of diamonds the new owners will haul. Van Artsdalen has asked it as a special favor."

She whirled away from him to find her tears of disappointment. "Oh, it is that Jenny! Can't you see? She would do anything to keep us apart. She is the reason her father is sending you to Africa."

His face darkened dangerously. "Lily, don't belittle yourself by speaking ill of Jenny. Do not credit *her* with your ideas. Jenny would never think of such a thing." His voice was dangerous.

She gritted her teeth. "I'm sorry, Joe. It's only that I'm so upset."

"There, little Mimi," he said, stroking her hair. "Of course you're upset. I am heartbroken myself. But it is a thing of honor. You can't have forgotten all the money I caused Van Artsdalen to lose on the boat race."

"No," she said in a small voice. She had learned about Joe's honor. She would never again try to squelch its fire with a bucket of common sense. "South Africa! You will be gone for months!"

"Not a moment longer than is necessary. I'll harness sea gulls to the sails to fly me home!"

"Oh, Joe! You'll have to wait for a ship—it will be forever. Marry me before you go!"

"It's impoossible. We've none of the papers. And I must go tonight." He held her fiercely as she sobbed against his linen vest.

One thing kept bothering her. One thing she must know before he left. "Joe . . . do you think Jenny Van Artsdalen is a better woman than I am?"

He had been looking as though he, too, wanted to weep, but now his laughter split the air. "Oh, you cannot be jealous of her, my little minx! I meant only that she is innocent. She has not the ability to be devious. Didn't I tell you in St. Pierre that no woman like that would ever claim me? It has taken you, my wanton little Mimi! I shall never sail home to anyone but you."

And then he begged her not to leave him the memory of her tears, and she did her best to smile for him as he loved her. At dawn he held her face before him a long moment, as though to memorize it.

"I wish I had a miniature to take with me," he sighed.

"I should have had one painted for you."

"Do you still have my watch?"

"Yes. To keep track of forever by."

"Good. I shall love you for that long. I still have your necklace—your *collier-choux.*

"You've kept it all this time?" She flushed with pleasure.

"I could never part with it. And I have your jupe dress, too. It's a strange garment to find in a man's sea chest! *Atô bô*, Lily. Kiss me, now." And with these words that he had used to ask her favors first at Carnival, he was gone, slipping through her fingers as he always had, dark and unpredictable as the volcanic beach sands of Martinique.

23

"Jenny Van Artsdalen is the thing that galls me, Susan," Lily said as they sat together over a Spode tea set at Snowdown. "It's bad enough that he had to go, but worse that she is the cause of it."

"Would you like to think of a way to get even?" Susan's gray-green eyes sparkled as she brushed the crumbs of a chocolate éclair from her elegant tweed skirt.

"Oh, you are never so happy as when you are plotting!" cried Lily. "I dare not lay a finger on Jenny for fear Joe should find out. Not that I have any idea of what I might do."

"Heaven is on her side," said Susan.

"Yes."

"You might as well have one of these éclairs and forget your troubles. It's what we used to do, remember?"

"I can't even do that."

"Why not?"

"I have got to have a nineteen-inch waist to fit into my wedding dress. Giles will not allow it to be let out. Oh, a pox on it all! I am sick of this purgatory!"

She wrote letters every day, telling him everything that was happening. She had bought a set of Rookwood pottery done with a double glaze that made the design look as though it were under water. Archer was teaching her to ride a bicycle. And Giles did not approve, even though she had read that Lillian Russell had one—gold with mother-of-pearl handlebars and her monogram in diamonds and emeralds.

> My bicycle is quite ordinary, thank heaven! It would be a shame to dent up gold plate, the way my vehicle is becoming damaged. I am forever running into something or taking a fall. I cannot get the hang of it. You should see the mud stains on my white cycling outfit! The laundress despairs of ever getting it clean. That, as you

might guess, is the basis of Giles's disapproval. He is so afraid that someone will get a photo of Salome with her posterior in a puddle!

She wondered if such letters would bore him when he received two dozen of them at once on the boiling coast of South Africa. She would determine not to write another too soon, but then when night fell and she was alone, she could not help herself.

Archer squired her, courtly as always, an excellent dancer, fun to be with. He teased her gently about Joe. "Are you sure you want to marry him? He's forever making you wait. But here I am, good old Archer, always at your side, ready to waltz with you or pick you up when you've wrecked your bicycle again."

"I'm a fool, Archer. Ask Giles. I'm sure he'll agree. And as for the bicycle, I rode the entire length of Snowdown's lane today without a mishap. Will you take me for a spin in Audubon Park tomorrow?"

"If you insist," he grinned. "But Giles will never forgive me if you go head-over-heels into a fountain."

Only in this sarcastic way did he tell her he grieved, and in truth, her marriage seemed to bother him no more than it did Giles. Perhaps he had become resigned long ago. Once or twice she tried to remonstrate with him. "Archer, you should find some other girl. New Orleans is full of lovely women who would appreciate your attention."

"No, Lily, I am content just now. I had been looking a long while for someone like you. We're having fun; let's leave well enough alone."

She shrugged and returned to the subject of the bicycle. "Do you think I should order some of those daring new knickers for riding? I think it's the skirts that cause me so much trouble."

"By all means, Lily. It would be a fine thing. Giles would like it."

Archer seemed happy in his work. He had embarked on a new project, and the opposition it was meeting did not seem to faze him. He had taken on the task of restoring a block of Vieux Carré homes for a French client who had come into enough money to purchase the area surrounding his family home. She was shocked the first time Archer took her to see his endeavor. It was the same block that contained the home of Madame Drapeaux.

"The businessmen here are all very upset at being evicted," Archer chuckled. "And beg pardon, Lily, but there's many a strumpet that'll have to find another crib."

"It won't be easy for some of them, Archer," she said, surprising him with her sympathy. "What about that house? The one with the pink brick and the tulip pattern in the ironwork?"

"Oh, that one. My client has allowed the old woman to remain in her house. It doesn't need much work, anyway. I ordered a new roof to protect the interior from the rain. It's a marvel, Lily. I would like to show it to you, but I can't. The old lady is dying, so they say."

Lily could not refrain from repeating this news to Susan the next time her friend came to call at Snowdown.

"Dying!" Susan said. "I don't believe it. That canny old wretch will never die. She's putting on again, like before. Well, don't tell me you're sorry. You almost look it."

"I'm not, of course. It bothers me in some way. I can't think what."

"Have you heard any more from Jenny?"

"Not a peep."

"Not a twang of her angel's harp? That is another canny woman, Lily."

"No, she's really as simple as she looks. It's only that love makes her clever."

"What matter? The result is the same. You'd better be careful, Lily. She will try to split you and Joe for longer than a sea voyage!"

"Yes, but what can she do? I am free to marry Joe, and Joe is wildly in love with me."

"Keep a weather eye anyway, sis."

She was bored in spite of all that Archer could do to entertain her, restless regardless of all the outings and soirees and the still-bright popularity of Salome that followed her everywhere. She lost appetite and fit easily into the nineteen-inch waist of the wedding dress. When would she ever get to use it? She received a letter at last, posted from the Canary Islands. There had been problems with the ship, and now it would have to be drydocked to repair a defect in the hull. It would take longer than he had thought. The letter was full of his yearnings for her, and she kissed it and put it beneath her pillow that night before she cried herself to sleep.

Archer invited dinner guests for next evening in an attempt to cheer her, but after a meal of her favorite turtle soup and an elegant *daube glacé* of cold molded veal, Lily was still lifeless. The brilliant chatter of her guests had not interested her, and when they were gone, she sat on the terrace rocking herself in the huge balata-wood rocker she had brought from Acelie.

Watching her, Giles Benton orated in a sonorous stage voice, " 'Where thinkst thou he is now? Stands he, or sits he? Or does he walk? Or is he on his horse? O happy horse to bear the weight of Antony!' "

"That is Shakespeare, Giles. It's the second time recently you've quoted him."

"I've been thinking about Shakespeare a lot. How would you like to play Cleopatra, Lily?"

"Cleopatra!" The rocker stopped moving as Lily gazed at Giles in astonishment. "The serpent of the Nile! Oh, she has always fascinated me! Once I saw it done at the theater in St. Pierre. But, Giles, I am not a Shakespearean actress."

"Of course not. Do you think women are born Shakespearean actresses? I will have to make you one. Just as I made you Salome. It will be a great deal harder, but I, too, have always been fascinated by Cleopatra. And you are the first actress I have believed could portray her to suit me. Everything about you is exotic—your dark hair and eyes, the strange mystique of love that clings about you. You were good as Salome—more than that, a sensation. But you will be even better as Cleopatra. You will be my masterpiece, just as Snowdown is Archer's."

"Giles, there is the backing," Archer said softly.

"Aren't you going to back it, Archer?" Lily asked.

"I'm a wealthy man, but even I can't afford to risk the whole amount that Giles wants."

"It's taken care of," Giles said exuberantly. "There is a man who wants to put money into the venture."

"Really? Who, Giles?" Archer asked.

"That I cannot tell you. He doesn't want his name connected with it. Thinks his wife will be angry. A secret admirer of yours, no doubt, Lily."

"I would just as soon he remained secret, then," she said. "But, Giles, why will this play cost so much?"

"I told you, Lily. It's to be my masterpiece. It's the play I've always wanted to do."

"What about the play you've always wanted to write, Giles? Why don't you do that? Are you afraid you can't?"

He sneered at her. "I will do it when I have found the

right subject. I will take my time about it, but it will be a great day for the theater when I do. In the meantime, we will do *Cleopatra* and that will be the next-best thing. We will not skimp doing it. You will see, Lily!"

And she did see. She stood aghast at his orders for Roman chariots and plumed helmets, dozen of silk costumes for Cleopatra's attendants, to be changed with the scenes, the colors matched to the play's varying moods. For herself there was a magnificent throne, wrist and ankle bracelets, heavy ornamental collars sewn with hundreds of glass beads, a dozen headdresses in various styles, and tight-fitting gowns exposing one shoulder created from materials woven with geometric patterns.

Nothing would be done in a shallow way. Battle scenes would be fought with a hundred soldiers with elaborate painted backdrops of the plains of Syria. Cleopatra's palace at Alexandria would be lavish.

"But what about my wedding?" Lily thought to say, visiting the theater one day amid the scurry of workmen. "When Joe comes back, I am getting married. I won't change my mind."

"Your wedding will make it perfect, Lily. When you are wed to Joe Beau Clair, it will be as if Antony himself has captured you!"

"Let me guess. My bridesmaids will all be dressed as Egyptian princesses, and Joe and I will drive away in a golden chariot."

"Excellent suggestions, my dear. And now, no more of this wandering about. Back to Snowdown to study your part. All this will be in vain if you don't conquer the character of Cleopatra!"

"Oh, Giles, I'm tired. I must have a holiday."

"Work, Lily. You will be heard of far beyond New Orleans if you make a success of Cleopatra!"

She wanted Joe far more than she wanted success, but she didn't have time now to languish over his absence. She rose early, ate a quick breakfast of waffles and *café noir*, and began to rehearse.

"Cleopatra was a great courtesan, a woman of gaiety and passion with no feelings higher than enjoying herself," Giles would tell her.

"No, she was more than that."

For once Giles did not argue. He allowed her instinct for the role to take its course. "It will require skill to make your audience feel Antony's desire for Cleopatra," he warned her. "Remember, he has a lovely wife in Octavia."

But Lily seemed well able to handle the role. She seemed to have an understanding of her own sex that went deeper than most women's. Giles wondered whether it was because of the struggles she had seen in her early days in New Orleans. She had never told him anything about that, but he guessed she had known hard times. She was a friend of Susan Wickersham's—a very old friend, it seemed, and Giles had long ago penetrated the myth that Susan had begun her career in New York. Susan Wickersham had come out of some concert saloon, and maybe Lily, too, though he'd taken her from a convent to be Salome. Giles didn't care. He was only delighted with the depth she brought to the part.

"Other women cloy the appetites they feed, but she makes hungry where most she satisfies." Giles had an idea that no one was better qualified to project those lines than Lily. He was correct in thinking that audiences would agree.

Opening night was a triumph. Lily left the theater still dressed in the gold-threaded tunic she had worn in the final scene. This time she did not reach the waiting carriage, but found herself lifted high in the air and propelled all the way to the St. Charles Hotel, her silver filigreed diadem glittering in the gas lights as she was passed over the heads of her admirers. She was gasping as she was set gallantly down, unharmed, except that the baubles from her costume had disappeared into the hands of souvenir seekers. Archer, all smiles, came to ask her to dance.

"Not now. I want a cup of punch and time to catch my breath. It's a wonder they didn't strip me naked out there!"

"There is a certain decorum about these things, Lily." He grinned. "You were in no danger. I wonder if those beads can be replaced by tomorrow. Oh, incidentally, I've found out who is backing the other half of the show. Do you see him over there, dancing with that rather attractive girl?"

She did not recognize the distinguished gray-haired man in the vicuña dresscoat, but did know his partner, who flushed prettily and looked utterly happy as she danced in a gown with great lace ruffles over large balloon sleeves.

Jenny Van Artsdalen! Trying to look sophisticated in that dress! And her father's adoring gaze on her made it obvious that he would do anything she asked. Jenny had arranged for him to back the play, just as she had arranged for him to send Joe away. And she had the nerve to seek Lily out and offer her little suede-gloved hand in congratulation.

Why had Jenny done it? The question bothered Lily all night. When the party was done, she lay sleepless in the dawn, and giving up slumber, came downstairs where Archer and Giles were still reading the reviews of the morning papers. They were both in a marvelous mood.

"Come look!" Archer invited. "It's all splendid. They are calling it the finest extravaganza of the decade."

"The nineties have a way to go yet. Better that they had said 'of the century.'"

"Lily, whatever is wrong?"

She burst suddenly into tears. "Giles, why didn't you tell me who put up the money? You should have told me, Giles."

"Then you wouldn't have done the play," he said mildly.

"You knew that!"

"I've heard you speak of Jenny Van Artsdalen's infatuation with Joe. What does it matter? Joe is not in love with that little sparrow. Anyway, she had nothing to do with this."

"Of course she did! But I can't figure why. She reminds me of Octavia, somehow."

Archer chuckled. "Low of brow and round of face with no majesty in her walk. It describes Jenny well."

"More than that. Octavia was a simple, virtuous woman who aspired to wed an Atlas. And she did. I will not have Jenny Van Artsdalen be my Octavia!" Lily's voice was shrill with emotion. She was exhausted, and yet she could not rest.

"Lily, Giles is right," Archer said comfortingly. "Jenny had nothing to do with the investment. You mustn't become afraid of shadows."

"Oh, you would know better if you had seen that smile she gave me—so sweet and condescending."

There was nothing to do but telephone Susan. "Did you see her?" she asked.

"Oh, I did indeed," Susan said. "Looking as if she'd just stolen the crown jewels—or a man!" But her friend's agreement was small consolation.

Then one night a sun-blackened sailor waited for her at the stage door. Ignoring her frock-coated admirers, she turned to him immediately, and he put an envelope into her hand. "Joe Beau Clair asked me to give you this." Her heart almost stopped at the sight of his handwriting on the paper.

"Wait a minute, I'll pay you."

"I've already been paid handsomely, ma'am. My, he didn't lie when he said you were pretty." Then the sailor was gone, leaving Lily to rip open the letter.

> Darling Lily,
> I expect to be able to deliver Van Artsdalen's ship within a day or so, and I have already found a likely vessel, the *Tropic Belle*, which I am buying to sail home to you. Look for me by the fifteen of June. . . .

She shrieked with excitement, for it was already the twelfth of the month. The letter had been a long time in the pocket of the sailor. "In three days," she cried jubilantly to Archer as she climbed into the carriage.

"I imagine you'd like it to be sooner." He sighed.

"Of course! Waiting is so much harder now."

"Well, then, it's time to stop waiting. You shall have him in less than three days."

She threw her arms around him. "Oh, Archer! How?"

"We will take a vacation and go to the Gulf Islands to wait for Joe. We'll send a ship out to intercept his, to tell him that you will be waiting for him."

"But the play—I can't leave New Orleans."

"We'll give your understudy her chance. It will make you more appreciated when you return."

"You can get Giles to allow that?" she cried excitedly.

He grinned at her happiness. "Yes."

He arranged it, just as he had arranged for the closing of *Salome*. She was up early the next morning, dressed for the journey in a blazer-style suit with a velvet inlaid collar and a full sweep skirt lined with rustling taffeta. A black braided-straw hat tilted over her face, and she opened her best star-ruffled parasol against the already glaring sun as she alighted from the carriage with Archer at the foot of old St. Louis Street. There, by the sugar landing, all kinds of small steam craft were maneuvering for places at the levee, like a flock of noisy ducks.

"Which boat is ours, Archer?" she asked. She was traveling without a chaperon, but then, Archer made a curiously good one. She was certain he would deliver her safely to Joe.

"It's that little white one," he answered, indicating a light, narrow steamer built especially for bayou travel.

At the last moment somebody recognized Lily, and she had to dash up the gangplank to safety as the crowd began to call her name. She waved and blew kisses as the Chinese gong sounded the last bells and the boat slid away from the clamor of drays and baggage vans. The smell of burning pitch pine and resin faded, and a long sable column of coal smoke blew out as the steamer moved down the river and slipped into the mouth of a canal.

"You're so good to do this for me, Archer!" she cried, almost beside herself with pleasure.

"I shall always enjoy doing things for you, Lily, even if it must be taking you to Joe."

The steamer puffed into a shadowed bayou, came out into yellow-green rice fields, and then slid into a swamp forest of moss-hung cypress. In the dining salon they lunched on oysters on the half shell and cold French apple pie as the forest thinned to reedy wastes, the bayou opening into lakes and bays.

The little steamer scraped over sandbars as it struggled for the open water. About sunset they felt the first burst of ocean breeze, and the boat began to pulse with the rocking tides. She tasted salt on her mouth, and the smell of the sea made her wild with eagerness. The water fragmented the vermilion ribbon of sunset, and straining to see through the brilliance, they began to catch sight of islets with white sand beaches and myrtle and palmetto blowing in the wind.

They slid past little Oriental villages where Malay fishermen lived in huts, and later on a Chinese settlement of wooden houses clustered around a wharf with great signs in Chinese letters.

"What do they mean?" Lily asked Archer over the cry of gray pelicans.

"They say 'Shrimp for Sale.'"

"Well, how do they expect anyone to read that?"

He grinned. "No matter. Everyone knows."

She shivered.

"Are you cold, Lily? I will go and get your shawl."

"No. I'm not cold. This place has a strange atmosphere about it."

"Yes. It's utterly isolated, and the sea is eating out these islands one by one. Some used to be sugar plantations. The war ended that."

"Have you come here often?"

"Yes. New Orleans is a depraved city. Sometimes it's too much for me. I must get away and search for peace. I am taking you to my favorite island. It's the prettiest. I wouldn't share it with just anyone."

She put her hand on his and leaned against his shoulder as they moved out of the sea marshes into the Gulf. Something of artifice was stripped from Archer here, just as the wind had stripped the barren little islands, leaving only weeds and ancient timbers and dead fish washed ashore. She saw again the haunted expression she had noticed the first time she had seen him.

"Dear Archer!" she said spontaneously. He smiled at her, and the expression was gone. She had had the impression that something was very wrong, but perhaps she had imagined it.

The boat docked, and she forgot everything else as she ran to explore his island. Here sugar fields had returned to sandy beaches with tramways over them to the water's edge. The square, two-storied plantation house, balconied all around, had been transformed into a hotel, already aglitter with lights for an evening of dancing. Orange and oak trees grew about the porches, their foliage all leeward, making them look like long-haired maidens trying to run against the wind.

"Do you want to go in for dinner, Lily?"

"Oh, I'm not hungry yet. I do love the sea, and I have seen so little of it since Martinique. Couldn't we go for a swim?"

"I would find that agreeable," he said.

Upstairs in a room furnished with a bed of white enameled iron and a mirrored chiffonier, she changed into her black serge bathing gear. When she went outside again, sharp-leafed oleander bushes sighed in the dusk and yellow fields of wild camomile seemed to protest the coming night with their sunny color. Archer, clad in knee-length jersey trunks and a shirt, was waiting for her as she walked out over the tramway.

"There's a splendid surf, Lily. It's perfect for swimming." He took her hand and led her into the water. It was that time of day when sea and sky merged into blue gray and became indistinct from each other. The sunset had gone, and the water seemed to lap more loudly than before.

"Archer, did your messenger bring an answer from Joe?"

He smiled at her. "How did you keep from asking for so long? Was it because you didn't want to spoil my pleasure in showing you the place?"

"Maybe. But it didn't seem real until just now when I swam out into the water and thought that he was sailing somewhere on these very seas."

"Borne on currents of love, no doubt," Archer teased. "Word is that we shall see the *Tropic Belle* in the morning."

They swam in the warm Gulf waters until the moon rose. "It's the last moonrise I'll see without Joe," said Lily poetically.

"True enough. But don't stand there gawking at it. A crab will get your toes if you don't keep moving." And he dived down to the sandy bottom and seized her little white feet and made her squeal with laughter. Then, as she ran out of the water, he dashed after her, chasing her across the tramway, one dark-suited figure after another in the pale of the moon.

She ate such a hearty dinner of crawfish bisque and red beans and downed so many orange-flower fizzes that Archer began to wonder aloud about the nineteen-inch waist of the wedding dress. "Take care, Lily. You'll wind up in a faint on your day of days. I shall have to be buying you one of those four-in-hand corsets for ladies with large hips whose corsets break down at the sides!"

"Why, Archer Snow! How should you know about such things? I'm going to have strawberries and sponge cake for dessert, and if I faint from too tight a gown, Joe will revive me soon enough!"

Archer enjoyed the saucy repartee. He had never seen Lily in a better mood. But he was disappointed when she refused to join him for the evening's waltzing. "I am going to be rested for tomorrow," she said, and blew him a kiss as she went upstairs.

Archer sighed and walked out onto the veranda. He was not interested in dancing with any other woman while his mind was on Lily. He smiled to think how happy she looked. Tomorrow she would have her Joe. She would have him a day sooner than otherwise, because of him, and somehow he felt proud of having arranged it. She would marry Joe now, and he knew he should be desolate that it was actually going to happen. But why should he waste himself in grief? Joe Beau Clair was an adventurer; soon the sea would lay claim to him again. And whom would Lily waltz with then? With her old friend Archer Snow, of course. He would always have a function in her life. Joe was not jealous of him, and when there were babies, who else should be their godfather?

He was almost content like this, he thought, and then suddenly he noticed that the wind had risen.

Lily, lying in the white enameled bed, saw carriage lights flickering far off, as wheels tracked soundless dreams of love into the beach sand. Now and then a laugh came over the roar of the surf. She could not sleep. Tomorrow night she would be in one of those carriages with Joe, she thought. Or perhaps they would ride horseback, breakneck, over the dunes until they found the proper place. Yes, that was the way it would be, not here in this bed. She, too, heard the wind begin to howl. "Good," she thought recklessly. It was as if the breath of his love had stirred the wind to bring him to her more quickly. She slept at last, dreaming of his kisses.

The sickly dawn lighted a terrible sea. Waves ran at a sharp angle to the shore, and a bellowing wind whipped foam from their tops to lie in white, woolly lines along the beach, as if there had been a shearing of sheep. Worriedly she sought Archer downstairs at breakfast. "Do you think he can come in this?" she asked.

"I've been talking to the natives of the place," he replied. "They say he will not."

"They don't know Joe."

Dressed in a French lawn shirtwaist and a skirt of heavy, scrolled grosgrain silk, she trained opera glasses on the horizon. A fog of spray obscured the view, and the wind grew louder, making the old hotel quiver and behind the whirlwind gusts came sudden, insane bursts of rain.

Noon passed and there was nothing but the incredible tumult of wind. She pressed her hands against her ears to avoid hearing it. Would it never stop?

"It will get worse," Archer told her grimly. "They say it's typical of such gales."

"But how long will it last?" she demanded.

"Nobody knows. Some storms have lasted a week."

"A week!"

"It may be less. But there's no way to get off the island, of course. Joe will have avoided this and stayed to sea, where there are no shoals. He'll sail for the Mississippi and be in New Orleans before us. You'll see. He'll be there. Spare some sympathy for me, Lily. Think what trouble I'll be in with Giles when you're not back. Giles does not recognize the calamities of nature as excuses."

"Joe will come here," she said.

He did not bother to tell her just how bad the gales sometimes became. He did not mention islands that had been submerged by colossal waves, swept clear of every living thing, as bare as though the hand of Creation had skipped over them in the very Beginning. He told her that she looked wan, and made her go and rest.

"Put witch hazel on your eyes, Lily. They are strained and red from all this staring at the sea." And he trained her pearl opera glasses at the frothing distance and took up her vigil.

In the evening the clouds broke suddenly in the west, showing a strange, ghostly sun, a giant, blood-colored devil-disk magnified out of all proportion in a greenish sky. Then the curtain of the storm rolled shut, as though the sun had been merely peeping in on children who now lay terrified for the night. In the utter dark the wind became alive, shaking the island with a murderous hand. People began to come to the hotel from the summer cottages, and in the ballroom the violins played louder, trying to cover the sound of its evil voice. Lily did not disdain to dance tonight. The waltz was an outlet for her need for motion, and she welcomed the comforting circle of Archer's arm about her.

"Oh, Archer," she whispered fearfully as the wind screeched with special fury.

"Hush, Lily. He has avoided the storm and gone up the river. It's what any good sailor would do."

She tried to believe him. She no longer wanted to think that Joe would dare these awful seas to reach her side. Joe was a good sailor. He would know what was prudent. But a stronger voice told her that Joe believed himself a *very* good sailor; it told her Joe loved a challenge. Joe was arrogant. He would take this tempest as a personal affront. *Joe is coming here.* She knew it in the very core of her being.

She fell asleep in a rattan chair in the lobby, her grosgrain skirt crumpled all around her, and in the first gray light of dawn, the disbelieving cry of "A ship! A ship!" told her she had been right.

She did not have to see the name on the prow to know that it was the *Tropic Belle*. And soon everyone knew what ship it was, for whom it sailed hell-bent to this besieged island. She hardly noticed how people looked at her with a mixture of wonder and pity. She did not move the opera glass from her eyes as the ship came on, now floundering, swaying, plunging, a whiteness of spray wrapped about it like a cloud. The *Tropic Belle* seemed to be floating on vapors, a specter of a ship, and then for a moment it would be out of sight behind a wave that towered even above the height of the mast.

"That's all for her! She's capsized!" someone would cry,

and then they would see the ship atop the waves again, coming relentlessly on.

"Who is her captain? He's a madman!" she heard someone say, but finally the comments gave way to silent awe. Onlookers nearly crowded Lily from the window as the *Tropic Belle* came closer. She could see now that a mizzen had been ripped away, and its ragged remains fluttered like the tattered clothing of a battle-scarred soldier.

"She's heading right for the sandbar!" said a voice at her elbow. "She cannot miss it!"

Lily felt Archer's arms around her tightly, protecting her from falling, but he did not try to turn her eyes from the sight. She saw the great hull of the boat lift and snag, twist wretchedly like a trapped animal. She could see figures on deck now. Joe, the tails of his shirt blowing, the wind tearing his hair. Even from where she was she could hear the rending of the mast as it tore away.

She pulled loose from Archer's arms with a sob, and tossing off other hands that moved to stop her, she ran out onto the veranda. The steps of the stilted porch had been blown away; she had to jump to the sand below. Landing on all fours, she was running even before she completely regained her balance. Sand stung her cheeks and bit at her eyes like fine shot. With lecherous gusts the wind jerked her skirts around her thighs, and sand burned against her bare legs, too.

She saw him catch sight of her as he stood on the careening ship. How could he miss her? She was the only living thing that moved on the beach, her hair streaming, her clothing askew. Words carried over the wail of the wind. Had he cried,"Lily, I am coming"?

She saw him jump into the terrible arms of the ocean, and she sank to the beach in dismay, burying her head against the wind. He was a strong swimmer. She remembered how he had swum away from her out to the banana ship at Grande Anse.

"Even the professional swimmers do not go out after dark," she had pleaded, and she had made him light a flare to show her when he was safe. If only there could be a flare this time! "Oh, Joe, why must you always compete with death?"

She was lost in aeons of eternity. The quivering sand beneath her seemed to heave with sobs, and she drank in an ocean of grief as errant green waves splashed against her. Lily did not notice the rising water. She was uncaring as the greedy sea reached to sweep her away. Then he was there, doing battle with the foaming jade tentacles, lifting her out of the deadly surf into his trembling arms. She dropped her head dazedly against his straining chest.

"Oh, Joe," she murmured confusedly, "your ship is wrecked."

"What matter, love? It has brought me safe to you."

24

The storm raged three days more. Lily did not have an easy time of it, although the hotel held firm. Most of the summer cottages had been submerged or blown to rubble. The tramways had long since splintered into the water, and the stables were gone. Now, through the shriek of the wind, they sometimes heard the banshee whinnying of those horses that had escaped destruction, the sound weirdly distorted in the convulsing air.

As for Joe, nothing would do but that he go back to his ship where it still tottered on the sandbar.

She could not believe her ears when he said he was going, and then she fell at his feet begging him unabashedly not to leave.

"But, Lily, it's my ship. I am responsible for all those men still aboard." And without any further comment he went, taking with him extra coils of rope and supplies in a frail dinghy.

Lily went to bed with chills. Archer, sitting beside her hour after hour, thought she had caught a fever from her exposure on the beach and dosed her with blackberry balsam.

Still the ship hovered precariously, ready each moment to split and go down, sucking its crew with it. Sometimes Lily struggled up to see, but she was dizzy and afraid and she did not fight Archer's arms gently against her, pushing her back.

"Is it still there?" she would ask.

"Yes, Lily."

"Would you tell me if it were not?"

"I don't know," he said truthfully. "But it is there. He has had them strip away the sails and spars and even most of the deckhouse to give the wind less to get at. It is only a hull, but it is there."

"Why must he torture me so?" she wailed.

"He is right about the crew being his responsibility, Lily,

but he risked them coming here, instead of sailing for the river. He is a difficult man to understand."

At last the wind waned. There was a ragged cheer from the *Tropic Belle* as its crew leaped into the sea and swam for shore. The dining salon boomed with coarse laughter, and the lilt of violins was suddenly replaced by concertinas. Her door banged back, and Joe charged in, still wet from the lashing rain. "Lily, get dressed and come downstairs."

"I'm sick, Joe."

"Sick!" He looked at her perplexedly. He had had a hard time out on the shoals, and he had expected to return to something more pleasant than this. "What is wrong? Have you seen a doctor?"

"There's no doctor here, but I can diagnose the malady easily enough. I am ill from worry over you!"

Joe Beau Clair was genuinely surprised. "But, Lily, there was nothing to fret about. I would have made it to shore again if the ship had capsized."

"Oh, that is easy for you to say now! Why didn't you go up the river?" she cried.

"Because I wanted to come here." He studied her with a frown of concern. "That's the way I live, Lily. There's always one danger or another. How do you think I spend my time when I am away? Do you think I sit beneath an awning drinking claret on the deck? Come, you are going to be my wife. You can't spend your life lying abed with worry. Get up and come downstairs. The men ought to see what they've risked their lives for."

She realized the validity of what he said, and she did as she was told. She put on a gown of Dresden silk, patterned in old rose against cream; coiled her hair in a Greek knot; and adding a dagger brooch against her bodice, went off to the dining room.

A feast was in progress. Platters of food were everywhere. Fish washed up in the wild surf had been collected and cooked into a huge stew, and the smell of roasting pork told her someone had found a hog to butcher. Joe lifted her up, and standing her on a chair, cried, "Gentlemen, my fiancée!"

To her surprise, they burst into applause, and those who had hats left threw them in the air. He took her about the room and introduced her to each member of the crew. She gave each one her attention, asked where some called home, and if they were married. Several unwrapped pictures, kept from the weather in oilskin, and showed her sweethearts and infants in lacy white cambric dresses.

She shuddered to think of all those women who had not been watching the floundering ship, but whose lovers had been in danger because of her, and recklessly she announced that she would like to dance with every man. Joe looked dubious as she took on the first, but she was bent now on showing him she was worthy of him, that she could be as strong and imperturbably a wife as he could wish. The sailor held her gingerly, lest his muddy garments stain her gown as the concertina struck up a gay tune.

"I am sorry you had a hard time because of the captain," she ventured, not knowing what to say.

"Oh, but we took a vote, miss, not to go up the river. We agreed. All of us."

"You did? But why?"

"Oh, I don't know. There was something grand about it. To follow a man like Joe Beau Clair and take him to his bride. We'll have a fine tale to tell!"

He could explain himself no better, and she shivered and said, "It's a wonder you lived to tell it!" And she danced with the next man and the next.

Finally in exhaustion she returned to her room and slipped into the enameled bed. She was drifting off into blessed sleep when he came to claim her. She was aware of his kiss on her forehead, and she struggled to rouse herself. She had waited so long for his love! But weariness won, and she heard him laugh fondly as he tucked the covers tenderly about her and went away.

The little steamer came again, and they all partied their way back through the bayous to New Orleans. As they slid through the shadowy swamp forest, Lily thought for the first time to tell Joe about her role as Cleopatra, and the plans Giles had for their wedding.

He laughed aloud at the idea that they should be transported from their nuptials in a chariot, and announced he thought it would be good fun. "But we must make Giles get someone else for the part soon, Lily. I am an impatient man!"

She was uncomprehending. "What do you mean, get someone else for the part?"

"Why, just that. You are not going to play Cleopatra after you are my wife. That would be absurd."

She was stung. "You said you would accept my acting," she said. "Have you forgotten so soon?"

"I remember what I said. I was as proud as I ought to have been of your Salome, and I am sure your Cleopatra will delight me. But when I said you might act, we could not be married. It's different now. Even Giles will object to a Cleopatra in a maternity gown."

She blushed happily. "Oh, that is what you mean. Well, I would not work while there was a baby, of course. But when they were older, we would have nannies and governesses anyway. I can't see that it would hurt for me to perform occasionally."

"Oh, Lily! Only think! Imagine how they would tease a little boy whose mother wore those costumes and played Cleopatra. Mothers don't do such things. Never mind, you'll be kept busy. You will always have a child in your belly when we are married."

A little thrill ran through her. "Then I will not complain, Joe. But I must play Cleopatra for a while. Van Artsdalen has money in it, and you won't want him to lose it. We were the cause of his losing money once before."

"Van Artsdalen? He's not the type to put money into theatrics. Do you know why?"

"I haven't any idea," she said.

Joe looked thoughtful. She had not dared to suggest that Jenny had had anything to do with it, not after the row it had caused the last time, when Lily had been certain Jenny had arranged for Joe to go to South Africa. But now she saw his features twist with amazement, as if he had thought of it himself. He shook his head in puzzlement. He wasn't going to admit to her the idea that so surprised him.

He agreed that under the circumstances she could continue to play Cleopatra, and as the afternoon passed, she would catch him time and time again staring down into the delicate confetti moss and hyacinths in the green water as if he were still pondering the matter. She was pleased that she had won his permission to go on with the role, but less pleased to know that he must be thinking of Jenny.

Had Jenny imagined that she and Joe would fight over her doing the part? Silly girl! Joe had been very reasonable, and even if he hadn't, she wouldn't have been likely to trade him for the stage. The stage was a mere fantasy world, pleasant though it was. Joe was right. She would be a mother soon, and that, not Cleopatra, was the role for which she was meant.

The weeks and the wedding preparations rolled on. Sometimes with a wrench, Lily would think that soon she would never stand on this stage again. Strange how much she had come to enjoy it. Even Giles had abandoned the pretense that she was not a natural performer. He was impressed by the energy she had put into the Shakespearean play and he was calling her the finest talent he had ever discovered.

"She is so full of emotion!" he would tell anyone who would listen. "I recognized it the first time I ever saw her dance. But even I didn't realize the extent. Lily Beau Clair is not content to simper on the stage and depend on her beauty as so many actresses are."

She was too glad to be in his good graces to tell him she intended to quit the stage on her marriage. It was Joe who mentioned it quite incidentally one night at dinner. Lily saw Giles go purple with rage, and she excused herself and ran up to her room. He came after her in a moment, bursting in behind her, before she had a chance to lock the door.

"Lily, you cannot mean you will let him do this to you! Don't you realize—any woman can have babies! It's a mere biological function. Only a very few women can be great actresses and move people to tears with their performance."

"I don't want any other woman to have Joe's babies," she whispered, close to tears herself.

He gave a roar of frustration, and seizing her about the waist, lifted her off her feet and shook her furiously. For one brief moment she was as terrified of him as she had been when she had first come to be his protégée. Then Joe was framed in the doorway.

"Put her down, Giles!" he roared. "Lily is not your possession!"

"She is not yours yet either!" the wiry little director countered, but he let go of Lily, just in time to be seized by the collar by his antagonist.

"Lily will be mine soon enough!" Joe said, and prepared to hurl Giles in the direction of a kizer plush bed lounge.

She stepped between them suddenly, her pretty features contorting. "Do stop it!" she screamed, and ran from the room.

On the stairs she met an agitated Archer, who had just come to Snowdown to look for her. "I have a problem you must help me with, Lily."

"I'll try," she sighed. "Perhaps I'll be better at solving your problems than mine." Anything was preferable to returning to the scene she had left behind.

"Do you remember the old pink brick house you admired in the Vieux Carré? In the block I'm restoring?"

"I remember."

"That old woman is all alone there now. She had a servant with her, but the girl has run off with as much as she could carry. The end is not far now; I suppose it was to be expected that her nurse would not stay that long. I sent an ambulance to remove her to the hospital, but she refused to let them take her. What am I going to do, Lily?"

"Let her die there, of course. People like her have struggled all their lives to keep their houses."

"But all alone...."

"I will go and see to her, Archer." Before he could protest, she slipped her shawl around her and hurried outside.

Why had she volunteered? Had it been just because she had needed to get away from Snowdown, away from Giles Benton and Joe, away from their argument, which had been frighteningly like the two sides of one that had been raging in her own mind?

She could admit that now as the carriage rolled through a rainy dusk into the decrepit streets of the Vieux Carré. A large part of her heart and mind agreed with Giles Benton. How had that happened? Had Giles done that to her? Or was it as he had said, a natural thing? But how could anything be really natural to a woman, except to give herself utterly to a man? To receive him and bear his children and submit ...

But how peculiar, too, that Joe should require these qualities in her. They were not what he enjoyed most about her, not what had made him love her. He could get those things so much more easily from someone else—someone like Jenny Van Artsdalen. She shuddered, whether from the threat of Jenny or from the threat of the big house with tulips in the ironwork, before which the carriage had stopped.

"Is this the place, miss?" Her driver handed her down.

"Yes, you needn't wait. Come back for me at eight, in time to get to the theater."

The carriage clattered away and she was alone in a steady fall of rain. Lifting her skirts over the wet cobbles, she went around to the side entrance, where red rambling roses hung heavy and sweet with raindrops. The door was ajar. She closed it behind her, noticing how chill the house was. The sugar chest loomed out of the dimness, and she remembered how she had once hidden there from Hetty, the knife ready in her pocket, her feet bare because Susan had not had a pair of shoes to lend her.

In the parlor the girandoles she had dusted so often tinkled in gusts of wind that blew the curtains out from the windows. The place was heavy with the smell of dust—American dust, Lily remembered. It was claiming the house at last. She closed the windows to keep the rain from marring the violet ebony tables beneath them and went up the gloomy stairs.

The door to the room she had once occupied was open, and the little rosewood bed in which she had spent her first nights in New Orleans was neatly made with a lace spread and a matching bolster pillow. What a simple child she had been then, as simple as the room itself! She had thought to do nothing but wait for Joe. Wait and say her rosary and pray at the cathedral. How differently it had all turned out! She seemed to see a ghost in that room as she stood there, a ghost of a girl she no longer was. It was not the first time, either, that someone had thought to see her ghost in that room. She saw now how she must have looked to Hetty. *You's a ghost, Miss Lily. Old river got you!*

"Yes, Hetty, something got me. Not old river, but that was part of it. I had been married to Edmond, and I had slept with Joe, but it was here that I really lost my innocence. Here I began to grow to a mature woman."

Most girls subjected to Madame Drapeaux's initiation would simply have wound up in bordellos, but Lily had handled herself better. It was not only Giles that had made her what she was. The process had begun here.

The darkened room she knew was Madame Drapeaux's reeked of sickness. It took effort to intrude where the old woman lay, a dim outline in the huge Seignoret bed with its great headboard that hovered above her like a bird of prey. There was a perfect silence. Once music would have blared; the entreaties of prostitutes would have drifted in. That was all gone now, since Archer had begun his work. But the silence was not entirely welcome—was it one of death? She lighted the rose-painted lamp, her heart thudding as the room came into focus.

"What is it? Who's there?" Lily felt faint at the sight of hideous eyes staring at her from behind a mist of mosquito netting. "I won't leave here! I'll never leave!" the voice wailed determinedly.

"There, now, I won't make you. I've come to see about you, that's all. I'm Lily Beau Clair. Don't you remember me?"

"Lily . . ." The old eyes strained to see her, and suddenly the old woman emitted a spine-chilling cry of despair. "Lily Beau Clair! I remember you! You've come to take me to hell!"

Lily had forgotten that she would seem as much a ghost to Madame Drapeaux as she had to Hetty, the specter of the worst of her crimes returned to haunt her and bear her to damnation. For a moment the idea fascinated Lily as she stood at the foot of the bed. Then she began to move briskly to see what could be done.

"I'm not a ghost. I haven't come to take you to Hades, though no doubt it's where you should be. My husband killed Jim Frey, so perhaps it's he who will meet you. You remember I warned Jim Frey about my husband. But I've only come to take care of you . . . and . . . and . . . to forgive you, because that is what God wants. I will pray with you if you like, or I will go for a priest."

Madame Drapeaux's eyes changed, but Lily could not be certain that the old woman had even heard her. "Evaleen!" she gasped so suddenly that Lily looked behind her. "Evaleen!"

"Yes, Mama." Lily had not thought to say the words. They spilled out unbidden in a burst of pity. She was somehow relieved not to be the ghost of herself anymore, but the ghost of Madame Drapeaux's ill-fated daughter who had been hanged for spying.

"Do not go behind Yankee lines anymore. You'll get yourself in trouble."

"But I must—"

"You must marry Captain Colliday. That is all you must do. Leave war to men."

"It's everybody's war, Mama. I must spy because I love Captain Colliday."

"Evaleen, I will keep everything as it is. . . ." The words were choked out in a fit of coughing, and the silence was complete again.

"Mama! Madame Drapeaux?" The old woman's eyes had rolled shut. The terrible gaze was gone forever. Lily covered her gently with the crocheted bedspread, and then, to her surprise, she wept. Why had she slipped so easily into Evaleen's character and said things that were truthful instead of comforting things that might have eased the woman's troubled mind? "The war is over, Mama, and Captain Colliday and I are to be married next week. . . ."

Perhaps it had been that she had thought such a charade would be belittling to her old employer. She had been a grand woman in her way. She had been brutalized by the men she had had to depend on for survival. And she had known no other way. When the guilt had become too much, she had lapsed into insanity. How often was the result of women's dependence on men such a brutalization! Like Susan using Etienne as her protector and then marrying Henry Wickersham.

How different the world would be if women were as free as men, she thought suddenly. It was not a new idea. She had heard about movements for women's rights, though they had all been in New York, not New Orleans. Women in New York were marching in the streets to demand the vote, while in New Orleans unmarried women still did not frequent restaurants without chaperons.

Yes, she wished the world were different. She wished she could do something to make it different, she thought, remembering the innocent girls she had seen being taken from Cuba, most likely to a life in a house of sin. She herself had been lucky. But all her fame and economic independence had not stopped men from treating her as a chattel. She remembered with distaste the argument she had left, Joe and Giles disputing over her as if over ownership of a puppy.

That was it, she decided. This possessing of women by men was the reason Joe's attitude toward her had changed, why he wanted her to change into a Jenny Van Artsdalen of a wife. She thought of him jumping into the waves, competing with the ocean for his life as he swam to her arms. He was always so alive, always on the fine edge of life. Perhaps that was why she loved him, perhaps because she was so much like him. She too had cut life with a fine edge since she had sailed away with him to Montserrat. She sat downstairs in the parlor until her driver returned, and then she locked all the doors, and having sent word to Archer of Madame Drapeaux's death, she went to the theater.

Several days later Joe caught Lily with her nose deep in a new script. "What are you reading, Lily?"

"It's *Hedda Gabler* by Ibsen. Giles was interested in having me do it once."

But, Lily, you're not going to do any more plays."

"Not even if I agreed not to dance anymore or wear skimpy costumes? If I did only dignified roles? It would mean so much to me, Joe. Please!"

"No, Lily. I don't want you on the stage."

She fumed for a day, and then asked advice from an unlikely source. "Oh, Giles, I am going to miss the stage!" she said.

He smiled. "Cleopatra could give you the answer, Lily."

"Cleopatra?"

"Who should know better than she about men? There is a line that will tell you. You speak it every night."

She listened with special interest to her own performance that evening. " 'What should I do that I do not?' " she heard herself say.

" 'In each thing give him way, cross him in nothing,' " answered her attendent.

" 'Thou teachest like a fool the way to lose him!' " she snapped scornfully, and then was stunned for a moment. That was the line Giles had been speaking of. Cleopatra would not have given in. She put the idea into action the next day.

"Joe, I am not going to give up the stage. You must let me continue, and we will marry as two equals, each with the right to make decisions."

He laughed. "Of course we are equals, Lily. But you are a woman. Behaving as a wife is part of being a woman."

It seemed she could not make him understand. "Joe, I will give up the stage if you will give up something you do that displeases *me*."

"Why, of course, Lily. That's only fair. What will it be?"

"I don't like your going to sea. It makes me lonely. Do not do it anymore."

He could not believe he had heard correctly. "Not go to sea!"

"You would find plenty else to interest you with investments and ship designing."

"No, never! The sea is part of me!"

"And the stage is part of *me!* Now, don't you understand?"

He didn't. They argued, and each argument they had became more acrimonious than the last. "Oh, Edmond did say this marriage would be a disaster!" she cried one day.

"Perhaps he was right!"

"Oh, he wasn't right at all. He thought it would be because I would tie you down, and it is you who are trying to tie me down."

"Women are meant to be tied down. That's why God gives them children."

"Don't turn religious on me, Joe Beau Clair! I want to have children like any woman, but once you are in the bedroom, you won't be waiting for God to bring them!"

"What sort of woman are you, anyway, Lily? You haven't got the makings of a proper wife!"

"That's what Jenny said. Maybe you'd sooner keep me as your mistress!"

"Perhaps I would!"

But even that part of their relationship had begun to turn sour. The wild anger they felt began to enter into their lovemaking. She began to realize that she must give in in order to save the situation. Cleopatra might have known everything about keeping men, but Lily had neglected to note that the *play* about Cleopatra had been written by a man.

Jenny Van Artsdalen had outsmarted her after all, for now that she wanted to give in, something inside wouldn't let her. She considered pretending to give in, marrying him and later doing as she pleased when Giles came to ask her to perform. But she knew it would not work. Somewhere she had lost the wiles for it. It was going to have to be an honest marriage. She was too proud to have him conquer her, but she was not too proud to fall on her knees to beg him to understand. It was more than the stage that was the issue. It was the sort of free woman she had become.

In the end they quarreled with awful violence, and she took off the ring he had given her and returned it tearfully. She was hoping this last gesture would shake his obstinance, but Joe had a terrible pride. Worse, she was not even certain he loved her anymore.

"Well, if this is the way you want it, Lily."

"It isn't!" she cried.

"Then put the ring back on and end this nonsense."

"I can't, Joe, unless you make it possible."

He gave a groan of disgust, and turning on his heel, walked away.

She hoped for days that he would return. She would waken in the night thinking that he had come, as he had once before, over the wall and up the trellis to win his victory in spite of anything she could do. But the sound that had disturbed her sleep would always be only the wind making a lonely rustle in the trees or the croak of a frog in the bushes.

At last Lily could help herself no longer. She was ill with longing for him, and her mind could not rest from imagining what advantage Jenny must be taking of the split. She drove down to the docks amid the coal smoke and the smell of burning pine resin, to give herself up to him, surrender herself like the plunder of war to be his utter possession forever.

Oh, Joe, you have won. I am only a woman. Do with me whatever you will.

But where the *Sea Bird* had been there was nothing but brown, lapping water, no one to accept her capitulation but an old gray pelican ruffling its feathers on a post. Joe had sailed.

She felt destroyed when she wandered onto Snowdown's patio that evening and wondered aloud to the roses, "Whatever shall I do?"

A voice at her elbow replied softly. "I am still here—dear old Archer. You could always marry me!"

25

Marry Archer! To her surprise, the idea was not completely unthinkable. "But I don't love you, Archer," she said simply.

"Yes, you do, Lily. You're always glad to have me around. I make you happy. And Joe Beau Clair did not. Oh, I know what you mean when you say you don't love me. But I promise you I'd be most considerate in that way. That sort of thing is fleeting. It's a small part of life. We would not have passion, perhaps, but we would have fine times!"

He grinned at her rakishly, looking immensely handsome and warm, his blue eyes teasing and sparkling, as if daring her to take him seriously. Dear Archer and his defenses against letting her see how sincere he was, how easily she could hurt him! Suddenly her heart went out to him. He deserved her as no other man in the world!

He had never made demands on her like other men. He had built her Snowdown and had asked only that she live in it. He had danced with her and asked only that she enjoy herself, comforted her and wanted only for her to be solaced. His was the most unselfish love she had ever known.

Almost unconsciously she began to think about the life they would have together. Unlike Joe, he would always be with her, making her life gay and entertaining. He would build wonderful palaces; she would create marvelous roles. She would do anything she liked, perhaps she would even come out in support of women's right to vote. Archer wouldn't care. Archer would champion her in everything, even when she stirred controversy. And what would he say to that line of little children when they came asking him about their unusual mama? "Oh, that is just your mother's way, dear boys and girls. Isn't she adorable?"

As time went by, her anger against Joe began to grow again. How dare he sail away without even telling her his destination? How dare he leave without even saying whether he would return to her? It was not the first time he had used such tactics. Would he deal with every marital disagreement this way? It was a male prerogative to which she could respond with nothing but helpless fury.

Perhaps he had thought to break her will by his maneuver. He expected that she would waste away from need of him, and he would return to find her begging him to accept her on his terms. Oh, yes, she had been ready to do that, once, but that time had passed. She was growing strong again. She had begun to resent her need of him, to fight it in a way she never had before, even when she had been "Married" to Edmond. The raw power of his love had always rendered her helpless. Even when she had run away from Martinique, it had not been from strength of purpose, but from lack of a strong enough will to resist.

But no more. How delightful if Joe were to return and find her quite happily married to someone else! She began to let Archer kiss her, usually during moonlight drives along the river.

Romance at Snowdown seemed impossible. There was Giles, always underfoot. Strange, it had not seemed so when it had been Joe she was kissing. Archer's kisses were nothing like Joe's. They did not set her blood to racing, but they were gentle and soft as a featherbed; and sometimes she wanted to go on sinking down into them forever, wrapped and pillowed in his devotion.

"When is Joe Beau Clair coming back?" Giles growled one day when they were alone together.

"Joe? I have no idea. He told me nothing."

"I thought he must have come to his senses. You seem very serene these days."

"Perhaps I've decided not to marry a man who torments me."

"What! You haven't brought him around yet? When we've got thousands of dollars invested in wedding gowns and champagne? You'll be a laughingstock if you don't marry after all this. It will hurt your career."

"Nobody can 'bring Joe around,' Giles. What would you say to a switch of bridegrooms?"

"Who?"

"Why, Archer, of course."

"Don't marry Archer, Lily!" he said, his eyes suddenly dangerous.

Lily trembled. It had been a long while since she had really been afraid of Giles. He had made her what she was, and once she had felt herself to be his creation, subject to his will. But she had grown now, as a child grows away from its parents. How could it be that she still felt the same terror she had the night he had threatened to show her degradations if she went driving with Archer again? That had been during her role as Salome, when she had been unformed as an actress, and Giles had needed her despair over men unabated. But that was all past.

"Why shouldn't I marry Archer? You will have to give me a very good reason, because I've already overcome a number of strong ones of my own. Are you afraid Archer won't make me suffer enough?"

"No, I am not afraid of *that*. Oh, go ahead, Lily; you won't listen to me now. That is the way of actresses. They forget where they owe gratitude."

"Giles, I haven't forgotten!" But he had already left the room.

A week later she told Archer Snow she would be his wife. His happiness was contagious. She became caught up in the festivities and felt through and through the happy bride. Snowdown reeled with parties, each grander than the last, as the day of the wedding approached. And to top it off, Archer told her he had received an offer to take *Cleopatra* to New York. "Would you like that, Lily? We could leave right after we are married."

"Oh, Archer, of course I would!"

To play on Broadway, on the famed Rialto! That, if anything, would drive thoughts of Joe far away. New sights, new triumphs. It would be a tremendous beginning for their marriage, she thought, and more than ever she was convinced she had made the right decision. She had been little more than a schoolgirl bent on mischief when she had fallen in love with Joe Beau Clair, and someday she would look back on her passion for him as no more than a turbulent ocean she had had to cross to Archer's mature love.

"Are you certain you're doing what you ought, Lily?" Susan wanted to know. "It's such a turnabout."

"Not really. Joe Beau Clair has caused me trouble enough. I'll show him now!"

"Well, it's certainly sensible. Archer's delightful as well as rich. I wish I'd snagged him. I wouldn't have made him wait so long."

"He is a catch. But I don't need to marry a man for money. I've plenty of my own."

"I wish I had," Susan said wistfully. Her career had not done as well as she had hoped, perhaps because Henry always put his foot into it when Susan seemed on the verge of a breakthrough. "If I could only tour once like you, then I might have enough to leave him." She sighed. "That is, if he didn't get his hands on it first."

"It's still so bad, being married to him?"

"Oh, I can't bear the sight of him! I stay away from him as much as possible; and then, once in a while he catches me and throws me down somewhere, anywhere, just to vex me. I scratch his face all the while, but he has the better of it, you can be sure!"

"To think the last time we walked down an aisle together it was at your marriage!" said Lily with a shudder. "Susan, suppose I persuade Archer to have you come with us? Giles has plenty of influence in New York. It might help."

"What—on your honeymoon?"

"It won't be much of an intrusion." Lily laughed. "We are already taking Giles and the entire cast of *Cleopatra*."

"Not much of a lovers' idyll, Lily. Are you sure it's what you want?"

"Oh, yes. It's the sort of thing Archer and I thrive on."

"Well, I'll come, then, if you can arrange it."

There would be a sort of safety in numbers, a kind of security in transporting their entire environment with them into their marriage, but Lily and Archer had not put that thought into words. It had been a stroke of genius on Archer's part to save them from being alone with their frightening new relationship.

For her wedding day she chose creamy camellias instead of the roses Joe had wanted her to wear. She knew a moment of supreme panic just as she slipped into the cool satin dress with its nineteen-inch waist and its proud gigot sleeves. This was all wrong! This dress had been made for Joe. She should have had another made, at least. And somewhere, deep inside, she must have been expecting Joe to appear and carry her off from this wedding, because when the last tiny button had been fastened and she was finally on her way down the aisle, she felt a sense of anticlimax and disappointment. Then from the gloom of the cathedral came Archer's face, shining with an adoration and wonder that blotted out everything else.

She spoke her vows strongly when they were made man and wife and looked up gratefully into Archer's eyes. She had done the ultimate, put Joe Beau Clair finally and utterly out of her life so that he could never trouble her again. The idea made her light-headed as they were borne away to the reception at Snowdown. They danced for hours while maids in Egyptian costume passed champagne and guests nibbled the tiered wedding cakes set on a lace-covered table with an enormous nougat sculpture of the sphinx.

"Lily, it's time to go," said Archer at her elbow.

"So soon? But I'm having fun."

"The train must keep its schedule, love. Never mind, we'll take the party with us."

She changed into a green bolero-style suit trimmed with black mohair, and she traded her veil for a hat with a sugar-loaf crown. A display of fireworks marked their departure in Snowdown's sky as they rode toward the train station in a gold-painted carriage with Egyptian motifs.

Bedlam reigned at the platform, where police cleared the way for Lily and Archer among their well-wishers, and the rest of Lily's entourage struggled to get aboard with their luggage. Giles had engaged a gilded private car for Archer and Lily, with an elaborately hung bed, thick carpets, and velvet seats. The company of *Cleopatra* filled it quickly, and the champagne continued to flow, served now by dark-skinned waiters in crisp white jackets.

She looked out the window as the train pulled away and the crowds of New Orleans faded. She sighed, thinking back on all her life there. "Lily, why so pensive?" her bridegroom asked.

"Oh, I don't know. I was only wondering if you think they will like *Cleopatra* as well in New York."

"They'd be fools not to. We'll have a lot of fun and get even richer!" He kissed her and turned her back laughing to the revelry.

It was long after midnight when the car cleared, leaving them alone together. They lay exhausted in each other's arms; she still in the bolero suit, he clad in his light-colored double-breasted waistcoat and striped gray cashmere wedding trousers. She had dozed against his shoulder when she became aware that the lulling clack of the wheels had ceased. The quiet was eerie, and the motion of the train had not stopped. She gazed out the window, saw moonlight on water, and realized that the car was being ferried across the Mississippi, she and Archer alone in the lavish coach floating across the great silvery river.

She shook sleep away, and remembering the obligations she had undertaken at the cathedral, she began to unbutton the bolero suit. When she was nearly naked in the waffling light, he startled her by asking, "What are you doing, Lily?"

"I am getting my nightgown, of course," she said, instinctively holding a silk petticoat in front of her.

"Come here, Lily, please."

She went and let him pull her to her knees on the big bed. It was most unusual, she thought. She couldn't remember any time before that a man had said "please." He pulled the petticoat from her hand and ran his fingers over her creamy, moonlit skin. "Oh, Lily, how beautiful you are!" he moaned in wonder.

She pressed her lips against his, eager to know what love would be like with this gentle, devoted man she had married. He drank in her kiss and then pushed her back, giving her buttocks a playful spank.

"Go and put on your gown, Lily."

"But, Archer . . ."

"You have no duty to me. I will never have it that way. It is I who will be your servant. For you it must always be perfect, and you are too tired tonight. Go to sleep again here close to me. I don't believe in the ritual of wedding-night copulation. It's barbaric."

How thoughtful he was, she thought with satisfaction, as she drifted to sleep again.

In Richmond a crowd mobbed the train, crying for a glimpse of the famed New Orleans actress. She stood at the back of the car and waved and blew kisses. The same thing happened at Baltimore, and then at Philadelphia. She clasped Archer's hand excitedly as the train steamed into New York. It was all marvelous—this great city, the people who had turned out to cheer or to look curiously at her and her husband. What room here for thoughts of Joe Beau Clair?

Giles Benton ushered them efficiently to the carriage that would take them to their suite at the Albemarle Hotel. Later there came a trip to the Fifth Avenue Theater, where touring stars brought shows for limited engagements. It was here on the northwest corner of Twenty-eighth Street that *Cleopatra* would have its New York home.

She made Archer take her and Susan back again at night to drive along the Rialto—a mile of wide avenue lined with hotels, restaurants, and theaters, their marquees and lobbies glittering with Edison's incandescent lamps, incredibly bright in contrast to the mellow gas streetlamps in their square glass covers. The sidewalks were jammed with theatergoers, and expensive lacquered carriages were drawing up in front of each playhouse. Archer pointed out the Standard at Thirty-third Street, famous for its productions of Gilbert and Sullivan, and the new Wallack's at Thirtieth. Susan sighed after the sight of the great yellow structure of the Metropolitan Opera, and nudging Lily, reminded her, "That's where I got my start, remember? Henry told everyone I'd had a small role at the Met."

"Maybe you'll sing there one day," Lily said.

"I hope so. I'd be free of him then." And she kept looking after the carriage had passed it.

Giles had tickets for them at Daly's, where beautiful Ada Rehan and elegant John Drew headed a brilliant stock company. Lily and Susan gaped at the Chinese boy in Oriental costume who handed them their programs in the long, ornate lobby; and Archer, who had seen it all before, grinned happily, pleased with their excitement.

As for Giles, he was in an irritable mood. It was nothing new. It had begun even before the wedding, but it had become worse. Now he caused a small furor by complaining loudly that the seats were not exactly in the center of the orchestra section. He drew attention to them, and soon people began to recognize Lily and ask for her autograph. Everybody was looking at them. What was the matter with Giles, anyway?

Was he still upset because she had married Archer? She had never figured out why he had objected so much. He had not tried to dissuade her further or given her any reason. Had he tried to discourage Archer too? Surely that would have been more hopeless than trying to deter her.

She reached for Archer's hand as the lights dimmed, his ring, with its circle of moonstones and rubies around the diamond, shining on her finger.

Later, at their hotel, Lily, wearing a wrapper of Persian percale over her silk nightgown, brushed down her hair with a cherrywood brush and told him it had been a marvelous evening. "Oh, Archer, think of it, Daly's!" she cried, her eyes glowing.

"Tomorrow, the Lyceum," he promised. "The two very best of New York theaters."

"And in a week we will open *Cleopatra* in the Fifth Avenue!"

"Are you happy, Lily?" He knew the answer, of course, but he wanted to hear her say it. He would have liked it, too, if she had told him that she had no regrets, that she did not think of Joe Beau Clair, whom she had loved so passionately and so long.

"Oh, Archer, I am ecstatic! Why is it I love theater so?"

"For the same reason I do, perhaps. For a little while you can pretend that life is noble and beautiful, all the good side of the fruit."

"But that's not make-believe anymore," she told him gaily. "Our lives will be all the good side of the fruit from now on. I owe so much to you for all this!"

"And to Giles. He made you an actress. He made you realize your potential."

"Yes, to Giles, too, of course. He is an irascible old thing lately, isn't he? The extras we hire are going to think they've met the devil himself."

"They may be right." She looked at him sharply, surprised that he didn't seem to be joking. Then quickly he smiled again and asked if she would like to open a bottle of champagne before bed.

"Oh, dear, I've had so much champagne the last several days that I must be all bubbles inside." She laughed. "But why not? Open it."

The cork popped, and he filled their glasses and sat beside her on the brass bed. "It has been a perfect night." She sighed as she raised hers to her lips.

"It will be dawn in three hours, Lily. Aren't you tired?"

"No. I think I would like to stay awake to see the sun come up."

"A perfect evening, and you are not tired. There must be a way to fill the time until sunrise. . . ."

She gave a little gasp as he untied her wrapper and pushed it down from her shoulders. She had not been thinking of this somehow. Her mind had still been on the evening at Daly's. It might have been different if Joe had been with her instead. He would have made her think of it at once. But she simply was not used to thinking of Archer as a lover. She put her glass down and closed her arms around his neck as he kissed her bare shoulders.

"I do love you, Archer," she murmured. She had never said those words before. Indeed it had not been long since she had protested exactly the opposite. And he had confidently told her that she did care for him. He had been right. She cared for him in a different way than she cared for any other man.

Edmond had been appealing before their marriage because of the power she had had over him. And Joe had had power over her. Love had always been a struggle, the bedroom a battle-ground. But she would lie with this man in simple sweetness.

The wrapper dropped to the floor, and her nightgown went after it, as he laid her back on the covers. He tugged at his belt buckle, while she herself worked open the agate buttons of his shirt. "Let me see you, Archer. I want to see the man I have married."

She was amused when a faint flush rose too his face. He had a beautiful body, lithely muscled and covered with a soft filigree of golden hair that caught the glow of the gas lamp and made him seem to glimmer. She found with a spring of joy that she had no hesitation in opening herself to him.

"I have made no mistake; he is the finest of men," she thought as they lay together.

Then she was aware that her husband had begun to shiver. It was a small tremor at first—she was not certain. Then it became stronger. The entire bed quivered. "Are you cold, dearest? Shall I pull up the covers?"

She was shocked at the misery in his voice. "I am not cold, Lily. I would like to tell you that and hide the truth, but I would never be dishonest with you. The truth is that I am afraid."

"Afraid of what? Of making love to me?"

"Yes, Lily. I can't help it."

She was astounded. In her experience, women might be afraid of sex, but never men. It was a force that drove them with the power of a steam locomotive. She tried to gather her wits as he floundered for words to explain.

"I . . . am afraid of disappointing you. I couldn't bear that. More than anything in the world, I want to satisfy you!"

"But I can't think why you shouldn't!" she cried.

"Giles says—"

"Giles! Has *he* been talking to you about me? Have the two of you been discussing how you shall bed me?" Fury overcame her bewilderment.

Bent on trying to make her understand, he ignored her change of tone. "Giles says you are a lascivious little whore—"

"Oh, how dare you use such language to me, Archer Snow!

Giles says!" She was sitting up in bed now, her naked breasts hard and erect with anger. "I hate Giles Benton! And you, you do not have to agree with him about your own wife!"

"Lily! I don't agree with him, of course. But he says you need a brute of a man in bed—a man like Joe Beau Clair—to work his will on you. I am no such man, Lily."

"Of course not. I don't expect you to be. But you are the man I wanted to marry. Come here, and I will show you."

Archer did not accept the invitation. Instead, he flung himself out of bed and hastily pulling on his clothes, went out of the room. When he returned, it was nearly day, and the sounds of trolleys and horses had begun to echo along the streets.

She turned away and closed her eyes so he would not see that she had been lying in stunned wakefulness, and she heard him stagger and hit the bureau before he fell across the bed. She smelled the reek of liquor on his breath.

The preparations for opening *Cleopatra* went on. In the midst of the unpacking of equipment and costumes, Lily rehearsed on the new stage. Giles advised her to accept a generous offer of money from Sarony, the leading theatrical photographer, for the privilege of making her portrait; and likenesses of her appeared also in the show window of Ritzman's near Madison Square, where pictures of all the current celebrities were displayed for collectors to purchase.

Archer kept up a round of activities that delighted and exhausted her. They went to see the fire-eaters and sword swallowers at Huber's Dime Museum and visited the Chamber of Horrors at the Eden Musée, where major crimes were reproduced in waxworks. They attended variety shows at Pastor's Opera House, and at Koster and Bial's, where half the audience seemed to be artists and writers. For a special surprise Archer took her to a performance of the Manhattan Ballet, hosting a party afterward that reunited Lily with her old friends from the days when she had danced her Martinique number at the French Opera.

The girls laughed and hugged her and congratulated her on her new husband. There had been a rapid turnover in the company. Lily did not know half of the dancers now, and it seemed to take forever for her to hear what had happened to each one who was missing—those who had married and were comfortable wives, those who had loved unwisely and sunk to drink or prostitution.

"Do you remember that party we had last at your pink

house in New Orleans?" they reminded her. "What a night! No furniture, but plenty of champagne, and your Joe danced with us all!"

And then they thought how indelicate it was to mention Joe. It must have been a great tragedy or Lily would be here with him instead of this other man. Oh, they liked Archer Snow well enough. If they had never seen Joe, they would have thought that Lily had made a marvelous conquest. But Archer Snow did not have the aura about him that Joe had had, and his skillful waltzing was nothing like Joe Beau Clair's caleinda.

"Dance, Lily!" they cried.

"No, I am through with dancing." She looked so sad that none of them pressed her. They understood that she could not dance because it had become too painful. It reminded her too much of him.

Lily wished each evening would never end, but inevitably there came that moment of quiet when she was alone with Archer in their bedchamber. She would dress herself in a lacy gown, and he would kiss and caress her. Then, just as she had begun to hope, Archer would seem to freeze, as though some dreadful force had risen inside him to cut off all his natural warmth and passion. He would make some excuse— or worse, leave abruptly with no excuse at all. Whichever, the result was always the same. He returned drunk and murmuring protestations of love and fell on the bed in a stupor.

Susan had found a position at the Casino Theater as a member of the chorus, and the last night before *Cleopatra* was to open, they went to hear her sing on the roof garden of the exotic Moorish building. Lily managed to be incognito that evening as she observed Lillian Russell, golden and queenly as the featured performer.

"I shall never match her voice," Susan said wistfully afterward. "But the pay is good, and I have never heard so much talk of money. I shall eventually become the mistress of someone who has plenty. . . ."

"You've decided to leave Henry, then?"

"Yes. He doesn't care. I don't think he'll bother to come looking."

"I'm glad you'll be rid of him," Lily said, "but I wish you'd learn your lesson about men. You'll only be in trouble again, behaving as scandalously as you intend."

"Nonsense! This is not New Orleans. In New York a flair

for leading an outrageous life is as important as talent. It did not hurt Sarah Bernhardt to be photographed in velvet trousers or even to be the mother of an illegitimate child. You can see how much Miss Russell's friendship with Diamond Jim Brady hurts!"

"Oh, Susan!"

"Oh, Susan, nothing! If I'd behaved as I ought, I'd be somebody's washerwoman by now. As for you, Lily, you do have all the luck. With a husband as glamorous as Archer Snow, you can afford to be virtuous. It's a love story all New York adores."

Lily sighed. If New York knew the state of her marriage, that would be scandal itself. She wondered, not for the first time, if it were all her fault. She might keep thoughts of Joe away during the day, but at night, did her longing show? Was it this that Archer sensed that made him always fail?

Still in her evening gown that night, she was standing in front of the mirror, about to let down her hair, when a knock came on the door. Archer, his shirttail hanging loose, admitted Giles Benton.

"Lily, there is a newspaperman downstairs in the lobby. Go and see him."

"Now? At this hour? Tell him to come back in the morning."

"Lily, don't start to become imperial. It's not good business. If he writes an article tonight, it will be in print tomorrow to promote our opening. Go now."

She went, just as it always seemed she did Giles's bidding. "Aren't you coming along?" she said in surprise as he made no move to accompany her.

"No, I'll stay here and keep Archer company." She had the strange feeling that something was not right as she went off alone. Giles had always liked to be in on her interviews, and he had enjoyed all the publicity. Was it something about the two of them left in the room together? What could be wrong about that?

And then she returned and found them, Giles Benton naked and grinning as he demonstrated his mastery over her husband. She seized a china water pitcher and sent it sailing at his head as though he were a mongrel she were routing from defecating in her garden.

It broke against the brass bedstead, sending a shower of glass over the covers. Then everything began to go black as she rushed into the bathroom to vomit.

26

She did not think that she fainted, but voices seemed to come from a long way away. She was lifted dizzily into someone's arms, placed on a bed.

"No! No! I won't lie on this bed!"

The horror of being where they had been together aroused her, and she looked into Archer's eyes. They had about them that deep, haunted gaze she had noticed when she had first met him. She understood it now and shuddered.

"Lily, you've been doing too much. You're ill. You've been dreaming something bad."

She flung herself up dizzily to an armchair. "No. I wasn't dreaming, Archer. I know why it is you don't behave like a husband. Giles Benton is my . . . my rival!"

"Lily . . . Lily . . ." He had begun to cry, sinking to his knees on the rug beside her. "Lily, it's you I love! I had looked so long for a woman who could make me want to be a man. You were the only one who ever could. When you cared only for Joe, it was easier. I built you houses and loved you from a distance. And now! Now marriage has made me face my depravity. Marriage proved me a worthless lover, just as Giles said. I have never given in to a man before!" His voice was choked away by sobs, and he was unable to make any plea other than his weeping.

The sight was almost as unbearable to Lily as the first scene had been. She stumbled to her feet, and giving him no answer, ran hysterically to Susan's room.

"What on earth's the matter, sis?" Susan asked wonderingly.

"Oh, it's too awful to tell." Lily sobbed, unable to speak words that would explain the situation.

"Come on; we're a team, remember?" Susan remonstrated, and Lily finally blurted out everything, picturing for her friend the thing that still revolved hideously in her mind.

Who else did she have in the world but Susan? Once Arch-

323

er had been a dear friend who would have listened to any problem, but she had made the mistake of marrying him. She had had a husband, but she had deserted him. She had had a lover, but she had renounced him. It was different with Susan; the sisterhood between them would endure.

"Get an annulment," Susan said when she had finished.

"An annulment!" Lily had not thought of this way out of the trouble.

"Yes, it's simple. There'd be nothing to it."

"Nothing but an awful scandal!"

"You would survive a scandal. It might be the making of you. Didn't I tell you that an outrageous life is no hindrance?"

"Archer wouldn't survive. What would happen to his beautiful gift for designing houses then? Few people would want him. I think it might kill Archer to have people know."

The shock was beginning to wear off a bit, since she had told someone. Despair was taking its place, but determination was gathering, too. "I must help Archer, Susan. It's as much my fault as his. I shouldn't have married him! I wasn't in love with him the way I was with Joe. Archer isn't the sort of man to be loved that way. It's the second time I've married someone I shouldn't have, but this time I must make it work."

"You're right that you shouldn't have married him," Susan cried. "Get out before it gets worse. You can't change a man like that."

"No. It would destroy Archer. And he was my friend."

"What you need is a lover. Can you teach him to be that? Can you even bear to let him into your bed?"

She sobbed and shook her head unhappily and wondered if she could.

She fought down contempt as she told Archer her decision the next morning. He was still the same gentle man she had cared for enough to marry. And what was she to do without him, and without Joe, too? She needed him; and he, her.

"We'll fight this together, Archer. It will be different now that I know. I'll help you to be strong. I'll help you to love me. I won't expect too much."

She had her reward in the light of the incredulous joy in his eyes. "I'll try to be worthy of you, Lily," he said.

"First of all we must get rid of Giles, of course." A strength was building in her now, a bitter certainty of purpose. She would not let Giles Benton have her husband.

"Get rid of Giles!" She had her first real intimation of how difficult things would be in the look of horror on Archer's face.

"Yes, of course, get rid of Giles. He's the center of the trouble," she said with an impatient frown. "I understand so much now. I know why Giles objected to our marriage, why he was so angry when I went driving with you, and I know, too, why you could always get him to do things that I couldn't. You wheedled him as a woman can. We will cleanse our lives of him!"

"How, Lily?" Archer looked almost frightened. "We are both his puppets, you and I. There is something about him— you know what I mean, because you feel it, too. That power he has that can drag a performance from you that you had no idea you could give. You need him, too. You are as much in his thrall as I."

She trembled, less sure of herself as she realized that there was truth in his words. "We must fight him, Archer; that is all. You must free yourself, and Lily Beau Clair, the actress, must learn to stand alone."

"Lily, can you do it? Let Giles stay. I give you my promise that what happened last night will never happen again."

"No. After *Cleopatra* I will never do another play directed by Giles Benton. I have always hated him, and as for you, you know he's stronger than you. He will come between us as long as he can. Do you love me more than him? If you do, you must send him away."

Archer was very pale. "I love *you*, Lily," he murmured.

"Very well. It's decided, then. When we return to New Orleans, it will be without Giles." She looked again at the bed where she had seen them together and shuddered. "We'll get another suite. I'll give the hotel manager some frivolous excuse—the sun glares in my eyes in the morning, or some such thing. He'll think nothing of it. Actresses are supposed to be temperamental."

The new suite was equipped with the new twin beds that were just coming into vogue. The bellboy must have become richer by more than the tip they gave him for hauling their luggage, because the matter was reported in the papers.

"We have no privacy," Archer sighed as they sat over coffee.

"I know. It's frightening. What if they should find out things less silly to report?"

"Don't think of it. At least the play got good reviews. You

are a hit again, Lily. You'll be asked to extend the New York run, no doubt."

"Then I'll refuse." Opening night had been no pleasure for Lily. She had been unable to concentrate because of her problems with Archer. She could hardly bear the thought that her success was shedding glory on Giles. "We're going back to New Orleans as soon as the engagement we've contracted is finished. We're going without Giles, and you're going to tell him!"

"Me, Lily!" he said, choking.

"You. You are the one who can make it stick. He already knows how I feel. He can see it in my eyes. You must convince him you don't want him, either."

Neither Lily nor Archer knew if he had the strength to do it. Archer grew thin and hollow-eyed as the weeks went on. She coaxed him to eat and to go for bicycle rides in Central Park, but he scarcely seemed to notice anything. He was consumed with the test that waited for him, and she trembled for him and tried to give him support.

"You can come to my bed, if you like," she said, fighting revulsion.

He thanked her and stayed on his side of the room. It was just as well. He was still drinking every night. She was glad to be away from the reek of him. The time passed, and the owners of the theater asked that *Cleopatra* be extended. Giles, all elated, came to them with the news. Lily kept quiet and looked at her ashen-faced husband.

"We are going back to New Orleans now, Giles," Archer said at last.

Giles whirled on Lily. "Tell him. We are going to continue here of course." She smiled and looked back at Archer, her eyes fiery.

He seemed to totter beneath Giles's glare, and his lips quivered before he spoke, but the words came out clearly. "We are not going to continue anywhere, Giles. Lily and I are going home—alone. My wife does not wish to perform in any more plays of yours. As for me, I will not put up backing."

Giles was dumbfounded, looking from one of them to the other. Finally he burst out in a tirade. "The two of you! Oh, it's absurd. Neither of you can manage without me, you'll see! You will both come begging me to help you. You're a pair of fools!"

Lily put a hand on the director's small, strong shoulder. "Do be a good sport, Giles. I have won."

He was more of a man than before. He was proud of himself and grateful to Lily for having made him stand up to Giles. On the trip home they were almost happy, and Archer began to tell her jokes again and be her friend. She was glad to see Snowdown again, glad to settle into a routine that was almost like the one she had first known there. Archer did not share her bedroom; but as before, she would see him puttering about the gardens in the morning, and he would come in to breakfast with her.

She missed Susan, who had stayed in New York; and much more than that, she missed Joe. At night he was always in her thoughts. What was her life to amount to now? She would have the stage and nothing else. Or would she even have that? She put off the matter of finding another director and choosing a play to try without Giles.

She wondered what Giles was doing these days. Was he writing the play he had often threatened to write? She had an idea that that would be very worth her while. She felt utterly lost without his certain touch. She did not have enough confidence in herself. She was afraid of being a disaster without him to guide her. And then there would be nothing—a complete emptiness. But she must try, and soon!

She had almost given up on Archer's ever loving her as a husband when her door banged back one night and he stood there clad in nothing but a pair of French balbriggan drawers. She gasped and closed the book she had been reading as he covered the distance between them and grasped her roughly in his arms, tearing at the buttons of her modest muslin nightdress. His hands bruised her breasts painfully. She struggled for breath as he kneaded her buttocks and thighs.

"Archer, stop!"

"I won't stop! I am going to show you that I am a man! Joe Beau Clair would not stop just because you asked him!"

She knew that what he said about Joe was true, but it was also true that she would not want Joe to stop, even if she were asking him to. Archer had not Joe's skill. It seemed to her that he didn't understand what he was doing. His lovemaking was words without music, and no passion rose in her to change his rough caresses into something other than an invasion of her body. He put his lips against her stomach to kiss her there, and she struck upward with her knee to kick him away. He gave a grunt and came back even more strongly. She twisted his blond hair in her fingers and pulled his head back. She fought him all the way to the door, and separating herself from him somehow, she slammed the door and locked it. Bracing herself against it for fear the lock might give, she felt her back jarred by the pounding of his fist against the wood.

"What have I done to him?" she wondered. "Have I created a monster?"

Perhaps Susan had been right. She should have taken the annulment. He was trying so hard and failing so badly. Would this happen again and again? Worse, what had become of the gentle person she had once known?

He hit at the door until she was afraid the very panels would splinter, and she was sadly relieved when the pounding was replaced by racking sobs. Her heart went out to him, and she wanted to comfort him, but she was still afraid to open the door. Hopelessly she tried to secure the ripped fastenings of her gown, and then, sinking to the floor beside the door, she sat there, head against her knees, until at last she tumbled over and slept to the soft sound of his crying, as steady and insistent as the crickets in the oaks.

The sun came up, filtering weakly through the gray overcast of Spanish moss. She stretched her cramped limbs, and turning the key, peeped out, to find him gone. She crept out to the bathroom to bathe in the big claw-footed tub, and then, wearing a lawn underskirt and camisole beneath her wrapper, she went down to breakfast. He was not there either, but his presence was very real in the empty chair across from her as she tried to give her attention to the morning mail, sorting more personal correspondence from fan letters to read first. He had tried, and she had rejected him. What sort of woman was she? What would her rejection do to him?

She frowned, beginning to worry about his whereabouts. If he tried to love her again, she must let him. She had been the one who had insisted on continuing the marriage. She must have the courage to finish what she had started. She should apologize and invite him to her bed tonight. But she knew she could not. Instead she would lock the door before she fell asleep.

Dear Archer! She did not doubt he loved her in his soul as she looked about the beautiful room he had designed for her.

Babylon

Why was it that nature decreed that love must be expressed in bed, and how was it that no man but Joe Beau Clair could satisfy her there?

"Good morning, Lily."

She jumped, not having seen her husband come up behind her. He smiled at her wistfully, wearing a maroon bicycle sweater with white stripes on the cuffs and on the shirt-style collar.

"Have you been out for a spin, dearest?" she asked.

"Yes, it's lovely along the river this early. The willow trees have such a lucent color, and when I stopped to rest, a family of muskrats was playing in the water."

"I would like to go with you sometime," she said, as he took his seat across from her. She poured his coffee, her hand only a trifle unsteady. How grateful she was to him for behaving as though it were any ordinary morning! She returned to the mail, glad for something that would save them from having to keep up a conversation. A cream-colored envelope with a familiar handwriting caught her eye, and she ripped it open quickly with her silver letter opener.

"Oh, here is a letter from Susan, Archer. We shall see what new adventures she is having!"

Archer looked up with interest as Lily removed the sheets from the envelope.

Dearest Lily,
   I know you are in the habit of reading your mail over breakfast, but if Archer is there, you had better put this away and read it later, if you don't want him to see how excited ...

"Oh, dear, this is very female!" She flushed, covered with confusion as Archer looked at her expectantly.

"Is it? Let me see, Lily!" All at once he was no longer himself, but the more abusive Archer of the bedroom. "What would make you look that way? It's about *him*, isn't it?" He seized her wrist and fought for the letter.

"No, Archer, it's not about Joe. Why should it be?" She pulled the paper back, little knowing what it was she was fighting to protect. The pages tore, leaving him with the bottom part of the letter. "Now see what you've done!" she cried.

Archer was devouring the letter, and when he looked at

her again, it was as though something horrid he had read there had focused in his eyes.

"Archer, no!"

Only on some primitive level did she know what she was begging him not to do. Then the blow hit her, sent her reeling to the floor, her silk wrapper falling open to reveal her breasts in her lacy camisole.

"Damn, Lily, damn!" She buried her face in her arms as she heard him kick over the table, sending the china crashing all around her. She felt his awful presence over her, dark and thunderous, not the Archer she had cared for and married, but this terrible new person that was beginning to take his place because of her.

She lay there unmoving until senses deeper than sight or hearing told her he had gone, and then she lifted her head and shook fragments of glassware from her hair and wrapper.

She touched the spot where he had hit her, knowing there would be a bruise along her cheekbone, and then, reaching across the rug, she cut her finger on a shard of glass as she retrieved the part of the letter he had dropped. Making no effort to stanch the bleeding, she read the passage that had infuriated him.

> You'll never guess who showed up as a stage-door Johnny last night and took me out for dancing and a fine dinner at a lobster palace! A certain old flame of yours by the name of Joe Beau Clair! I was the envy of everyone, naturally—even the stars! Lillian Russell stared at him, and Pauline Hall asked me who he was. I hope you don't mind that I didn't tell any of them that the reason he had eyes only for me was you!
>
> He'd docked in New York and heard about the run of *Cleopatra,* and was he in a rage about your marriage! My dear, he plied me with champagne and he knows everything! I hope you'll forgive me for telling him, especially since I probably would have done it even without the champagne.
>
> He is a man who gets what he wants from women! Now he's sailing hell-bent for New Orleans, and you know what he wants from you! Oh, Lily!
>
> P.S. Don't forget the advice I gave you about the annulment. There are still ways in which I am wiser than you!

Babylon

She stood up shakily, her head still swimming, but now not because of Archer's blow. She looked at the date on the top half of the letter and wondered how soon. Dear heaven, what would she do when he came?

No answer came to her, only the message from the servant she had sent to the docks each day since Susan's letter. The *Sea Bird* was arriving!

She dressed in a gown of sheer India linen and swept up her hair quickly, fastening it with big crimped tortoise-shell hair pins and covering it with a straw hat. She must hurry before Joe could come here. He must not come to Snowdown and cross paths with Archer!

She had a little two-seater hitched and drove down to St. Louis Street, dodging creaking wagons and baggage vans. "Have you seen the *Sea Bird* docked?" she called to a dark-skinned girl who was gleaning rice spills from the levee with a broom.

The girl lifted her hand and pointed, the ends of her madras whipping. Lily followed with her eyes and saw the ship, its mizzens flapping as they were lowered. She caught sight of Joe Beau Clair on a tour of inspection high in the rigging.

"Joe!" she cried, forgetting everything else. "Oh, Joe!"

The wind carried her voice, and he heard her. He made her heart stop as he swung around and let go of the lines with one hand to wave her a greeting.

She ran along the pier, stumbling over uneven boards as she watched him descend, swaying hand over hand, his silhouette graceful as a gull against the sky. She crossed the gangplank just in time to have him drop in front of her, landing lightly on the deck. There was that marvelous spice-colored hair, the strong body with its magnet of masculine excitement that almost pulled her into his arms before she thought, before she saw his eyes, cold and mocking.

"Well, Madame Snow! How nice of you to call! And so soon! You simply couldn't wait! Go into my cabin, and I shall come in a minute."

"Joe—"

"Go, Lily. I'll give my crew leave to go ashore now. They're too delicate a lot to hear the row we are going to have!"

She went, quaking. But the anger in his voice sent a thrill through her, too, and in a way she anticipated the approaching storm. She paced the cabin with nervous eagerness, her blood racing as she listened to him calling instructions to his men. She had done the worst possible thing that she could do to him: she had married another man. He would know how to punish her. He would know how to deal with her, though she didn't know herself. He would master her as he always did, and somehow put things right. A soft, heavy rain began to fall, the big drops sighing as they plunked into the river to join the great stream. She lighted a lamp and waited for him to give her her due.

He came in wetly, threw a slicker aside, stared at her with those bice-blue eyes that rendered her helpless. She trembled, half in fear, half in ecstasy. He took a step toward her and lifted her chin with both his hands. She almost swooned, thinking he was going to kiss her, but instead he only held her face up to his, so that she could not shift her gaze from the terrible accusation in his eyes.

"So, Lily, you thought to call my bluff by marrying that excuse of a man Archer Snow! Do you think I will hesitate to take you from him, when I once took you from my own brother?"

She gulped and said nothing, her neck aching from the position in which he was holding her.

"I admit I underestimated you, Lily. I thought you would wait for me when I sailed off. I thought you would be waiting for me on your knees, begging me to have you, ready to give up the stage and do anything at all I wanted. I am forever learning about you!"

"Yes, Joe." She smiled weakly, thinking how nearly right he had been about her. He did not know how she had been ready to surrender when she had found he had sailed.

"It was a dangerous thing to do, Lily. You meant to devastate me with your marriage to Archer Snow, and then, when you had me hopeless with despair, you would reveal this quirk of Archer's and offer to end the marriage if I would let you have your way about the stage!

"That was your game, Lily. You never meant to stay married to Archer. You only did it to hurt me, to get your way. But you are going to get an annulment and marry me, and you are going to give up the stage as well."

"I've promised to try to make the marriage work," she found strength to say. "I'm not going to marry you or be your mistress just now. My reasons for marrying Archer weren't the best, but they weren't the ones you think. I didn't know about him, and now that I do, I'm going to give him a chance to change. He deserves it. He loves me, and I'm going to help him."

He let go of her chin to shake her vigorously by the shoulders. "You're more of a fool than I thought. We've wasted time enough already, you and I. You can't help Archer Snow! You can't teach him to make love to you while you are longing for another man, as you are for me! And you *are* longing for me, Lily. If I but touch you, you will have no power to resist! I know every way to your undoing!"

And he showed her, running his hand expertly beneath her bosom, his caress so charged that her breasts tightened and fought to break from her corset and her legs seemed unable to support her. He smiled with magnanimous understanding of her weakness as he threw her on the bed.

"No, Joe," she moaned. He paid no attention to her entreaties. Why should he? In desperation she began to pray to the Virgin, hoping she would hear her pleas, if Joe would not.

"Let me be strong for once! Let me resist him and not be again in sin!"

Suddenly his hands were gone from her body. She felt a wave of resentment at the thought that her prayer had been answered. She had wanted so terribly to transgress. "Joe?"

"Sh, Lily. I heard footsteps outside. It may be only some of the crew returned, but I don't like it. Wait here. I'll go and see."

He went out into the rain, and she lay too dazed to make any move to straighten her clothing. She gazed down at the floor at the straw boater she had been wearing. It had fallen from her head and he had crushed it under his feet. She had liked that hat, but nothing had a chance when Joe Beau Clair wanted his way. If she could pull herself together, she might escape while he was gone. Go back to Snowdown—to Archer? But Joe might follow her. Her stomach tightened as she imagined just how horrible it might be if Joe tried to wrest her from Archer at Snowdown itself.

While she was trying to decide what to do, it was all at once too late for action again. The door opened, and she closed her eyes, knowing that it was out of her control now. She could not fight her desire for him.

She felt hands on her thighs, heard a chuckle of laughter. Not Joe's voice! Her eyes flew open, and she looked on a weird sight. A face with a mask drawn across the eyes, a stubby, unkempt beard, a dirty flannel shirt on a reeking body. The eyes behind the mask gleamed with desire.

She screamed and heard the laugh again. "No one to hear you, little lady. He's not coming back, that fine gent of yours! What a shame! Never mind! I've got what you need!"

She heard more footsteps outside and struggled against him. "Joe! Joe!"

"That's not him. It's only more of me gang. Keep yelling, and they'll all be in here for a piece of you!"

"What have you done with him? Have you killed him?"

For answer the intruder only grasped her waist roughly and tore at the fastenings of her dress. She flung herself up from the bed, kicking at him with all her strength. There was a crash, and the room was in flames. The lamp, she thought, hearing him curse.

Just as she reached the door, the hem of her skirt took fire. She ran on deck, screaming to God for mercy, thinking that she had already burned to death and that the flames that shot from the cabin to devour her were the very fires of hell.

Then hands seized her again. She had never thought such worldly demons would be seeking after her in Hades, but after all, where would such creatures go except to damnation? She fought against him and lost and felt herself lifted.

"Stop hitting! I'm trying to save you!" a gruff voice said.

Then she was falling, falling, like an angel from grace, and the waters of the Mississippi closed over her.

27

She opened her eyes and saw the roses of her imported French wallpaper at Snowdown. Across the way was her satinwood dresser with its half-moon front and its oval Art Nouveau mirror, trimmed in flowing tendrils of silver. The mirror held a reflection of the back of a man with blond hair, and looking up, she came upon Archer's tragic face bending over her.

"Oh, Archer," she said compassionately, "it's all right. I'm not dead."

"No credit to me you aren't!" he moaned. "They were river pirates, and I sent them."

"You!"

"I didn't know you'd be there! That wasn't part of the plan. Don't you see, Lily? I had to be rid of him. I could never really possess you while he lived. No man could."

She shot up in bed and clutched at him. "Archer! You had him murdered! He's dead? Is he dead?"

Archer's eyes went strangely blank. "I arranged it, Lily. I wanted him dead. I saw your face when you read the letter, and it only told me what I knew already. I did it, and yet I can't believe that I did. I had never felt such a passion before—I, Archer Snow, a murderer!" He shook his head as though trying to clear away a fog to understand what had happened. "You must not say I'm not a man, ever, Lily. I have loved a woman enough to kill—"

"Is he dead, then?" she screamed.

"How could he live? The ship was burned to a cinder, and him lying unconscious on it. But it will be a while before his body is discovered, since no one knew he was still aboard when the fire started. Lily—you will not betray me to the police? It was you I did it for."

"Betray you! I will kill you myself!" She pushed away from him and reached for the drawer where she kept her scissors. He caught her hand and shoved her back into the bed.

"You're hysterical, Lily. The doctor left laudanum in case of that. I will give you a draft."

"No!"

She had never guessed how strong he was. He held her securely, crushing her breasts with his thighs as he forced her mouth open. She gagged and choked, clawed at his hands, and managed to spit a part of the potion back into his face. He clamped his palm across her nostrils and forced her to swallow to get her breath. He looked at her with satisfaction. "There, now, love; you'll sleep."

"I won't, Archer! I'm going to kill you!"

He did not relinquish his brutal hold. Gradually the room blurred, and she drifted into unconsciousness, weeping in fury.

When she woke, he was gone. She dug frantically into her drawer and found that the scissors were gone, too. So was everything sharp and dangerous, even her hatpins, which she might have used to put out his eyes. Downstairs she would find something. She ran to the door and found it locked. She was puzzled at first. She would have loved to lock him out, but how had she done that? Then she realized that the door had been locked from the outside. She was a prisoner!

The lock rattled, and Archer came in bringing a tray of food—coffee and sandwiches and little yellow roses. "Are you feeling better, Lily?"

He seemed so natural, so much his old self that she felt she must have been in a delirium. He looked at her with adoring eyes and offered to butter her toast.

"Please do, and put some of that elderberry jam on it," she answered. "Archer, I have decided not to notify the police about the thing you did."

"Of course you won't love. And you are not going to bury your scissors in my heart or any other such foolish thing." He spoke with no more emphasis than if she had announced that she did not intend to plant cockscomb in the flowerbeds.

"I want an annulment, Archer. This marriage has been a hideous mistake."

"It's too late for an annulment."

"Too late! But we have not—"

"I've killed for you, Lily. That is consummation enough. I've killed for you, done things beyond my wildest nightmares. Oh, I have felt myself evil before, ever since I first recognized my weakness. But I never imagined it could be like this. I have lost my very soul for you, and at least I am going to have you!"

"No, Archer. I am not going to give myself to you. Not after what has happened. I never could." Something about his voice frightened her. It was still calm, but there was a cold certainty in it.

He made no move to come any nearer. "I am going to have you, Lily. I'm going to keep you here with me always. Did you notice that your door was locked? It won't be anymore. I've completed the work now. I've had padlocks put on all the outside doors. The shutters have all been locked, and there are guard dogs on the grounds. It is the finest prison anyone ever had. You are going to spend the rest of your life here."

"Archer, you're insane!"

"Yes. We used to say that about Giles Benton, too. But he was not nearly as insane as I am! I've sent for him to come back, by the way."

Spend the rest of her life here, the prisoner of a pair of depraved men! She dropped the tray onto the floor and ran about the house, up and down stairs, testing windows and doors. He had thought of everything, even the servants' door and the pantry. He followed her approvingly, sipping a snifter of brandy.

"What about the housemaids? What will they say?" she cried, out of breath.

"I will choose them carefully to be loyal to me. And when they see the way you are, they won't doubt it's you, not me, who are insane.

"I can't just disappear! I am too well-known. People will come looking."

"Famous actresses often become recluses, love. The world becomes too much for them, as it has for you. And of course, there will be the disappearance of your lover, Joe Beau Clair. It is just the sort of thing New Orleans loves. There will be legends about this place, about you and about Snowdown. And people will be forever trying to peer through the hedges to try to catch a glimpse of you. Maybe some will succeed, because if you are very good I will take you out to walk in the gardens. And if I die before you, you can tell your story. . . ."

The house took on a ghastly atmosphere with its airy windows all shut. It grew dank, and everything mildewed. Even her gowns and the fresh linen smelled of it. She had nothing to complain of in Archer's treatment of her; in fact, she rarely saw him. She would find little gifts of flowers at her door, or books or new records for her Victrola, and knew that he was about.

What could it all lead to? Where could it end? Would it be as he said? She grieved for Joe as she thought back over the muddle of her life, wondering where she would change it if she had it to do over. She thought of girlhood days in Martinique, riding horseback through marvelous jungles of lianas and acajous, swimming in sapphire waters. She dreamed of her father, and of being cradled again on Yzore's comfortable lap. She thought of the golden fields of Acelie and wondered what was happening there. Did Cyrillia still sleep sweetly in Edmond's bed? And was there still another child ripening in her womb, fresh and promising as a big peach mango?

She lived more and more in her imagination, until she almost smelled the sweet reek of green jungle against the salt breeze and the charry aromas of frying codfish *akras*. She took refuge in sleep, lazing away long afternoons in slumber that was often filled with dreams of Joe. In those dreams she walked down the aisle of a cathedral in her satin wedding dress and Joe instead of Archer waited at the altar. Just as the golden carriage whisked them away toward paradise, she would laughingly begin to tell her husband this silly idea she had once had about marrying Archer Snow.

Once, waking abruptly, she ran out into the hall, wearing nothing but her cream-colored lisle camisole and Swiss ribbed drawers. She was in the parlor before a maid caught her, threw a cloth hastily snatched from the dining-room table about her, and led her away.

"What's the matter with you, honey?" said the plump black-skinned woman.

"I heard a voice. Wasn't there someone at the door, Yzore? A man with wonderful blue eyes and light brown hair, with his face all tanned by the sea...."

"Wasn't anyone. Get you back to bed! And my name ain't Yzore; it's Opal. Don't be callin' Opal that again. It don't sound Christian!"

"Who is that Opal?" she asked Archer later when he came to bring her tea.

"A kind old Negress I hired to take care of you."

"Take care of me! I don't need anyone—"

"Yes, Lily. Of course you do. In your condition you need a

nurse. Would you like to walk in the garden with me later when it's cooler?"

A nurse! Could he be right that she needed one? Was she beginning to go insane from imprisonment, from grief over Joe? It seemed to her that she heard his voice over and over. She could never tell when it would come, in the morning or dead of night, and in the shuttered house she had begun to lose track of the hours anyway. The voice spoke in snatches, muffled and incomprehensible, angry. Was he speaking to her from the grave?

"Archer, have they found Joe's body?"

He struck her hard across the face and sent her reeling against a wallpaper styled with flowers and peacocks, a design that had delighted her when she had first seen Snowdown. "I don't ever want to hear that name again, Lily!"

"Only tell me, and I will not mention him again," she begged.

He turned on his heel and walked away, as if, suddenly aware of the violence he had done, he could not trust himself not to do more.

"Oh, Archer, please let me go! Give me an annulment, and let things be as they were before!"

He stopped and looked back at her, his eyes full of terrible sadness. "No. You could never forgive me for all this. You could never be my friend again. It's too late to turn back, Lily; and I must have you. You are the only person I have ever truly loved. I'm sorry, for whatever that is worth."

She must think of some way to escape the house! If she could only bribe one of the servants to mail a letter to Susan! But the ubiquitous Opal precluded anything like that. God seemed her only hope, and she spent hours praying.

One day as she sat trying to read, a small green lizard crawled in at a crack between the shutter and the window ledge. It seemed such a long time since she had seen any such little creature that she caught it between her hands and set it down on the skirt of her dress. "What a fool you are to come in here!" she told it. "You could be out in the sun, and how will you find your way out, any more than I?" She felt absurdly happy, watching the little reptile blow out the red balloon under its throat, appearing unafraid on the expanse of her gown.

"And then an idea came to her. "I could . . . perhaps I

could. Oh, but I don't know enough about such things! But who knows when I might have another chance? I must try!"

Her jaw set with decision, she dumped out her teacup onto the floor and thrust the lizard inside. Running down to the kitchen, she found it deserted and put a pot of water over the fire. When it came to a boil, she gave a sob and tossed the little lizard in.

She felt sick to her stomach as it struggled against its death, and then, steeling herself, she began to mutter everything she could remember of the native incantations of Martinique. Poor lizard! If only its death turned out to serve her cause!

A dried lizard's head had been in the gris-gris bag that Madame Drapeaux's Hetty had left on her doorstep in the dark of the moon. And the yellow dust—had that been sulfur? Could she substitute something else? She could sew the little bag herself. Was there a chance it would work? The lizard was dead now, and she wondered grimly how long she should boil it. Then a dark hand closed over her arm.

"Dear Jesus! You's a witch! Yo husband said you's crazy, but he never did say you's a witch! You's been makin' a brew!" Opal seized the pot and headed for the door, leaving it open behind her in her terror to dispose of the boiled lizard. The whiff of fresh air swept Lily into it. She was running, mindless with the ecstacy of escape. She felt grass beneath her feet, saw the dim forms of oaks sighing in the hot afternoon breeze as her eyes tried to adjust to the brightness of outdoors.

The wall was before her, if she could but scale it. It wasn't high, and there was a peach tree beside it with low, spreading branches. The barking of dogs did not register at first, so intent was she, but suddenly a huge form leaped at her, knocked her flat in a planting of elephant ears. They were all around her, and she cowered and wept, covering her face with her arms as she waited for them to devour her.

"They are well-trained, Lily," came Archer's voice. "They will not touch you now, as long as you don't move." He gathered her tenderly in his arms and carried her back inside the house.

Word spread quickly through the household that Lily was a witch, and servants scurried away at her approach, leaving her more isolated than ever. They had been leery of her before, but now they were terrified, and if only dogs could have been made to believe in witchcraft as well, she could easily have threatened her way to freedom. As it was, she could only support that the story of her sorcery had made its way from the house to become part of the legend of Lily Beau Clair, which Archer had predicted would grow.

Then Giles Benton returned to Snowdown. The shutters in the downstairs rooms were opened to air the house, and every girandole of the chandeliers was polished. Archer was in a great state of excitement as he dressed in a French madras shirt and silk four-in-hand.

"Wear something nice, Lily," he told her. "We'll all have a pleasant evening, like old times."

"A pleasant evening! When things are as they are!"

"Yes, why not? Things are always going to be as they are. Why shouldn't we try to enjoy life a little?"

She sighed and understood him better. He had always been the way he was, and he had tried to make the best of it. He had been doing well until she and Giles had come into his life.

"Very well, Archer. I'll go and make myself more beautiful than my rival." And she spun swiftly away for fear he would hit her.

She did her hair in a Psyche knot and put on a yellow surah gown with big puffed sleeves and a low neckline above which she wore a pearl collar.

"The table was set sumptuously on a cloth of Turkey red damask when Giles arrived. He was the perfect guest, fresh from New York and full of theater chatter. Susan had won a small featured part at the Casino and was reputed to be sharing bed with a railroad tycoon. The new Harrigan and Hart musical was uproarious, but the new play at the Fifth Avenue Theater had not been nearly so well-received as *Cleopatra*.

Lily was caught up in it all. It was a tremendous relief from the usual routine, and though she could never have thought she would be delighted to see Giles, she was glad he was back. "Oh, I wish I might do another play!" she cried impulsively over the charlotte russe.

"Without me, Lily?" said Giles with a smirk.

"Of course without you. I haven't changed my mind about that!"

"Lily will not do another play for a while," Archer said dangerously. "She is in poor health."

Giles wiped his chin with his napkin. "So I have noticed," he said thoughtfully.

She realized he knew everything, without Archer's having told him. Was it possible that he would help her?

When the house was dark and quiet, she crept in to the hall and knocked on his door. "Come in, Lily," he said, without asking who was there.

She turned the porcelain knob and fought down revulsion at the sight of the wiry lines of his body beneath a blue pearl-buttoned nightshirt with rose-colored embroidery on its collar and cuffs. She set her candle on the square oak dresser and saw her dark reflection in the German bevel mirror.

"Giles, I must get away from him. I will do anything you say."

"Anything, Lily?" He leered at her. "Are you aware that there are many shocking things a person like myself could ask?"

"I can only imagine, Giles. But I'll try to do whatever it is."

"Ah, you are really desperate! I knew as much. You would do anything, no matter how repugnant. If you had only listened to me! I told you not to marry him."

"You gave me no reason!"

"It should have been enough for you that I told you. You shouldn't have had to think for yourself. I didn't give you a reason, because Archer would have been furious if he'd found out. But he is mine, anyway. Marriage has not made him yours. Or you his, despite this maneuver of fences and locks."

"They are talking of it already in New Orleans?"

"Indeed. It's the gossip of the day—how no one ever comes here anymore, and you are insane or a witch and cast spells on everyone who ventures near the gate."

"Get me out, Giles! Tell me your price!"

He sighed and swung his bare calves down over the side of the bed. Her flesh crawled, and she took a step backward. He laughed at her. "What are you thinking, Lily? If I asked you to a *ménage à trois*, what would you do?"

She gulped and felt faint and noticed with fury how much Giles Benton was enjoying her discomfort. "You are not going to ask me to do any such thing, Giles," she said, suddenly intuiting the truth.

"No. I'm going to ask for something I want much more."

"Yes, I know, Giles."

"You must act for me again. I am hungry for more triumphs."

She sighed with relief. "All right. I'll do that."

"Go back to your room now, Lily. I'll arrange everything with Archer."

In the morning they told her they had decided that a sea voyage would be good for her health. A new Van Artsdalen ship was leaving for Australia on the grain route. It was hoped that the design would beat all records, and Lily might go along as a "good-luck omen." It would be useful publicity on both sides.

A week later, when her trunks were all packed and standing in the hall, Archer came to her room and kissed her good-bye in a most husbandly way. "I'm sorry for everything, Lily. You'll have the annulment when you return."

She touched his cheek, pity welling up. "Archer, don't give in to Giles Benton again. Go away from him!"

"No. I'm beaten. There is no use my denying I am a depraved creature. I have tried and only caused terrible suffering. Be happy, Lily!"

"I can never be, Archer."

He smiled sadly. "You're wrong, Lily. It's I who will never be happy. You will be, you'll see. I promise!"

She shook her head. How could he think she would be happy? She would never be that again until she reached the next world and danced the caleinda again with Joe Beau Clair.

"May I come to see you off, Lily? Shall we let New Orleans see us together one last time—the brilliant, elegant Archer Snow and the beautiful, talented Lily Beau Clair?"

"I should like that, Archer."

A large crowd had turned out to watch the ship sail. People called her name as she went aboard. She waved and smiled and saw her new mystique in their faces. The sails filled, shimmering in the sun. She was amused at the speed with which they left the city behind. Looking back, she saw that the crowd had scattered, concerned with other things. But for as long as she could see, one figure still stood there, alone at the pier, growing smaller and smaller, his fair hair like the flame of a dark candle against the horizon.

Part III

Holocaust
(1897-1902)

1

The water of the Gulf of Mexico changed from the pale blue of the coastal shelf to cobalt, and the sky took on a dusky steel-gray hue as they raced for the Straits of Florida. The speed of the ship remained incredible, and a member of the crew told her they would see Cuba on the morrow.

"Joe Beau Clair worked on this ship, didn't he?" she asked.

"Yes, ma'am. How did you know?"

"By the name."

"*Mimi*. A silly name for a ship. Not grand enough for this vessel. But he insisted. She was some beautiful dancer, he said, and the *Mimi* is a dancer, too, as light and graceful as her namesake."

"There's going to be a storm tonight, isn't there?"

"Yes. A good gale, I shouldn't wonder. But don't be afraid. She's a fine ship, and you can trust her captain."

Whoever her captain was, he was terribly rude. He must have resented having her aboard, because he did not send the customary invitation for her to dine at his table. Perhaps he was only too busy the first night out. Whichever, she did not mind. She had been alone for so long that it was unsettling to be facing people all at once.

Through the afternoon there were squalls and fretful cobble seas. Rain had begun to pelt down steadily by the time she supped in her cabin, and the darkness beyond her porthole was complete. She locked her door and lay in her cozy bunk, content not to worry about the increasing pitch of the waves.

But the wind rose, too, and in its sound she seemed to hear the voice that had haunted her in the halls of Snowdown. Did he haunt this ship that he had named for her, too? Or was she losing her mind? Would the stories about her turn out to be true? Was she going mad? She buried her head beneath the quilt and tried to blot the voice away.

If only she knew that his body had been retrieved from the river! Perhaps it was the lack of a proper grave that made his spirit so restless. "Take in the skysails!" she heard the voices cry, torn by the wind. That could not be Joe's voice! It was only the voice of the captain. No reason but madness to think it was her lover's.

She got out of bed and put on a wrapper. She would follow the sound and put an end to the matter once and for all. The wind caught her loose hair, blowing it across her face as she stepped out of the cabin. The wrapper whipped, and her bare feet slid on the tipping, rain-wet deck. She fell to her knees, hearing the voice ahead of her in the darkness.

Take in the topgallant and pull in the sea braces!

A lantern swung ahead of her, like a wind-spun firefly. Stumbling to her feet, she tried to follow it. The ship hit a powerful wave, plunging into the trough behind it, and Lily lost her balance again. She gave a scream as she rolled helplessly, clawing at the slick deck.

The lantern was suddenly above her, and the voice declared, "Good evening, Lily." She looked up into Joe Beau Clair's decidedly unghostly face. She was unable to speak for joy as he hung the lantern aside and took her into his arms.

She clung to his neck and buried her face in the wet cloth of his coat. "I'd have come to your cabin before this, but the storm delayed me. I should have known we'd meet some odd way—you careening down the deck in your nightdress. It is your way always to be turning up in strange places."

"My way! What about you? You are supposed to be in your grave. You might have told me you weren't!"

"I came to Snowdown every day for weeks and tried to see you. And I always got the same answer: 'Madame is not at home to visitors today.' You were playing another of your games, I thought, like marrying Archer. But Giles told me differently. We will take up where we left off, you and I, when Archer Snow's river pirates interrupted us."

"What about the storm, Joe?" she protested as he bore her over the heaving deck.

"The ship will stand it. Come, I know you are not afraid of storms. I am going to show you one that will make the ocean seem quiet as a pond."

He laid her on the bed, and helping him strip away her clothes, she protested no more. A bolt of lightning cracked into the sea as she opened her body to him. She started at the sound of the splitting ocean, but he shoved her back, loving her. The ship heeled violently, and they were thrown to the floor with the violence of the pitch. He threw himself on her again, smothering her with kisses. The storm within her rose then, and, except as a distant accent to the turbulence within her, she was unaware of the thunderbolts dropping all around. She felt herself burst into a thousand parts, and then, with a rending crack, the ship did, too.

"We're hit! We're hit! Where is the captain?"

Joe floundered up, yanking at his trousers and leaving the door open behind him as he charged onto the deck. Lily ran out in her nightdress, smelling char where the lightning had struck, destroying the mast. Sails fluttered ineffectually, like the broken wings of a bird. Sailors scrambled everywhere in a silver downpour, getting tangled in sails and fallen lines.

She heard Joe's voice shouting, trying to bring order to the panic. Then an arm went around her waist, and she was lifted off her feet. She kicked with her bare heels at the tough shins behind her. "Don't fight me," said the sailor. "I'm only taking you to a lifeboat. Captain's orders."

"I don't want to go to a lifeboat!"

"Yes, you do. You're only in the way here." He passed her over the side to another sailor to take down a rope ladder. She wondered that the little dinghy did not swamp as she was rowed away from the ship with a dozen of the crew.

"Why are you all going?" she harangued them. "You're all cowards! Go back and help! Captain Beau Clair has not left the ship!"

"He's a fool! He'll go down with her!"

A gray dawn came, and through the tasseled rain she saw a handful of men still struggling with the crippled ship. The angry waves vomited foam and debris, and once Lily saw a lifeboat like her own floating upside down. Nowhere did she see another, and she knew that many had already paid the price of their cowardice.

"Go back," she commanded her sailors. "Save those that are left."

"We can't! We'd sink, too, then. And she's going under any minute now. We'd get sucked in!"

She watched in horror as the *Mimi* slowly lifted her bow to the sky, her figurehead seeming to lift its eyes to heaven in supplication. Then suddenly the ship stood upright in the water and, rigid as a saluting soldier, plunged straight beneath the surface.

She knew that she was screaming, but the whole ocean seemed to be encompassed by an unearthly silence. She fought to jump over the side of the dinghy in search of him. She had always followed after him; her soul called for her to do so now, and she could not understand the hands that held her back as the dinghy fought the paroxysm of the *Mimi*'s death throe.

She did not know how many hours passed as she lay moaning, her head in the lap of a burly sailor. She had thought Joe dead, and then she had had him back, known his love again. Had it all been a dream of insanity, like the dream voice she had heard at Snowdown? Would she waken to find herself there again, Archer's prisoner, with the dogs prowling the grounds beyond the locked shutters?

Day drifted on, and the clouds parted to let the sun beat upon them. The sailors took what extra clothing they had and built an ineffective canopy. "Did you see anyone else from the *Mimi*?" she asked them.

"No. If he'd been tending to business instead of you, he'd not be at the bottom of the ocean, and neither would his crew!"

"That's not so! Joe wouldn't have left the deck if he were needed. What could he have done to keep lightning from striking? Oh, I'd like to kill you!" And in truth her hands trembled with desire to get at the sailor's throat.

"Oh, never mind, little lady. The sun will do that job for you, most likely. We've only one cask of water. As for your question, the *Mimi* had auxiliary steam, and if Beau Clair had been on deck, he'd have seen how bad things were and got up a head of steam. The sails would have been down, and we'd have had more control."

"I saw no funnel!" Lily protested.

"It was beneath the deck."

Lily knew the design had been common to many of the boats Joe had helped plan. The opening for the smokestack was covered over, but it could be got up in good time. "You're wrong that it would have helped!" she cried.

"It couldn't have hurt. Things couldn't have turned out worse, could they? Or maybe you don't mind a shipwreck, as long as you've had your fill of him?"

She clawed his face, much to the interest of everyone, until the struggle threatened to capsize the craft. Then other hands held them apart; and falling back weary and dizzy with the heat, she heard another of the men chuckle. "There, now, leave her be. Can't nobody say the captain didn't have plenty of steam."

Lily was too exhausted to protest the weak round of merriment the comment produced. Her skin was blistered when darkness fell, and she was too fevered to try to pick out the North Star. What good would it do? They would drift where they would. They had drawn lots to see who would be in charge of the water cask, and now the sailor who had won whispered in her ear, "How would you like a drink as cool and long as you want?"

She drew in her breath with delight, and he added, "Wait until the moon has set, and don't make a sound. I want to know before I die what is so wonderful about you that a man would sink a ship—"

She fought his hands away from her burned flesh.

She had lost track of the days when the man whose face she had clawed succumbed. They threw him overboard and watched the water vibrate as the sharks feasted. Nobody was really sorry. They had more room in the boat and more water for each of them. By the next afternoon another two were dead. She felt hatred all about her, deadly and penetrating as the sun. They blamed her for what had happened to the *Mimi*, and for what, inevitably, was going to happen to all of them. Yet they gave her water and saw that she sat in what shade could be managed. It was as if they needed to keep her alive, as if their growing hatred of her were an amulet against death. But then the water they had rationed for so long was gone. They threw the cask over, too, and then nothing could protect them.

Seaweed raked against the boat, and they knew they must be coming close to land. Close, but how close? Would anybody find them? They pulled the brown clusters into the boat and searched for shellfish and little crabs they could eat or use for bait to fish. Lily took a silk ribbon from the skirt of her gown to make a line and gave away stray hairpins for hooks, but she herself was beyond such endeavor.

The sun seemed purple behind her closed eyes as she lay in a stupor in the bottom of the boat. And then she knew blackness and silence.

2

Someone was singing. And over her head there were palm trees. She was still moving—strangely, as though the boat had gone on sailing onto land—and the song was soft and secret, sung in Spanish that she did not comprehend. Suddenly there was a cry, and the motion and the song stopped.

"Se levanta," someone whispered.

"Sí. Es bonita!"

These voices were musical themselves, nothing like the coarse ones of the sailors. Looking up, she saw half a dozen delicate little brown faces. Little schoolboys, she thought, no older than twelve or thirteen, each one charming, beautiful, and smiling.

"Como se llama, señora?" one asked. She smiled back at them and wondered what it meant.

"Do any of you speak English?" she asked.

They laughed and punched each other, and somebody offered her a juicy guava. The youngest might have been ten, all of them barefoot, wearing white trousers and loose white shirts. They had been carrying her on a makeshift hammock of sugar sacking.

"Where are you taking me? Where are the men that were with me?"

"Cállese!"

She did not have to know the Spanish word to understand the command for silence. They had all flattened themselves in the swamp grass beside the road, everyone alert and earnest. She heard the sound of a horse picking its way over the damp ground. A lone rider appeared, wearing a blue-and-white striped uniform and a white panama hat. Lily recognized the uniform of the Spanish Army that she had seen in Havana, and for the first time she saw that the boys were carrying rifles with bayonets.

With a soft cry of *"Cuba libre!"* they leaped into the road, and stuffing a bandana into the soldier's mouth to stifle his death scream, they jerked him from his horse and flung their knives eagerly into his body. These sweet children were a band of rebels!

They stripped his still-twitching body of money and goods, admired his Mauser rifle and his bedroll. Then hastily they dragged him aside and brought his mount for Lily. Sensing she could do nothing else, she let them set her astride it. They applauded the easy way she rode a horse as they led her along a trail lined with banana trees and vines covered with ripe yellow fruit. Once they made her leave the path and hide as a whole company of soldiers rode past, and they all held their breaths for fear the horse would whinny to the others. Then they went on again until they caught sight of the ocean.

There on a small promontory stood a gray castlelike building of lichen-covered coral stone. They all pointed and chattered to tell her that was where they were taking her. She balked and looked uncertain. Was it a prison?

The boys laughed, encouraging her, and said over and over, *"Las monejas! Las monejas!"* She could not make anything of it, but then she caught sight of a black, flowing figure on the ramparts.

Las monejas—the nuns! They were taking her to a convent. She wept with relief as she was given into the hands of the sisters, and asked again if anyone could speak English or French. This time a nun answered, "I do."

She learned at last the story of her rescue. The boys had been fishing on the beach when they had seen the boat drifting. They had swum out and found her, all alone, like some sea nymph. She shuddered, thinking of the sailors from the *Mimi*, who must have jumped out and left her to die at the very edge of land.

"Tell the boys I am wealthy, and I will reward them someday," she said.

The nun translated and returned with the answer. "They say it is not necessary, but that guns for Cuba are the only reward they will take."

"Guns! These boys should be in school!"

"Should they, madame? The teacher has been executed. And little Juan and Pablo are brothers who should still be at their mother's knee—except that she was shot while running after their father as he was taken to be deported to a penal colony in Africa."

"Are things so bad? In Havana, when I was there—"

The nun made a grimace of distaste. "Life goes on in that

sinful place. But even there—have you heard of the ditch of laurels?"

"No."

"It is a place at the Morro, the fort. The brave Cuban patriots die there every day, staring at a gray stone wall splattered with the blood and brains of those who have gone before them. The Spanish have to have a band to play waltzes to drown out their cries of liberty."

"That is horrid, Sister. But these are little boys, and they should not be fighting. How can you condone it?"

"You'll find out, I fear."

The nuns gave her a cup of hot soup to drink and bathed her parched skin with a lotion of alligator pears. One of the young rebels came bringing a bolt of bright calico to make her a proper dress. He grinned mightily, pleased with himself, and only laughed when she asked if he had stolen it from a Spaniard.

The boys came to the convent every day or so to be petted by the nuns and fed sausages and fried bananas. They gathered around Lily and looked at her adoringly. When she kissed each one's forehead, some squirmed happily and some made protestations of love in Spanish. They were doing their best to teach her the language, and she was learning.

She was learning about other things as well.

As soon as she was able, she went with the nuns on their missions about the dilapidated little town. There were two squares, covered with unkept grass and palm trees, and between them was the priest's house and a church with two little towers and a Spanish-style *azotea* roof with only enough slope to allow the rain to run off. Many of the houses were vacant; some of the *bohíos* of thatched palm were beginning to disintegrate with the weather.

"Where are all the people, Sister?" she asked.

"Driven away," the nun answered shortly. "You have heard of General Weyler?"

"Vaguely. He's the Spanish commander-in-chief, isn't he?"

"Yes. It is his plan to eliminate all Cubans from the island and replace them with colonists from Spain. He thinks it is the only way that Spain can achieve control."

"Genocide! How incredible!"

"Yes, but he's right. As long as one Cuban is left, there will be resistance."

"But whatever will he do with all those people?"

"They will not take up much room in graves. He has already begun to deport the educated class, the leaders. Juan and Pablo's father was a university man at Mantanzas. He won't survive in Africa. Nobody does. There have been thousands like him. For peasants, starvation will be simpler. It will save bullets. The houses here are empty because people have been killed or have run away. People are afraid to go to till the fields or to run the sugar mills. Now you understand better why *los hermanitos*, the little brothers, have run away to fight in the long grass."

"Where will it end, Sister?"

"It would end at *Cuba libre*, if only *the* Americans would help. You will tell everyone when you return, won't you?"

"Yes. I'll do what I can."

But how would she ever get back? And what did she have to return to? She didn't have the heart to do the play she had promised she would for Giles. And her health was not improving, even with good food and fresh air. Lying exhausted on a lounge in the convent garden, watching the nuns troop down to the jetty to fish, she would listen hopefully for the sound of boyish voices.

They came sometimes one or two at a time and sat at her feet and made her tell them about the places she had been— about electricity and trolley cars and men who had unhitched her carriage to draw her through the streets of New Orleans. She was something special to them, their own Lily. They let her sing to them as they leaned against her knees, and once when no one was about, Pablo, the youngest, crawled into her lap, and weeping, told her she reminded him of his dead mother.

Finally the nuns told her grimly that she should leave. "But why? What harm am I doing?" she asked. "You know I will repay you."

"It's not payment we worry about. It's the little brothers. They are too fond of you."

"I am fond of them, too. They have no one, and I have no one. We are meant for each other."

"No. You aren't meant for each other. The little brothers come here more often now than they used to. They are young and will take chances to see you. They will be caught someday. It's not good for you, either. Do you think that a convent wall makes you safe from the Spaniards? Already there have been rumors about the beautiful lady who lives in this isolated convent. God help us all if the soldiers decide to enter the convent, if they accuse us of aiding the rebels. We are all Cubans here, and they might deport us. As for you, the punishment would be worse."

"I'll leave, Sister," Lily said. "If I can get to Havana, I can find a ship to take me home. Pray for me—and for the child I am carrying." She flushed as she uttered the words for the first time.

She had been growing surer every day that before Joe had gone down with the *Mimi*, he had left her with his child. How long she had wished for the child of Joe Beau Clair! Day by day she carried herself more carefully, more proudly, as if she herself were in awe of her precious burden. Joseph was his name, but Joseph who? In New Orleans she could not give him the name Beau Clair without marking him as illegitimate. Joseph Snow, then? She was still married to Archer, and the child was legally his. Nobody would know. Of course, there might be talk. She had sailed away on a ship captained by a man she had once been going to marry. He had gone to the bottom, and she had come home pregnant. Yes, there would be talk, especially if any of those sailors lived to return and tell their ribald tale.

Whether they did or not, Archer would know whose child it was. She couldn't guess what he would do. One Archer she had known might have accepted the child, glad to be of use as a surrogate father. That was the Archer who had accepted her engagement to Joe so easily. But the other Archer, the one who had been called upon to perform as a husband, the one who had sent river pirates to murder Joe—what might *he* do? Dare she risk going back to New Orleans? There could be no annulment with her in her present state!

Her child would grow up hearing a confused myth about his mother. Perhaps he would even fight a duel over her someday beneath the oaks. Too late she saw how right Joe had been about the stage being no place for a mother.

She became determined to raise the child at Acelie. She could call him Beau Clair on Martinique. There everyone thought she had married Joe after becoming free of Edmond. Joseph Beau Clair would carry on, the boy her father had wanted for Acelie. Oh, there would be stories about her on Martinique, too, but stories she was not ashamed of—how she had fled her marriage for love of her husband's brother and how a fluke of the plague had made her free to wed him.

These stories she could explain to her son, she thought. She could make him understand the sort of man his father had been, and how she had had no choice but to love him.

She did not feel like traveling, but she knew the nuns were right. She had better leave as soon as possible.

"Don't go, Lily," the little brothers said when she told them.

"I must. You see, I'm going to have a baby. And I must get the guns I've promised."

They were only a little consoled. "Will you come back someday when Cuba is free?" they asked. "Will you come out here to the long grass and look for us?"

"I'll come, but most likely I'll find you in the palace in Havana." She laughed.

"Will you send us the baby's picture? And the guns, Lily? How many guns will you send?"

She had not thought of how many. The word conveyed to her one awful deadly mass that did not need to be counted. "Five hundred?" she asked.

"Five hundred!" Their eyes lighted as though she had said so many lollipops.

They built an open fire in the courtyard of the convent and spent the last evening frying fish and singing songs together. The boys threw blankets into the grass and slept, and Lily went from bedroll to bedroll pulling up covers, giving goodnight kisses as though she had been in a nursery. They clung to her in the darkness, knowing they would never see her again, like many of their own mothers.

In the morning, before it was light, they brought around the horse they had taken from the Spanish officer. The trail was dewy, and the palms sighed in the night breeze as they set out for the town of Mantanzas, where a packet ran regularly to Havana. Finally, dull gold beams struck through the trees, and a sun more heat than light made the vegetation give off a warm, woodsy reek.

"Go back now, boys," Lily said. "I can find my way."

She didn't see them again, but she felt their presence alongside in the tall grass and knew they had disobeyed her. Hoofbeats came along the path. "Hide, Lily!" cried one of the little brothers.

But remembering how frightened they had been before that the horse would whinny and warn the Spaniards of their whereabouts, Lily remained in the road. This time no one would have any reason to think that half a dozen little rebels were concealed by the palmetto and green-gold bamboo.

A company of soldiers rode into sight, going single file in their blue-and-white-striped uniforms. She inclined her head modestly and turned her horse to the side of the road to let them pass. But the leader drew up, intrigued at seeing a pretty foreigner on this jungle path.

"Who are you?" he demanded. "Where are you going?"

"My name is Lily Beau Clair. I'm from New Orleans, and I've been to visit my sister, who is a nun at the convent. Now I am going to Mantanzas to catch the packet." This was the story they had all agreed she should tell. It was simple, and had a touch of truth that made it believable.

The Spaniard sighed with frustration. He would have liked to detain her just for the fun of it, but he was unlikely to win a promotion for forcing himself on an American lady whose family would lodge a protest. "You may pass, *señora*," he said.

She flicked the reins, her hand trembling, but now another soldier spoke. "That horse, Lieutenant. It belonged to Captain López."

The lieutenant brushed aside her skirt, which she had arranged to cover the brand on its flank. "What are you doing with an army horse, *señora*?"

"I found it running free."

They weren't convinced. One grabbed the bridle, and another reached to pull her from the saddle. "She's the one we've heard the stories about, the rich Anglo woman who is going to send guns!"

She kicked at them, fighting to stay on the horse. Then shots stabbed the air, splitting fronds from palm trees and dropping bodies on the swampy path. "*Vaya*, Lily! Go!" the little brothers were yelling. A sapling whip struck against the hindquarters of her mount, and she could only cling to its back as it catapulted her through the palmy jungle.

Half an hour later the horse stood exhausted on a little white beach. Lily bathed her face in the surf and let the animal get its breath. Then she found the path again and rode back cautiously the way she had come. At the spot where the shooting had occurred, men lay with flies already buzzing loudly about their faces. Her stomach crawled, and she was afraid to look closely, but when she did, she saw with relief that there were no small bodies among them. None of the little brothers had met death here.

She must go on to Mantanzas before the soldiers decided to look for her again. There could be no doubt in their minds now that she was with the rebels. But what had happened to the boys? Almost without willing it, she was riding toward the convent.

The nuns were not glad to see her. "Oh, Lily, why didn't you take the chance the little brothers gave you? The soldiers have been here—"

"I must know about the boys!" she cried.

"They were captured, every one."

It was more than she could bear. They had saved her, in more ways than one, from the wreck of the *Mimi*. When she had lost Joe, their affection had saved her from the wreck of her life as well. She loved them all as though they were her six little sons, and they were almost as dear to her as the one Joe had sired in her belly.

"Where have they got them? What will they do to them?"

"They are holding them in the church," the nun told her. "Perhaps they will take them to the prison of San Severino at Mantanzas."

"And there?"

"There they have trials that amount to nothing, and they shoot rebels on the esplanades where all the town can see."

"But the little brothers are only children, sister! They would not shoot them!"

"Come into the chapel and pray with the rest of us, Lily."

She knelt in the cool gloom for more than an hour, focusing her soul on heaven. Finally she rose shakily, a ghostly, light-colored figure among the black habits. She stared at the cross over the altar for a long moment and then walked out into the courtyard. An evening breeze had struck up, and a wan, cadmium sun cast shadows over a whispering blue surf. She followed the beach until she came to a swift little river, a ribbon ruffled with thickets of banana and palmetto. There she began to struggle with the buttons of her simple calico dress.

"What are you doing, Lily?" The nun had come up behind her.

"I am going to bathe."

"It's a strange thing to do when the rest of us are praying."

"I have finished praying," Lily answered steadily. "I must do something."

"To save the boys? Whatever could you do?"

"I wouldn't expect you to understand, but there are certain options that I have. . . ."

"I understand better than you think, Lily. I was not born a nun. You are going to make yourself pretty and offer yourself to the Spaniards for the little brothers. It won't work. No doubt the soldiers would rather have you than the boys, but when you go to the church in the village, what is to keep them from having both? Would you like the children to see you raped, when it would do them no good? You can't help the boys. You must think of what you owe your own child."

She sobbed, realizing that, as usual, the nun was right.

"There must be some way we can help them escape!"

"What! With a ring of soldiers all around the church?"

"Surely the priest will help us!"

"The priest is a Spaniard, Lily!"

She returned to the convent and paced the stone corridors all night while the sound of prayers mingled with the drone of crickets. Defiantly she wondered if God distinguished one sound from the other. Hour after hour she tried to devise some plan of escape, until at last she drowsed, her numbed brain still working feverishly in her sleep. She woke as light pearled the rim of the ocean, and she heard a cry from a parapet.

"The little brothers! They are taking them out!"

She rushed to a window and saw the boys in the distance of the soft morning, moving along the sandy road beside the unkept square. They were singing, and before she noticed that they were hobbled and bound, her heart leaped at the sound of a wistful song she had taught them.

> Little feathered lovers cooing,
> Children of the radiant air
> Sweet your speech, the speech of wooing,
> You have not a grief to bear.

When had that song become so sad? Once it had been gay, when she had danced with Joe at Carnival, but they had learned from her the rendition they gave it now. Then they started to sing some martial song in Spanish, a song of patriotism to which she could not quite catch the words.

She ran down to the nuns. "What are they doing with them? Are they taking them to San Severino?"

"We don't know, Lily. They are not going in the direction of the road."

The nuns crowded the windows as the soldiers marched the boys down to the beach near the convent. She could see all the dear little faces now, each one frightened and defiant, each one looking as though he were denying a need to run to his mother's arms.

She heard a command that she did not understand and saw Juan arguing with an officer. "At least unbind my arms, *por favor!*" she heard the boy beg.

"So you can fight, you cockroach, you filthy rebel?"

Juan's chin tilted upward. "It was only because Pablo is so little that I asked. I wanted to put my arms around him when the bullets came. But Pablo is a Cuban. He will be brave!"

"No!" She was running down the stone steps, knowing only that she must stop the atrocity. Through the haze of horror she saw the soldiers push the boys down in a neat row, each three feet from the other.

The nuns caught her as she reached the courtyard, before she could run through the gate, beyond which the little boys were working their knees furiously in the sand to be closer together.

"Apunten!" came the command, and the rifles pointed at the back of their heads. She could see that the dark curls had been clipped away from their necks so that aim could be taken easily.

"Fuego!" The little brothers had squirmed shoulder to shoulder and cheek against cheek as the smokeless fire of the Mausers lifted their bodies from the sand and blew them to the edge of the sea.

The nuns gave Lily a black habit so that she would look like the rest of them as they gathered the broken children to bury. She kissed each one as she laid him in his grave, just as she had kissed them when she had tucked them into bed.

Still wearing the habit, she left on foot for Mantanzas. The nuns all hugged her and wished for Godspeed.

"Watch out for snakes, Lily."

"Yes, I know about snakes."

"If you must spend a night on the road, go to the beach and make yourself a little hideaway away from the path."

"Yes, Sister."

"Lily, do not forget the guns."

"I will send them. Nothing can stop me!"

3

She was home again. Martinique loomed from the water, vapory gray, then bluish, then green, with gold plains of sugar-cane, warm and sparkling as a hearth. Long emerald arms, formed of old volcano flows, reached out to receive her. And there was St. Pierre, seeming to tumble down the mountain to meet her in a cascade of yellow walls, stone-flagged streets, and red roofs.

When the ship had docked by the sugar landing of La Place Bertin, she made her way up the clifflike flight of mossy steps, past the sashless windows with their slatted blue shutters, and stopped to drink at a fountain of mountain Gouyave water, spurting a glittering thread through lion lips of stone.

She sighed as she tasted the sweet current on her tongue, and lifting her eyes to the purple mornes beyond the town, she thought that nothing could stir her from this island again. Joe Beau Clair had been like the beat of the *ka* that her heart had followed, and now that he was dead, she would put aside passion for a contentment that in its way was as profound as the love she had known. The tattered strands of the life she had left behind her would fade into the tropic mists, unreal as the apparition of the ghost woman in the quiet, cloudless noon. They would all vanish—Archer Snow and Giles Benton and Lily Beau Clair, the sensation of New Orleans.

Only one vision would not diminish, the vision of six beautiful boys on their knees in the sand, pressed together cheek to cheek. She wondered if she would ever rock her own son in the huge soundless rockers of Acelie without remembering . . .

She picked her way to the cathedral, among the fruit-colored, madras-turbaned crowds, past the pastry seller in his white apron and cap, vending sweet maize cakes wrapped in banana leaves. She paused and looked up toward Morne d'Orange again, to see the creamy towers of the church and get her direction. At last she walked between the twin palms at the cemetery gate and knelt in the burning heat at her father's grave.

"Papa, I have come home for good. It will be all right now. I have brought with me Acelie's son. Oh, Papa, he has been worth waiting for, this little son. He will be more special than any son Acelie has ever had, a child of thunderbolts and passion, the son of Joe Beau Clair."

She found Acelie polished and shining, sweet with the scent of bougainvillea, and beyond the banana trees the fiery green of the high woods rose into displays of sun and shadow beneath the blazing violet sky. But something was wrong, Lily thought as she stepped down from the carriage Edmond had sent to meet her. The bananas looked too small, and the trees seemed affected by some sort of blight. The canefields were ragged with jungle tangle encroaching from every edge, and weeds were as high as the creaking stalks.

She frowned as she went inside, and then, hearing singing in the kitchen, she went to see if the singer were Cyrillia. A strange, chocolate-skinned girl looked up at her, startled. Lily smiled at her and went back to the main part of the house, where another person startled her as much as she had startled the native girl.

"Edmond!"

"I hope you don't mind my coming without being asked, Lily. I'm so used to having the run of the place. I have had it all cleaned for your arrival."

"It's wonderful, Edmond. Thank you. And thank you for sending the money to Cuba for my passage."

"It was a pleasure. Oh, Lily, I can't believe that you are here again! It is so marvelous to see you. But Joe died in the shipwreck? And you are a widow?"

"Yes. But, Edmond . . ." She saw with amazement that he was still in love with her. Joe was all that had ever come between them, and now Joe was dead. She saw hope ill-concealed in his tired eyes. Everything about him seemed exhausted now, worn and dropping as the fields of cane. Though he had been born on the island, the tropics were taking their toll of him. French families had not been in the Indies long enough for nature to make the proper changes, the deepening of the set of the eyes, the changing of blood to protect them from the ravages of motionless heat and vaporous atmosphere.

He had worked too hard for the land, and after he had

worn himself thin with saving it, the inexorable jungle had begun to move back, stupid and mindless of his accomplishments. It seemed to Lily that the fields themselves were betraying him, nurturing the enemy weeds and wild logwood and seaside grapes, just as they had nourished the cane and bananas. But was it something more than that that was wrong with Edmond? The fevered glint of his eyes told her how much her return meant to him. It spoke of an insane dream.

"Lily, I haven't married anyone. I am still waiting. When a year or so has passed, do you think you might consider—?"

"No, Edmond, it's impossible. I shall never marry again." She was, after all, still married to Archer, but she would never tell him about that. Everyone on Martinique was to assume she had married Joe, and as for Archer, he doubtless thought her dead.

"But only think, Lily, if you do not marry and I do not marry, who is to inherit all this?"

"I have brought Acelie's heir with me," she said, unable not to smile with pride.

"You have brought—"

"I am going to have Joe's baby," she said, and he seemed to crumple with defeat. "Edmond, you are a foolish man!" she cried. "You have got your heir, too. You have had him long since!"

He looked at her with a blankness that made her angry. "I am speaking of Cyrillia's son, of course. Why don't you marry her?"

"Marry Cyrillia? A native girl! You are still full of ridiculous ideas. I will never get used to them."

Her old servant came to see her the next morning, walking from Beau Clair, where she now lived at Edmond's beck and call. She came up the lane, slender and graceful as ever, wearing a *douillette* of rainbow stripes, and behind her in a line came the children.

Rilla was not jealous of her children as she had been before. She grinned happily and let Lily pick them up one at a time to admire them. The eldest, the boy, was a handsome little fellow with a steady gaze that reminded her of Edmond. The girl, Yzore, who had been born during Lily's last trip to the island, had beautiful skin like the palest yellow rose. The last, Lele, was a pretty toddler who smiled at everything, and still unsteady on her feet, sometimes resorted to crawling to keep up with her busy brother and sister.

Lily invited Rilla to come and sit with her on the veranda,

but she had forgotten native ways, and Rilla would only stay if they worked together over cloth she had brought to make maternity gowns for Lily.

"Rilla, don't you try to make him marry you?" Lily asked as they cut a skirt with a placket to expand with Lily's girth.

"No, missy, there's no hope."

"How can you say that, the granddaughter of Monsieur Bon! What would your grandmother say?"

"I suppose my grandmother was not in love with Monsieur Bon. It's easier to manage a man, even a Creole, when one doesn't really love him."

"What of little Yzore? You swore she wouldn't be a servant girl. And now there's Lele, too. He'd give in if you'd hold yourself back."

"You think I haven't tried it? Why do you think I have no child coming now? But here you are again, and he will never give up marrying you. Oh, I had a chance while you were married to his brother."

"I won't marry him, Rilla!" she cried in frustration.

"He doesn't believe you."

Edmond spoiled her peace at Acelie. It seemed that if she but went for a walk, he was there, sitting on his horse, watching her with a smoldering gaze that made her naked with embarrassment. And hardly a day passed that he didn't come to sit with her in the evening and remind her of his devotion.

"The crops are not doing well," she would tell him. "Can't you do something about it? You were always good at making things grow."

He would call the servant to bring him another *cocoyage*, and slumping back, would tell her, "Let the crops do what they will. It's not the crops I care about. My brother, Joe, did not tend bananas, and you loved *him*."

"Edmond, please . . ."

"Find another manager for Acelie, Lily. I have more than I can do with Beau Clair."

She knew that would be an impossible task, but she asked around St. Pierre when she drove in to price guns for her shipment to Cuba. The shopkeeper looked on in wonder as she examined his stock, compared Belgian-made and English-made, hammerless and semihammerless; and he gasped when she asked if he could sell her five hundred smokeless rifles. Having secured his promise to order them, she went to the bank to make arrangements to withdraw the money.

There she met an unpleasant surprise. Not only was there no money for her to withdraw, but Acelie owed payments to a dozen merchants of St. Pierre.

"Perhaps you will make a good crop, Madame Beau Clair," the banker told her. "Then there will be no need for a new mortgage."

Going straight to Beau Clair, she found Edmond dozing on the veranda. "You've got to do something about Acelie, Edmond," she demanded. "I've been to the bank, and I know how matters stand."

He lifted his head as though he were heaving a great boulder, his face white and hollow. "Oh, go away, Lily. Acelie is nothing to me now. Get someone else to help you."

"There's no one else. Where could I get anyone as capable as you? Anyone the workers respect like you? Please, Edmond!"

He did not answer, staring out over the canefields, as if beyond the cacao and calabash trees he saw something fascinating in the piercing dazzle of the sun.

"Will you lend me five thousand dollars, then? I'll pay you back after the baby is born. I'll let them know in New Orleans that I am alive."

"Five thousand dollars!" That at least interested him. "Whatever for?"

"Guns. I have got to send five hundred guns to Cuba."

"What a ridiculous idea! No doubt it's the result of your condition. Women always get foolish ideas at such time, I'm told; and since your ideas are never quite ordinary, it's no wonder, I suppose." He chuckled, and she realized it was the first time she had heard him laugh since she had come home.

"It's no whim, Edmond. I must have guns!" But no matter how she insisted, he refused to believe it more than a feminine trifle.

"Go home and tend to having Joe's baby," he told her bitterly. "And don't bother me again about Acelie. It's not my son or my plantation, either."

She tried to manage the plantation herself after that, riding about the fields in a high-waisted native *douillette* that easily concealed her pregnancy. She was filled with joy as she felt the infant begin to kick inside her, seeming to keep a kind of rhythm to the beat of the *ka*. He was a child of the land already. She smiled to herself. Already he understood.

Then one day the sun was too much for her, even beneath her wide-brimmed hat. She had no warning of what was going to happen. One moment she was trotting briskly off to see if a certain portion of cane were ready for cutting; the next she lay in a dreamlike blackness. She came to herself in her big *bateau* bed, with an old native woman from the workers' cottages standing over her.

"You're lucky, missy. You still got your baby."

She knew then what chances she had been taking. No tragedy could have been worse to her than to have again conceived Joe's child and then lost it. She knew she must let happen whatever would happen with Acelie. She didn't go to the fields again. She sat and rocked in the shady house and drank cocoa water and guava juice, ate little coconut cakes brought to her on a tray.

The scrawny cane would not bring the price she would like of course, but there was no help for that. She had set her workers to picking bugs from the banana trees, but she suspected they had forgotten about the insects without her there to keep them at it. Perhaps the bugs were not the reason for the poor yield, anyway. Who knew how long it might be before the fruit grew lush again?

She asked Cyrillia about these things when the girl came to help her sew for the baby. "What is the price of cane now, Rilla? Do you see as many bugs on the banana trees?"

"Don't think about it, missy. It's bad for you to think." Rilla used a native word that meant "to think intently," an unhappy word, for to Martinique minds such activity always caused unhappiness.

Lily knew that Cyrillia was right. Such thinking would not help her with her most important task. But how could she keep from having such thoughts? And where was she to get the guns? She must honor the promise she had made the little brothers! There was money in New Orleans, but she could not go there pregnant and endanger her annulment. If only Edmond had not let her down about Acelie!

"Missy, couldn't you remarry him, after all?" Cyrillia asked one day.

"You, Rilla! You want me to marry him? When you love him so much! What is it? Has he treated you badly?"

"No." Tears stood in Cyrillia's dark eyes. A hummingbird flashed by above the Rose d'Inde, and the girl sighed. The sound seemed like a current of wind in the midday stillness, and Lily was all at once aware of an atmosphere of resignation all about her. Edmond was resigned to a life of unfulfillment. Acelie seemed resigned to be reclaimed by weeds and snakes. Even proud Cyrillia, who had been so determined to marry her Creole, was resigned.

"Why, Rilla?" she asked again.

"Oh, missy, he has the Creole fever. He doesn't eat, and if I but lay a sheet across him at night, he screams that it is burning him. He cries out with a pain in his head, and nothing anyone does helps. He hasn't been the same since you went to marry his brother, but now, with you here every day, I am afraid he will die."

"I can't marry him, Rilla. You must make him see that it's you he loves."

"Are you so sure he loves me, missy?"

"I have never been more certain of anything."

After the girl had gone, Lily wept. What was she to do? If she went away from Martinique, he might be better, but she could not do that, not now. The promise she had made the little brothers haunted her, and in nightmares the boys reminded her, their earnest faces bathed in the blood of their execution. She would awaken screaming, then be unable to sleep again, as though some terrible presence lurked in the flood of weird moonlight. And Acelie, which must belong to her son—even Acelie seemed hostile, as though she were preventing a death journey it longed to take.

She would have her son soon now, and he would make up for everything. Already he was company for her, beating against her fiercely in his eagerness. All the others could not wait to die, it seemed, but her Joseph could not wait to live.

One morning she heard a terrible clap of thunder, and looking out the window, saw a black cloud over Pelee. Calling a servant girl, she sent her to the river to make sure that no children were playing there. Though the sun was shining over Acelie, a thunderstorm on the volcano would send torrents into the riverbeds, and never a year passed that laundresses who washed on the rocks of the Roxelane did not drown in such floods.

She sat languidly sewing after the girl had gone, listening to the sound of the *ka* and wondering how many more days it would be until she held Joe's child in her arms. It could not be many, and she smiled as she sewed, thinking how sweet it would be. A son! When she had raised him, he would go out into the world and do exciting things, all the things a woman could never do. And he would come home and tell her; she would see it in his eyes, and it would be as if she had done it all herself. She would love him with a passion different from that she had felt for his father, but stronger than she would ever feel for anyone else.

The sky went dark suddenly, and she looked up indifferently, thinking it was going to rain. She should go and close the shutters, but it was hot, and the rain would bring a cool breeze. But the wind that swept in was dry and dusty. There was a sound like hail on the roof. She ran to the door and met her workers racing for the shelter of the veranda.

"Get inside, quick, missy!" they called to her. "It's the volcano!"

Pelee! Around the green mountaintop where she had once stood beneath a rainbow with Joe swirled clouds of steam and firebursts of volcanic lightning. The sound she had thought was hail was instead a rain of pebbles and small rocks. It went on all day while she sat wih her workers inside Acelie's main rooms, the shutters fastened against dust that was making it almost impossible to breathe. The wind howled, twisting banana trees, beating down unharvested cane. Rosary beads clicked as the hours went on. "It is going to erupt, missy," they told her. "We are all going to die!"

"It will not erupt," she told them. "It is only sputtering. Pelee will not erupt."

She remembered standing on its summit, feeling it groan and heave like a live thing, and she was not so certain. But Joe had laughed at her then. Joe had said it would never erupt, and she intended to trust his word now.

Some of the workers wanted to hitch up the wagons and brave the rock storm to go across the island to Fort de France, where they would be far away from Pelee. She exacted a promise that they would come back when the trouble ceased, and gave them permission.

"We'll take you, too, missy," they offered.

"No. I will have to take my chances here," she said. "The baby . . ."

In the end, the fear communicated itself to every one of them, and they left her alone. The dust had seeped in everywhere, and there was a haze like evening. "It is not going to erupt," she told herself. "Joe said it would not!" Then, feeling a sharp pain as she tried to stand, she knew that her time had come.

"Oh, little Joseph, you were waiting for this moment, for a storm the equal of the one in which you were conceived," she thought, and then she was lost in pain and struggle.

She heard the sound of soft laughter as she awoke, lying in

her bed, all fresh in a muslin nightgown. The wind was quiet, and Cyrillia was sitting beside her. "Rilla! My baby! I was all alone!"

"You were not all alone, missy. I came to you. I knew when Beau Clair's workers began to run away that Acelie's would, too."

Lily was filled with a weary joy. "Rilla, come, show me my beautiful son!"

Again the soft, secret laugh. "Oh, missy! It is not your beautiful son. It is your beautiful daughter."

The clouds broke away from Pelee, and the sun blazed above it. Dust lay everywhere, a strange tropic snow of ash, swirling from the red-tiled roofs with every breeze, lying over fern and acajous, breadfruit trees and tamarinds. Mountain whistlers called among the thick, ashy foliage of flamboyants and from the branches of ancient silk-cottons. At night the wood crickets sang quietly. The world was as it had been before. Except for the ash and the memory of the fiery clouds. In his hut up the mountain, the witch doctor was doing incantations to cleanse Pelee of its devil. The workers had not returned.

Lily named her little daughter Mimi after the ill-fated ship on which she had been conceived. The child had Lily's dark hair and vivid blue eyes. "Joe's eyes," she said to Edmond.

"Don't be so sure, Lily. All newborn babies have blue eyes."

"Not like these. It's as if Joe is looking at me."

"Time will tell. Are you really set on that name? It makes her sound like a native. Mimi—it's familiar, somehow. Did we have a Mimi working on one of the plantations?"

She rocked her child and loved her, but her heart was uneasy. Her responsibilities to a daughter would be different from those to a son. And this daughter was not just any daughter. It was not only because of the ship that Lily had named her Mimi. She knew now that when the child had seemed to respond to the beat of the *ka*, she had been dancing, even in the womb! Those eyes already burned with eagerness as they began to focus for the first time on the world. The daughter of Joe Beau Clair! How would Lily know how to deal with her? How to defend her from men and protect her from herself?

"My wild, wonderful child, shall I be equal to raising

you?" she whispered into the soft curls, as Mimi lay on her shoulder, her shell-pink lower lip thrust out in slumber.

Flies swarmed about the rotting fruit on the dusty banana trees and she begged Edmond again, "Can't you do something about the workers? Remember how you got the crops harvested when Pascal put the curse on us? You have a talent for such things."

He had roused himself more since the trouble had begun. At first she had thought it was because he was challenged; then she had realized that it was because of Mimi. She did not have her son for Acelie after all, and he was hoping again that she would marry him. She knew she should tell him she never would, but she knew, too, that Cyrillia had been right. The delusion was what he needed to keep him alive. Why, oh, why couldn't he see that it was Cyrillia he loved, Cyrillia, who had cared enough to give up her dreams for him?

The workers came trickling back, brought by Edmond's reassurances, but the losses had been great to both Acelie and Beau Clair. There was small satisfaction in the knowledge that most other plantations on the north end of the island had fared as badly.

Lily thought more and more of the wealth she had left behind in New Orleans. She had had fine furniture and clothes, jewelry and lush bank accounts. It was all there waiting. She had only to return from the dead and claim it. As much as she dreaded seeing Archer again, she would have to go. Otherwise Mimi would grow up in poverty; otherwise there would be no way to keep the promise she had made the little brothers.

She held her baby close to her, breathed its sweetness, and her heart broke at the thought of separation. "I have waited so long for you, Mimi, so many years. How can I leave you so soon?"

Week after week she put the matter off, telling herself it was forgivable for her to remain on Martinique. Then, one morning, awakening from a particularly vivid dream of the little brothers, she was overcome at last by guilt. She rode to Beau Clair and asked Cyrillia if she could find her a healthy wet nurse.

"But, missy, I thought you liked to do that yourself."

"I do, Rilla. But I'm leaving Martinique. You will take care of Mimi for me, won't you?"

The girl's face lighted. Now at least Edmond would not

look at Lily every day. She would have him to herself. "I will love her like one of my own, missy."

When she ceased to nurse, her breasts ached, and she had to bind them and lay cloths wrung in icy river water on them. For days it seemed that nothing would help, and Lily almost gave up and returned to feeding the baby, as she longed to. She wept in the night when the child cried, and she heard the footsteps of the wet nurse going to her.

"Oh, Joe, why couldn't you be here to take care of us?" she moaned. "Then I could be a mother and only that!" But in a larger sense she knew that it was because she was a mother in every pore that she was leaving Mimi to go to New Orleans to get money for them. And it was because she had been a mother to the little brothers that she was so determined to send guns.

On the last morning she had to tear herself away from the cradle. When she reached the door of the room, she was overcome with weakness and turned back again and again to touch the plump little hands and kiss the baby's cheeks.

"I shall be back in less than a month, Mimi, and then nothing shall ever part us again," she promised. She drove away, leaving to the ancient yellow walls the charge of all she loved.

4

She had her luggage brought to the St. Charles Hotel and asked at the desk if she might use the telephone. The boy in charge looked at her goggle-eyed. "Aren't you Lily Beau Clair, the actress?" Then, looking at her again, he took in her outdated gown from Acelie with its waterfall flounce at the back, and grinning sheepishly, corrected himself. "No, I guess you can't be. She was lost in that shipwreck, you know."

"I heard." She allowed herself a small smile. Lily Beau Clair, the actress! Let her remain at the bottom of the ocean where she belonged. "Is the telephone in a private spot? It's a very important call."

He led the way to an office and offered to look up the number on the subscriber list. "Don't bother; I know it," she replied. When he was gone, she lifted the receiver and asked Central to connect her with Snowdown. The voice that answered the ring made her stomach lurch with revulsion.

"Hello, Giles," she said acidly. "So you're still around. It's Lily."

"Lily! So you're still around, too."

"You don't sound surprised. Didn't you think I'd gone down with the ship?"

He gave a languid sigh. "Oh, I did for a while. Then those two sailors swore you washed up alive on the shore of Cuba. Even after that, I thought you were probably dead. But when Joe Beau Clair showed up, I knew you'd be close behind."

"Joe is alive!"

"That is pleasant news to your ears, no doubt. He'd fashioned himself a sort of craft out of torn sheeting and a piece of flotsam, when he was picked up delirious off Yucatán. It must have been quite a voyage for the pair of you, while it lasted, to hear those sailors tell it."

"I'm not interested in their filthy stories, Giles."

"Filthy, but true, eh? What a night you had! Well, wherever you are, you'd better come right to Snowdown.

There's no other place in New Orleans you can successfully hide."

"Hide! Why?"

"Because those sailors are telling their tales to a board of inquiry. If anyone finds out you're back, you'll be called to the stand in an instant. You can make your miraculous return later."

"I am not making any miraculous return, Giles. I am going to marry Joe."

"Marry Joe! What an idea, Lily. Archer will have to give you an annulment, and I shall have something to say about that. You promised me another play."

She sighed. "Oh, Giles, surely you're not going to hold me to that now!"

"I'm going to try. Come along, now, before someone sees you."

"Giles . . . is that awful Opal gone? And the dogs?"

"Yes, yes. All gone and forgotten."

"Very well, then, I'm coming."

Snowdown did seem to have forgotten. The gardens were blooming with jasmine and plumbago, and mimosas waved feathery fingers in the river breeze. The windows stood open, and Archer met her, looking fit and tan in a pin-striped percale shirt and Russian linen trousers. She stepped cautiously inside, half-expecting to hear the door slam and lock behind her, but instead, there was only Archer ringing for a pretty little Irish maid to bring them orange-flower fizzes and chocolate éclairs.

"You will have missed such things in Cuba, Lily," he said with a grin. Then, turning serious, he declared, "Oh, Lily, I am so glad you came here! I thought you would be afraid."

"I was afraid, but I had no choice. Giles said there was no other place I could hide. He was right, as always. But I'm not frightened anymore. It is easier for you now, isn't it, Archer?"

"Yes, since I have admitted to myself that I am what I am. But I still love you!"

"But as a sister, Archer. You must only love me as a sister. We were good friends before we tried to become lovers."

"We shall be good friends again, I hope," he said.

There were three drinks on the satin-finished silver tray, and in a few minutes Giles came in to join them. Both men were elated to have her back. Archer because he loved her, and Giles because he foresaw some future triumph on the stage. They wanted to hear everything that had happened from the moment she had been forced into the lifeboat, and she related it all, without omitting a detail.

She told about the sun that had boiled her skin away, how the sailors had all hated her and how they had died one by one, to be thrown to the sharks. But she did not tremble until she began to talk about the little brothers who had saved her, then ambushed a Spanish officer, stolen his horse, and left him dead. Her voice broke as she told how she had come to love them. But the nuns had said the boys were taking risks to come to see her, so she had decided to leave. Even then they had risked for her carelessly when the soldiers had stopped her on the path.

"I'm not surprised," Archer said softly when she reached this part of the story. "Every man who loves you risks for you."

A perfect silence settled over Snowdown as she told of the executions—how she had prayed, and giving up prayers, had schemed, how they had all been marched to the beach with their hair clipped to make a better target for the bullets.

Giles sat with a strange stare as she finished and collapsed weeping, her head on the black ebony pier table. "It is a powerful story," he said finally.

She should have realized then that Giles thought about stories with only one purpose, but she was too overcome with grief. Archer lifted her gently in his arms and carried her upstairs to the bed that they had once thought to share. She pushed his hands away in mute protest as he sought the buttons of her dress.

"There, Lily, it's all right. You're exhausted, and I will undress you. I am still your husband."

She remembered that he had unfastened her once before like this, on the first night of *Salome*, when he had showed her Snowdown for the first time and she had said that she could not marry him. She sighed, allowing him to strip her to her silk undervest and petticoat. "Archer," she said as he pulled a white damask spread over her, "you will give me the annulment, won't you?"

"Of course. Why shouldn't I?"

"Giles said—"

"I can't imagine why Giles would oppose it."

"You must promise to give it to me even if he does."

"I promise. I've hurt you enough, Lily. Go to sleep now."

She gave a satisfied murmur. There was no way Giles

could make her do the play, nothing he could hold over her.

"Archer, you'll send the guns for me, won't you?"

"Yes, first thing in the morning." He kissed her forehead as he went out.

Her body throbbed with weariness, but she could not sleep. The sound of tree frogs in the oaks was different from the wood crickets of Martinique, and it was that she longed to hear—that and the cries of her little Mimi. "I'll be back soon, my precious," she whispered. "I'll bring you your father. He will be surprised to hear of you, no doubt! He shouldn't be, though, the rascal!"

They were going to marry and go home to Acelie. He would sail his ships, and she would wait for him, ready each time to be filled body and soul with his love and his children. "Little Mimi, you are only the first. We shall be handing down cradles and christening gowns until they are in tatters."

She had told Giles and Archer nothing about having returned to Martinique or having given birth to Joe's child. It seemed better to tell no one before she was safely married to Joe. He must be the one to know first. Then, even as she thought of him, there was a rustle at the window. The dado-fringed shade jerked up, and he let himself in, crossing to her bed with long strides.

"Oh, Joe! Oh, my love!" Her arms snaked about his neck, and she pulled his lips close to hers joyfully.

"This is where we left off, Lily," he said, resisting her.

"Yes. I am ready to take up again, my darling. Oh, I have so much to tell you...."

"Shh! I have something to tell *you*. Be quiet and listen. You were recognized today. Tomorrow they'll be coming with a subpoena for you to testify at the inquiry about the *Mimi*."

She drew in her breath. "Then I must leave tonight. Have you a carriage waiting?"

"You are not leaving. That's what I've come to tell you." His eyes were fierce in the moonlight. "You are going to testify. You are going to tell the truth. I will not flinch from the consequences of my deeds!"

"You have done nothing wrong, Joe! That is all I can tell anyone!"

"You know better, Lily. That's why you came to Snowdown to hide. I was so preoccupied that night, I couldn't think of anything but you. I wanted to go to your cabin as soon as it was dark, but I could see the storm coming. I knew that it and night would meet the *Mimi* together. I neglected my duties, Lily. I was consumed with wanting you. I did not have the smokestack put up or build up steam in the boiler. If *Mimi* had been under steam, I might have controlled her when she was demasted."

"You thought she could ride out the storm under canvas, Joe! The ship was a new, untested design. And you are not to blame for an act of God!"

"Don't tell me; tell the board tomorrow! Tell them everything, Lily. There can be no peace between us if you don't."

"All right, Joe," she said, trembling. "Come and love me, then. Come and hold me; I'm frightened."

But he brushed away her arms and turned toward the window. "I am not in the mood for that. We have done enough damage with our love. There is something about it that makes it different from the loves of other people. It is like the difference between a breeze and a gale. It destroys anyone who comes in its way. We began with Edmond, and now we have progressed to an entire ship's crew. Ours is a love that sees nothing beyond itself. I don't want to love you anymore, Lily."

"But you can't help it, Joe! she cried, horrified.

"I'm going to try. Don't bother to show me out. I've come this way before." There was a ghost of his old grin as he swung his legs out onto the trellis.

"Joe!" she cried after him, heedless that she might rouse Archer and Giles. Not love her anymore! Oh, but that was impossible. And she had not told him about their baby, about their beautiful Mimi.

In the morning, as she had promised, she was dressed and sitting in the parlor waiting when the subpoena was brought. Wearing a blazer suit of black ladies cloth trimmed with tiny pearl buttons and a hat with a spray of roses beneath its tilted brim, she entered the hearing room and waited her turn to be called. The place was jammed, and she knew that word must have gotten out. Here they were, her old admirers.

Were there some among them who had helped to pull her carriage on the first night of *Salome* or who had passed her above their heads to the St. Charles Hotel? Here they were again, panting to see a drama even more lascivious than those, they hoped. Such was the quality of their devotion! She caught a glimpse of a face she knew, and shuddered. Good heavens! Henry Wickersham! She had not seen Henry since that night years ago when he had tried to rape her, but the leer on his florid face informed her he had not forgotten an instant of their tussle in the house on Coliseum Square. How would she ever be able to face the ordeal with him there to watch?

She turned her head and saw someone else she did not want to see—Jenny Van Artsdalen, her fair hair tucked under a dainty hat with a brim of starched, pleated chiffon. Jenny looked embarrassed and even a little frightened, but everything about her demeanor seemed to match the hat. She was made of delicate fabric, but well-fortified with stiffening. Jenny was no voyeur; what was she doing here, so out of place in a gallery of men and only a few women, mostly beer jerkers from the concert saloons? Jenny's presence, more than anything else, unnerved Lily. Jenny was in love with him still! That could be the only explanation. Through the bonfire glare of Lily's passion, her love had remained, quiet and steady. Most little lights like Jenny's would have been easily extinguished by experiences like this one, but Jenny's only seemed to leap higher, fed by the winds of trouble. Joe appeared, wearing a willow-patterned vest beneath his brown twill jacket, and to Lily's horror, he did not look at her, but up at Jenny, who flushed with self-consciousness and delight.

"She has announced to all New Orleans how she feels about him," Lily thought. "Now her name will be linked with the scandal as well as mine." She heard her name called and went forward to take her place on the witness stand.

"You are Mrs. Archer Snow?"

"Yes." It startled her to be called that. Even in the days that she and Archer had lived together, she had almost never been addressed by that name. She had been Lily Beau Clair, the actress. It had not occurred to her before that the hearing would drag Archer's name with hers into the mud.

"Where were you, Mrs. Snow, when lightning hit the mast of the *Mimi*?"

"In my cabin."

"Were you alone?"

"No." Every ear was strained to hear her answer. "The captain of the *Mimi* was with me, Joe Beau Clair." The room seemed to breathe a sigh. The questions grew more intense, and Lily struggled to answer with equanimity.

"How very odd, Mrs. Snow. And you were making the voyage alone? You a bride of but a few months?"

"I had been asked to sail on the ship to publicize her voyage. My manager, Giles Benton, thought it a good idea, and my husband agreed."

"You succeeded very well in publicizing it, I would say, Mrs. Snow!" A roar of laughter greeted the comment. She looked to Joe for strength and saw anger staining his face. He was talking to his counsel, and in a moment the lawyer made an objection, demanding that the questioner refrain from extraneous remarks. Lily's eyes caught Jenny's in the gallery. They held for a moment; then Jenny looked away.

Lily's questioner warmed to his task. "But why was the captain in your cabin?"

She felt dizzy, overheated on the sultry New Orleans day in the too-heavy conservative clothes she had chosen. "He was an old friend from the plantation next to my father's in Martinique." Then Joe's displeased stare made her blurt shrilly, "He was my lover!"

With that she thought surely the worst of it was over, but it seemed to go on and on. She must confess that he had been with her in bed at the instant that lightning had struck, and even that it had been necessary for him to find his trousers and shoes before he could go on deck.

When it was over she sat drained and limp and watched the galleries clear. Nobody seemed to care whether Joe was judged guilty of negligence. Her testimony had been all that mattered; the conviction she had dealt him, the only important one. Silence rang in her ears, and then someone came to tell her that Joe waited for her in a private room. Her heart leaping with hope, she stood shakily, adjusted her hat, and tugged at her wilted skirt. She opened the door the attendant indicated and found herself alone with him. His blue eyes studied her, and she blushed, thinking how unattractive she must look after her ordeal. Then he put out his hands and took hers. He smiled, his eyes sparkling. "I am proud of you, Lily!" he said.

"Proud? What a strange choice of words, when I have just been so humiliated."

He held her against him, removing her hat so that he could kiss the nape of her neck more easily. She curled into his embrace. She had been through hell, but it had been worth it to win his approval. The nightmare that had begun when he had climbed in her window and told her he was not going to love her anymore was over.

"Oh, Joe, there is so much I did not have a chance to tell you last night. You were right about the stage. I have given it up. Archer has promised me an annulment, and there is nothing to stop us from marrying. We will go far away from here when this is all over."

But oddly the nightmare did not know it was over. He was pushing her away from him again, looking at her sternly. "No, Lily, whatever the decision of the board may be, I know I am to blame. We have done enough damage."

"Joe!"

"You were strong today. You did something not many women could have done. Go back to Snowdown. Don't fail me now!" He turned his back, and she saw his fists clenched in his effort to stop himself from reaching for her.

"Joe, if we don't love each other, what else have we to live for?"

"I would never be able to forget the *Mimi!*"

"Nor I, Joe," she whispered. But she was thinking of their baby, the beautiful life that had flowered amid the death. She must tell him that all had not been disaster and dying when the ship had gone down. She must tell him about the little girl with his eyes who lay in the acajou cradle at Acelie. But suddenly she knew she could not use a child to bring him to her. He must make peace with himself, come of his own accord. She longed to touch him one last time, to kiss him good-bye. But if she did, she could never leave gracefully, as she must.

Outside, the police cleared a corridor for her, and she rode back to Snowdown in a carriage with every window closed.

5

She did not expect to be cheered by her return to the house Archer had built for her. Ordinarily its smooth, airy spaces and clean detail were a balm to her spirit, but today things had gone too wrong. Then, in the hallway, she saw a familiar pile of suitcases—tan alligator bags and canvas Gladstone suitcases with leather straps.

She ran upstairs calling, "Susan! Susan, are you really here?" Rounding a corner, she bumped into her friend, saucy as ever, her brilliant hair done with a loop in the new doorknocker style.

"I was in town, sis, and I heard about your trouble. So I came on over. You don't mind a houseguest, do you? I've been expecting you to turn up. You always have, ever since that time I found you washed up on the riverbank."

"When I jumped from Jim Frey's boat. I don't drown easily, do I? Maybe better if I did!"

"There, now. Tell me everything. Perhaps it can be fixed."

Giles and Archer weren't about, so she had coffee brought, and they spent hours bringing each other up to date on everything that had happened.

"Henry's divorcing me," Susan said gaily.

"Is he? He was at the hearing today."

"He hasn't changed one stripe, old Henry. He still remembers it was you he wanted, too. Well, he can go after other game now. I've plenty of money and don't need his."

"But it will be only a civil divorce. You'll still be married in the eyes of the church."

"I don't care. I'll be rid of him. Until we're both in hell together, anyway."

"Are you still the mistress of that railroad magnate?"

Susan stuffed a date praline between her dainty teeth and asked, "Which one? I am forever meeting them."

A tension broke inside Lily, and she laughed until tears streamed from her eyes. She had thought that nothing would ever make her laugh again, but Susan was a wonderful comfort.

"He'll forget it, sis!" Susan insisted with a vehemence that almost made Lily believe her. "You'll have Joe yet!"

"He said never."

"He may never forget the *Mimi*, but he'll never forget you, either. All you have to do is stick."

"Wait for him the way I did when we worked at the French Pigeon? But I can't do that. I have a baby on Martinique."

"A baby!" Susan cried, incredulous. "Archer's?"

"No, his—Joe's."

"Well! Well, there you have it. Tell that idiot he's a father. He'll want to marry you quick enough when he hears he has a son."

"A daughter. She is like him, though. Even to the last little curl of her hair. I'm afraid for her without the protection of her father."

"Don't tell me, sis. Tell Joe."

"No. It mustn't be that way."

"Oh, you are a puzzle, Lily. The perfect answer to your problem right in front of you, and you refuse to recognize it. It's no wonder your gumbo's always burning! I'm going out for a while." She went upstairs and returned carrying a large crepe de chine parasol.

"Susan, you are not to tell him, either!" Lily cried suddenly as she made for the door.

"Me? Tell Joe? I shouldn't be likely to meet him on a simple drive, should I?"

"Promise!"

"Oh, fiddlesticks!" said Susan.

The next morning Archer came in from an early spin on his bicycle, wearing an elegant sack-style bicycle coat, and found Lily in her room, where she had been having breakfast.

"I missed you downstairs this morning, Lily."

"I didn't feel up to it after yesterday," she answered, and dropped her eyes. It was the first time they had spoken of the hearing.

"It was very upsetting," he said, and she saw in his face the greatness of the understatement. "I rode a very long way today. The river is up, and I have never seen the current so strong."

"The rains have been heavy, I hear."

He interrupted her impatiently. "That is the way I feel about my life, Lily. The current has never been so strong, and I've lost my grip on the bank. Could you possibly wait awhile for the annulment?"

"But why? What's to be gained by waiting?"

"I don't know. It's just that it couldn't be a quiet thing, now. The papers would have it, after yesterday. They would dig out everything. Everything—you know what I mean! It is bad enough too be called cuckold. I can't bear to be known for what I am!" He dropped his head on her silk bedspread to weep.

She stroked his hair and soothed him. "There, now, Archer, I'll wait if you wish it. There's no rush, since Joe isn't going to marry me. And as for what you are, why, you are a kind, generous man with a gift for creating beauty. There is more to life than bedding women. I still care for you."

He kissed her fingers and held them to his cheek, unable to speak with gratitude.

"I'm going back to Martinique soon," she told him. "It was only the guns I came for, and the money I need for Acelie. You'll help me tend to legal matters about that, won't you?"

"Yes, but what about Giles's play?" he said, surprised.

"I am not going to do a play."

"But you promised him, Lily."

"I had to, then. But promises can be broken." She drew a deep breath, studied him, and said, "Archer, I have a baby daughter at Acelie."

"A baby? Joe's! Why didn't you tell me before?"

"I didn't know how you—"

"Yes, yes, I see! After the way I acted before. I'll never hurt you again, Lily, dear. A baby! But all the same I think you'll do Giles's play. It's going to be his own. He's writing it!"

Poor Archer. He didn't realize that no matter how much of a man he had been, he could not have overcome the force of her passion for Joe. Perhaps it was just as well that he had been no man at all.

Lily checked boat schedules and made a reservation. Meanwhile, Susan's divorce proceedings rolled colorfully on. New Orleans turned its attention from Lily Beau Clair to her friend Susan Wickersham, who was even more delightfully scandalous. Taking the stand in an outrageous sunray skirt, the newest fashion, cut tight to the body until it flared at the knees, Susan blithely admitted all the charges against her, sometimes professing to have lived such a full life that she couldn't remember all the exciting details. Had she taken diamonds from a certain gentleman? Susan would knit her pretty brow and declare with a merry laugh, "Well, I'm sure I did, if he offered them!"

The comment would be repeated, and the city would rock with laughter. Susan was ever so much more fun than Lily, whose case had been tragic and who had turned pale with the admission of sleeping with only one man. Here was Susan confessing to a score of indiscretions, and although she already had enough money to make her independent of Henry, she soon had more, as men hopefully showered her with jewels.

Henry Wickersham squirmed, and that in itself was enough to cheer Lily. Henry had intended making a public spectacle of Susan, but she had accepted the role with such aplomb that it was he who was the laughingstock. "He's winning the divorce, keeping that horrible house and all his money, and he's not happy," Susan exulted. "Oh, it's choice! Help me pick my gown for tomorrow, Lily. Shall it be demure for a change?"

"Have you really done all those things they say you have, Susan?"

"If I haven't, I hope I will! There were occasions when less champagne would have been better. But there has never been a time when love itself was the champagne, like for you and Joe. I've missed that, Lily. But I'm satisfied. I've had a lot from life. I don't expect everything."

"I suppose I did expect everything." Lily sighed. "Everything being *him*, of course."

"Your baby will be everything now."

"Yes. Susan . . . you had better be careful. Henry'll be out for revenge."

"Oh, don't be so pigeon-hearted, Lily. He's defanged, I tell you!"

"I hope so."

She was waiting for her own personal serpent to strike. Giles Benton had hardly been seen about the house since the day that Lily had returned. He was still writing his play, Archer said, and Lily only hoped that she could manage to leave Snowdown quietly before it was finished. The arrangements for the separation of her property from Archer's and its transfer to Martinique seemed to be taking a long while. Archer said it was all standard procedure, but she wondered if the two of them were in league to keep her here so Giles could try to make her fulfill her promise. She could not understand why he seemed so sure of himself the rare times that he put in an appearance for dinner.

"I tell you, Giles, I'm not going to do it," she told him flatly, as he rhapsodized about the future over a steamy shrimp creole.

"You'll do it, Lily," he said, looking so smug she almost hurled a fluted Havilland sugar bowl in his direction.

"You can't make me, Giles. You've no hold on me. Even if you expect to get Archer to withhold the annulment, it won't work. I don't care just now."

"You care about nothing but getting back to your sweet baby," he mocked. "Motherhood! That is even more debilitating to an actress than love. You will leave the child to her native nursemaid, Lily, because, as I have told you before, any woman can be a mother, but no one else can be the famous Lily Beau Clair!"

"I am not Lily Beau Clair, the actress, anymore. I'm Mimi's mother. You know nothing about motherhood, Giles!"

"No. But I know a lot about *you*."

In the end, he did nothing at all to pressure her. He simply left the finished manuscript at her door. The name of the play was *The Little Brothers*.

When she had read it, she wept and pounded her bed with her fists. He had told the story with a genius that would stir the most unfeeling heart, and she realized that it would make people aware of the Cuban plight in a way that news dispatches couldn't. Damn Giles! Why had she had to be the one to bring him the perfect story for his talents? Giles didn't care about Cubans. Giles only cared that it was a compelling tale to be told. And if he cared at all about the dilemma he was causing Lily, it was only to anticipate his triumph over her.

"I won't do it!" she decided. "Let Giles get another actress. There are plenty. I'm going back to my baby."

But Giles had other ideas. "I am not going to produce *The Little Brothers* with any actress but you, Lily," he said when she told him. "It would be poor theater. You lived it, and you will bring feeling to it that no one else can."

"I'm not going to do it. I can be as stubborn as you, Giles!"

"Can you, Lily? We'll see."

She did not sleep that night, lying awake until the

mockingbirds began to sing outside her window. Then, falling into an exhausted slumber, she dreamed of the littlest brother, Pablo, crawling into her lap and telling her she reminded him of his dead mother. She dreamed of laughter and music and of flowers they had brought her. She was tucking them into their beds, and then the beds had become graves. She was screaming, and an evil-faced Spaniard in a blue-and-white uniform had hold of her . . ."

The Spaniard turned into Susan, shaking her. "You have got to get up, sis!"

"Why? Why have I got to get up?" she moaned.

"Open your eyes, and I'll show you. Come on, you've got to get ready. It's almost eleven! Good heavens, you're all bleary. What will Joe think if he sees you like this? Maybe that you've been out for a night of fun with someone!"

"Joe!"

"I thought that would bring you around," Susan said. "Look!" Lily's eyes focused on the morning paper Susan was holding folded to a headline: JOE BEAU CLAIR EXONERATED.

She scanned the story eagerly. Joe had not only been cleared of the charges, but commended for heroism in his attempts to save the *Mimi* and her crew. A study of the plan of the ship had led the board to believe that steam would not have saved the disabled craft, and indeed might have caused it to catch fire. "Only the bravest and most skillful of captains could have kept the ship afloat as long as he did," she read happily aloud.

"Get dressed, Lily," Susan urged. "He'll be coming here!"

"No. He said he felt to blame, whatever the board's verdict."

"He was only upset. He'll feel differently now. He's been commended. Get up, you goose!"

Lily did what Susan commanded and let her friend fuss over her, brushing her hair into a soft bun on top of her head and fastening her into a gown of lace-striped zephyr gingham. "There, now! You are the very picture of a beautiful young mother. You have nothing to do but say yes to everything he suggests."

She wandered the halls and peered out windows all afternoon. Once there was the sound of a carriage, but when she hurried to the door, it was only Giles the maid was letting in.

He gaped at her, and then his mouth turned in a sneer. "Playing the ingenue today, eh, Lily? It's not convincing."

She went upstairs, studied herself in the mirror, and decided he was right. She let her hair down, redid it in a twist like Susan's, added a dagger brooch to the throat of the dress, and splashed on cologne. She sat out under the oaks in the quiet twilight, letting her tears flow as it grew dark. Still he did not come.

"*You* go to *him*," Susan urged. "He is easing his guilt at your expense. Go and tell him about his responsibilities. It'll put an end to this nonsense!"

"But suppose he really doesn't love me anymore? And my telling him about Mimi makes him feel he has got to marry me?"

"Joe not love you! Oh, pooh!"

"Well, I will give him time."

On the third day she knew she had given him too much time. The newspaper carried a picture of a smiling Jenny Van Artsdalen, and beside it was the announcement of her marriage to Joe Beau Clair.

6

"At least he's out of the way," she heard Giles say to Archer."

"Oh, him! Joe Beau Clair is trying to settle down and become respectable. He's trying to be something he's not, and he won't have any better luck than I did when I tried to be a husband to Lily."

"You're drunk, Archer."

"Yes, but I got that way in the best of style, on mint julep. Do you want one, Giles?"

"Perhaps I'd better, if it will keep you from drinking it. Cheer up, Archer. We'll have Lily with us indefinitely when we do the play. You'll like that, and think of it—you're little Mimi's legal father!"

"Oh, damn you, Giles! Get somebody else for your play and let Lily go home to her baby. If she stays, we will soon be treated to the spectacle of her having an affair with a married man. Or worse, the spectacle of my trying to behave like one!"

"Don't be so dramatic, Archer. Lily is perfectly free to go. It's nothing like when you kept her imprisoned here with locks on the windows and dogs in the yard."

"Don't remind me of that, Giles. I'll kill you!"

"I suppose you think if I were dead you could go back to being whatever you were before. You think no other man could seduce you. Perhaps not, but that wouldn't make you a husband. Dear me, we were doing so well, weren't we, before she came back!"

No longer shocked by their arguments, she wandered in between them, her face freshly washed in an effort to erase the traces of weeping, her silk wrapper closely fastened. "Giles, I want to be alone with Archer," she said imperiously.

"Certainly, my dear," he said, more amused than amazed, and smirked as he took himself to another part of the house.

"Do you feel better, Lily?" Archer said. "You've been crying all day."

"I don't think I'll ever feel better." She sat beside him on a velvet sofa and let him stroke her hair as she leaned against his shoulder. "What are we to do, Archer? We are two miserable people."

"Do? Why, it's simple. You are going back to Martinique, and I am going to have another drink."

"I'm going to do the play, Archer." She sighed.

"And let Giles win? Oh, Lily! You are doing it just to stay near Joe."

"Not because of Joe. Because of General Weyler. Giles brought me the latest reports. He has herded all the noncombatants into camps and burned their homes and fields. The camps all lie in malarial swamps, and people are starving and dying of disease by the thousands, while sentries with rifles and machetes kill anyone who dares to try to cross the line to dig potatoes. They say that every morning the soldiers drive pack mules through the lanes of the camps, loaded with the mutilated bodies of men and women who tried to prevent their children from starving. It is just as the nuns said, Archer. It's part of Weyler's plot to exterminate Cubans from the island."

"Calm down, Lily. It's all exaggeration. These yellow journals are always trying to top one another. Like the matter of the Spaniards undressing the American lady on the *Olivette*. Everyone was ready to go to war before it was found to be untrue."

"We *should* be at war! These stupid newsmen! They are forever crying wolf, and when it is the truth, nobody believes them. Well, I will make people believe it when I do *The Little Brothers*!"

"Nothing has changed, Lily. We'll both do what Giles wants. But you at least shall do it in a holy cause. Go and fix me another drink. It'd be a disgrace to call the maid and have her see me in my condition. There's a love."

A month later the play opened to packed houses. Patrons who had come to be titillated by another *Salome* or *Cleopatra*, or merely to lay eyes on the seductress of the *Mimi*, stayed to cry as Lily knelt in the spotlight in a calico dress, her face registering the horror of the shots fired in the wings. The little bodies would be carried in, and she would kiss each one and cover it.

"Good night, little brothers," she would whisper as the

lights dimmed, leaving the stage in blackness. Taking curtain calls, her gown still streaked in blood, her face still wet with the heartfelt tears she cried every night, she would send a basket into the weeping audience to ask for contributions for Cuba.

One night she found the door to her dressing room blocked by an officer in a Spanish naval uniform. Still in the mood of the play, she gasped and flinched, thinking of the incident on the Cuban road, when she had been caught riding the stolen horse.

"Don't be afraid of me, Madame Beau Clair," he said, seizing her arm. "I only want you to have coffee with me."

"With you! You are the enemy, sir!"

"I want to convince you I am not."

"I can't be convinced, I'm sure."

"Of course not, if you don't listen. We aren't beasts, not all of us. General Weyler is gone now. Things will be better soon."

"That is what they say. But it hasn't happened. And people who are starving won't live to see that time!"

"I want justice for Cuba as much as you!" he snapped. "But Spanish justice. Can you imagine what would happen if the peasants were left to govern themselves. It would be chaos. Then America would step in to annex the island. That is what this is all about—imperialism. That is what you are aiding with this play. You are a fine actress, but you should stick to acting and leave affairs of state to President McKinley. This play of yours is nothing but rabble-rousing sentimentalism!"

"Young boys murdered? That is not sentimentalism. That is atrocity."

"Perhaps, but they were murderers, too, though they were so young."

"They were heroes!" she cried, yanking her arm free to strike his face.

He reeled, and with a hand to his cheek, bowed low. "Heroes! I should like to be a hero to you, Madame Beau Clair. You are a woman of conviction. My name is Captain Eduardo Rodríguez. Call on me if I can ever be of service in a way compatible with honor."

He turned on his heel, and she did not see him again. But she did not forget him. He was different from other Spaniards she had known.

Since she was allocating most of her share of the play's

profits to relief for Cuba, she soon had a shipload of food and medical supplies in a warehouse near the docks. But now another problem arose. Ships' captains all demanded a premium to sail to Cuba. It was only fair, since there was the risk of being arrested, as several Americans had been, or of having shots fired at the ship.

Lily was outraged. "Is this the quality of American manhood? Are they all so cowardly and avaricious?"

"I don't know, I'm sure," Archer said mildly. "I expect you'll find your man."

And she did. "There's a gentleman to see you, madame," was all the maid said to announce him. She went downstairs and found Joe Beau Clair in her parlor, compelling as ever, his body straight, lean, and inviting, his eyes shadowed like evening at sea. When he walked across the room to meet her, the rhythm of his step made Carnival drums pound in her ears.

But he made no move to touch her, and she had to clasp her hands tightly to keep herself from reaching for him. He was, after all, a different Joe, a married Joe, who had determined to give up his reckless ways.

"I saw the play last night, Lily."

"With Jenny?" She choked on the words and knew that her mortal hurt showed in her face.

"No. Jenny is not well. She's . . . you know—in a certain condition."

A deathlike coldness gripped her at the pride in his voice, pride that should have been for her and Mimi and might have been if she had told him, as Susan had advised. "You're to be a father! I congratulate you."

"Lily, I am the one who will sail your supplies to Cuba." His face lighted in a different way, and she was reminded of the sudden sunrise over the dark mornes of Martinique. She laughed to know that he had not changed at all. They would be together in this adventure at least. She would raise the money and buy the goods; he would run them into Cuba, delivering them hither and yon about the coast wherever they were needed. Jenny could have little to say about what he did for so noble a reason.

The days were tedious while she waited for his return, and the emptied warehouse began to bulge again in expectation of a second voyage. In the evening after the performances, she went about town with Archer as she had used to, playing another role, that of his adoring young wife who was deeply regretful of her moment of folly on the *Mimi*.

"It'll never wash, sis," Susan said.

"I know. But he likes it. It will give him something sweet to remember when the play is finished and I go away to Martinique."

"I'm going back to New York soon. Are you planning to take *The Little Brothers* there, to the Fifth Avenue Theater?"

"Giles would like to. I don't know."

"You don't want to be away from Joe," Susan said wisely.

"No, I don't. Not unless I can be with Mimi on Martinique. It's terrible of me, isn't it? I should at least try to stop loving him."

But she did not try, especially when he returned from Cuba and came to Snowdown about teatime, his duck-cloth trousers thrust into boots still grimy with mud from Cuba's swamps, his face full of conquest and success. The situation was even worse than the dispatches said, because none of the correspondents had been deep enough into the long grass. Nowhere had Joe seen fields under plow, and between the Júcaro-Morón Troche and Cape San Antonio he had seen no houses left standing. *Pacíficos* were dying by the thousands, and a part of the order that had established the camps had also forbidden the moving of food supplies on land or sea without the government's permission.

She caught her breath. "What happened to the supplies, Joe? Did they give you permission?"

"Do you think I asked?" he said with a grin.

"No. What did you do?" she asked eagerly.

"Stuck to the Florida Straits, then ran in straight from the sea. Spanish gunboats chased me twice. But most of the camps aren't on the coast, so I found myself a band of rebels and we commandeered an old train. I've seen it all, Lily, and left a few dead Spaniards to mark my trail. Have you got another load? I must tend to Jenny for a few days, then I'll go back again."

"I'll have everything waiting, Joe," she said.

"Good-bye, Lily." His eyes burned into hers, and she reeled as though he had kissed her.

Jenny came to see her the next day, looking delicately wan. "Oh, Mrs. Snow! Can't you stop him from going back to that horrible place? I am afraid he'll be killed! And I—"

"You are going to have a baby. He told me. But I won't

try to stop Joe from doing what he thinks is right to do. If you love him, neither will you."

"Oh, I do love him!" Jenny said, her little lips pursing.

"I know you do. If you try to change him, you will only make him care for you less."

"I must accept it, then. You are right. I am glad I came to talk to you, Mrs. Snow. It's good of you to advise me after I schemed to get him from you. But you are married, too, and that is all in the past, isn't it? We'll be friends now, won't we?"

Lily smiled, accepted Jenny's hug, and watched in admiration as her carriage drove away. Now that Jenny had declared them friends, it would seem worse if she betrayed Jenny with Joe. Jenny knew that. And she knew she was in danger of losing him, even while she carried his child. Poor Jenny! It was going to happen. It could not be stopped. Joe could not help himself. She had seen it when he had returned from Cuba. And if Joe couldn't help it, neither could she. If he put his hands on her, she would succumb instantly. They were about to destroy someone else, the two of them. And might Jenny's destruction destroy Joe, too? If only she could resist!

She might get another captain to carry her goods. That, after all, had been what Jenny had been hoping she would do. But it was too late for that. He had seen bloody Cuba. He was committed.

"Giles, I would like to take *The Little Brothers* to New York," she said that night.

"All right, I'll make arrangements. We'll go in a month or two."

She was certain that would be too late.

The thought depressed and elated her at the same time. Joe was married to Jenny and bound to feel his obligation. Perhaps it would never be the same as during that marvelous time when they had both been free and had planned to garland the horses of their wedding carriage in roses. But she would be his mistress again and feel his arms about her. His love for her was greater than his tremendous will, and she wondered fearfully what the toll of his battle to do without her would be. Would failure in that resolve diminish him? Would he be in a fury at himself and at her?

But Joe must be making a good fight of remaining true to Jenny. Day after day passed, and he did not come to Snowdown. Could she have been wrong? Did he really love Jenny as a husband should? Jenny had been smart enough to claim him, quick to provide him with a potential family. Had she managed to secure his heart, after all?

Then one night as she stood onstage listening to the sound of the execution, the crack of the rifles seemed oddly close. She smelled the acrid odor, and the ribbon that held her hair at the nape of her neck snapped loose. How careless of the wardrobe mistress, she thought as her dark locks spilled warmly about her face. It would spoil the scene.

But the scene was spoiled anyway. Acres of red and blue spun before her eyes; then the stage rocked upward to meet the plummeting curtain. Somebody was yelling for a doctor, and Archer was holding her head in his lap while a crowd of cast members gathered around.

"Are you all right, Lily? It was a Spanish sympathizer—an assassin. He shouted '*Viva España!*' Didn't you hear him?" He lifted her hair and found a fiery red mark where the bullet had passed close enough to stun her.

"Archer, hadn't you better go and announce that I am all right?" she asked, hearing pandemonium beyond the heavy curtain.

"No. The police haven't caught the fellow yet. New Orleans has a Spanish heritage, you know, and he will find someone to shelter him. If he thinks you're dead, he won't try again. Can you walk? I'll help you, and we'll get you out of here."

Someone threw a hooded cloak around her for disguise, and she was led to a tightly closed carriage. She could hear a hubbub of frightened theatergoers and police on the sidewalks as they drove away.

She didn't protest when Archer and Giles insisted she go straight to bed at Snowdown. She shivered even under quilts, and the hot coffee they brought her didn't really warm her. "Is Susan home?" she asked.

"She's out."

It was the answer Lily had expected. Susan had too many admirers to spend an evening at Snowdown since her divorce had become final. But Lily had been close to death, and she needed someone with her tonight in the huge bed. Could she ask Archer? He was her husband. But that, after all, was the trouble with that idea. She smiled and kissed him good night, bidding him leave the lamp burning.

Outside in the hall she could hear him talking to Giles.

"They haven't caught the man yet. Lily mustn't perform again. For all we know, there may be others, too!"

"Oh, come, Archer. It was a fluke. They'll have him by morning. *The Little Brothers* is a hit, and if we close, Lily won't do another play. She'll go to Martinique to be with her baby. After tonight, we could run for years!"

"Giles, can't you think of Lily's welfare for once? I won't stand for her to risk her life, do you understand?"

She shuddered and drifted into a nightmarish sleep, wishing that she could keep tomorrow from coming, because ultimately it would be she, not Archer or Giles, who would decide whether the play would continue.

Then, through her dreams, she heard a third masculine voice in the hall, more demanding and urgent than the others. "Where is Lily? Is she hurt? I want to see her!"

"Shh! Not now, old man. You'll wake her!"

"I don't care. I'm going to see her!"

She knew it was Joe even before the door flung back, then slammed hard behind him. She clung to him as he took her in his arms, his jagged breath a storm of passion against her cheek. "I couldn't stay away, Lily. I couldn't wait to read in the papers if you were dead or alive."

"It's all right, Joe. I'm very much alive."

"And I am alive, too, though I have not felt it for the longest time," he said. His hands fell to the warm orbs of her breasts. Moving aside the cloth of her gown, he laid his lips against her yielding flesh. Then his hands were everywhere at once; her body quivered with mindless rapture as he tore off her clothing, making her naked for his love.

When he was finished, she lay damp and glowing, the cold death of the Spaniard's bullet vanquished. She thought of Jenny, shivered once, and chased the thought away. That would come soon enough. Whatever time she had him, she was going to have him without worry of what might come tomorrow. She had made another decision as well.

"Joe," she whispered, "I am going to do the play again."

She wondered if he would try to dissuade her, but the time had passed when he had thought he could dictate her life because he loved her. He had come to realize that it was not only in bed that she was more than a submissive little creature in petticoats.

"It's what I expected, Lily," was all he said, and she thought he was proud of her.

In the morning Archer told her that he intended to move from Snowdown with Giles.

"Archer, no! Stay here. You are most welcome."

"It's a large house, Lily. We could almost lose each other in it. But it is not large enough for me to stand your having your affair with Joe in it. I'd become jealous and not content to be your friend."

"Then I'll leave."

"No. It's your house. I built it for you, and you must have it."

"Oh, Archer." She sighed.

The Loyalist who had tried to assassinate her had managed to elude the police that had searched the city and the river front during the night, but the play went off without incident, with guards at the entrance of the theater to check gentlemen's pockets for revolvers.

Each night now her body shuddered in a new way as the guns sounded in the wings, and her gesture of supplication was as much a plea for her own life as a piece of dramatic business. When the donation basket was passed, audiences responded to her courage. She would laugh with pleasure at the sums collected and with joy at being alive. Joe would be waiting at the stage door—to see her home safely, he said. Once they were inside Snowdown, she was anything except safe, but it was a sort of peril she relished.

Would things go on like this always? They never spoke of Jenny, never admitted her presence between them. She knew that the *Sea Bird* was loading for Cuba again, but they did not talk, either, of their impending separation. One night he loved her with such yearning that she knew, and the next night after the performance, there was only Giles to take her home.

He made her ask him in for coffee and took his time about leaving, stalking the empty house. "So, all alone, Lily? All your fine gentlemen left. Beau Clair's off again, the knight-errant of the Cuban cause, and Archer Snow, the famed architect, has removed himself from the scene of his crimes. Poor Lily."

"Where *is* Archer, Giles? Why doesn't he come to the theater anymore since he moved from Snowdown?"

"I expect it's because he's too drunk. He's developing such vices, tch, tch!"

"New ones? Tell me."

"No. Too dreadful for your tender ears."

"My ears! Tender! It's Lily, Giles. You can't shock *me*!"

"Why not? I have done it before. Do you think you've seen the bottom of the barrel of degradation?"

"I've tasted the very dregs because of you, Giles!"

"There's worse," he said with satisfaction, daintily licking a bit of sugar from his shell-patterned silver spoon.

"I don't believe you!" she answered, and rang for the maid to take away the tray.

He accepted the hint and reached for his soft felt trilby hat. "You do still hate me, don't you, Lily?"

"Terribly."

"That's as it should be, of course. But I'm telling you the truth. I'll arrange for you to find out. Do wear a flannel gown tonight. It's coming up a norther, and there's no one to keep you warm. You'd be ridiculous sneezing your way through *The Little Brothers*."

She slammed the door behind him, and then proceeded to take his advice. It was early November, and though the mosquito netting had long since been put away, it had not been cold enough for a fire. But at evening there had been a line of puce clouds along the horizon, coming in low and flat and threatening in a way that meant a touch of winter. There had been excitement in the air as night had fallen and the oaks and mimosa had begun to blow. Such weather did not come often to New Orleans, breaking its languid spell for the vigor of other climes. Lily had always liked the cold, a novelty after a lifetime on Martinique, and she curled into bed, sighing as she pulled the quilts around her.

She began to think of Captain Rodríguez as she lay there. Would things get better in Cuba, as he had predicted? Or would there be war? If there were, she could close the play at once and go home to Mimi. That, in a way, would be as much a wrench as leaving the baby had been. To go away, leaving Joe to Jenny, not even knowing that he had a daughter. But that was too painful a thought, and she turned her mind to Joe, wondering if this northern wind were sweeping him across the warm Gulf waters to the Straits of Florida and beyond.

7

Dimly she heard the telephone ringing, civilized and insistent over the rapping of the rain. Beyond the windows it was still dark, the Spanish moss shaking phosphorescent tails in the nightglow. "Whoever that is can call back in the morning," she thought. But the phone kept on ringing self-righteously. Braving the chill, she went down to answer it.

"Mrs. Snow? Mrs. Archer Snow?" said a woman's voice as she lifted the receiver.

"Yes."

"If you want your husband, you'd better come and take 'im off our hands. Bring money, too, if you want it kept quiet."

Her stomach went cold as she realized that Giles was arranging for her to see the bottom of the barrel, as he had promised. Dear heaven, whatever could it be?

"Isn't Mr. Giles Benton supposed to take care of this?" she asked.

"Yes, sis, but he said tonight you would. He said to call you. Those were his exact directions. If you don't want to bother, I'll toss him in the street. I don't care a feather how wet he gets, and he's taking up space that others are wanting."

"How much money?" Lily sighed.

"A hundred dollars would do it. It's Dr. Stone's Pleasure Club, sis. Villere Street. Have you got a driver? He'll have heard of it."

"I'll find it," she said, and hung up.

She dressed quickly in a skirt and jacket of blue cheviot and fastened a wool cape over them. She woke a maid and sent her to the stables to have her buggy brought around. "You mean the brougham, ma'am," the maid corrected her. "You'll not be wanting to drive yourself tonight."

"The two-seater buggy," Lily insisted. "I'm going alone."

There would be gossip, but it would be about her, not

Archer. And a little more gossip about Lily Beau Clair would hurt nothing. Archer, on the other hand—she shuddered and tried not to imagine just what gossip it would have been if she had taken the driver with her.

She was glad tonight for her knowledge of the Vieux Carré. It was still its dirty shabby self, but the footpads and prostitutes had been driven inside tonight by the rain. The tawdry signs, the beckoning lights in the windows of cribs, still announced her arrival in the business district of sin— soon to be so by law, for at the beginning of next year it would be illegal to operate bordellos in any section except between the lower side of North Basin Street and the lower side of North Robertson Street and from the south side of Customhouse Square to the north side of St. Louis Street. The Story Ordinance had been passed only recently, but already property values in the area had doubled and the area had gained a reputation as Storyville. Poor French New Orleans. It seemed destined to bear the brunt of the city's sin forever!

Music wafted out into the rain, the lascivious tones of a trombone and the racket of an upright piano on which the hammer pads must be worn to the wood. The lights of red and blue globes reflected like rouge and paint on the wet street, streaming with the muddy runoff down to the river. The Arlington Annex at Customhouse and North Basin Street was doing a good business at the gateway to the district, and so was the French Pigeon, which had landed happily in the middle of the region. Lily urged her horse to go faster as she remembered the art poses that were probably going on inside. She drove by Lulu White's Mahogany Hall, and in spite of her urgent mission gaped at the huge fishbowl out front, where lights changed the water from gold to crimson, then to purple and green. Across the way St. Louis Cemetery Number One was dark and silent, housing many who had paid the wages of sin.

When she drove down Villere Street, she could not find the place at first. Then, turning back, she saw the sign, a hand with a finger pointing down an alley between two balconied bordellos. Wishing now that she had someone with her, she secured the buggy at a rusting lion's-head post and walked cautiously into the narrow blackness. Nothing marked the entrance of the pleasure club except a door showing light behind an olive-green shade. Lily knocked tentatively. The lamp was carried closer to the door, the shade moved, and then a key turned in the lock. Light flowed into the alley, eddying around a large woman in a black lizard-cloth dress.

"Yes?" Lily thought she recognized the voice on the telephone.

"I'm Mrs. Snow. I . . . I've come for my husband."

It seemed an ordinary parlor, with its tasseled Turkish suite of tête-à-tête couch, rocker, and easy chairs. The very lack of any appearance of evil made Lily all the more apprehensive. What sort of place could this be that a man like Giles would call it the very bottom of the barrel?

"Come with me, sis," said the woman. She was in her fifties, a worn-out prostitute, Lily guessed. Was she the madame here? Was Archer trying to find his manhood in a brothel? But no, she knew it must be worse than that. Giles knew enough of her past to guess that she wouldn't be shocked by the usual Vieux Carré fare.

She followed the woman through another door into a long hallway. "Hello, dear," somebody called in the dimness. She turned, and as her eyes became accustomed to the light, she made out a woman stretched on a cot, her face heavily painted, her body naked except for a chemise pulled suggestively over her thigh. The cot was inside a cubicle across which a heavy velvet curtain could be stretched for privacy. Beside that cubicle was another, and another, along both sides of the hall, and in each a girl similar to the first sat or reclined in some alluring position. A cheap bordello, after all, but something was wrong. Something about these girls seemed different. They were all so slender about the hips, and the voices rang falsetto.

"No fair, Mae!" someone protested. "That one's too pretty. The rest of us'll lose business."

"Shut up, you lout," another answered. "Can't you see she's the real thing?"

They were men, she realized suddenly. A house of protitution, but a very different sort than the likes of Lulu White's.

"A woman! What's she doing here, Mae?" somebody wanted to know.

"She's Mrs. Snow. She's come for her husband."

"Mrs. Snow!" came voices. "Oooh, Archer's wife! Would you like us to show you how to love him, dear? Archer Snow—he's a peach, and he pays well. Would you like to hear what he does to me?"

She blanched and was speechless, but the "prostitutes"

were more interested in bantering among themselves than in taunting her. "He paid me more than you!" one asserted, and another declared, "He's been with me four times. He's sweet, that Archer!"

Lily was in tears by the time Mae threw back one of the velvet curtains and disclosed Archer seated on the floor, his head lolling onto a bed, his shirt unbuttoned, and one shoe off. He was drunk, snoring gently, the expression on his face not one of lechery, but of lonely sadness. She bent and touched his cheek and called his name.

"He can't hear you, sis," Mae said, putting out her hand. "The bill's a hundred dollars, remember?"

Lily nodded and dug out the banknotes.

"I'm in a generous mood tonight," Mae said, stuffing the bills into her bodice. "I'll have him carted to your carriage for nothing extra."

She was gone for a moment and then came back with one pair of toughs she had whistled up from the alley. One seized Archer's feet, another his shoulder, and they carried him away, much to the amusement of the "whores," who hooted and giggled at the spectacle of their lover leaving the premises feetfirst, followed by his wife.

Outside, rain splattered into Archer's upturned face, and suddenly she was afraid that it would revive him, and he would realize his predicament. But Archer only groaned as he was dumped beside her in the buggy. She set off quickly for home, breathing in great gulps of the wet November air, as if to cleanse herself of the miasma of the degeneration she had witnessed.

Archer sat limply, his head almost unbearably heavy against her shoulder, and she had to drive with her arm about him to keep him from tumbling out into the street. She began to think about what she would do with him. If only she could reach Snowdown before he regained himself, it would all be better. He would not need to know where she had found him.

She had to wake stableboys to carry him inside, but she forced herself to smile at them and tell them that he had drunk too much at the faro club and that she would add something extra to their wages for their trouble. They grinned at her, understanding, and carried him upstairs and put him in bed.

She sat downstairs, rocking in her Martinique rocker until nearly dawn, wondering what to do. Archer could not go on this way. She must think of some way to help him. Finally she rang Giles and gave him an ultimatum. "Giles, you'll see to it that that woman does not let him in anymore. Pay her whatever is necessary."

"Ah, Lily, do you think there is only one such place in New Orleans?"

"There are more? Then you will see to it that he doesn't frequent any of them. If I hear of such an incident again, I will quit the play, Cuba or not!"

"Lily, that's not fair!"

"I don't care about fair, any more than you do, Giles," she told him. When she had hung up, she still felt dissatisfied. She knew she had not really solved the problem, but she had a cheery breakfast ready for Archer when he came downstairs.

"Lily, what am I doing at Snowdown?" he said worriedly.

"You were very drunk."

He put a hand to his head and sighed. "Yes, I can tell that I was. But, Lily, what did I do?" he asked anxiously. "Did I ... did I try to be a husband?"

"No, dear, no," she soothed. "Nothing like that. Come and have some coffee."

"Oh, Lily, you are good to me," he said. "I don't deserve it, of course. I am so miserable. I am glad at least you don't know what my life is really like."

And Lily was glad that he could not guess that she did.

In two weeks Joe was back from Cuba. Delightedly she forgot everything else in the ecstasy of his embrace. He would be home nearly a month, thanks to Jenny, who had made him promise not to sail again until after Christmas. Lily shopped for toys and sent Mimi a box of pegs, alphabet blocks, Scripture cubes, and bisque dolls. She was too young for most of the things, Lily knew, but she had to do something. It was her baby's first Christmas.

Joe came on Christmas Eve and helped to put the star on top of the tree. His gift was a silver-and-gold peacock pendant set with pearls. That day, too, President McKinley appealed to the country for contributions of food and medicine for Cuba. On Christmas Day she had thought to be alone with Susan, who had proclaimed the holiday the most boring day of the year, the day when all her suitors went home to their families. But about noon another homeless soul blew in, and they shared their meal of turkey and candied yams with Archer.

It was a cheerless feast, despite the red Christmas candles

on the table and the garlands of fresh white-berried mistletoe. Susan, always chipper, had gone into a funk, and after a few efforts at gaiety, Archer lapsed into silence, too. As for Lily, she could think only of Mimi, and finally tears ran down her face.

"Oh, that does it!" cried Susan, throwing down her Dresden-patterned napkin. "You are the last one of us who should be crying. You at least have someone you ought to be with—your baby—and her father loves you! Oh, I am so tired of not having anyone. I would give anything—"

"And then there's me," Archer interrupted. "Poor old Archer, who is never going to have anyone. Let's all go for a drive and see the decorations."

He herded them out into the gray afternoon and made them all sing Christmas carols as they rode along. There was a kind of nobility about him as he sang with false ebullience into the chill, debilitating air, she thought. Would life ever change for him, or for Susan, or even for her?

She was still depressed on the twenty-seventh, when Joe came to say good-bye as he left again for Cuba.

"Don't fret, love. I'll be back soon. It'll be Carnival time. We'll dance together. It's been too long since we danced at Carnival."

"And I'll be your little coaling girl again," she burst out. "That's all I'll ever be now! It won't be Carnival you'll be hurrying back for. It'll be the birth of Jenny's child!"

"Lily—"

"I'm sorry, Joe," she said quickly.

He sighed as if he almost wished for an argument that would make him feel less guilty about his marriage. "I should have been strong enough not to come back to you, Lily. But since I wasn't, I'm still going to make Jenny the best husband I can."

"I know, I know," she said, and parted her lips for his kiss.

Carnival opened on the fifth of January, the Eve of Epiphany, the holy day on which the Magi, following the star, had found the Christ Child. It was that day on which the Twelfth Night Revelers, one of the most exclusive of the krewes, gave its great ball and crowned as its queen the girl who found a golden bean in her piece of frosted cake. It seemed that every night now there was a parade, with papier-mâché floats made in France, each parade with a theme, such as a story from tales from the *Arabian Nights* or one of Aesop's fables. The floats were all ridden by men who were members of the krewes. Women were not allowed to exhibit themselves in such an unseemly way, except in the Krewe of Venus, where the Queen of Love sat among paper lilies and violets with bluebirds and butterflies overhead.

The demand for theater tickets grew with the Carnival atmosphere, and Giles urged Lily to add more performances. The air was filled with the whistles of steam calliopes playing the Carnival song:

> May fish get legs and cows lay eggs,
> If I ever cease to love.

Lily was weary from all the extra work, but Susan seemed to thrive on the season. Wherever there was a party, Susan would be content, Lily thought. But Susan's eyes were sparkling in a way Lily could not attribute to revelry, and she had begun to wear constantly a paste bracelet in Carnival colors of purple, green, and gold.

"Where did you get that, Susan?" she asked finally, curious as to why Susan's diamonds and moonstones had been discarded in favor of imitation jewels.

"From a float."

"Some member of a krewe threw it to you?"

"No. I didn't even catch it myself. A man next to me did. And he gave it to me. He wasn't anyone important."

He wasn't in the social register and he wasn't a cotton broker, but Lily wasn't sure that he might not be important in another way. Susan was singing a lot, her beautiful voice ringing through Snowdown's halls.

> May the moon be turned to green cream cheese
> If I ever cease to love.

Joe returned early in February to find Lily's warehouse already bulging again with response to McKinley's request for aid. "That foot-dragger will never support war," Joe said disgustedly. "And now there is the *Maine* in Havana harbor, on a goodwill mission. The Spanish have sent out a case of sherry, and the crew is all sporting on the shore. I saw it myself when I came up from the long grass."

"Oh, I don't see why we cannot go to war! It would be nothing for the Americans to capture Havana, would it?"

"Victory could be had almost for the asking, Lily. Have you got another load?"

"No."

"No!"

"I'm going to dump it all into the river to have you stay here with me. Anyway, you can't go again. What about Jenny?"

"Oh, that's still six weeks away. I have time to make one more trip. But I did promise we'd dance at Carnival, didn't I? I'll stay until Valentine's Day. How does that strike you?"

"I'm sure that will please Jenny and me both."

Lily wondered if she weren't more pleased than Jenny, since he spent the greater part of each evening in her company instead of his wife's. There would be no official street dancing until Shrove Tuesday, but there were plenty of cabarets where the season was in full swing. He would arrive at Snowdown at nine or ten, and they would dance the night away. Sometimes they would stop at the French Market for doughnuts and coffee, just as Lily once had with Susan and Etienne, her fencing master; and those times Lily would wonder where Susan was these days. Dancing with someone, but who?

More often when Joe and Lily tired of dancing they would drive straight back to Snowdown, Joe, amorous already, using only one hand on the reins; and the horses, as if sensing his urgency, dashing off toward home at a breathtaking pace, along the moss-hung river road.

One night, however, he did not come until after midnight, and apologized wearily, telling her that Jenny had been ill.

"Oh, but is she all right? Should you have come away at all?"

"It would have been useless to stay. The doctor has given her something to make her sleep, so this is one night at least when she will be oblivious of our love."

"Isn't she every night? What do you tell her when you go out?"

"I say I'm going to play faro."

"Does she believe you?"

"She acts as though she does. Come, Lily, since we're going to deceive her, let's do it cheerfully. I'm still to go to Cuba, so let's enjoy ourselves while we can. The doctor says there's nothing to worry about so long as she rests in bed."

She went with him to the Vieux Carré and smiled and let him love her. Punishment for wrongdoing always came soon enough, if not in this world, in the next. Joe was right. It was a shame not to enjoy sin, since one would pay eventually. She was miserable enough already, being away from Mimi and not being able to tell Joe about their baby. And things might get worse. When Jenny's baby was born, Joe would become more of a family man, and she, too, must be thinking of her return to Martinique. It was a last fling, this Carnival season, an ending of a well-rounded story that was finishing as it had started, with a pagan caleinda.

On his last day, February 14, she arranged for a holiday from the play and found a huge gilded valentine in her mail. Inside was a train ticket for the resorts of Lake Pontchartrain.

They were to have the whole day together! He met her at the station, impish as a schoolboy with this runaway excursion, as they chugged out of town through cypress swamps and palmetto thickets. They walked promenades and gardens laid out in pretty walks and labyrinths. In the summer these gardens would be greener and filled with blossoms, but knowing it would be wise to seize the moment, she led him on until they had seen every cranny.

Then, because the weather wasn't cold, they rented a rowboat and drifted for hours along the banks of the enormous lake. They were ravenous at dinnertime and ordered fried river catfish and hot, oniony hush puppies at a restaurant built on poles over the water. After dark there was dancing, and Lily, losing all sense of time and place, felt as though she would waltz on forever in Joe's arms.

Too soon he was pulling her outside, telling her it was time to catch the last train to New Orleans. She dozed on his shoulder as they rode toward the city, trying not to think that when he sailed in the morning, he would not be coming home to her but to imminent fatherhood. At the New Orleans station he hired a Cooke's taxi, and suddenly she realized they weren't heading to Snowdown, but to the docks.

"Where are you taking me, Joe?"

"To the *Sea Bird*. That way we can be together every moment until I sail."

"But you must say good-bye to Jenny!"

"I did that this morning. I told her there was work to be done aboard and I wouldn't be back again before I sailed."

"Joe! She is lying there unable to get out of bed for fear of losing your child, and you are spending your last night with me. It's not right!"

"No, but I'm beyond caring. If I am to go back to her tonight, you must send me!"

It was too much to ask of her, especially when she remembered that all during her own pregnancy she had not had him for even one night, and she stepped out of the cab quickly and waited for him to lead her across the moonlit deck to make love to her in his cabin.

Time drifted sweetly on, the rocking ship a cradle of passion. Each clung to the other, denying forces more powerful than oceans that were tearing them apart. There was commotion outside along the piers, but they were heedless of what they thought was Carnival revelry. The singing of "The Star-Spangled Banner" drifted in, and there was a popping of firecrackers.

Then, nightmarishly, the door burst open, and Jenny stood gasping, her eyes burning, her hands clasped against the taut, round protuberance of her unborn child.

"Joe! Thank heaven I've found you in time! You mustn't go to Cuba. Not now! You must think of the baby if not of me. The *Maine* has blown up in Havana harbor! There will be war."

Her gaze met Lily's as she collapsed over the doorframe, her body contorted with agony. "Oh, Joe, the baby!" she sobbed. "Can you ever forgive me?"

"Forgive *you*!" he said in confusion, as he lifted her and ran to put her into her carriage. Lily held to Jenny to keep her from being hurled to the floor as he took the reins to race through the streets.

"I loved him, Lily, was that so wrong?" Jenny whispered.

"Nothing is wrong with *your* loving him," she replied, her eyes full of bitter tears.

"But it has all been for nothing, Lily. I have lost his child for nothing! He will go to Cuba, won't he? And he will go on forever loving you. Oh, you did tell me I should not interfere with him!"

She waited through the night at the hospital, Joe sitting apart from her, his face closed and stony. The sun was well up when a nurse called Joe away. When he came back, his expression was unchanged.

"She is dead, Lily, she and the baby," he said, and without another word walked past her outside.

8

New Orleans was afire with the excitement of war, and that added to the spirit of Carnival, which had risen to a peak with the approach of Shrovetide. Only ninety of the *Maine*'s crew of three hundred and fifty had returned alive, yet no state of war existed. McKinley had ordered a naval board of inquiry and was using every diplomatic power available to force Spain to grant Cuban independence. Queen María Cristina was resisting adamantly. War would come, and already there were long lines outside enlistment offices.

Lily had made no effort to follow Joe or find him. She knew well what he was thinking; his thoughts were hers, too. If Joe had been with Jenny on Valentine's night, she would not have disobeyed her doctor's orders to come to find him. If Lily had sent him back, or if he had had strength to go, Jenny would be alive. No matter that Jenny must have known the risk she was taking. No matter she should have known better. Joe would always see her as an innocent, always think that it had been the shock of finding them together that had caused her death.

Their love had become a demon of a thing to him, a fire that consumed not only their lives but also those of others with its awful heat. He had tried to put out its flame with the water of every sea, and now she was certain he would try to extinguish it in the conflagration of war. She heard a rumor that he had obtained a naval commission and had headed for Key West to join the North Atlantic fleet.

A kind of hysteria had seized the city. Even while everybody was dancing, they were talking about the Spanish fleet, which was said to be steaming toward the Atlantic coast. New Englanders were mounting cannon along the beaches, news reports said, and New Orleans, thinking of its proximity to Cuba, began to arm, too. Everyone told Lily she should wait until after the war to return to Martinique. In a few weeks it would be all over. Lily herself was in a quandary.

She longed to return to her baby, but she did not relish the prospect of being on a ship seized by the Spanish.

Torchlight parades began the week before Shrove Tuesday. Lily, a heroine of the moment because of *The Little Brothers,* was invited to sit with the mayor. But next to the mayor's grandstand was one for orphans, and there were the children from the convent where she had taught long ago, recognizing her and calling her name. She sat with them instead, remarking on how they all had grown and buying them a big sackful of pralines.

The day before Shrove Tuesday, Proteus, God of the Deep, rode through the city in a pink seashell, and Archer asked her if she would spend Mardi Gras day with him. She was surprised because she hadn't thought he liked that sort of thing. He had always preferred the elegance of ballroom waltzing to the coarseness of street dancing.

"I don't know, Archer. I always go to pray with the Poor Clares on Shrove Tuesday."

"Not this year, please."

He smiled at her in his old, winning way, and she agreed. A shift at the Blessed Sacraments was worth an indulgence, but Lily was so far from a state of grace that a mere indulgence ought to be worthless, anyway. Archer was in an unusually happy mood when he called for her early Tuesday morning and drove her down to Canal Street, where the lampposts were wearing masks.

"It's barely daylight, Archer," she complained.

"But we don't want to miss King Zulu's parade."

"All right, if I can keep my eyes open to see it. You'll have to buy me coffee first."

"Coffee, then. But do wake up! We're going to have a wonderful day. It will be something to remember always."

Something to remember. She began to understand, and patted his hand and tried to feel less sleepy. But when King Zulu arrived, surrounded by his spear-brandishing Bushmen, wearing his tin-can crown, and carrying his scepter of a loaf of French bread, Lily forgot to be tired and laughed and shouted with the rest of the crowd. The black king of Carnival burlesqued the white festivities, throwing coconuts and old shoes from his royal float as the throng moved with the parade from bar to bar.

She worried about Archer at first. How could he start to drink so early in the day? But after the first stop or so, he didn't take any more, but joked among the black warriors and baby-doll-costumed women until King Zulu cried, "I abdicates!" and amid great hilarity plonked his crown onto Archer's head for him to try.

At noon, Rex, King of Carnival and Lord of Misrule, paraded, preceded by a masked captain on horseback, wearing a velvet cape and white-plumed helmet. Behind Rex came the great bands of Carnival and floats drawn by white-garbed mules led by black men in red turbans. Archer took her to dinner and then to the Sazerac Bar, which opened to women only on Mardi Gras. Then it was time for the parade of Comus.

The streets glowed with lights of Carnival purple, green, and gold; and torches made eerie waffling shadows as pirates, animals, devils, and cowboys cavorted. Archer produced sequined masks for himself and Lily and led her out to dance.

"Oh, Archer," she said suddenly. "I am going to miss New Orleans!"

"Hush, Lily, don't think of it. You'll come back someday."

She shook her head. The night had the air of a finale of more than Carnival. It seemed that an era was ending—not only for her, but for many who were dancing tonight who would go to war and never return to see another Carnival. Catching the beat of the drums, she thrust the idea away to lie with her sad remembrances of Joe and that other Carnival where she had danced long ago on Martinique.

Jays and mockingbirds were beginning to sing when he took her home to Snowdown. "May I come in, Lily?" he asked. "There's something I want to show you, if you're not too tired."

"Come in, then," she answered. She was indeed very tired, and she almost didn't care what was in the brown-paper-wrapped parcel he took from the back of the carriage. As she lay back exhausted on the sofa, he kissed her on the lips like a lover, and she was afraid for a moment that he wanted to try to begin their marriage again. Then, with a laugh, he told her he would be back in a moment, and went upstairs. She smiled to herself, sure that the package contained a Carnival costume that he had been too self-conscious to wear.

She drowsed off, to be awakened by his shaking her. Her eyes blinked open to the sight of him in a blue army uniform.

"Archer! But you? You are not . . ."

A blaze in his eyes warned her not to say more. "I can fight for Cuba as well as any man! I am going as your champion! Haven't I watched you appeal to men to fight for freedom every night for months? And I have had to stand idly by while Joe did all the deeds of glory. But now my time has come!"

"Archer, I don't want . . ."

But suddenly he was his old teasing self. "I'm bound for Tampa now. Aren't you going to tell me to come back with my shield or on it? No? Well, I shall do it anyway. Good-bye, Lily. Thank you for today." He blew her a kiss, and while she was still trying to decide what to do, he was gone.

She called Giles and woke him up. "Giles, do you know what Archer has done?"

"Taken up arms. I heard."

"Well, can't you do something, for heaven's sake?"

"Of course, if you want me to. I have only to tip off someone, you know. He'd be ousted at once if they found out he was my kind. Do you want me to do it?"

"No." She hung up resignedly. Having failed to prove himself a man in her bed, he was going to attempt to prove himself another way. She could only let him try.

She started wearily down the hall to bed, but sobs from Susan's room stopped her. "May I come in?" she called.

"You might as well, sis. An hour ago there'd have been good reason not to, but he's gone now."

Lily opened the door and saw her friend sprawled elegantly on the bed, her fiery hair mussed, the hoop skirt of an antebellum Carnival costume riding up to show her pretty thighs. But Lily noticed none of this as quickly as she noticed the ring with the oval diamond on Susan's finger.

"That did not come from a float!" she cried.

"No," sobbed Susan, "but it did come from the same man."

"The one who gave you the bracelet."

Susan nodded. "He asked me to marry him when he comes back from the war. What will he say when he finds out I can't marry him in church? Oh, Lily, I knew better, and now I've done it—fallen in love, like you! Damn Henry!"

"He'll settle for City Hall, if he loves you. And if you're worried he won't come back, that's silly. Joe said the war would amount to nothing."

"Everybody *is* saying that, aren't they?" Susan said, brightening. "Oh, there was a telegram for you, Lily, from Edmond."

She could think of nothing but Mimi as she tore open the

telegram with the Martinique dateline, but the message was not about the child. "Lily, I can't hold out any longer. Send cash quickly. Edmond."

He had never truly regained himself, and the hope that she would marry him must have eddied away with the months. Perhaps he had even let things degenerate, hoping that the saving of the land would be a bond between them as it had in the beginning. Spanish fleet or not, she must risk going to Martinique. The next day she packed a bag, and having arranged for a transfer of cash, said farewell to New Orleans.

9

On shipboard the talk was of nothing but the Spanish fleet. People hung over the railing staring off at the horizon, and hardly an hour passed that someone didn't cry that he had sighted what later turned out to be a fishing vessel or even a formation of low-lying clouds. At first Lily rushed to the rail with each alarm. Somewhere Joe was out there with Admiral Sampson's fleet, searching for the elusive enemy that had been reported to be everywhere from Newfoundland to Trinidad. She spent hours staring off into the distance, until at last she sighted, not the dark hulks of the Spanish Navy, but the purple and lilac heights of Pelee, yellow-banded, like a magnificent madras, by a rising sun. Palms curved out to meet her from the black beach of volcanic sand, and a blue glow rose like a halo from the water. Home! She could hardly wait to get to Acelie, and she kept urging the driver to go faster over the mountain roads.

She had never seen Acelie as dejected as it looked that morning, as mountain whistlers and hummingbirds flew among the bougainvillea and silk-cotton, and a parrot scolded coarsely in a breadfruit tree. The windows were all shuttered against the breeze, and the rockers, which had always been themselves like a human presence to welcome her, were gone from the veranda. She had expected the house to be open, of course. She had wired Edmond she was coming.

Most of the *ajoupas* were shuttered, too. The gardens of yams, couscous, and camanioc seemed as untended as the desolate canefields and banana trees twined with encroaching liana vines. She scared up a chicken or two among the workers' huts and then came to an old grandmother tending a baby.

"Where is everyone?" she asked.

"All gone, missy," came the answer in sweet, native French.

"Gone?"

"Looking for work. This place was sold."

"Auctioned!" she cried in horror.

"Yes, missy. Monsieur Edmond said so. We did not know who bought it."

"He never came here?"

"No, missy."

She walked the way to Beau Clair, noting the state of neglect, even on the larger estate. Auctioned! How could Edmond have let it happen? It was as well for him that he was not at Beau Clair when Lily reached it. There was only Cyrillia to greet her and to point out a beautiful toddler with blue eyes and cinnamon curls playing with Cyrillia's children. Mimi looked at her mother seriously when she picked up her daughter to kiss her. Her little lip thrust out, and she held back tears.

"She will come to know you, missy!" Cyrillia laughed.

"Yes. Oh, Rilla! She is so like Joe! Rilla, what has happened to Acelie? How can it be that it was auctioned?"

"Edmond didn't work it anymore. Or even Beau Clair. Not the way he used to. He doesn't care about anything. He said that he was tired of keeping his promise to you, when you had so long forgotten yours to him. If you could only have married him again!" Her dark eyes filled up with tears.

"Rilla, who bought it?" Lily demanded.

"Some American gentleman. I don't know his name."

She arranged to rent a house in St. Pierre and moved there with Mimi and a native nurse Cyrillia had recommended. She inquired at the bank to learn the name of the person who now owned Acelie.

"The gentleman asked that his name not be disclosed," she was told.

"Oh, but that's absurd. I have a right to know who bought my property. I want to try to repurchase it."

Still they wouldn't tell her, and she wondered how much the buyer had paid to remain mysterious. And why? Why on earth did Acelie's new owner wish to stay in the shadows?

"Edmond Beau Clair will tell me," she threatened. She was certain she could make Edmond tell her, but she did not want to have to face him.

"Monsieur Beau Clair does not know either," came the answer.

She would find out. Sooner or later the name would appear in a deed book. Then one day a note arrived for her in an expensive cream-colored envelope. Inside, the letter from the banker told her that Acelie's buyer wanted to see her. She was to call on him at his hotel. Her heart leaped. Had Acelie's buyer had second thoughts about acquiring the home of a "widow" and her child? Or had he discovered she was wealthy and decided to try for a fine profit? Well, she would give him that! Charged with hope, she descended the sea road from her house on Morne d'Orange. Instinctively her gaze turned toward the roadstead, searching among the ships for the *Sea Bird*, which could never be there. But today there was a ship that made her gasp and stop to look more closely.

"Dear Mary! There is a ship with a Spanish flag!" It was not a passenger ship, either, not with those cannon! She stared again at the great silk standard waving bloodred against the sky, its edges trimmed with gold. It must be some vision of the tropic morning, she thought, but the ship remained as she descended, seeming to float in the sky as her way led down a street of zinc-roofed houses, where the sea line cut the blue space at the level of the upper stories.

Hurrying down the mosaic-tiled sidewalk, she came close enough to see the line of coaling girls moving gracefully toward the Spanish vessel. Coaling! Could the rest of the fleet be far behind? She shaded her eyes to look seaward and saw shapes against the horizon. They were here at Martinique, all of them! In an instant she had forgotten her errand concerning Acelie, and picking up her skirts, she ran for the telegraph office.

Inside it was dim and quiet at a time when it seemed to her every line should be clattering. "I want to send a message to President McKinley," she gasped, and from somewhere a knife shot out and plucked a little rosette from her summery dimity dress. She wheeled indignantly and looked into the barrel of a Mauser rifle.

"We must not disturb the president today, *señora*," said a voice softly.

Of course! She should have taken time to think that they would be guarding this place! One of them grabbed for her and put his hands over her mouth. She dealt him a swift kick and twisted away, darting out through a side door. Glancing back, she saw that they weren't going to be content to oust her from the telegraph office. They were following!

Dear heaven, what did they intend to do with her? The moment of rage was past now, and she was frightened. She darted into a narrow street, knowing that at least she had the advantage on them, since she knew the city. But where could she hide? Her rented house was a long way, and she did not want to risk bringing murderous Spaniards down on little Mimi.

Then she remembered the hotel where Acelie's buyer was waiting to see her. Quickly she headed for it, with the Spaniards close behind. She lost them in the twisting streets, gained the hotel, and ran inside, not pausing in the lobby to ring for the gentleman and ask to have him called down, as a lady should.

Straight up the stairs she ran, hoping against hope that none of the Spaniards had seen which building she had entered. Urgently she banged on the door that had the number she had been given. When it opened, she was stunned, seized with an impulse to turn back to meet the Spanish.

"Lily. Do come in. It's been quite a while."

She made up her mind, and stepping inside, closed the door behind her. Acelie's buyer grinned with success.

"Henry Wickersham! I don't believe it!"

"Of course you don't, my dear. You've been too busy being famous and kicking linen with Joe Beau Clair to notice what I've been up to. But when I want something, I get it eventually, and I've always wanted you. You wouldn't share my mansion on Coliseum Square, but maybe you'll live with me at Acelie, now that I've divorced Susan. Such a drear little place, Acelie. But since it's what you want, I'm amenable."

Henry's face was redder than usual with tropic heat. His collar was unfastened and standing away from his twill French shirt, and she could see the pulsing of a vein in his thick neck as he regarded her lustfully. He seemed drunk from the effects of a bottle of white rum beside the bed.

"You can't mean marry you, Henry!"

He chortled gleefully. "What else? I've been keeping an eye on your affairs on Martinique for years. And now I'm going to have you. I'll make you sorry for the tricks you played on me!"

"I'm sorry already. And I won't marry you. You are still married, in the eyes of the church. And I am married to Archer Snow. Sell Acelie back to me, Henry. It's no use."

"Archer Snow!" Henry waved a hand. "That is not a marriage."

She was aghast. She loved Acelie more than anything. She could not stomach having it in his filthy hands. "I'll give you twice what you paid for it," she offered.

"No, no, it's not for sale," he chirped delightedly. "If you won't marry me for it, offer me something else I'd like."

She cocked an ear and heard a disturbance downstairs—feet clattering, voices calling in Spanish. She was trapped here! He took advantage of her moment of distraction to seize her and press his mouth hard against hers. She squirmed and struck at him, but her efforts only seemed to please him.

"I've waited a long time for a sample of you!" he declared, and flung her onto the brass bed, which shrieked itself like a ravaged woman as he added his heavy weight atop her.

"Stop it, Henry! I'll scream. There are Spanish sailors following me, and I would rather have them violate me than you!"

"Spanish sailors! On Martinique! You'll have to do better than that, Lily. I'll rape you at least, if you won't marry me. I won't fall for another of your tricks." He laughed and pulled up her skirts. She heard footsteps coming and began to scream in Spanish, *"Socorro!"*

It was only an instant before the door slammed back, and dark and dangerous, they surrounded the bed. "That is no way to treat a lady, *señor*," one advised in exactly the tone he had used to tell Lily not to disturb the president.

But Henry had waited long enough to have Lily. He had gone to so much trouble, and now everything was spoiled again. Desire and drink were heavy upon his soul, and these Spanish sailors could be nothing more than a delusion of the liquor. He cursed and struck out at them, thinking of a little derringer he had hidden in his bags. "Get out! Get out, you bastards!"

The room was shattered with the sound of a rifle fired at close range, and Lily, her senses numbed and shaken, screamed again as he fell back across her, as if even in death his lust for her had not deserted him. A Spaniard had hold of her arms. She fought, certain they were about to finish what Henry had started.

"Get up! Get up, *señora*," he said. "Don't stain your dress with the life's blood of that *quita*, that bird dung!"

She let them help her then. She was unsteady on her feet as they took her outside. "What are you going to do with me?" she thought to say as they reached the landing. "Aren't you going to kill me, too?"

"No. But you are going with us."

"Why? Someone else will give your position away when you leave here. I have a child—"

"Someone will wire our position, but at least it won't be you, Lily Beau Clair! You've caused enough trouble for Spain! Don't you remember me, Lily?" The Spanish officer swept off his hat.

"Captain Rodríguez!"

"We have both come a long way since we met in New Orleans after a performance of *The Little Brothers*. But you are going to thank me for saving you in a proper way. You are going to be a sort of talisman. It will lift the morale of the fleet to know who we've captured!"

By nightfall they were on their way to Cuba.

"Susan, Henry is dead and you can marry your soldier in church if he returns," she thought, and wished she could send that telegram, at least.

10

Joe Beau Clair saw no reason not to volunteer for a hazardous mission. It did not bother him, either, that there were plenty of men who felt he wasn't worthy to go. That was as it should be. He had lost the *Mimi* and her crew. But that itself was the reason he must be with the scuttling crew of the collier *Merrimac*. He had helped to set the dynamite, and now in the dark of night he had bribed his way aboard the cantankerous old tub that was soon to be sunk under the nose of the Spanish fleet in Santiago harbor.

"Putting the cork in the bottle," everybody called it. Hurricane season was coming, and Admiral Cervera must be counting on that to blow the American ships away from each other so that he could come out. The *Merrimac*, scuttled across the harbor's channel, would put an end to that. It would be a decisive blow for Free Cuba, and Joe, his adventurer's blood stirred, could not be left out. Maybe all the ghosts of the *Mimi* would be proud of him tonight. Maybe the ghosts of Jenny and her unborn child.

Some would have said that a child who had never lived could not have a ghost, but Joe knew better, for it haunted him day and night. He had hoped to lose these spectral companions in Cuba, but the sight of the long blue ridge on the horizon, its flowing blue and green hills merging into amethyst mountains, had done nothing to banish them. Nor had the knowledge that the Spanish fleet lay inside the harbor, its entrance almost indistinguishable from the jungle around it. On the ridges and hills he had seen the little Spanish *fuertes*, the blockhouses, built for protection against General García's insurgents, and the pink ocher of the old Morro, which, loaded with modern guns as well as bronze cannon, defended the city of Santiago. Joe was tired of this game of cat and mouse they had been playing all over the Caribbean. He was tired of this blockade. He, a Frenchman, had not joined the U.S. Navy to take part in a mere blockade.

Lily would be proud of him—the thought filtered in, and he tried ineffectually to deny the ache in his body and soul. He had wronged his own brother when he had made love to her on Montserrat, when his feet had burned their way to her bed as if of their own will. But even then he had thought it would only be one fevered night. He had never guessed she would follow him to New Orleans.

Lily behaved with a passion that made her unpredictable; it was the reason he loved her and the reason that that love was his special demon. If he could have admired her from afar as his brother's wife or loved her without responsibility as a coaling girl, it might have been all right. But he could not love her either of those ways. Lily was always presenting challenges; his blood was always hot with the thought of her.

Never again. It was the promise he had made the ghosts. The sailors of the *Mimi*, and Jenny, who had innocently been his penance for the lost ship, herself an anchor that had failed to hold. The baby—he sighed and wished he knew if it would have been a boy or girl. If he had asked, he could at least grieve for a son or daughter. He would never have a child now, he supposed, and he felt the loss. Lily had been right when she had said he needed children.

Hobson knew he was coming tonight, and that was what was important. Hobson had command, and the others, if they recognized him in the dark, could do little about it. He knew Santiago harbor better than any of the rest, having himself run this channel many a moonless night on his missions to the Cuban rebels. Hobson had said he should navigate.

"Straight north," Joe said. "Steady." He had stripped away his shirt and shoes against the time when he would swim for the lifeboat, and now he lay on the deck as Hobson had ordered everyone to do to reduce the chance of being hit by enemy fire.

They were making good time, not like last night, when they had been delayed by a press boat that had lost its bearing and had had to turn back before dawn revealed them to the Spanish. Making nine knots, the old ship moved silently on its way to its end. Joe searched the shore for landmarks and saw light shining through a cleft in the hills. Punta Estrella—Star Point. Somewhere over there in the utter darkness was the Morro, its guns ready to shower death. Water foamed below the surface where the *Merrimac*'s anchors were dragging; below, the engines hummed distantly. It was so quiet he could hear the sound of the bow wave. They changed course to the west.

They were beneath the Morro itself. Joe could see the awful, looming shadow against the sky now, and he tasted excitement; a honeyed sweetness almost tangible lay in his mouth, spread in deep, hot currents through his body, mixing with his blood, dissolving into the essence that was Joe at his finest. The ghosts that rode the collier with him were quiet now, awed into submission. The ache for Lily subsided as though he had taken a powerful drug.

There was an explosion, and he saw her face in a blast of fire. A picket boat off Canones Point, he guessed, cursing. It had missed, but now the enemy was alerted. Cannon belched from the Morro, answered by batteries on shore and from somewhere across the channel.

"Now!" Joe yelled. "Now!"

They were almost in position. They were going to make it. Hobson was signaling to stop the engines. Joe grabbed an ax and swung himself into the hold to help hack off the seacocks. Topside again he heard a shout, "The rudder! They've shot off the rudder!"

Out of control, the *Merrimac* was careening up the channel, past the spot where it should block it. An entire regiment seemed to be shooting at them from each side of the channel. The order came for the scuttling torpedoes to be fired, but only number one and number five had not been shot away by the enemy, their battery packs ruined by shells and flying fragments. Then came an enormous shock, and the bow of the *Merrimac* rose straight up. They had hit a Spanish mine! Everybody cheered, no matter that the lifeboat had been destroyed. The Spanish had outsmarted themselves and sunk the *Merrimac* in time!

But no, the old collier was not sinking fast enough! It was going on up the channel, carrying its crew beneath the fire of batteries on Socapa Point. They heard the din of rapid-fire guns and revolving cannon, the roar of nine-inch mortars. Spanish ships were in front of them, blistering the spar deck and the deckhouse. They were being carried into the very jaws of the Spanish fleet!

"Goddamn, we've become the whole war!" Joe thought, and feeling an odd thirst in the heat of the gunfire, he drank heavily from his canteen.

The cruiser *Reina Mercedes* was in front of them, and the crew nourished a last hope of being sunk before the

Merrimac reached open water. But the ship swung farther away from the intended scuttling point, and as torpedoes struck her, went down bow-first.

Joe was washed over the bulwarks, then swept back as water rushed over the deck. Blood was dripping from a wound in his forehead where the percussion of a cannonball had knocked him against a winch, as he began to breaststroke toward a catamaran adrift above the wreckage. Failed. All for nothing. Joe stroked slowly, drawing breath deliberately, glad that he had become such a strong swimmer in his youth on Martinique. The Spanish guns were quiet now; there would be sharks, though. A fin cut the water near him, and he threw a wet revolver to frighten the creature. Perhaps better after all to be dinner for a shark. Then the ghosts would be quiet. But he would not have liked to admit, even to himself, that it was the thought of never seeing Lily again that made him struggle on.

"Were there any survivors? Please tell me!"

"Dance with me, and I will."

"You are a beast, Captain Rodríguez!"

"No, no, Lily. You must save such language for when you really need it. That man who was trying to rape you in St. Pierre was a beast. I am merely a man who wants a dance. You have been refusing me all this time!"

"You are a man who took a mother from her child. That is the kind of man you are!" she blazed.

"Don't be so dramatic. Your child is safe with her native nurse. You didn't mind being away from her while you provoked war in New Orleans. Now that you've had your way, you ought to be around to see the consequences."

"I'll see a glorious victory for the Americans, Captain!"

"No doubt. If yellow fever doesn't fight on the Spanish side. Our fleet is no match for the *Yanquis*, despite that little incident last night. Eat your dinner. That marvelous roast beef is to celebrate, and there'll be strawberries for dessert."

Lily pushed back her plate and dropped a linen napkin over it. No matter that the Spaniards had been courtly, feeding her in the officers' mess, seeing to her every need. No matter that Captain Rodríguez had given up his cabin to her. Tonight, at least, she would not eat. She would not share the victory feast. She knew the satisfaction her presence gave every sailor. They had captured the flower of insurgent womanhood, and it delighted them more than if they had sunk the battleship *Oregon*. At first Lily had thought they would taunt the Americans with her, but they had kept her quite to themselves. Perhaps when it was time to exchange prisoners, they would find her valuable.

But Lily would not dance with them. It had become something of a contest among the officers to see who could persuade her. But now Lily wanted to know about the Americans from the *Merrimac*. Only a handful of sailors from Sampson's fleet had made that daredevil ride, and yet she had little doubt that Joe had been one of them.

"One waltz, Captain, and you must tell me while we dance."

"You trust me that little?"

"I want to be sure you think of business and don't enjoy yourself too much while we are dancing."

"Ah, Lily, all right. I could fall in love with you, but that would be so futile. More futile than the Spanish Navy!"

He called for music, and a pair of concertinas struck up. He waltzed her around the dining room to the applause of his fellow officers. "Now, Lily, I'll tell you. They are safe, every one of them. It's a miracle that not a one was killed."

"Where are they now?"

"Imprisoned in the Morro. But treated like heroes. Admiral Cervera himself pulled some from the water. I'll tell you an odd coincidence. One had the same last name as you. Your brother, I suppose."

"No."

"I thought not. Nothing very brotherly in the way he called for Lily when they brought him delirious from the water. Not your husband, either—you were married to that Archer Snow—I don't imagine you'd tell me the secret. Would you like to see him?"

"Could I?"

"I'll arrange it. But you'll have to dance with me again."

In the morning a launch took Lily ashore at the Morro of Santiago de Cuba. She climbed a flight of stone steps past a courtyard with bloodstained walls, where Lily thought patriots must have been executed. She shuddered, went on, and was ushered into a little drawing room. She grew weak as limping footsteps came down the hall. She had not seen him since the night Jenny had died, and she had no indication that he wanted this visit. He might curse her, for all she knew.

But when he came in, he merely gaped at her in astonishment, and she was so overjoyed to see him that she entirely forgot their estrangement and ran into his arms, which he opened instinctively to hold her. "Lily, whatever are you doing here?" he cried.

"The same thing as you. I mounted a mission that failed. Mine was in a telegraph office."

"On Martinique? The *Havard* sent the news, finally. I wondered if you were there. We're two of a kind, Lily. We can't stay out of trouble!" He smiled at her, and she trembled.

"Joe, what's going to happen now? Will you try to escape?"

He laughed. "From the Morro? I'm not that much of a fool! But never mind. The days of General Weyler are over. There is not as much barbarism now. And I am the prisoner of Admiral Cervera, who lives for honor."

"Joe, when the war is over . . ."

His smile vanished as he read her meaning. "No, Lily. We are not a good match, you and I."

"Not a good match! But you said we are alike!"

"That is exactly why we aren't good together. One bonfire doesn't need another. Perhaps you should think of returning to Edmond. He is still waiting, I'm sure."

"It has never worked, this staying apart!" she cried. "Can't you see, it's what causes all the trouble."

She would have argued more, but the guard came and told them their time was over. "I won't be coming home to you when the war is over, Lily," Joe told her as he was led away.

His ghosts were still with him, and who was to say that what they whispered was not right? Only Lily, who wasn't sure herself and who wasn't ennobled by having died while carrying his child. Alive, Jenny had never really possessed him. Dead, she had claimed his very soul. She had him at last, clever Jenny, though she had gone to her grave for it.

Lily tried to put Joe out of her mind, listening each day to all she could about the movements of the American forces. First she thrilled to the news that the marines had captured Guantánamo Bay, and then one morning someone lent her field glasses to watch a line of transports steaming past Santiago harbor. "Giving us a show," the Spaniards said.

Next she heard that there had been a successful landing at Daiquirí, and wondered if Archer had been with those volunteers.

There was deep gloom now in the officers' dining room;

nobody asked Lily to dance. Captain Rodríguez told her there was a rumor that when the fall of Santiago was near, the fleet would be ordered out to face the Americans.

"But why?" Lily asked. "Is there a chance you could win a battle?"

"Not a prayer. We will have to steam single-file through the channel under American fire."

"Oh, that's ridiculous! Why don't you all refuse to do such a stupid thing?"

"The government thinks it's better to let the Americans destroy the fleet than for them to capture it. We will do as we are ordered, and try to do it bravely. There will be much dying. I am going to have you put ashore where you will be safer."

They made an occasion of her leaving, though every man knew why she was being sent away. A band played, and the sailors lined the decks to cheer. Captain Rodríguez kissed her hand and thanked her for her visit, and forgetting they were the enemy, she waved her handkerchief back at the doomed men as the launch moved off.

She was relieved to be on land in the pretty town of Santiago, with its narrow streets of balconied houses. From the roof garden of the army officer's house where she was quartered she could see the opera house, and diagonally across from it, priests strolling before the grilled gates of the Archbishop's Palace. Cuban children played in the fountains of the plazas, and down by the docks the corrugated roofs of empty cargo sheds gleamed in the sun. Soldiers were everywhere in their blue-and-white uniforms and their broad-brimmed straw hats with the red-and-yellow insignias. But nobody seemed to think much about Lily's being on the opposite side, and they even talked in front of her about fortifying a place called El Caney. In no time she discovered that her maid was a rebel.

"*Señora*, would you like to escape to American lines?" the girl asked as she turned down the covers on the cane-plume mattress.

Escape! Do what was impossible even for Joe! "Oh, I should love it!" she whispered. "But how? The city is surrounded by Spanish troops."

"It will be easy. They'll let you through with the bullets for the insurgents."

"With the *bullets for the insurgents!*"

"*Cállese!*" The girl put a finger against her lips. "The bullets for the Mausers. Don't you know about that? The rebels kill Spanish soldiers and take their rifles, but they don't have enough ammunition to fit, so that is what the prostitutes do for the cause. They charge cartridges for their favors. From a regular soldier they ask a hundred; from an officer, a thousand. Then the wood-seller goes from house to house and collects all the bullets and hides them in his cart. The soldiers all know him. They always let him through. If they stopped him, they would stop the good times, too."

"They actually do that, knowing that the rebels will use the bullets to try to kill them?"

"Yes, that is the way some men are. They will die for their filthy pleasure if they have to. Do you want to go with tonight's shipment? Tomorrow there will be a battle . . ."

The Spanish blockhouses were silhouetted against the dusk on every hill as she rode out of town with the cartload of bullets, wearing white pantaloons and shirt that the maid had supplied. Nobody challenged the wood-seller or his cart. Nobody challenged her. Beyond, above a rolling jungle, she saw the fires of the American troops.

Entering a tangle of liana and banana trees, they forded a creek under an arch of bamboo, and immediately were surrounded by Cubans, each carrying a machete and burlap bandoliers. *"Quién pasa?"* they challenged, and then, recognizing the cart, fell upon the ammunition. They were less certain what to do with Lily, who swept off her hat and told them she wanted to go through to the American lines. But then, in her broken Spanish, she told them who she was, and when they heard the name Beau Clair, they connected her quickly with Joe and the supplies from the *Sea Bird*.

"Where is Joe Beau Clair now?" they wanted to know.

"In prison in the Morro."

"We will get him out tomorrow. Tomorrow will be a great victory."

Riding a commissary mule among cooking pots and baskets, Lily Beau Clair, the toast of New Orleans theater, arrived in the American camp. Word of her presence spread along the lines, and Rough Riders, dismounted cavalry, and regulars took turns leaving their posts to have a look at her. For a while she sat in a colonel's dog tent while they discussed who should have the honor of escorting her to the rear. Then someone piped up, "Aren't you Mrs. Archer Snow? I know your husband. A damn good soldier for a volunteer. He was with the troops that came to the aid of the

Rough Riders when they were ambushed at Las Guismas. Fought at bayonet range and never turned a hair. You'll be wanting to find him. He's with General Hawkins, somewhere east of here."

There were a lot of volunteers to show her the way, and when one was assigned to her, she waded off again through the pitchy jungle, where crickets chirped and land crabs crackled in the underbrush, their five pairs of legs sounding like entire patrols of Spanish. Hours passed as they journeyed from encampment to encampment. They found the Sixteenth Infantry and the Second Artillery. Though she supposed she didn't look very glamorous in her peasant outfit, everyone was delighted to see her. Teddy Roosevelt came out of a tent to shake her hand and congratulate her on the help she had been to the war effort. "If it hadn't been for the *Maine*, you might have started the war all by yourself with *The Little Brothers*, like Harriet Beecher Stowe." He chuckled, and Lily shivered, not sure she felt complimented. It was all too near, now. The feel of battle hung heavily in the humid night.

Roosevelt called someone over and introduced her to J. Stuart Blackton of the Vitagraph Moving Picture Company, who said he wanted to take pictures of the American troops in action. "I hope you aren't going too far to the rear, Mrs. Snow. I'll be looking for you to photograph. It'll be wonderful to have a woman! You can be binding up some poor private's wounds, and they'll love it back home!"

"I shall try not to be available, sir!"

Roosevelt laughed, finding it all very amusing.

She still hadn't found Archer, and she began to wonder if it might not be better if she didn't. She had heard the jokes that went along with her, about what memories he would have of tonight, even if a Spanish bullet found him in the morning. Only one man in all of the Cuban expedition could have a woman this night before battle—and it was the very man who did not need one! Maybe better if she did not remind him of his failures. He was in control, by all reports, for whenever she met someone who knew him, the word was always of his valor. "No scrimshanker, Lieutenant Snow!" everyone told her. Could it be that this battle would give him confidence to fight that other, more personal battle?

Reveille blew in the dark. Lily helped boil coffee on a Buzzacoat stove to go with hardtack and sowbelly. The dawn was a heavy gray; then, as though a page had been turned, the sky went blue. Parrots twittered in the trees as the bugle sounded Troops filed out of the chaparral, and with the colors encased in black oilcloth, marched into the road. Some soldiers thought they were headed for Havana; others thought they were going to march across the island. But Lily, who had come up that cactus-lined trail in the night, knew that it led to Santiago.

William Randolph Hearst galloped by, dressed in snappy civilian clothes, with a flat-brimmed straw hat with a scarlet hatband, and a scarlet tie to match. Lily tucked up her hair and tried to look like a peasant. She didn't want to be in the *Journal*, any more than she wanted to be in the Vitagraph movie. She stared at Hearst, thinking that it was he who had almost started the war, of course, without the help of the *Maine*. She was sure that Hearst had not been putting the profits of his yellow journalism into Cuban relief, either, as she had done with the proceeds from the play.

She began to hear the rat-a-tat of gunfire. There came a whine, and a little branch snapped from a tree and cartwheeled gracefully to the ground. "You'd better go farther to the rear, Mrs. Snow," someone suggested.

"Yes."

The wounded had begun to return, Cubans first, because they had been in the fore of the advance. One, who had given her the ride on the mule the night before, passed her, smiling at her from a sapling-slung hammock that dripped blood into the trail.

The movie crew came running back, white-faced and panting. Lily put an arm around a limping soldier and helped him down the path, away from the fighting toward the field hospital. She didn't know where the surgeons had set up, but that was unnecessary. One had only to follow the splotches of blood.

As the day wore on, she did what she could to help, and listened to the news the soldiers brought. A bright yellow observation balloon had gone up right over the path, marking it for the Spaniards. Four hundred men had died on that trail, especially at a place called Bloody Ford, where the blood of the dying had made slippery mud beside a creek. Then she learned of the charge of San Juan Hill that had broken the bottleneck. Kettle Hill, with its pot-shaped sugar-refining equipment, was also in American hands. El Caney had fallen, too, after bitter fighting, and the Americans had been horrified to learn that women and children had been in the village during the attack.

It seemed the day would never end. Ashy clouds of gunsmoke made a false twilight before night came, and at last the darkness settled, filled with the ghostly cries of wounded figures moving through the mist. She began to ask stragglers if they had seen Archer. Some said they thought he had been on San Juan Hill. Another told her that Archer had paved the way for an American advance, charging a blockhouse in the face of Spanish fire. Others began to confirm it. "It was a dangerous spot he was firing from, ma'am," they told her gently, trying to prepare her. But she would not believe that he was dead. She kept searching and asking through the night, and in the early-morning hours, as the sun began to heat the damp jungle, a pair of soldiers told her they had found him.

She threw down the bandages she had been unrolling and followed them to where he lay in a clutter of wounded and dead beneath a palm tree. Around his wrist was a doctor's tag listing wounds so horrible she could not even bear to finish reading them. She shuddered, knowing the rumor that the tags were put only on hopeless cases left to die. Archer opened his eyes and saw her.

"Oh, Lily, I am glad you found me. They told me that you were here."

"Be quiet, dearest," she murmured. "I will get some water and find a doctor."

"No." He put a hand on her arm. "Let the doctors work on those whom it will do some good. Not me, Lily. I have a tag."

"It doesn't mean what they say!" she cried, her voice breaking.

"Shh, Lily, don't spoil it. It's a beautiful way to die. In the long run it wouldn't work. But just now, you're proud of me."

His eyes searched hers for confirmation. "I am proud you are my husband, Archer," she whispered.

"Oh, Lily, I love you! I am the luckiest man in this war to have you with me while I die!"

She put her lips to his and felt his weak but ardent response. Then his head fell sideways, and he was dead.

11

She walked stoically back to the hospital tent and began to help again. At home she might have been prostrate with grief, but there did not seem to be time for that here, and she let her courage be tribute to Archer's gallant death.

Several days later she heard that the Spanish fleet had come out of the harbor and had been destroyed. It was then that Lily wept—for Archer and for all the brave Spanish sailors and all the Americans who had gone to their death for atrocities others had committed. Nobody could understand Lily crying over a victory. Didn't she understand it meant that there would have to be no new attack on Santiago? It was a good thing, too.

There was dysentery now, and yellow fever. Almost no food was coming through. Faces were lean and bellies bloated. The men wrote letters home, and because there were no envelopes, sewed them shut with thread. Already the ridge around Santiago had been dubbed Misery Hill. If the Spaniards held out, disease might win, but at last there was a truce. During it, the prisoners from the *Merrimac* were exchanged.

Lily, now wearing a uniform supplied her by a group of nurses from the *State of Texas,* stood with the troops that lined the road as the group drove out in a wagon pulled by six mules. There was a moment of silence first, and the soldiers took off their hats. Then there was cheering. She strained for a glimpse of Joe and saw him grinning on the wagon seat, his hair swirling into the breeze as he waved his hat and yelled at the mules to run faster toward the American lines.

If she called his name, he didn't hear her, but somehow he must have sensed she was there. Just as the wagon rolled past, he glanced at her. His face went stern for an instant; then he looked away and yelled at the mules again. She knew that he had meant what he had told her at the Morro, and at that moment she felt that the war ended, not several days later with the surrender.

She found her way back to Martinique, where she managed to repurchase Acelie from Henry Wickersham's estate. Joe had gone on with the American forces to Puerto Rico. Edmond almost never came to the plantation now, though she had forgiven him for having let Acelie slip through his fingers.

"I promised to keep it safe for you, Lily." He sighed.

"Oh, but that was long ago when we were to be married."

"That *was* long ago," he said sadly.

She had told him that Joe was alive, and since he still thought she had married Joe instead of Archer, she had put an end to any hope he had had of marrying her again.

"What is this rift between you and Joe?" he asked.

"Oh, the *Mimi*. He blames me for that. That is, he blames our love. That is not all he blames it for! It has unholy strength."

"Ah, my foolish brother! Would that I had the opportunity he wastes!"

"Would that I loved you, Edmond!"

"Hush, Lily. You would have if you could. We are at peace, you and I."

At peace. She supposed she was as close to it now as she was ever going to come. She rode about the plantation, overseeing the planting of new crops of cane and bananas. In the shade of silk-cottons she played with Mimi and told her stories about her papa, the way Cyrillia told her children native folk tales.

"When will my papa come?" Mimi always asked.

"I don't know. But you must learn to dance. Your papa loves to dance." She would take a banjo and strum a rhythm into the quiet day.

He had taken an oath never to return to Martinique years ago, when he had thought that Mimi, the coaling girl, had betrayed his love with the snake, the deadly fer-de-lance. He had never broken that vow. Would he ever? She supposed he knew she was here. If he didn't guess where she had gone, he had only to ask in New Orleans. It seemed to her that Giles wrote once a month, trying to tantalize her into some new venture, and she had kept close track of Susan, who had married her soldier and already given birth to a son. Singing was still in Susan's blood, and she wrote that she intended to sing at the French Opera again, as soon as she "got her figure back."

Lily smiled to think how little life seemed to have touched Susan, how unchanged she was, even in love. The day when she herself had battled Joe over her right to continue her career seemed far away. Her life in New Orleans seemed dreamlike, a fancy party she had been to, an excitement built of fantasy, irrelevant in the golden morning. She had no more use for it; it could be tossed aside like a sun-bleached madras.

Suddenly it was a new century, the year 1900. She looked out on the purple shadows of the mountains and thought they seemed smug with the knowledge of the ages. Her gaze fell on Mimi, playing beneath a ceiba tree with a Martinique doll that wore golden five-cylinder earrings. "This will be your century, Mimi," she thought.

Another year passed, and Teddy Roosevelt, still riding high on the glory of Cuba, became president. The Americans had taken over the Panama Canal project, and Lily heard that Joe was in Panama again, this time as one of Roosevelt's advisers. He was doing the things he liked best, and she imagined he was happy.

Had he conquered his love for her? She wanted more than anything to know. He was missing so much, not knowing he had a daughter, but she could not go to him and trap him with Mimi's existence. He would have to come home to them, home to Martinique to face her and the brother he had wronged. The year changed again, and it was Carnival time.

"Why don't you go, missy?" Cyrillia asked. "You have no papa to stop you now. I will make you a pretty dress, one with red flowers. Go and dance. You will find another man."

"No, Rilla. I don't want to go to Carnival. I don't think I'll ever want to go to Carnival again."

The season slipped away, and it was Easter. Pelee began to rumble ominously. Hibiscus blossoms, bougainvillea, and rose d'Inde were all covered in a hoary fall of ash. As she walked across the wintry lawns of Acelie, a mountain whistler fell at her feet, asphyxiated in its flight.

She ordered her workers to beat the snowy ash from the banana trees, but soon she abandoned the idea. Even the natives were all frosted white in the endless ashy twilight. The Roxelane had risen to a furious torrent, and all the other streams of the island had followed its example, the rampaging waters strewing wreckage along the way, rolling huge boulders down their powerful streams. Lily drove to Beau Clair and asked Edmond if it might not be better for all of them to leave Martinique.

"The experts say everything will be all right, Lily," he told her, and showed her a copy of St. Pierre's newspaper, *Les Colonies*, in which an expedition was announced for the curious to climb to the volcano's summit.

"Well, I suppose it would be silly to leave," she said. But at night the mountain kept her awake with its shaking and groaning. Her eyes burned from lack of sleep and from the blowing ash.

On the afternoon of May 5, Edmond rode in to ask if she had seen Cyrillia. "She was here this morning," Lily replied. "She was on her way to the sugar mill to see what had become of a load of cane from Beau Clair."

"Yes, I sent her to see," he said, his voice oddly strained. "How long did she stay here, Lily? Did she stay until noon?"

"No. She must have been at the mill by then."

"Oh, God!" Even through the haze she could see that he was very pale, and his hands trembled on the reins of his horse.

"Are you ill, Edmond? Come in, and I will fix you a *cocoyage*. These times are hard on us all."

He shook his head and did not dismount. "Oh, Lily! I have just learned that the sugar mill was swept away shortly after noon!"

"I will go with you to look for her!" Lily cried. She found a hat with a veil to give her some protection against the ash and sent a boy to saddle her mare. All along the way they stopped people coming from the other direction to ask if they had seen Cyrillia. Nobody had, and when told she had been at the sugar mill, they shook their heads in pity.

"*Monsieur*, if she was at the sugar mill, there is nothing you can do for her now!"

"*Monsieur*, go back and don't even look! Don't take a lady there!"

Lily and Edmond sensed the hopelessness without comprehending it, and they urged their horses faster toward the mill. Even in the worst disaster, there must be a chance—but then they saw the sugar mill.

A flood of boiling mud had been hurled from a fissure of the volcano. It had raced down the river to the sea, burying the mill so that its proud chimney was only a grave marker in a desert of seething black volcanic mud.

Impossible indeed to help her or even to recover her body. The beautiful *capresse* had been buried alive.

When they were back at Acelie, Edmond wept openly. "Oh, Lily, you were right! I loved her, and I never told her!"

"It's all right, Edmond. She knew it."

Only death had made Edmond realize how deeply he cared. Death had done what Cyrillia's native charms had not. Nothing could console him.

"Don't worry about the children, Edmond. I will take them to live at Acelie, the poor motherless dears."

But suddenly he seemed to gather himself. "No, Lily, you will not take them. They are motherless, but not fatherless! They are my children, and I will see to them. I will . . . adopt them, Lily. Rilla would like that, wouldn't she? I'll adopt them, and I'll make Beau Clair grand again for them!"

What Cyrillia's grandmother had begun when she had won her freedom was finished at last. The thing that Cyrillia had been so determined to do was accomplished.

Lily would have liked to leave the island after that. The flow of volcanic mud had unnerved her. But Edmond needed her in his grief, and for the time being Cyrillia's children did come to Acelie.

The paper, which she now sent for every day, was still saying that there was no danger from the volcano except along the rivers. She peered at the journal under the glow of the oil lamp as she read that most businesses in St. Pierre were still open. Ships were coming into the harbor, too, loading and unloading. The print swam before her eyes as she read the name of the newest arrival.

Sea Bird!

It must be some other ship of that name! She forced her eyes to focus again and read that the ship was out of New Orleans and just come from Panama. Her cry of joy brought Mimi running.

"What is it, Mama?"

"Nothing, love," she said. It would not do to tell Mimi yet. She must go to St. Pierre at once and find out if this meant he was coming home to her. He must not come to Acelie if he did not intend to stay.

When she set off the next morning, Pelee was roaring hoarsely. She passed cane and cacao bent to the earth with mud and ash, and she had to give way time and again to cattle and horses that were wandering aimlessly over the ash-coated road. The volcano itself was enveloped in an immense cloud. Thunder rolled over its summit, and lurid lightning streaked its smoking column.

Her horse was wheezing, having difficulty breathing the sulfurous air, and seeing that she must pause to preserve the animal, she stopped to pray at a roadside shrine, its white light gleaming, soft and feeble, against Pelee's glow.

The stricken look of St. Pierre shocked her as she looked down from the shrine. A blizzard of ash blew about the deeply coated streets, and the dazzling ocean water was filled with islands of debris swept down from fields and forests, and there were floating wastelands of pumice and jetsam.

Dear heaven! How could anyone think there was no danger? Out in the harbor she caught sight of the *Sea Bird*, and for the moment she forgot about the volcano. What was a mere volcano, compared with the ecstasy of seeing Joe again? She seized her mare's reins and flung herself recklessly up.

"It's only the same as always," she thought. "It's no worse today. I'm going down."

Why not? She had always gone where she wanted to go. To Carnival. To Montserrat. To New Orleans. She had been to many hells made by man. Now she would enter one made by a greater power.

She could see that there was panic in the city. People were crowding toward the Moulliage, the landing place, and several small steamers were setting out toward Fort de France, their decks crowded with refugees. She heard the great iron bell of the cathedral chime, and thousands hurried toward another sort of protection—it was Ascension Day, the day of Christ's rising to heaven, a day of holy obligation. She pressed her heels against the mare's side, and sent her galloping down the slope, the *Sea Bird*'s sails a beacon flag. In a few minutes she would be with Joe—in his arms, God willing.

Then the ground trembled, and the horse faltered. The volcano roared with mighty internal thunder, and a small white pennant floated out from the cone and drifted lazily on the gray morning sky.

A colossal blackness spilled out of the mountain, and the volcano beat like a giants' contest of *kas*, as the dark torrent swept toward the city. A terrible burning wind whipped over Lily as the mare reared and flung her to the ground. The shrine at which she had been praying shattered, and the head of the Virgin's statue rolled against her shoulder. She caught it and held it to her, shock making this desecration more horrifying than anything.

Volcanic lightning flashed as the coils of the appalling column expanded, plunging the city into an unnatural night. The saint's head in her hand was lost to her sight, and she did not know what had become of her horse. Suddenly there was light again, as a stream of fire beat down on St. Pierre, racing toward the sea, as if to consume it. Lightning flashed again, and from within the cloud came blinding explosions and rending detonations.

St. Pierre was a brazier, burning as though with one monstrous flame. Tiny figures ran darkly, then took fire and fell. The flame had raced into the sea itself, and every ship was afire. The ocean seemed to leap and boil, and where the *Sea Bird* had been, there was only fire, seeming to rise from the sea, as if the water itself were burning.

Instinctively she tried to run toward the fiery city, but the searing wind shoved her rudely back. She could not believe that Joe was alive. Nobody could be down there. She strained her eyes and saw that the valley were Acelie lay was a volcanic hell, a chaos of vapors shot with awful electrical scintillations.

"Mimi, oh, Mimi!" It could not be that this must be her final punishment! She tried desperately to go back the way she had come, but that way, too, lay in the path Pelee had chosen. Only the height of the ridge had prevented her being burned in the conflagration. Dazedly she took refuge under the roof of the shrine that had sheltered the Virgin, as a shower of brimstone pelted down. A torrential rain of mud followed the rockfall, beating palmetto and fern to the ground and splashing onto her even where she hid, clothing her with a grayish putty that made her look like a clay casting of herself.

She knelt for hours in a frozen daze, unable to move toward the city, unable to join the line of refugees that were fleeing from the surrounding countryside toward Fort de France. The sun came out, a dull red ball hanging over the harbor, showing the charred mast of the *Sea Bird* in a smoky haze. Northward, a malevolent ash fall obscured the sky, and Pelee itself was wound in a black shroud. No one had come out of St. Pierre. No one at all.

She saw a rescue boat approach, and then turn back, finding the way blocked by the awesome heat. Great thunderstorms burst over the surrounding mountains now, as though

God had decreed the fires should spread no farther. The icy deluge poured through the inadequate roof of the shrine, drenching her, and she shook with chills at the sudden change of temperature.

It must have been afternoon before she saw another rescue boat nearing the city. Men came ashore, the first human motion in the volcanic desert of still-smoldering ruins. She rose as if in a trance and began to walk down the slope. The heat grew and pressed down on her as she came closer. It seemed the only presence besides the rescue party, which, tragically, was finding no one to rescue.

Thirty thousand lay dead, as ash fell quietly, almost tenderly, onto their grotesquely postured bodies, most fallen on their faces, their hands over their noses and mouths in a futile attempt to avoid the asphyxiating vapors.

On the ruined beach Lily was aware of an incredible sense of loneliness. The streets merged into a vacant nothingness, completely devoid of color. Gone were the red roofs, the lemons and pinks and blues that had marked the city. The only building Lily could recognize was the cathedral, with its three arched doors still intact. Worshipers lay dead by the hundreds inside, buried mercifully in the continuing fall of ash. Outside, the park was jammed with untold numbers who had died beneath the shadow of the Cross, but somehow the great statue of the Virgin stood intact, overlooking the destruction.

At one extremity of the harbor, the river rushed madly seaward, crowned with a vapor of steam. Farther out, an American packet was still blazing, and everywhere charred bodies floated in the water. Lily could not bring herself to look at them. One might be Joe, any one of them, for now one looked no different from another.

She waded through the ash with a sense of unreality, touching a house front four feet thick which crumbled under her fingers. She saw the clock of the hospital, stopped historically at three minutes to eight, where time had ended for St. Pierre. Gone were the theater, the bright shops of Rue Victor Hugo, the Lycée, even the ballroom where she had danced the wicked *danse du pays*.

Her eyes fell on the body of a young child, its arms tight about its dead mother, who pressed it close against her. Her heart broke then, her soul as devastated as the ruined city. "Oh, Mimi! Oh, my darling! If only I could have held you like that when it came, I would have been content to die, too!"

Perhaps after all she had died; she had become a walking phantom of native lore. She left the city gates and walked toward Acelie, meeting survivors from the outlying districts, some trying to hurry away from the volcano's furious shadow, others struggling toward St. Pierre, bent on searches for loved ones that could only end in tragedy. Seeing the terrible expressions of doom on their faces, Lily knew they mirrored her own as she walked on toward home, toward the body of her child that she must at least find and hold.

They were all ghosts on this road, all of them, remnants of life that no longer existed. Whitely they moved, covered in grave clothes of ash, all colors of humanity as indistinguishable as the pastel tints of the buildings of St. Pierre. *Capresses* and Negresses, banana-skinned or white—who could tell? And who could tell which might be true ghosts and which the living dead?

The lane to Acelie was marked only by the still-blazing crowns of palmistes that had lined it, twin columns of torches to light her way through the dusky ash rain to the desolation beyond. Rays of hazy sun filtered weakly across her path as she came out before the ruins of the house that she had so loved, that she had promised her father she would save for generations to come. It was what she had been expecting, but the finality of it caught her unawares, and without the courage to look inside the crumbled walls, she dropped sobbing onto a fan-shaped flow of mud that covered the veranda steps.

The second floor was gone altogether, the nursery tumbled into the rooms below. Had Mimi been there, sleeping in her little balata-wood bed? It had been the time of day when she would have just been waking, calling to Lily to come and kiss her.

She must go and search, just as people were doing everywhere Pelee's mad tongue had passed, but she seemed to have become part of the wreckage. Beneath the mud covering her body, there was only more ash.

"Mimi! Oh, Mimi!" She felt the wail come from her departed spirit.

And another spirit answered, "Mama! Mama, where have you been? My papa's come home!"

She raised her head in wonder and saw her daughter running toward her. Behind the child hurried the tall figure she had never expected to see again, looking more glorious all hoary with cinders than when they had first danced together.

Holocaust

Lily's soul returned to her, forsaking a bleak hereafter for earthly paradise. Mimi's arms were around her, then Joe's were crushing her in an embrace that blotted away Pelee's destruction, obliterated the years she had done without him.

"Oh, Joe, I thought you were in St. Pierre!" she sobbed when she could speak.

"No. I was afraid *you* were! But no cataclysm can part us, Lily. It has been proved once and for all today. I have come home forever. I surrender to this love of ours!"

"As I did long ago," she murmured, safe in his arms. "But where is Edmond?" she cried suddenly, as Cyrillia's pretty children came running from somewhere in the ruins.

"Dead, Lily. My brother died at Beau Clair."

"But ... did you see him first? Did you fight?"

Joe smiled. "We fought. But not over you. He lectured me on the responsibilities of fatherhood and told me of the joy he had had in these children of his. I ought to look after my own, he said. Imagine my astonishment. I had come looking for one Mimi and found another. I went straight to Acelie and made the *bonne* let me in to see her, asleep in her bed. When she opened her eyes, I thought she might be afraid, but she smiled and held out her arms and called me 'Papa.'"

"I'm not surprised she knew you, Joe. I had told her of you so many times. And then?"

"Then the earth shook and I ran with her, calling the other children to follow."

"But where? Where could you have gone?"

"To the *case-à-vent*, Lily, the hurricane house. You remember—where once I nearly lost my life to the snake. We were inside only an instant before the whirlwinds hit. If the walls had not been so thick to withstand hurricanes, if there had ever been a window for the heat to enter, we would have been burned alive!"

"And now, Joe? What will we do now?"

"Now we must find a priest who will take time from the last sacrament for a happier duty."

It was growing dark when they reached the town of Morne Rouge, which Pelee's destruction had not touched. They walked through streets of little wooden cottages screened with banana trees, Indian reed, and pommiers roses, until, following a road lined in the dark red hedges of rose d'Inde, they found the church, a shrine where miracles were said to have been wrought. And to these miracles they added one more, their marriage.

They remained in town for several happy days, and then Joe, listening to Pelee's rumbling, declared that it was not safe and took the family across the island to the sweet isolation of Grande Anse, where once he had swum away from her through the great surf to his banana boat.

It was there at the end of the summer she told him she was pregnant again.

"Joe, I would like to rebuild Acelie someday," she said as she saw his face light at the news.

"Yes. I wouldn't have it any other way. I am not the sort of man Edmond was, but I know that I need a home. We will rebuild Beau Clair, too."

"Edmond's plan for his children," she guessed.

"Yes."

A few days later Pelee spewed its devastation again, and Morne Rouge, where they had been married, was destroyed. She found Joe packing a valise.

"What are you doing?" she asked.

"I am a free man again, Lily. The church in Morne Rouge is gone, and the marriage records have been lost."

She gaped at him in horror and made him laugh. "I do not like being a free man, my love. I have learned a lesson from my brother about unrecorded marriages. There is no priest here at Grande Anse, so go and make ready. I have a ship waiting. What do you say to Montserrat, where first we bedded together?"

The island with the slender palms where she had lain in Joe's arms and understood what love was. She smiled as she thought of it. "Are we to be married again?" she asked.

"Yes. And again and again, if need be. I would marry you a thousand times to have you mine, Lily Beau Clair!"

"And I you, Joe!"

Her heart beat like a Carnival drum when he kissed her.

ABOUT THE AUTHOR

Gimone Hall was raised in Texas and lives in Bucks County, Pa., where she is working on a new novel. Married to a writer, she has two young children. Previously, she has written gothics and an historical romance.

Other SIGNET Bestsellers You'll Want to Read

- ☐ **MISTRESS OF OAKHURST—Book II** by Walter Reed Johnson. (#J8253—$1.95)
- ☐ **OAKHURST—Book I** by Walter Reed Johnson. (#J7874—$1.95)
- ☐ **OF DAVID AND EVA: A Love Story** by Gertrude Samuels. (#E8262—$1.75)*
- ☐ **I, JUDAS** by Taylor Caldwell and Jess Stearn. (#E8212—$2.50)
- ☐ **THE RAGING WINDS OF HEAVEN** by June Shiplett. (#J8213—$1.95)*
- ☐ **THE TODAY SHOW** by Robert Metz. (#E8214—$2.25)
- ☐ **HEAT** by Arthur Herzog. (#J8115—$1.95)*
- ☐ **THE SWARM** by Arthur Herzog. (#E8079—$2.25)
- ☐ **BEWARE MY HEART** by Glenna Finley. (#W8217—$1.50)*
- ☐ **I CAME TO THE HIGHLANDS** by Velda Johnston. (#J8218—$1.95)*
- ☐ **BLOCKBUSTER** by Stephen Barlay. (#E8111—$2.25)*
- ☐ **BALLET!** by Tom Murphy. (#E8112—$2.25)*
- ☐ **THE LADY SERENA** by Jeanne Duval. (#E8163—$2.25)*
- ☐ **SHADOW OF A BROKEN MAN** by George Chesbro. (#J8114—$1.95)*
- ☐ **LOVING STRANGERS** by Jack Mayfield. (#J8216—$1.95)*
- ☐ **BORN TO WIN** by Muriel James and Dorothy Jongeward. (#E8169—$2.50)*
- ☐ **THE HOURGLASS MAN** by Carl Tiktin. (#E8083—$1.75)
- ☐ **TWO DOCTORS AND A GIRL** by Elizabeth Seifert. (#W8118—$1.50)
- ☐ **LOVERS IN A WINTER CIRCLE** by Jonathan Kirsch. (#E8119—$1.75)*
- ☐ **JULIE** by Florence Stevenson. (#J8121—$1.95)*

*Price slightly higher in Canada

Have You Read These Bestsellers from SIGNET?

- [ ] ROGUE'S MISTRESS by Constance Gluyas. (#E8339—$2.25)
- [ ] SAVAGE EDEN by Constance Gluyas. (#E8338—$2.25)
- [ ] WOMAN OF FURY by Constance Gluyas. (#E8075—$2.25)*
- [ ] BEYOND THE MALE MYTH by Anthony Pietropinto, M.D., and Jacqueline Simenauer. (#E8076—$2.50)
- [ ] CRAZY LOVE: An Autobiographical Account of Marriage and Madness by Phyllis Naylor. (#J8077—$1.95)
- [ ] THE SERIAL by Cyra McFadden. (#J8080—$1.95)
- [ ] HARMONY HALL by Jane Meredith. (#E8082—$1.75)
- [ ] THE INCE AFFAIR by Joseph Morella and Edward Z. Epstein. (#E8177—$1.75)
- [ ] DAMIEN—OMEN II by Joseph Howard. (#J8164—$1.95)*
- [ ] THE OMEN by David Seltzer. (#J8180—$1.95)
- [ ] THE RULING PASSION by Shaun Herron. (#E8042—$2.25)
- [ ] TWINS by Bari Wood and Jack Geasland. (#E8015—$2.50)
- [ ] CONSTANTINE CAY by Catherine Dillon. (#J8307—$1.95)
- [ ] WHITE FIRES BURNING by Catherine Dillon. (#J8281—$1.95)
- [ ] THE WHITE KHAN by Catherine Dillon. (#J8043—$1.95)*
- [ ] FEAR OF FLYING by Erica Jong. (#E7970—$2.25)
- [ ] HOW TO SAVE YOUR OWN LIFE by Erica Jong. (#E7959—$2.50)*
- [ ] KID ANDREW CODY AND JULIE SPARROW by Tony Curtis. (#E8010—$2.25)*
- [ ] THE MESSENGER by Mona Williams. (#J8012—$1.95)
- [ ] WINTER FIRE by Susannah Leigh. (#E8011—$2.25)*

* Price slightly higher in Canada

NAL/ABRAMS' BOOKS
ON ART, CRAFTS AND SPORTS
in beautiful, large format, special concise editions—lavishly illustrated with many full-color plates.

- [ ] **THE ART OF WALT DISNEY: From Mickey Mouse to the Magic Kingdoms** by Christopher Finch. (#G9982—$7.75)

- [ ] **DISNEY'S AMERICA ON PARADE: A History of the U.S.A. in a Dazzling, Fun-Filled Pageant**, text by David Jacobs. (#G9974—$7.95)

- [ ] **FREDERIC REMINGTON** by Peter Hassrick. (#G9980—$6.95)

- [ ] **GRANDMA MOSES** by Otto Kallir. (#G9981—$6.95)

- [ ] **THE POSTER IN HISTORY** by Max Gallo. (#G9976—$7.95)

- [ ] **THE SCIENCE FICTION BOOK: An Illustrated History** by Franz Rottensteiner. (#G9978—$6.95)

- [ ] **NORMAN ROCKWELL: A Sixty Year Retrospective** by Thomas S. Buechner. (#G9969—$7.95)

- [ ] **THE PRO FOOTBALL EXPERIENCE** edited by David Boss, with an Introduction by Roger Kahn. (#G9984—$6.95)

- [ ] **THE DOLL** text by Carol Fox, photographs by H. Landshoff. (#G9987—$5.95)

- [ ] **DALI ... DALI ... DALI ...** edited and arranged by Max Gérard. (#G9983—$6.95)

- [ ] **THOMAS HART BENTON** by Matthew Baigell. (#G9979—$6.95)

- [ ] **THE WORLD OF M. C. ESCHER** by M. C. Escher and J. L. Locher. (#G9970—$7.95)

THE NEW AMERICAN LIBRARY, INC.,
P.O. Box 999, Bergenfield, New Jersey 07621

Please send me the SIGNET and ABRAMS BOOKS I have checked above. I am enclosing $_____(please add 50¢ to this order to cover postage and handling). Send check or money order—no cash or C.O.D.'s. Prices and numbers are subject to change without notice.

Name_____

Address_____

City_____State_____Zip Code_____
Allow at least 4 weeks for delivery